PENGUIN BOOKS

Home Fires and Spitfires

Daisy Styles grew up in Lancashire surrounded by a family and community of strong women. She loved to listen to their stories of life in the cotton mill, in the home, at the pub, on the dancefloor, in the local church, or just what happened to them on the bus going into town. It was from these women, particularly her vibrant mother and Irish grandmother, that Daisy learnt the art of storytelling.

D0103973

Home Fires and Spitfires

DAISY STYLES

PENGUIN BOOKS

PENGUIN BOOKS

UK | USA | Canada | Ireland | Australia
India | New Zealand | South Africa

Penguin Books is part of the Penguin Random House group of companies
whose addresses can be found at global.penguinrandomhouse.com

Penguin
Random House
UK

First published 2020
001

Copyright © Daisy Styles, 2020

The moral right of the author has been asserted

Set in 12.5/14.75 pt Garamond MT Std
Typeset by Jouve (UK), Milton Keynes
Printed and bound in Great Britain by Clays Ltd, Elcograf S.p.A.

A CIP catalogue record for this book is available from the British Library

ISBN: 978–1–405–94519–6

www.greenpenguin.co.uk

Penguin Random House is committed to a
sustainable future for our business, our readers
and our planet. This book is made from Forest
Stewardship Council® certified paper.

For my sister and my mother, Kate and Emily
Redmond, with a hundred happy memories of
growing up in the North West of England,
close to the Lake District and the Irish Sea
where this book is located. Happy days!

1. Mary Vale

May 1940

Ward Sister Ada Dale came swinging out of Matron's office with a radiant smile on her beautiful, young face. Only six months ago she had worried that a scandal that had rocked both the Sisters of Holy Mary and Mary Vale, their Home for Mothers and Babies, would destroy their reputation. But the Home's former Matron, along with the shamed chairman of the Board of Governors, had been imprisoned for what they had done thereby vindicating Mary Vale Home and the convent too. During the trial the previous resident doctor had been struck off the list for his drunken misdemeanours, leaving the Home free to appoint a new young doctor – one whom everybody was keenly looking forward to working with. With the dark memories of the past regime laid to one side, Ada could only thank God that justice had been seen to be done, and they could carry on with the work they loved.

Smiling to herself, Ada headed back to the ward, but as she passed the front door, which had been left wide open to let in the fresh air, she couldn't resist slipping outside for five minutes. She walked quickly across the garden to the end of the terrace, from where she was

1

always sure of getting the best views. Ada's deep blue eyes sparkled with pleasure as she took in the vast dramatic sweep of Morecambe Bay, where the tide was making its way out.

'God!' she murmured softly to herself. 'How I love this place.'

Rock pools appeared in the sweeping, silvery, sage-green marsh, rich pickings for long-legged oystercatchers, redshanks and godwits, pecking and dibbling in the shallows for razor shells and rag worms. Gazing raptly from her vantage point on the terrace, Ada recalled a story she'd read in a local history book. Centuries ago, after docking at Heysham, Irish friars and pilgrims had hired expert guides to lead them on donkeys along the safe pathways that threaded through the treacherous quicksand of Morecambe Bay. Once safely on the eastern side of the bay, the pilgrims broke their long journey at Mary Vale, which had once been an ancient priory. After being given food, drink and a bed for the night, the pilgrims continued on their way to Furness Abbey.

With the breeze teasing tendrils of golden-auburn hair from under her nurse's cap, Ada's thoughts returned to the present, and, even though she was warmed by the late-spring sunshine, she felt a shiver tingle all the way down her spine. It was becoming terrifyingly evident that the enemy were outpacing Britain on land, sea and sky. Nazi troops were making rapid progress across northern Europe, relentlessly pushing the British, French and Belgian troops back westwards. Even the new Prime Minister, bulldog-like Churchill, couldn't provide the number of fighter planes the RAF would need to outpace the Luft-waffe's supply of Messerschmitts, when the air war began in earnest.

With the capital under the threat of attack from bombing-raids, evacuees were leaving London in their droves. Surely married pregnant women evacuated from their homes would be part of the movement north and might soon be making their way to Mary Vale? Ada wondered how their arrival would go down with the residents who came to the Home to hide away their shame and have their babies in private. Respectable, married evacuees would feel no shame about their condition, and they would have no secrets to hide. How would the two very different types of mothers-to-be react to each other? Ada's wandering thoughts returned to the long-ago pilgrims breaking their journey at the ancient priory.

'Mary Vale has been providing shelter from the storm for nearly a thousand years. Nothing much has changed,' she thought to herself, smiling as she headed back into the Home.

The appointment of a new and much trusted Matron could not have come at a better time. The promotion of Sister Ann, a nun of the order of the Sisters of Holy Mary and an experienced midwife too, filled the Mary Vale staff with hope and excitement.

'I never in the world of God expected it,' Sister Ann had humbly confessed to Ada when she was told of her promotion.

Laughing, Ada had given her old friend a reassuring hug. 'God made you for the job – you'll be perfect!' she had exclaimed. 'After all the upsets we've had, the Reverend Mother is wisely taking no chances. She needs a Matron of impeccable character – who better than you?' Ada reasoned. 'An excellent midwife – and a nun to boot!'

Sister Ann's gentle brown eyes twinkled as she blushingly dismissed Ada's praise. 'Get away with you, Ada.'

'I'm not saying I won't miss you,' Ada blurted out.

Sister Ann wagged a finger in the air. 'I can be a midwife as well as Matron, don't you go forgetting that. My only request on taking the job was that I'd still be nursing our mothers and babies.'

Ada beamed. 'Thank heavens for that. I'd be lost without you.'

'The new nurse should ease the situation,' Sister Ann added thoughtfully. 'She comes with a lot of experience and was highly recommended.'

Ada gave an indulgent smile. 'Dora.'

'Nurse Saddleworth,' Sister Ann added.

'How she loves those babies,' Ada reflected.

'Just as well,' Sister Ann replied. 'Mary Vale has plenty of them.'

Checking her fob watch, Ada quickly said, 'I've got ten minutes before I go back to work – might now be a convenient time to discuss Shirley?'

Sister Ann positively glowed with pride. 'Miss Shirley. Our newest postulant.'

'Exactly,' Ada agreed. 'Her new life is now with you in

4

the convent, but you know better than anybody how much Shirley loves to help out in the Home.'

'Baking bread in the kitchen, tidying the wards, mopping the floors and lending a hand with feeds in the nursery,' Sister Ann said, smiling.

'Really, there's no stopping her!' Ada cried.

'It's a transitional period between convent life and the life of the Home,' Sister Ann answered calmly. She gave a small sigh as she recalled her first sight of Shirley, heavily pregnant and barely more than a child herself. 'She was barely able to speak when she first arrived here.'

Ada's blue eyes swam with tears as she too recalled the terrified young girl who had arrived after years of abuse from her own father.

'Staying on here after her baby's adoption, working as a ward assistant, gave Shirley not only a role but dignity and status too,' Sister Ann added thoughtfully. 'And it led her to God.'

Returning to the immediacy of the moment Ada continued, 'As much as we appreciate Shirley's unstinting help, I worry that she might be spending too much time on her knees on the wards rather than on her knees in the chapel. She always says she's closer to God when she's on her hands and knees beside a mop bucket,' she giggled. 'But I would hate the dear girl to get into trouble.'

Sister Ann waved a hand in the air. 'There's no fear of that, Ada. Shirley's commitment to becoming a nun is rock solid; her only problem is she'd like to have been received into the Church yesterday rather than in five years' time. Part of Shirley's spiritual training will be learning how to balance her time between her studies, her prayers and her vocational work. Don't worry, the child will get there in the end,' she said with confidence.

Ada scraped back her chair and rose to leave. 'I just needed to check the situation with you. I wouldn't like to be accused of exploiting a nun,' she quipped as she left the room.

After her heart-to-heart with the new Matron, Ada felt easier in her mind about Shirley, whom she found sitting on a chair beside the new nurse, Dora, busy changing babies' nappies. Shirley was competent enough when it came to handling babies, but she seemed a novice compared to Nurse Saddleworth, who confidently lifted each baby on to her aproned lap and deftly removed the pins from their dirty nappies, which were then removed and dropped into a bucket containing sanitizing fluid. After gently cleaning each baby, she slipped on a white terry-towelling nappy, then lifted it on to her shoulder and gently stroked its back.

'Clean and fresh as a daisy,' she cooed, as she bounced each contented child.

Shirley gaped at her in awe. 'How did you learn to change nappies so quickly?'

'Years and years of working at the coal face,' Dora replied with a grin.

Impressed, Shirley shook her head, as she struggled to balance a baby on her skinny lap.

Dora whacked her own hefty thighs. 'Get some flesh on you, girl!' she cried. 'You need thighs as big as a coffee table to change a baby.'

Picking up a mewling baby boy, whom she laid across her wide lap, Dora demonstrated what she meant. 'Look! Solid as a rock!' she boasted.

'I see you two will be busy for a while,' Ada remarked as she approached. 'Shall I get rid of the dirty buckets and bring you fresh ones, Nurse Saddleworth?'

Dora beamed at Ada. 'Aye, thanks very much – a fresh bucket would be right welcome. Yon one's stinking the place out.'

Ada picked up the heavy bucket. 'Back in a tick,' she said.

After rinsing the dirty nappies in the sluice-sink, Ada quickly filled up the empty bucket with warm water and sanitizing liquid.

'There you are,' she said, as she returned it to Dora.

Settling the baby she had just changed in his little canvas cot, Shirley quietly informed Ada that she had to be in the chapel by eleven.

Ada's loving heart lurched at the sight of Shirley's sweet, earnest face. Who would ever have thought that this lovely young woman with eyes that seemed to reflect the beauty of her soul was the same person who had tried to take her own life in the vast, dangerous waters of Morecambe Bay?

'Of course, dear,' Ada answered warmly.

As Shirley rose to go, Dora spoke with an emotional catch. 'Say one for my boys, sweetheart.'

Shirley nodded kindly. 'I always pray for all the brave lads fighting for our country,' she answered sincerely. 'I even pray for the German lads we kill,' she admitted with tears in her eyes.

Dora rolled her eyes. 'Well, you would, being a nun and all. I'm afraid my prayers don't extend that far. I worry myself sick about my lads, both serving in the Royal Navy, not together unfortunately – and nowhere either of them can mention in their letters home,' she said miserably.

Shirley gave Dora a soothing pat on the arm. 'Of course, I'll say extra special prayers for your sons,' she promised, before leaving for the chapel that was attached to the convent.

'She's a sweet little lass,' Dora murmured as she watched Shirley go.

Ada smiled in complete agreement. 'The girl's a treasure,' she said fervently. 'Is it all right if I leave you to finish off here while I check the ante-natal ward?'

'Off you go, Sister,' Dora replied. 'Don't you worry, I can manage.'

Ada had no doubts that Dora could manage. They had had a number of applicants for the post of Ward Nurse, but Dora Saddleworth had literally stood out head and shoulders above the rest. Before joining the Mary Vale team, she had worked as Senior Nurse in a number of maternity homes in the area, her references positively glowed, and, an added perk, she lived locally and never baulked at the long shifts. In Dora's short time at Mary Vale, the staff had been impressed by her warmth and compassion both with the mothers and the babies. She was skilful and unflappable in the delivery suite, and her easy-going nature made her popular with staff and residents alike. Ada was sure that buxom Dora Saddleworth, with her greying, curly hair, twinkling eyes and ready smile, was an asset to the Home and a friend in the making.

After Ada had checked her patients with the most imminent delivery dates, she popped into Father Ben's office, which was close to the chapel and always smelt of candles and incense. The minute she saw the priest's beaming smile she knew he had good news for her.

'Come in, come in, Ada,' he cried, as he beckoned her towards his desk. 'Our prayers have been answered: we finally have our own doctor!' he announced as he drew out a chair for her.

Ada grinned as she sat down opposite Father Ben. 'You're within spitting distance of the chapel,' she teased. 'You must be first in line for getting prayers answered.'

'God is good,' he agreed. 'But we haven't got it all our own way: we'll be sharing the new doctor with a GP's practice in Barrow.'

Too relieved to quibble, Ada shrugged. 'Some of a doctor is better than none at all.'

'My feelings entirely,' the priest agreed. 'With so many

doctors serving at the Front, I'm sure the ones who remain have to spread themselves thin.'

'What's his name?' Ada asked.

'Dr James Reid,' Father Ben told her. 'The Reverend Mother and I were very impressed by the young man's credentials, especially when we heard that he had specialized in obstetrics at Leeds Infirmary.'

Ada threw the priest (who had become a dear and trusted friend during her time at Mary Vale) a curious look. 'Wonder why *he* hasn't been called up?' she enquired.

'We had to ask the exact same question at the interview,' Father Ben admitted. 'It was a bit awkward, to be honest.'

Knowing full well the depths of Father Ben's compassion, Ada gave the priest an indulgent smile. 'I'm sure you were very sensitive, Father.'

'Poor chap, he told us at that he had contracted polio as a child, which left him lame in one leg,' Father Ben explained. 'He was declared unfit when he tried to sign up with the Royal Army Medical Corps.'

'Heavens!' Ada exclaimed. 'He must spend a great deal of his time justifying his civilian status to the straight-talking folk of Barrow-in-Furness.' Her sparkling blue eyes widened as she added excitedly, 'I for one welcome him unconditionally and with open arms.'

'Absolutely, my dear,' Father Ben agreed. 'But bear in mind, Ada, if the war continues, as I'm quite sure it will, Dr Reid may well be called up, lame or not.'

Ada rose to leave but, before she did, she fondly planted a kiss on Father Ben's bald head. 'Ever the realist,' she teased.

Beaming, Father Ben called after his favourite nurse, 'God bless you, my child!'

Walking back on to the post-natal ward, Ada found a few girls lying on their beds, clearly feeling a little weepy. Experience had taught Ada that high emotion was only to be expected after the trauma of childbirth, which was inevitably followed by radical changes in the girls' bodies. Engorged breasts, sore nipples and their hormones all over the place inevitably reduced new mothers to tears; in addition, most of them were shortly to lose the baby they'd only just given birth to. Ada quietly approached a young girl whose baby girl she had delivered that morning.

'Oh, Sister!' the girl cried when she saw Ada. 'How's my little girl?'

'She's fine,' Ada assured her. 'She had a few sips of sterile water, then fell fast asleep. I'll try her with a bottle later on.'

The poor girl pointed to her large, tender breasts. 'I've got enough milk to feed an army.'

'You can feed her, dear, if you really want to, but is that wise?' Ada gently asked.

The girl's eyes flooded with tears. 'You mean feeding her might make it harder for me to part with her?' she cried. 'I want to keep her, I love her,' she said wildly. 'Mi mam said she'd look after her when I go back to work at the cotton mill, but mi dad said 'e's 'aving no bastard child under his roof.'

Ada gave a deep inward sigh. How many times had she heard the same tragic story? Mary Vale provided for rich and poor women alike; the better-off girls paid for their stay from their own funds, while the poorer girls (who made up the majority of the Home's residents) were dependent on the convent's charitable trust. In exceptional circumstances (like a young homeless woman found wandering the streets) the convent could offer an entirely free place. Women arrived at the Home when their pregnancy started to show; their stay normally consisted of the four or five months before their due date. Once the babies were born, the mothers were expected to leave within a month to six weeks after their delivery; some girls couldn't get away from the place fast enough, while others clung on, dreading the moment when they would be forced to hand over their child for adoption. The girl sobbing on the bed was one such.

Ada, who had comforted many heart-broken young women, knew exactly what to say. 'You've had a long, hard day, dear, you must rest,' she murmured, as she settled her patient back on the pillows that she'd banked up. 'I'll pull the curtains around your bed to give you a bit of privacy,' she whispered, and her patient slumped backwards on to the pillows and closed her eyes. 'I'll be back in a few minutes with a nice cup of tea.'

By the time Ada returned with the hot tea, the girl was sound asleep. Ada gazed sadly at her patient's face, young but worn with fear and worry and streaked with tears.

'Poor child,' she said, as she tucked the bedding cosily around her. 'Get some rest while you can, sweetheart – you're certainly going to need it.'

2. Barrow Shipyard

With her heavy welder's mask pulled down over her face, nobody could see Gracie Price's long, wavy brunette hair, or her sparkling green eyes and full red lips. The masculine work overalls (allocated to all welders, male and female alike) drowned her small, slim, wiry body; even so, nothing could fully disguise the swell of her full breasts and the swing of her shapely hips.

Completely absorbed in welding plates of heavy sheet metal that would form the hull of the latest warship presently being built at Barrow Shipyard, Gracie was grateful for her clothing (ugly and mannish as it was), which protected her body from the red-hot sparks that flared and hissed as she welded together two metal sheets. Gruellingly hard though the job was, Gracie loved it with a passion; her family, like most others in Vickerstown, had been shipbuilders for generations, but now, with the war on, women were urgently needed to take over men's work in the shipyard. Though keen to do their bit for the war effort, some of Gracie's workmates disliked the heavy, dangerous job of welding, but tomboy Gracie loved it. Admittedly, in the early days of her apprenticeship, her back felt like it would snap in half, while her eyes burned from the glare of the welding torch, and her ears rang with the constant clamour of the shipyard. Now accustomed to the work, Gracie had developed strong muscles in her arms, legs and back, which eased the strain of the constant heavy lifting of tools and sheet metal essential to the job.

Gracie took pride in her welding when a new ship was launched, sometimes by the King and Queen, who regularly visited the shipyard to support and encourage the workers. As the ship that she had helped to build or repair slid down the runway, then out into the open sea, her heart would beat with patriotic zeal.

Adjusting her position in order to get a better grip on the welding iron in her thickly gloved hands, Gracie glanced anxiously towards her friend Ethel, whom she could just make out through the narrow visor in her welding mask. Married and pregnant, Ethel lived just a few doors down from Gracie's family. The two girls had been playmates since childhood, learning to walk in the cobbled back streets that separated the rows of redbrick terraced houses, where washing flapped on lines strung between the backyards.

Seeing Ethel struggling to manoeuvre her bulky belly around some heavy machinery, Gracie frowned. 'She would have been better off staying at home,' Gracie fretted to herself.

Glancing over to the vast number of ships lined up in dry dock awaiting urgent repairs, Gracie knew full well why even pregnant women had to drag themselves into work. The ships were always needed by the Royal Navy but especially so now, with the Germans forcing British,

French and Belgian troops to retreat towards the coastal beach-heads.

Returning to the seal she was painstakingly welding, Gracie blinked as the fizzing sparks bounced off the red-hot metal plate. Feeling the heat through her mask, Gracie was glad that nobody could see her face, which right now was creased with worry. Here she was, worrying about her friend's health when she was increasingly sure that she was pregnant too. Determined not to think of her situation right now, Gracie concentrated harder than ever on her work, until a sudden tap on her shoulder made her jump.

'Take Ethel home, lovie,' the Charge-hand yelled over the din of the clattering machinery. 'I don't want the poor lass going into labour on the job.'

Gracie quickly switched off her welding rod and removed her visor. 'I've been worrying about her too,' she admitted.

'Tell her, for the love of God, not to come back to work until after she's had her baby,' the Charge-hand added. 'I know she's a good lass, but there is a limit.'

Leaving their work clothes in their lockers, the two women linked arms and made their way through the busy, bustling shipyard. Gracie never ceased to marvel at how many skilled men and women were needed to build a ship – platers, shipwrights, hammer-boys, drillers, welders, riveters and riggers – many of whom she knew by sight.

'Oi!' one man called. 'Clocking off early?'

As they made their way past the Time-keeper's office, a sharp sea-breeze caught Gracie's long brunette hair, sending it flying around her pretty, smiling face.

'Don't worry, I'll be back,' she called over her shoulder.

On their way home, Gracie gently chided her breathless friend. 'You're due in less than a month – you should be at home, with your feet up.'

'I know,' Ethel guiltily admitted. 'But the thought of sitting on mi own all day, worrying myself sick about mi husband, drives me outdoors. I've not heard from Gerald in weeks!' she cried.

'Gerald wouldn't want you working like this,' Gracie firmly pointed out. 'Promise me you'll stay at home until after the baby's born?'

Ethel gave a feeble smile. 'I promise.'

Making slow progress through the network of terraced streets that provided housing for the fifty thousand inhabitants who lived in Barrow, they finally reached Ethel's house in Steel Street, where Gracie settled her friend on the sofa, with her legs up.

'Stay right where you are,' she commanded. 'I'll make us a brew before I head back to the yard.'

Ethel gratefully accepted a mug of strong hot tea, and, by the time Gracie had washed and tidied away the cups, her friend was fast asleep on the sofa. Creeping out of the house, Gracie retraced her steps through the back streets, dodging drying sheets flapping on washing lines. Alone, Gracie's thoughts immediately returned to her own problems. She knew her mother wouldn't throw her out into the street. Tough, working-class Vickerstown had seen many a local lass get wed in a rush! Nevertheless, if she really was pregnant, Gracie dreaded the moment when she would have to tell her parents that she was in the family way.

Before he had bolted, her cowardly lover had left Gracie a hundred pounds inside a farewell letter in which he had revealed that he was married and the father of three. The letter she had immediately thrown on the fire, but the money she had carefully kept. If she had to go away to have her baby, Reggie's guilt money would pay for her stay in a Mother and Baby Home. The sight of a gleaming Ford motor-car cruising down the main road into town caught Gracie's eye. Blinking away hot tears of anger, she roundly cursed herself. 'Stupid, stupid woman,' she seethed. 'You should have walked away the minute he offered to take you for a ride in his blasted car!'

Tall, handsome, thirty-something Reggie from down South had turned quite a few heads on his arrival, an experienced Foreman from London's Dockland, he had been transferred to Barrow, where he had given every impression of being single and unattached. Nobody could fail to notice the good-looking new Foreman with his sweep of black hair, flashing dark eyes and elegant high cheekbones.

'He reminds me of a film star,' one of the welding girls had giggled. 'Cary Grant or Robert Mitcham!'

Gracie drained her mug of tea and lit up a Woodbine. 'Don't be daft!' she had mocked. 'He's a Southerner, he won't want now't to do with the likes of us poor Northern lasses.'

But Reggie's wandering eyes had lingered on the stunning, slim brunette sitting on the dockside with seagulls winging overhead and a fresh sea-breeze blowing her long, dark hair around her sweet young face. Determined to make a play for the sexiest girl in the shipyard, Reggie had flirted with the welding girls whenever he passed their way.

'Cheek!' one of them had grumbled. 'Coming up here with his flirty Southern ways.'

'He is gorgeous,' another girl sighed. 'So mature, and he talks dead posh too.'

Pulling on her thick protective gloves that finished at the elbow, Gracie rolled her eyes at her silly, infatuated friends. 'I wouldn't trust him as far as I could throw him,' she declared.

'How right I was,' Gracie murmured under her breath as she re-entered the shipyard. 'If it hadn't been for his damn fancy car, I might have followed my instincts and stayed well out of harm's way.'

Gracie knew now, with the wisdom of hindsight, that it had been Reggie's stylish Hillman motor-car that had broken her resolve. She knew nobody in Barrow who could afford a car like Reggie's, or any car at all in fact; plus petrol was regarded as a precious commodity.

Gracie's love of cars had begun in her childhood, when she and her dad had taken an ancient Morris apart; dismantled, the old heap had stood on bricks for months while her dad tried to work out how to put it back together again. Gracie, a regular little grease monkey, who loved the smell of the engine oil from the time she was a little girl, had always dreamt of learning to drive.

Working at the yard, watching the crane drivers skilfully swinging their mighty cranes out over the sea to hoist goods from the ships lining the dockside, made Gracie's heart race. What must it be like to be up there, seated in the driver's cab?

'It's always fellas that get to drive the cranes,' Gracie thought resentfully. 'Would the gaffers ever allow a woman to drive one?' she wondered. 'Maybe they'd have to if the war continued, and more men were called up. Who else would replace them but women?'

When Gracie had first seen Reggie cruising out of the shipyard in his Hillman Fourteen, with its shiny chromework and expensive leather upholstery, her green eyes had all but rolled out of her head. Having systematically ignored the brash interloper for weeks, she found herself gaping at his car in open-mouthed admiration.

'Smart little number,' she had murmured under her breath.

Reggie had smiled and waved at a blushing Gracie, who had quickly turned away from him, but not before he had seen the rapt expression on her face. Smirking, Reggie had slammed his foot on the accelerator and roared away; after weeks of trying to engage with aloof but gorgeous Gracie, Reggie realized that he might have just discovered her weak spot.

3. Scandal

On a sunny morning in early June, Sister Mary Paul, the Home's beloved cook and housekeeper, opened Mary Vale's front door to a pin-thin waif of a girl with hollow cheeks and big, dark, almond-shaped eyes. The nun's habitual welcoming smile fell from her face at the sight of the stricken girl, who was wearing a floral headscarf over her long red curly hair and a coat that drowned her. Standing on the doorstep, she clutched the handle of her old battered suitcase so hard her knuckles shone through her pale skin. Struggling to communicate with the bemused nun, the visitor spoke in a faltering mixture of English and German.

'My name is Zelda, Frau Fischer . . . I am refugee from Germany.'

Some of the residents, passing the open door, stopped dead in their tracks when they overheard her German accent. A tall, big-boned girl called Annie dramatically rolled her eyes. A born gossip who loved a bit of scandal, Annie laid a finger on her lips as she crept closer to eavesdrop.

'Zelda Fischer . . . are we expecting you, dear?' Sister Mary Paul gently enquired.

'*Nein*, no, I come for help, to have my baby.' Zelda rolled her hand over her tiny tummy.

Catching sight of snooping Annie, Sister Mary Paul bustled Zelda past the gathering crowd of girls in the hallway. Seeing their curious expressions and raised eyebrows, the nun briskly dispatched them. 'Off you go, ladies, I'm sure you've all got plenty to do.'

Annie threw quaking Zelda a filthy look before she moved off with her friends. As soon as they'd gone, Sister Mary Paul led the visitor into the dining room, where she managed to communicate to the girl that she should wait until someone came to help her.

Leaving Zelda in the empty dining room, Sister Mary Paul scuttled down the corridor to Ada's office, where she burst unceremoniously into the room.

'Ada!' she gasped. 'Come – quick!'

Rushing after the nun, who breathlessly retraced her steps, Ada wondered what on earth could have panicked Sister Mary Paul. Hurrying Ada into the dining room, the nun introduced her to Zelda, who jumped up from the chair she'd been sitting in.

'She's just arrived,' Sister Mary Paul announced before dropping her voice to a whisper. 'She turned up on the doorstep.'

Seeing the obvious feeble state of the girl, Ada gently urged Zelda to sit back down again, then, smiling kindly, she took a seat beside her. 'How can I help you, dear?' she enquired.

Looking increasingly agitated, the visitor repeated virtually the same words she'd used to Sister Mary Paul, who had already left the room intent on making a pot of strong tea.

Suddenly pulling a letter from her pocket, she thrust it into Ada's hands; gabbling nervously she added, 'From relative in London, she explain me . . .'

To whom it may concern,

My niece, Zelda Fischer, arrive from Berlin, she escape to England on train with false papers. Her husband, a Jew, he shot dead by Gestapo. Zelda is very weak and ill, London is bad place for her, she frightened it will be bombed. She hear from doctor that Mary Vale is nice quiet home in countryside to have her baby, I pray the child survive. Zelda decide to make long journey to you. She will pay. Please God protect her, I can do no more.

Ada read the letter calmly before refolding it and handing it back to Zelda, whose resolve completely crumbled as she started quietly to sob.

'Please, please, I stay?' she wildly blurted out, before lapsing into a torrent of words in German.

The little German Ada had been taught at school didn't help her to understand, but one thing she did recognize was the abject misery of the woman before her. Laying an arm around Zelda's shuddering shoulders, Ada murmured, 'Shhh . . . don't upset yourself.'

Zelda paused to wipe her streaming eyes on a grubby hankie. 'Help me?' she begged.

Trying desperately to think of words that the wretched girl might comprehend, Ada said, 'I go and talk to Manager.'

Leaving Zelda in the good care of Sister Mary Paul,

who had returned with hot tea and coconut biscuits, Ada went in search of Father Ben. Mercifully, he spoke some German and was able to comfort Zelda with assurances that they would do everything they could to help her and her baby.

'I have money,' Zelda told him in German. 'I can pay for my stay here.'

'Good, that will make things easier,' the priest answered in German. 'I'll speak with the Reverend Mother; meanwhile I'll leave Sister Ada to settle you in.'

Seeing Zelda literally wilting before their eyes, Ada took her off to a bedroom that had already been prepared. After they had both left the room, Sister Mary Paul turned to Father Ben with a frown on her face.

Seeing her expression, Father Ben spoke first. 'We must do all that we can for the poor soul.'

'I agree, Father, but what if the residents see her as the enemy?' she asked nervously.

The priest threw his hands up in the air. 'For the love of God!' he exclaimed. 'We can't throw her out just because of other people's prejudice.' Agitated, Father Ben paced the room. 'For the time being, I think we should let the poor child settle in and avoid questioning her.'

Sister Mary Paul nodded in agreement with him. 'God only knows what horrors she must have been through,' she said sadly.

On the Home's second floor Ada led Zelda into a large, airy room that had two single beds and a wide bay window overlooking Mary Vale's lovely gardens and the Irish Sea. The newcomer actually gasped with pleasure when she saw the clean, quiet room with its stunning view.

'*Danke, danke,*' Zelda whispered repeatedly. 'You, kind lady,' she added, as she threw off her coat and lay back on the nearest bed.

Ada stifled a gasp at the sight of Zelda's stick-like, white legs poking out from underneath her long skirt. Leaving her patient curled up on the bed, Ada crept out of the room hoping that the newcomer might get some rest. Sadly, rest didn't come easily to Zelda: left alone, she rolled over to face the wall and all too soon felt the familiar coursing of hot tears on her dry cheeks. As the pillow beneath her head grew damp, Zelda forced herself to will up her dead husband. The process might tear her apart, but she needed to remember Izaak, to etch his face forever into her mind. His soft, intelligent, dark brooding eyes, his silky jet-black hair, his gentle mouth and even gentler touch, and his wonderful brilliant mind.

'Izaak, Izaak, my dearest darling,' she wept, '*mein Lieber, mein Schatz.*'

News of Zelda's arrival spread like wildfire around the Home.

'I couldn't believe mi ears,' Annie gossiped. 'A bloody Hun in our midst.'

Her equally spiteful friend, Bessie, melodramatically rolled her eyes. 'She dun't even look like she's up the duff,' she whispered. 'She could be lying, pretending to be expecting just to get herself into the Home to spy on us!'

In the sluice-room Shirley and Dora were also discussing the newcomer.

'I'm not sure how t'other lasses will react to the new girl, her being a German,' Dora said, as they refilled the nappy buckets with hot water and sanitizing fluid. 'She might come in for a bit of ragging.'

Shirley's pale brow creased under her starched white wimple. 'The poor girl's more to be pitied than picked on,' she exclaimed. 'Sister Ann told me there are thousands of Germans who have been made homeless by the Nazis just because they're Jewish. She said it was' – she stopped in order to accurately recall Sister Ann's exact words – 'it's a crime against humanity.'

Grim-faced, Dora carefully set down the heavy buckets. 'Let's just hope the Mary Vale residents see it that way too. The poor lass looks like a strong wind would blow her over. I don't think she's in any state to be bullied.'

Dora's prediction turned out to be right. Most of the residents united to turn against 'The Foreigner'. Rather than pass her in the corridor, they would blatantly turn their backs to Zelda and walk off the other way. A few publicly sneered at the sound of her voice, while others, like Annie and Bessie, were downright vicious.

Nervous Zelda felt safe only with the nursing staff, especially Ada, whom she quickly trusted implicitly.

Blushing and embarrassed, she tried to articulate her fears, which Ada in turn tried to ease.

'They will get used to you,' she insisted. 'In this place you're all the same.' Ada patted her own tummy to demonstrate her point. 'Pregnant, waiting for a baby to come. *Baby* is important in Mary Vale – not war.'

Nevertheless, Ada kept a close eye on Zelda. Whenever she ate with the residents, she always made a point of sitting beside her and trying to integrate her into the group, but they nervously kept their distance. Even though Ada chatted to her, Zelda only smiled and nodded in response; she didn't dare speak for fear the other diners would mock her German accent. It was a wretched situation that angered Ada and humiliated Zelda, who hid in her room as much as possible and avoided speaking to anybody.

'It's intolerable,' Ada seethed to Sister Ann in private. 'I really don't know how the likes of hard-hearted Annie and Bessie sleep in their beds at night.'

Sister Ann fingered the little wooden cross that hung from a chain around her neck. 'We must pray for the poor child,' she said softly.

Ada adored Ann and would never utter a word that might upset her, but her thoughts at that moment were anything but pious. 'It will take a lot more than prayers,' Ada quietly fumed. 'It will take nothing short of a blasted miracle,' she added under her breath.

A few days later Ada asked to see Zelda in her office.

'Good morning, dear,' Ada said, smiling.

Ada handed Zelda a thick English grammar book and a German-to-English dictionary that she had borrowed from the convent library the previous night.

'These books will help you to improve your English,' she explained.

Zelda's pale, thin face lit up as she flicked through the pages of the books. 'I study English in *die Schule*,' she told Ada. 'I have English books in Germany, I study but then I leave.'

As tears flooded her deep, dark-brown eyes, Ada leant forwards and laid a comforting hand on Zelda's arm. 'Tell me what happened to you,' she said softly.

Zelda stared at her for several moments before she whispered, 'You hear story of *mein Leben*?'

'Yes, please, dear. I want to hear your story.'

Using the grammar book and the dictionary to help her formulate sentences and jotting down odd words and pictures in a notebook, Zelda managed to relate her recent history to Ada.

'I study botany at university in Munich; my Izaak, he read law, he is a clever student, always discussing politics,' she said with a proud smile. 'We marry and move to Berlin, but dangerous times come to us. One night my Izaak away from house.' Her voice broke, but she bit back her tears and continued, 'Nazis stop him for passport, when they see he is Jew they kill him in street. My Izaak is dead because he is Jew.'

Ada covered the poor girl's trembling hands with her own. 'I'm so sorry,' she murmured.

Determined to finish, Zelda took a deep breath and went on. 'My parents buy me false identity; I get train to Belgium, then cross sea in fisherman's boat. I go to relation in London, but London not good for my baby, so I find good place here to live.'

Zelda hadn't the words to describe her long journey north, how heartache and fear had given way to relief when the train had left the grime of the industrial cotton towns. Puffing black smoke in its wake, the train had stopped at Lancaster and Morecambe, then, after passing through a long dark tunnel, it emerged into a wide, sunlit bay. Zelda had gasped in disbelief when she saw that the train was speeding along on tracks secured on wooden piers drilled deep into the sea. Feeling like she was travelling between the sea and the sky, Zelda had gazed in wonder at the vast stretch of ocean that merged with the shimmering blue of the far western horizon. Filled with a rush of hope, Zelda was suffused with a deep instinctive feeling that Izaak had guided her to this bright, beautiful place to give birth to his child.

Struggling to explain herself, she stumbled over her words. 'His spirit was close, I feel him near to me,' she said, and, cradling her tiny tummy, Zelda concluded her story: 'And now, this baby is *mein Lieber*, I need to keep him safe.'

Ada smiled gently as she made a promise that she vowed that she would keep faithfully: 'Don't you worry, dear,' she said. 'We'll look after your baby and we'll look after you too.'

4. Good News

Unaware of being observed by two pairs of quizzical eyes, Dr Reid, struggling with his ancient car's clunky gears, arrived at Mary Vale House in order to briefly introduce himself to the staff before officially starting work in the Home the following week. Like two naughty schoolgirls, Ada, who was supposed to be leading the breathing and exercise class taking place in the garden, jostled behind a privet hedge with Dora to get their first glimpse of Dr Reid.

'He looks young,' Dora whispered. Squinting hard, she added, 'He's got a nice head of hair.'

Ada burst into giggles. 'Stop talking about the man like he was a horse at an auction!'

As the new doctor climbed out of the driver's seat, Dora hissed at her friend to be quiet.

Fed up with lying flat on her back with one leg up in the air, a girl on the lawn called out, 'Sister Ada! Can we relax yet?'

Feeling guilty that she had abandoned her class, Ada immediately turned her wandering attention back to the group of heavily pregnant women. 'Yes, of course, lower your legs, nice and slow now, all the time breathing out . . .' Ada said, as she talked them through the exercise.

'Phew!' one of the class joked. 'Any longer and I might have gone into premature labour.'

As the girls chatted to each other, Ada nipped back to join Dora, who seemed to be glued to the privet hedge. 'He's taking in the view,' she informed Ada.

Ada noticed that, as Dr Reid strode along the garden path, he showed no evidence of a limp. She was impressed by how tall and broad he was, young too, as Dora had noted, with a mop of tawny-brown hair that fell in a boyish sweep over his brow.

'Hell fire,' Dora continued lugubriously. 'Yon fella's too good-looking to be working in a place like this – he's bound to get the girls' pulses racing.'

'For heaven's sake, Dora!' Ada exclaimed. 'They're all pregnant!'

'That doesn't mean to say they've no imagination,' irrepressible Dora chuckled. 'Let's hope he's as good at his job as he is good-looking.'

Returning to her class, now recumbent on the sunny lawn, Ada enquired,

'Are you all sufficiently rested, ladies?'

'I'm so rested I could nod off right here on the spot,' a sweet young girl called Marie said, and yawned.

Ada threw her an encouraging smile. 'It's worth the effort, believe me: these exercises will strengthen your pelvic muscles and help you to breathe deeply, both of which will be useful when you go into labour. Ready for the next lift? One, two, three, nice and slow now, slowly raise your legs . . .'

As the class groaned good-naturedly, Dora whispered to Ada, 'Yet again, no sign of Zelda.'

Ada sighed. 'No matter how hard I try I can't persuade to join this class.'

'If only she could find a friend,' Dora murmured wistfully.

'If only . . .' Ada agreed.

Inside the Home, Dr Reid was welcomed warmly by Sister Mary Paul, who escorted him, with her long veil fluttering out behind her like a dark cloud, to Father Ben's office. Rising from his chair to greet the new doctor, Father Ben shook him warmly by the hand.

'Dr Reid! It's such a relief to know that we finally have a doctor on board.'

After a welcome cup of tea and home-made bread and jam (Sister Mary Paul couldn't bear the thought of Father Ben ever going hungry!), the priest led Dr Reid back to the Home, where many curious females stared at him as he made his way on to the maternity ward.

'Ah!' Father Ben cried when he saw Ada, who had just finished her class, walking down the main ward towards them. 'Let me introduce you to Sister Dale.'

Jamie found himself gazing at a tall, slim nurse with a neat waist and long shapely legs. Though her flame-coloured auburn hair was tucked under her cap, little golden curls escaped to frame her pretty tanned face, which was lit up by her large dark-blue eyes. As Ada smiled warmly, the new doctor admired the sweep of her wide, generous lips, which revealed perfect white teeth.

'God! She's beautiful,' he thought.

Even though Ada had already observed Dr Reid from a distance, now at close quarters she was even more struck by his wide-open smile and unusual hazel eyes that were beguilingly flecked with gold.

Realizing that she had held his gaze for far too long, blushing Ada shook him by the hand. 'Delighted to meet you, Dr Reid,' she murmured.

'Jamie Reid. Lovely to meet you too, Sister Dale.'

'You have no idea how very welcome you are. Come,' she added enthusiastically, repeating Father Ben's words in a voice that hinted of a soft Northern accent. 'Let me introduce you to the staff – they're all keen to meet you – then I'll give you a tour of the wards and the delivery suite.'

After bidding farewell to Father Ben, Dr Reid followed in Ada's wake, all the time trying not to gaze at the seductive swing of her shapely hips. Unaware of what was going on right behind her, Ada pointed out the ante- and post-natal wards as they passed through them.

'The delivery room separates them off,' she explained, when they came to a stop in the middle of what he considered to be quite a small room. 'It's a bit cramped,' she admitted. 'Luckily we don't usually deal with multi-births, so we get by,' Ada said, smiling. 'And when it gets hot and stuffy, which it often does at this time of the year, we can just throw open the window,' she said, and she stepped back in order to allow him to gaze out at the view.

The sharp wind borne on the tide swept into the room, along with the tang of the salt marsh and the piercing call of the oystercatchers and redshanks hunting on the sandbanks.

'It's an extraordinary place,' Jamie commented. 'Homes like these are usually dark and forbidding, more like prisons, but Mary Vale is surprisingly pleasant.'

Leading him out of the delivery room and along a corridor to the sluice-room, kitchen and the nursery, Ada agreed with his sentiments. 'I thought exactly the same thing when I came to Mary Vale for my interview,' she said. 'To be working in a lovely big house like this, right by the sea and so near the mountains, was a very attractive prospect.'

Aware of her patients' curious eyes following the handsome young doctor, Ada hurried him along the corridor to his office, which Shirley had mopped and polished until it shone, going so far as to pick a bunch of fragrant, heliotrope-coloured sweet peas that she had arranged in a crystal vase on his desk.

'I know it's a bit poky,' Ada said with an apologetic smile, 'but you'll have somewhere private to keep your belongings and sleep overnight if necessary,' she said, nodding towards a neatly made-up narrow single bed.

'This will do me just fine,' Jamie said gratefully.

'Matron's next door,' Ada continued. 'I'll fetch her,' she added, as she left the room.

*

Leaving Dr Reid with Ann, Ada made her way back to the main ward, where she found Shirley helping Dora with the feeds.

Above the mewling cries of the hungry infants, Dora gave a sly smile. 'I've just been telling Shirley what a good-looking fella the new doctor is.'

Shirley smiled shyly. 'I'm not interested in men, good-looking or otherwise.'

Undeterred, Dora, who knew every bit of local gossip within thirty square miles, lowered her voice to a whisper. 'I've heard tell that he's in high demand at the Barrow surgery, working every hour God sends.'

Shirley looked concerned. 'I hope that won't affect his hours here.'

Incorrigible Dora winked in the direction of Ada. 'From the way his eyes were following Sister Dale's every move, I'd say we'll have no trouble keeping him close to Mary Vale.'

Before Ada could respond to Dora's cheeky comment, Matron reappeared with Dr Reid at her side.

'Thank you for taking the time to pop over and meet us all before you officially start next week,' Sister Ann said, as they shook hands.

Dr Reid's eyes were again drawn towards Ada. 'It's a pleasure to have met your staff, Matron.'

After Dr Reid had driven away, Sister Ann turned to her friend with a satisfied expression on her face.

'Thank God!' she exclaimed. 'At last, a decent, respectable young man.'

Recalling the last doctor who had worked in the Home – the drunk and liar who had been struck off the medical register – Ada nodded vigorously.

Smiling at the memory of the new doctor's boyish grin and unusual gold-flecked hazel eyes, Ada replied, 'We're very lucky to have him.'

Behind the driving wheel, Jamie Reid was also smiling. Only a few hours ago he had regretted his rash decision to drive the twenty miles from Barrow to Kents Bank to meet the Mary Vale staff. After being up all night, initially with a woman who was suffering a miscarriage and then with a middle-aged man who was dying of tuberculosis, Jamie could barely see straight. Though he had felt deeply sorry for both patients, he nevertheless longed for some sleep, but the sight of lovely Sister Ada had driven all thoughts of sleep from his mind.

Bumping along the narrow lanes to Newby Bridge, Jamie had a fleeting, tantalizing glimpse of the Langdales in the far distance, and he briefly fantasized about ignoring the call of duty and driving north to Keswick. He reckoned he could be in the Borrowdale Valley within two hours, from where he could strike out in any direction to walk his favourite fells: to the north, Scafell Pike, east to Watendlath, west to Catbells and south to mighty Skiddaw. After a long, yearning backward glance, Jamie put his foot on the accelerator and headed back to work.

As he drove along the narrow lanes to Barrow-in-Furness, Jamie's thoughts drifted to his fellow medics from Leeds Royal Infirmary, who were, as far as he knew, behind the Front Line in northern France, treating soldiers wounded in battle. He and his pals had volunteered for active service, but after the obligatory medical Jamie was the only one the wartime medical board had rejected. Instead of fighting for his country, he was easing the workload of a hectic GP's practice. Jamie originally considered his new role in the back streets of Barrow a bit of a comedown, but he soon grew to admire the toughness and tenacity of his Barrow patients, who welcomed him warmly into their community. When Jamie was informed that he would be splitting his workload between the Barrow surgery and a home for unmarried mothers and their babies, he had been quite pleased; it would be useful to keep up his obstetric research, and now there was the added attraction of a beautiful, long-legged midwife nurse with shapely hips and sparkling, deep-blue eyes. He was counting down the days until he saw her again.

5. Gracie

Feeling hot, heavy and exhausted after a hard day's work, Gracie walked slowly home with the din of the shipyard still ringing in her ears; the clattering, drilling, riveting, banging and hammering of shipbuilding machinery pounded inside her head until it ached. It seemed to Gracie that, no sooner had they repaired one battleship, than two more came back with their hulls blown out. With the British and French forces stuck like sitting ducks on the beaches of Dunkirk, ruthlessly strafed by German aircraft, every sea-worthy vessel was desperately needed for the evacuation of men stranded on the beaches.

Patriotic though she was, Gracie longed for a day off. The thought of not having to conceal her ever growing tummy under her heavy overalls and lie in bed, wearing only a cool nightdress, sleeping undisturbed for hours, was her idea of heaven right now. With every passing week Gracie knew it really was time to tell her mam of her condition; plus, she needed an ally, and Gracie knew that her mother (once over the shock) would support her. She had been delaying making her announcement until she had located a home where she could go to have her baby. Thanks to the advice given by Dr Reid, who had recently joined her local GP's practice, Gracie had booked herself into a nearby home called Mary Vale. Well aware that she could not afford to prevaricate any longer, Gracie would have to tell her mother that, not only was she pregnant but she was also going to a home for unmarried mothers.

Breathing heavily, Gracie dragged her leaden feet along the narrow, terraced streets, where washing flapped in the salty sea-air and children played marbles in the gutter. Once inside her own backyard, Gracie manoeuvred a pathway round a heap of car, propped up on bricks, that she and her dad were forever tinkering with. Gracie gazed fondly at the ancient Raleigh, whose rusty engine they had painstakingly taken apart more than once.

'It'll be a bloody miracle if you ever get that wreck going!' her mam regularly complained. 'It's blocking the path to the privy, and I can barely get to the coal hole too.'

'We'll 'ave it up and running in no time,' Gracie's dad, an eternal optimist, always answered cheerfully. 'Me and my little helper,' he had added, with a fond wink at his grinning daughter.

After unlocking the back door, Gracie was relieved to find the house empty. Her mother was helping out with the evacuee children at the local church hall and would be home later to make supper; for now Gracie had the place to herself. Sighing heavily, she curled up on the sofa in front of the old black cooking range and did what she'd been longing to do all day: fell fast asleep.

Sometime later the sound of a whistling kettle woke Gracie with a start.

'Want a brew, lovie?' Mrs Price asked.

Blurry-eyed and suddenly nervous, Gracie struggled to sit up, frightened that she might lose her nerve and further delay telling her mother the news she'd been holding back for too long. She drew a deep, shuddering breath and blurted it out. 'Mam . . . I'm expecting.'

Mrs Price stared at her daughter for a long few seconds before bursting into tears. 'Oh, Gracie, love,' she wept. 'You were always so independent-minded – how could you have got yourself into this mess?'

Gracie didn't even try to defend herself. 'Because I was bloody stupid!' she cried, and started to weep too. 'It's the oldest trick in the book – married man sweeps young girl off her feet.'

Looking white and tense her mother asked, 'Married? So there's no chance of him marrying you?'

'Mam, he's long gone,' Gracie angrily blurted out.

'Who is this fella?' Mrs Price insisted. 'Your father will have a thing or two to say to him.'

'You're wasting your breath,' Gracie sighed. 'He ran back to his wife and children the minute he heard I was pregnant.'

Reaching for her packet of Woodbines, Mrs Price, in a voice thick with fury, said, 'The pig! How could he do a thing like that to an innocent young girl?'

'It takes two to tango, Mother,' Gracie answered bitterly. 'I blame myself just as much as I blame him. God! I was so bloody stupid!'

Mrs Price took several deep drags on her cigarette before she asked, 'Are you planning on keeping the baby?'

Gracie vehemently shook her head. 'No, I'll have it adopted; a lass as witless as me is no fit person to bring up a child,' she muttered miserably. Now that she had started to confess, Gracie rushed on. 'Mam, I've booked myself into a home for unmarried mothers in Kents Bank,' she gabbled nervously. 'It's run by nuns – they're expecting me there soon.'

Gracie's green eyes brimmed with tears as she gazed into her mother's sad and bewildered face.

'I have to get right away from Barrow: I don't want you and Dad shamed by what I've done.'

Mrs Price slowly nodded her head. 'Aye, mebbe you're right, love.'

'Please, Mam, will you come to the Home with me?' Gracie asked anxiously.

Mrs Price gathered her daughter into her arms. 'Aye, lovie, I'll take you,' she replied. 'We'll go together as soon as you're ready.'

Gracie's last week at the yard was more miserable than she could ever have imagined. Hiding her burgeoning tummy behind her overalls and protective clothing was difficult enough, but that, combined with the heat from the soldering iron and the flying sparks, made her sweat until she felt almost faint. As much as she loved her job and her workmates, Gracie was forced to acknowledge to herself that her timing to leave was spot on. Only a few weeks ago she would have been able to manoeuvre her way around any sheet of plate metal she was welding; now she felt awkward and clumsy, and the soldering iron she had handled with such dexterity seemed to weigh a ton.

It wasn't just her pregnancy that Gracie was hiding; she was also keeping to herself the fact that when she finished work on Friday she wouldn't be back in the yard until well after Christmas. She would behave perfectly normally when the hooter blew to announce the end of the working week; she would wave goodbye to all her pals, just as she always did; then quietly slip away. When awkward questions were asked, she would be miles away.

After an emotional farewell with her heartbroken father, who had been informed of his daughter's condition by his wife, Gracie and her mother boarded the train. Gazing out of the window at the passing landscape, Mrs Price gave a deep sigh. 'My . . .' she murmured, as the train sped along the track that skirted Morecambe Bay glittering bright in the sunshine. 'When you think there's the shipyards just around the corner and all the RAF bases up near Walney . . . but here,' she said, gazing out of the window, 'you wouldn't even know there's a war on.'

'Unfortunately, there is a war on, Mam, a terrible war,' Gracie said grimly. 'All them poor lads shot down or drowned at Dunkirk, massacred as they waited for transportation to get them back home. So many thousand dead or wounded.'

'Don't go forgetting how many thousands were saved

by them little boats crossing the Channel, volunteers of all ages, risking their own lives to bring our boys back,' Mrs Price reminded her daughter. 'When I think of the nation's response to Churchill's call for help, it makes me want to weep – if I'd had a boat I'd have set sail myself!' she said, wiping tears from her eyes. 'Hitler might think he's winning, but I tell you, our Gracie, he may have more weapons and planes, but us Brits have got more guts,' she finished proudly.

Gracie smiled at her mam's passionate expression. 'You're right, Mam,' she agreed. 'We'll win in the end.'

She carefully avoided adding, 'Though God only knows when the end might be.'

As the train shunted past Cark and Flookburgh, bringing her ever closer to Kents Bank, Gracie couldn't stop herself from thinking of handsome, two-timing and two-faced Reggie, who, as she herself had said, was long gone but who nevertheless haunted her thoughts. How she wished she could turn back the clock. If only she had followed her instincts instead of allowing him to charm and seduce her. Thank God she had the loyal support of her mother who, Gracie knew, would never let her down. Mrs Price would see this ordeal through to its conclusion, and she would be waiting faithfully for her daughter when she returned home after the baby's birth.

At Kents Bank they were the only passengers to disembark from the steam train, which, as it halted, sent out great clouds of thick black smoke that briefly obscured the lovely view of the salt-marsh. Following the guard's directions, they took a leafy track through a small wood, then entered the spacious grounds of Mary Vale, where Gracie's pretty face suddenly crumpled.

'I'm scared, Mam,' she sobbed like a terrified child.

With her arms firmly around her trembling daughter, Mrs Price nodded in the direction of Mary Vale. 'You're in the right place, our Gracie. Now come on, chin up, let's go and introduce ourselves.'

Oddly enough, once Gracie was inside the Home, she immediately felt calmer; some of the residents passing her in the hallway smiled briefly in Gracie's direction, and as usual Sister Mary Paul came bustling out of the kitchen to greet the visitors.

'Welcome, welcome, ladies. I'll get one of the girls to fetch Sister Ada, but, in the meantime, do you fancy a cuppa and a slice of cake, only coconut and carrot,' she chatted on. 'You've missed dinner, so I fancy you might be feeling a bit peckish?'

Mrs Price immediately accepted her kind offer. 'I'd love a cuppa tea,' she replied.

'What about you, dear?' Sister Mary Paul politely asked Gracie.

Too nervous to eat anything, Gracie shook her head. 'I'd like to unpack first, if you don't mind?'

'Of course, you settle yourself in, while I see to your mother. This way, Mrs Price, you'll be comfortable in the dining room,' Sister Mary Paul said, as she led Gracie's mum out of the hallway.

No sooner had they moved off than Ada arrived.

'You must be Gracie!' she said cheerily. 'We've been expecting you.'

Ada's wide-open smile and her welcoming, big dark-blue eyes immediately put Gracie at her ease. 'Hello,' she answered a little shyly.

Grabbing the handle of Gracie's suitcase, Ada said, 'I'm Sister Ada – let me take that.'

Gracie followed Ada up the stairs to the second floor, where she was relieved to find the room she had been assigned was, in fact, beyond her expectations. Rather than the dark, dingy accommodation she had envisaged, this room, with its two single beds, was big, bright and spacious. After placing Gracie's suitcase on the bed by the bay window, Ada said, 'You'll be sharing with Zelda, but, before I introduce you to her, I need to explain something about her background.' Ada paused briefly before she added, 'Zelda is German.'

Gracie gave a little gasp of surprise. 'German?' she spluttered.

Ada nodded. 'She's Jewish, a refugee who's recently arrived in this country. She's a widow; her husband was killed by the Nazis,' she said starkly. 'She's only recently arrived and she's still getting acclimatized.'

'Acclimatized,' Ada mused to herself. 'More like shell-shocked, punch-drunk, a complete nervous wreck.'

Though shocked to find herself sleeping in the same room as a German, Gracie made an effort to remember her manners.

'I look forward to meeting her,' she said diplomatically.

*

After unpacking her clothes, Gracie walked downstairs with Ada and joined her mother in the dining room, where, now starving, she gratefully accepted Sister Mary Paul's offer of a cup of tea and a slice of bread and butter.

'The butter is from the Mary Vale Farm, just across the meadow,' the old nun quickly explained. 'We're not fiddling the ration books,' she chuckled.

In the shabby but comfortable dining room with sunshine flooding in through the wide-open French windows and jars of wildflowers dotted along the windowsills, filling the room with a fresh fragrance, Gracie started to relax. Her mother beside her suddenly became very emotional. 'So, what happens now to my little lass?'

'You needn't worry, Mrs Price: Mary Vale isn't a prison,' Ada assured the tearful mother. 'Gracie can take herself off for a walk whenever she needs a bit of peace and quiet.' Turning to the newcomer, Ada explained, 'When the tide is out, I often walk out on the marsh. It's beautiful, full of wildflowers and sea-birds. I love the place, especially in the evening, when you can stand and watch the sun go down over the Irish Sea.' Turning back to Mrs Price, Ada added, 'You can visit your daughter whenever you want; the residents generally look forward to their family's visits.'

'Thank you, Sister. I'd like to come and see how she's progressing, especially after she's er . . . given birth,' Mrs Price ended awkwardly.

'Of course!' Ada cried. 'Come on, let me show you around before you leave.'

*

46

In the nursery, Gracie and Mrs Price were unexpectedly moved at the sight of cots covered in stout white canvas, lined up side by side in neat rows. As they passed them, both Gracie and her mam peered into the cots, where some babies lay wide-eyed, staring out at the new world they had only recently entered, while others whimpered either from hunger or for attention. Ada quickly introduced the visitors to Dora, who was supervising the never-ending bottle-feeding rota.

'The babies need feeding every four hours; sometimes we can have as many as a dozen babies at a time in the nursery. The only way we can make the rota work is by asking the residents to get stuck in and help with the shifts; otherwise we would have every baby in the place screaming blue murder,' Dora explained. Rocking a new-born baby girl in her arms, she went on, 'The girls don't complain too much about the rota, not unless they're on the 4 a.m. feed in the middle of the night – nobody likes that,' she chuckled. 'All the girls have chores to do, bottle-feeding is just one of them.'

'We appreciate the residents' help; the Home couldn't function as it does without their input,' Ada continued. 'We try to keep the chores as light as possible: general cleaning, lending a hand in the kitchen and helping out in the nursery, as you've just seen. We limit the housework to the mornings, so that the residents can rest in the afternoon or do some gentle exercise classes, which I lead most afternoons.'

After an inspection of the ante- and post-natal wards,

Ada led the visitors into the delivery room, where Gracie's big green eyes filled with tears.

'I can't believe I'll give birth in here,' she gulped, as she reached for her handkerchief.

Ada smiled. 'Hopefully that will be the case, though I have had the occasional girl give birth in the corridor!' she laughed.

'Are the babies taken to the nursery immediately they're born?' Gracie asked curiously.

'We go by whatever the mother wants,' Ada told her. 'Some want to hold their babies for hours on end and visit them in the nursery. Not many choose to breast-feed: they worry that if they do so it will be harder to part with their babies. Most of the new mums opt for bottle-feeding, which they can do themselves if they wish. Our aim at Mary Vale is to assist the mothers who will be leaving, while nurturing the babies that are left behind.'

'Do most of the babies get adopted?' Gracie asked.

Ada nodded. 'The majority do. Occasionally a mother will leave with her baby; that will start to happen more, now that married pregnant woman are being evacuated out of the cities. Since the start of the war we've had a few evacuees here, and their older children too,' she informed the listening women.

'Who arranges the adoptions?' Mrs Price asked.

'Father Ben,' Sister Ada replied. 'He's attached to the convent; he's a genius at matching up babies and families.'

'Do the mothers have any say when it comes to choosing the adoptive parents?' Gracie asked.

'Yes, if they want to get involved,' Ada responded. 'To be honest, Gracie, most of the girls prefer to leave it to Father Ben's good judgement. You'll get to meet him soon,' she promised.

After they'd completed the tour of the Home, Gracie accompanied her mother back to the railway station, where, as they waited for Mrs Price's train to arrive, Gracie told her about her new room-mate.

'Sister Ada told me that her husband was shot by the Nazis,' she explained.

Big-hearted Mrs Price exclaimed, 'Poor little bugger! You make sure you keep an eye on her.'

'I'll do mi best, Mam, but I must admit to feeling a bit shocked,' Gracie admitted.

Mrs Price looked her daughter straight in the eye. 'You might think you've got troubles, lovie, but think what that poor kid's going through – it can't be easy being German in this country, refugee or no refugee, and on top of that a widow *and* pregnant,' she murmured compassionately.

'I'll try my best, Mam,' Gracie promised.

As the train loomed into view, the two women clung on to each other. 'I'm sorry I've let you and Dad down,' Gracie whispered.

Mrs Price gave her daughter a long, hard look. 'What's done is done,' she said firmly. 'Time to move on, eh?'

Struggling to hold back her tears, Gracie gave a feeble nod. 'I'll miss you, Mam,' she cried.

'I'll miss you too, my lass,' Mrs Price gulped as she boarded the train. 'Be brave, sweetheart, God bless.'

For all of Ada's warning, Gracie was alarmed by her first sight of the girl she was to share a room with. Pale-faced, with huge, dark, sad eyes, Zelda looked more like an abandoned child than a pregnant woman. Glancing anxiously at Ada, who had just introduced the two young women, Zelda held out her hand to her new room-mate.

'Hello, I happy to see you,' she said in a low, trembling voice. 'I hope you are happy with me?'

Ada, who knew what an enormous effort Zelda had put into her welcome, and how much she must have rehearsed it, was relieved and impressed when Gracie responded warmly. 'Thank you, I hope we will be friends?' she said, as she firmly shook Zelda's hand.

Ada could have hugged Gracie; she was a good girl, straight as a die, just like her mother. She was the perfect room-mate for Zelda, who needed all the friends she could get.

6. RAF Duxford

Diana Bishop's slender waist and narrow hips weren't built to disguise her advancing pregnancy. Her years at an exclusive boarding school in Surrey had taught her deportment and a passion for tennis and hockey, which (with her long legs and muscular frame) she excelled at. Diana also excelled at mathematics, and, had it not been for the war, she would most certainly have gone on to study at university level. The demand for smart, analytical women with a flair for maths soon drew Diana into the WAAFs, where her talents were quickly spotted by her senior officers. They agreed that Miss Bishop would be perfectly suited to the work of a radio locations plotter. Shortly after Diana was transferred to Duxford, an RAF air base a few miles outside of the ancient university city of Cambridge. Diana's smart Women's Auxiliary Airforce uniform, of which she had originally been inordinately proud, was presently causing her great concern. The tight-fitting, blue barathea wool skirt (worn with a black tie over a crisp white shirt) was bursting to the point of ripping at the waistband. Diana had bought larger shirts to replace the ones she had outgrown, which she draped artfully around her thickening waistline in the hope that nobody would guess her condition. Diana's biggest fear was that her colleagues at Duxford would guess that she was pregnant before she even had a chance to inform the father.

Her beloved, RAF Senior Officer Harry Ferguson, whom she had met in Duxford's Control Room, was regularly absent. 'Working the Field' was the official term. Harry's colleagues never referred to his unexplained absences, which got longer and longer, and, because they didn't mention it, Diana felt that she should not do so either. Right now, she longed to know when Harry would be returning. She had to tell him he would soon be a father, but, if the truth were known, Diana was dreading it. What would his reaction be when she dropped the bombshell? She was sure he would be shocked rigid, possibly disappointed; he might even be angry with her. When Harry finally showed up in the officers' gallery, Diana's knees went weak with relief. Just the sight of him standing tall in his pale-blue RAF officer's uniform, broad-chested and in command, puffing studiously on his pipe, instantly made her feel calmer. His still powerful presence dominated the space as he studied the gridded table-map, around which several WAAFs were working. Though the atmosphere in the Ops Block was always one of high tension, Harry's focus and composure never faltered as he made swift mathematical decisions that would save lives. The sound of his deep, strong voice on the line to Radar Intelligence soothed her addled nerves, and, taking her place around the mapping table, Diana put on her radio headset.

*

Feeling light-headed and queasy from the clouds of cigarette smoke circulating in the stuffy room, Diana was relieved when it was time for her break; desperate for some fresh air, she made her way outside, where she smiled when she heard Harry's quick step behind her.

'Sweetheart,' he cried, as she rushed into his arms. 'It's wonderful to see you.'

Diana could barely speak for happiness; all she wanted was to stay just as they were, locked in each other's arms.

'Then he can never go away again,' she thought wistfully.

Smiling into her beautiful, radiant face, Harry kissed her soft pink lips. 'I've missed you, my darling.'

Knowing just how vital it was for her to talk to him as soon as possible, she quickly said, 'Can we go out for dinner tonight, somewhere quiet, away from here?'

Harry gave a roguish smile. 'Certainly, and spend the rest of the night making love.'

Hoping that nobody had heard his passionate declaration, blushing Diana quickly glanced over her shoulder.

'Sweetheart,' she warned. 'People might hear.'

'I don't care who hears,' Harry declared as he lifted Diana up and swung her around. 'You're my girl, Diana Bishop – and I love you!'

Harry booked a cosy, candle-lit table for two in the village pub, which served good ale and surprisingly good local game that enhanced the usual dreary rationed food.

'You look more beautiful than ever, darling,' he whispered softly, as they sat facing each other.

Diana smiled. She'd taken a lot of trouble dressing for the occasion; she longed to wear one of her gorgeous, silk-crêpe feminine dresses, but none of them fitted her any more. In the end she relied on her three-strand pearl necklace with matching droplet earrings (a twenty-first birthday gift from her parents) to add glamour to her rather plain mauve-coloured twin set and pleated black skirt.

With Harry's eyes lingering over her face, Diana felt, for the first time in weeks, like a desirable woman again. Wanting to hold the moment for as long as possible, she decided to drop her bombshell at the end of the evening rather than at the beginning, little knowing that Harry had his own bombshell to drop. After they'd been served a bitter blend of chicory coffee, Harry surprised her by taking a small velvet box from his pocket and laying it on the table. Her heart in her mouth, Diana watched as he flipped open the lid to reveal a ring with a cluster of diamonds and sapphires set on a thick gold band.

'Love of my life, darling Diana, will you marry me?'

Astonished and completely overwhelmed, Diana gasped at the sight of the beautiful ring that glittered in the candlelight. Gazing into Harry's handsome face, which was presently suffused with emotion, she cried out joyfully, 'Yes! Oh, yes!'

Reaching for her left-hand, Harry slipped the ring on to her wedding finger. 'It fits,' she cried in surprise.

'Of course, it fits!' he chuckled. 'I've been planning every detail of this moment for weeks.'

'Oh, Harry, Harry,' she sighed, as she gazed dreamily at her engagement ring. 'I never expected this.'

He leant across to tilt her chin, so he could look into her eyes, which sparkled almost as much as the large pale-blue sapphires on her finger.

'You didn't think I loved you enough to want to spend the rest of my life with you?' he teased.

Diana tensed; she couldn't go on deceiving him. The moment of truth really had come.

'Sweetheart,' she started nervously. 'I've got a bit of a surprise for you too.'

Seeing her lips quiver, Harry sat bolt upright. 'What is it?' he demanded. 'Is something wrong?'

'Well, yes . . .' she mumbled nervously.

Now quite alarmed, Harry tone was sharp: 'For God's sake, what is it?'

Taking a deep breath to steady her nerves, Diana blurted out, 'I'm pregnant.'

For several long seconds Harry just stared at her. 'Pregnant –'

'Three months' pregnant, to be precise.'

'God!' he gasped. 'Why didn't you tell me before?'

Diana protested in her own defence: 'Because you've been away so much! I never know where you are when you go away – I couldn't even send you a letter,' she told him pointedly.

Suddenly aware of her pale, strained face, Harry asked anxiously, 'Are you all right, sweetheart? Have you been ill?'

Diana pulled down the corners of her mouth in a

grimace. 'I've been pretty sick,' she confessed. 'A number of the Ops girls have commented on how awful I look.'

'You could never look awful, my darling.'

With Harry's sweet proposal fresh in her mind, Diana was more than aware that what she had to say next might shatter the romantic atmosphere, but knowing that Harry might suddenly disappear at any time made her resolutely push on.

'We don't have to keep this baby,' she started. 'I've had plenty of time to consider and ...' Her voice wavered. 'Maybe it would be a good idea to think about having it adopted?'

Harry's brow creased. 'Really?'

Forcing herself to be practical, Diana continued, 'We never planned for a baby; the timing right now, with you away so much and me working around the clock on the base, is all wrong.'

Looking sad, Harry reached out to take her hand. 'I'm not sure that I altogether agree with you.'

Struggling to hold back her tears, Diana added angrily, 'I could kick myself for getting pregnant in the first place; I'm old enough to know better.'

'We're both old enough to know better,' Harry said, giving her a sly smile. 'We have got rather carried away in our love-making recently.'

Recalling their nights of passion, Diana blushed. 'We should have been *a lot* more careful.'

Across the table Harry leant in to wipe tears from

her cheek. 'I have no regrets, my darling,' he responded passionately. 'I've just asked you to marry me; what you've just told me makes me want to marry you even more.'

'Because you pity me?' she asked miserably.

'No! Because I love you, Diana, and . . . I don't want you to have our child adopted,' he added honestly.

'You want to keep it?' she asked incredulously.

'I most certainly do!'

Looking confused, Diana said, 'Won't being a father hamper your career?'

Harry burst out laughing. 'No, but it might hamper yours!'

Knowing that his lovely young fiancée was pregnant filled Harry with a huge wave of protective love for her; so far nobody but he knew of her condition, though he saw with new eyes over the next few days how his fiancée's previous flat belly now had a gentle swell. If he had noticed, surely it was only a question of time before others did. Worried that he might be called away from base sooner rather than later, something that he was anxious to play down for fear of upsetting Diana, Harry made a surprising announcement one night after they'd eaten their tripe-and-onion supper in Diana's kitchen, pleasantly warmed by the Aga that Diana kept well stoked up with wood and coal.

'Darling, it might be a good idea to have a chat with the local vicar fairly soon,' Harry suggested. 'If he could procure a special licence for us, we could get married right away.'

Overcome with emotion, Diana rose and went to sit on Harry's warm knee. 'I'd absolutely love that,' she told him, as she brushed her lips against his cheek.

'Well, then, let's try to see the vicar this week.'

Diana blushed shyly, 'Do you plan to tell him I'm pregnant?'

Kissing the top of her head, Harry said, 'No, my sweet. I'll just say I'm required for urgent duty and we would like to be married before the RAF whisks me away.'

'Do you really think that might happen soon?' she asked, as she laid her head against his strong shoulder.

Stroking her long, beautiful hair, Harry could feel Diana's body tense as she waited for his answer. The last thing he wanted to do was to upset his beloved, but, given the circumstances, he could hardly lie.

'It's more than likely,' he admitted. 'But, young lady, posted elsewhere or not, I want us married right away.'

'We'll have to notify our parents,' Diana reminded him. 'Mummy's bound to want to invite the world and his dog, and she'll insist on bridesmaids and a lavish wedding breakfast,' she sighed.

Harry stopped her wandering thoughts with a kiss. 'What do you say that we keep it a private affair? Just me and you and the vicar? After all it's not so unusual these days,' he added. 'With men briefly home on leave lots of couples tie the knot without any pomp and ceremony.'

Delighted by his suggestion, Diana smiled in relief. 'Yes, darling, let's keep it a private affair.'

The morning the vicar's letter arrived, Diana cycled to the air base faster than she had ever cycled before. She was desperate to show Harry, who had been working throughout the night, the letter in which the vicar had suggested a few dates for their wedding day. Giddy with excitement and breathless with exertion, she signed in, then hurried past the armed guards to dash into the Ops Room, where her eyes immediately flew up to the gallery. As usual there were the officers, chain-smoking as they barked instructions to the WAAFs surrounding the mapping table. Diana did a startled double-take when she realized that Harry wasn't at his usual desk, talking down the line to Radar.

'Where is he?' she thought.

Thinking Harry might have popped out to stretch his legs, or even be in the officers' mess eating breakfast, she went in search of him, but found him nowhere. Realizing that now she would be late for work, she ran back to the Ops Block. She had just taken her place around the mapping table when her friend pushed an envelope into her hand.

'Your young man asked me to make sure you got this,' she said with a saucy wink.

Throughout the morning shift Diana didn't have a private moment to open the letter, which burned in her pocket; finally, when she was granted a five-minute tea-break, she went outside and (hardly daring to breathe) read Harry's letter.

My Darling,

*The call that I've been expecting came last night. By the time
you read this I'll be on my way. Stick to the plan we made,
arrange the wedding, I'll be back next week at latest. I love you,
sweetest Diana, be brave.*

Yours,
H

7. Dunkirk

A few days later Dora arrived for work looking like she'd been to hell and back. Seeing her colleague's haunted expression and red puffy eyes, Ada quickly removed Dora from the nursery and took her into the privacy of her own office, where Dora all but collapsed into Ada's arms.

'We got a telegram last night,' she wailed. 'Our Perce is dead!' Almost incoherent, she slumped into the nearest chair, where she lit up a Woodbine that she drew on heavily.

'Oh, Dora, I'm so dreadfully sorry. What happened?' Ada gasped in horror.

'We can only go off what we read in the papers about Perce's ship, HMS *Wakeful*,' Dora explained. 'They loaded up at Dunkirk but on their way home they were torpedoed by a U-boat. Sunk . . .' she sobbed.

Recalling the horrifying radio announcement describing the evacuation of Dunkirk, Ada gave an involuntary shiver.

'Dear God,' she thought. 'What must poor Perce and his crew have gone through?'

But for the courage of the crews of the little Dunkirk boats, who had stepped in at the request of the government, the British Expeditionary Force might have been lost altogether. Just thinking of the Allied troops, thousands upon thousands of men and boys, all lined up in ranks awaiting rescue, brought tears to Ada's eyes. After a humiliating retreat through the countryside just ahead of German forces, the troops must have thought, once they were on the beaches almost in sight of the White Cliffs of Dover, that they were nearly home and dry. As it turned out, they were tragically stranded, sitting ducks for the Luftwaffe, who ruthlessly strafed them where they stood. Ada would never forget Churchill's speech to the nation after the event.

'We shall fight on the seas and oceans, we shall fight with growing confidence and growing strength in the air, we shall defend our Island, whatever the cost may be.'

Against all the odds little crafts had braved the Channel (and the Luftwaffe) to bring home over three hundred thousand troops. Yet again Hitler had been denied victory but at a high cost: three thousand British troops had been killed during the evacuation, one of whom was Dora's young son, Percy.

After Dora had smoked three cigarettes in rapid succession, Ada implored her to go home, but poor Dora, utterly distraught after receiving the telegram that every mother dreaded, refused point-blank to leave Mary Vale.

'I can't be in the house with memories of the boys all around me,' she sobbed. 'Mi husband couldn't face it either – he's gone to't shipyard and I've come 'ere – working's the only way we'll ever get through this,' she said, pinning her cap firmly on her head and setting off resolutely for the nursery.

Shirley's gentle heart ached for Dora. 'God help the poor woman,' she said to Ada. 'To lose a boy so young, and in such a horrible way.'

'I don't know how she'll ever get over it,' Ada murmured.

'Would you mind if I went to the chapel, Ada?' Shirley begged. 'I need to be close to God to pray for Dora's lad and for all the others that died alongside him.'

'Dearest!' Ada exclaimed, as she hugged Shirley tightly. 'Please go and take all our thoughts with you; for sure, your prayers will go more quickly to heaven than anybody else's.'

While Shirley found solace in the chapel, Dora found some solace from the babies she nursed. Holding their warm bodies close to her heart eased some of the agony that racked her, and seeing their little hands eagerly reaching out to her as she bent to lift them from their cradles even brought a shadow of a smile to her lips. When Ada found Dora (half asleep herself) cradling a baby, she begged her to take a break.

'Come into the kitchen and I'll make you a nice hot cup of tea,' she suggested.

After she'd drunk her tea and chain-smoked several more Woodbines, Dora spoke with a catch in her throat.

'Our Jack doesn't know about Perce, and we can't tell him 'cos we don't know where he is.' Burying her face in her hands, Dora started to sob. 'God spare our Jack,' she wept. 'If anything should happen to him, me and his dad would have nothing to live for.'

The following day when Dr Reid arrived for his first day on duty, Ada gave him an update on all his patients and informed him of the latest arrivals too.

'I gather you know Gracie Price, from Barrow,' she said.

Jamie nodded. 'She came to my surgery, a strong young woman. I recommended that she should come here to have her baby. As I recall I had no concerns about her pregnancy.'

Closing the surgery door so they could continue in private, Ada came straight to the point. 'I do have concerns for a relatively new arrival, a young German woman,' she started. 'Her name is Zelda; she's the first patient on your list this morning,' Ada added, as she nodded at the list she'd drawn up and left on his desk. 'I was hoping that once she had settled into the Home, her condition might improve but if anything it's worsened.'

Jamie frowned as he buttoned up his laundered doctor's coat. 'How has it worsened?' he asked.

'She barely eats, takes no exercise and, once her chores are completed, she hides away in her room.' Ada took a deep breath. 'She's not popular among the residents either; the only person I've ever seen her talking to is Gracie, with whom she shares a room.'

'Are the residents hostile to her?' Jamie enquired.

'They've certainly not put themselves out to welcome her,' Ada told him hotly. 'I've overheard some of them whispering behind Zelda's back: they call her 'The German – the enemy', that kind of bigoted rubbish!'

Jamie couldn't help but notice that when Sister Ada's blood was up her blue eyes flashed with passion; he also couldn't fail to see how her tight belted uniform emphasized her slender waist and hips, and the stout black brogues and thick black stockings that she wore did nothing to take away from her long, shapely legs. He dearly wished that he didn't find Mary Vale's Senior Sister quite so attractive, but every time he saw her (and this was only his second visit) his heart involuntarily skipped a beat.

Even though Ada had forewarned him, Jamie was nevertheless shocked by Zelda's wasted appearance. Seeing how tense and nervy she was when she walked into his surgery, he attempted to speak to her in rusty, faltering German, which she responded to eagerly.

'Women here – hate me! Call me Fascist, Nazi.'

Shocked, Jamie struggled on in German. 'I apologize for their unkindness; they are prejudiced.' He frowned as he tapped the desk searching for words. 'The most important thing is you must take care of your baby,' he insisted.

Zelda's huge, sorrowful dark eyes brimmed over with tears, and, abandoning herself completely, she gave an agonized sob. 'I have NOTHING to live for!' she cried in German.

Realizing how desperate his patient was, probably on the point of a nervous breakdown, Jamie replied in a mixture of English and German. 'Zelda, you have something to live for; if you die, your baby dies. Is that what you want?'

As his patient's tears subsided, Jamie turned to Ada. 'I need to examine her,' he murmured.

Ada stepped out from behind the desk where she'd positioned herself and laid a comforting arm around Zelda's shuddering shoulders. 'Shhh, sweetheart,' she said softly, leading her to the narrow examination bed and helping her to lie down.

When Zelda's skirt and underclothes had been removed, Ada was yet again shocked by how thin she was; the only shape to her was the bump between her skinny ribcage and her bony pelvis. After Jamie had washed his hands, he carefully felt Zelda's swollen tummy then, after fixing his stethoscope to his ears, he moved the instrument around her tummy in order to hear the baby's heartbeat. Zelda lay as stiff and rigid as a plank.

'Take some deep breaths,' Jamie instructed.

'Like this,' Ada added, as she breathed slowly and steadily in and out.

Zelda copied her pattern of breathing and gradually her pale body relaxed enough for Jamie to complete his examination. When he had finished, Ada helped Zelda to get dressed, then she returned to the chair across the desk from Jamie. In the best German he could muster Jamie spoke slowly and firmly to his patient.

'Your baby is weak; the heartbeat is weak.'

Zelda went so pale that Ada grasped her arm to stop her from fainting.

66

Speaking in a mixture of English and German, Jamie purposefully didn't avoid stressing the danger of Zelda's delicate condition.

'If you want your baby to live, you must eat, Zelda, you must rest, sleep and exercise.'

With an agonized expression on her thin, pale face, Zelda replied, 'I want my husband's baby.'

'Then you MUST take care of yourself,' Jamie concluded. 'It is the only way to keep your child.'

Gracie's examination with Dr Reid could not have been more different from Zelda's; as Jamie had said previously to Ada, Gracie was strong and healthy. He did take the liberty of asking her how she got on with her new room-mate. Gracie was both kind and forthcoming.

'Zelda cries a lot, especially at night when she thinks I'm asleep; she has nightmares too – she always calls out the name of her husband, "Izaak". She's frightened to death of t'other girls,' Gracie informed Jamie. 'When we go down for meals, I can see how scared she is, so I try to do the talking, but long term that's not going to help her, is it?' Gracie looked enquiringly from Jamie to Ada. 'Surely things can't go on the way they are?'

Ada's eyes flashed with anger. 'You're quite right, Gracie, things definitely can't go on the way they are!'

Later that day, at tea-time, Ada sat down at the large mahogany dining table, which was spread with plates of spam sandwiches and bowls of jelly. The residents weren't taken aback by her presence, Sister Ada often joined them for a cup of tea when she had time to spare. Noticing that Gracie was there, though not her roommate, Ada poured herself a strong cup of hot tea before helping herself to a spam sandwich as she sat back in her chair and calmly started to eat.

'Off-duty, Sister?' cheeky Annie asked.

Ada shook her head as she set down her cup and saucer. 'No,' she responded. 'Actually, I need some advice and I thought you might be able to help me.'

Curious, the girls paused in their eating and drinking. 'What kind of advice?' ever suspicious Annie asked.

'I wonder if any of you know how many refugees there are in Britain today?' Ada started.

A stunned silence met her question. Ada paused before she continued. 'Over seventy thousand, most of them Jews, women and children seeking asylum. They come here with nothing, from France, Italy, Spain, Germany.' Ada paused to sweep her eyes around the circle of women before she purposefully added what some already knew and others chose to ignore. 'Zelda is one such, widowed by the Nazis, who shot her husband simply because he was a Jew.'

A dumb embarrassed silence followed Ada's delivery. Pushing her point home, Ada asked, 'Have any of you taken the trouble to speak to Zelda?'

Apart from Gracie every girl present shook her head. 'So not one of you has taken pity on a poor refugee who has arrived here seeking sanctuary?' Ada persisted.

Heartless Annie shrugged. 'She don't speak English and I don't speak German.'

Feeling like she was going to lose her temper, Ada took a deep breath. Bessie lit up a cigarette before she boldly said, 'She could be a bloody German spy for all we know.'

Ada laughed mockingly at the very idea. 'A pregnant German spy – I don't think so! Disguised as a Jew on the run is a bit far-flung, Bessie,' she scoffed.

Impatient with their pathetic excuses, Ada continued with a sharp snap in her voice. 'She's scared stiff, she's not at all well, and she's very lonely. Would it be too much to ask, ladies, that you give Zelda a little respect, an occasional smile, a kind word?'

Marie, one of the kinder girls, asked a genuine question. 'It's hard to communicate when you're not sure how much she understands,' she said with an embarrassed blush.

Gracie intervened at this point. 'I share a room with Zelda, and she understands more than you think. Just smile and say hello when she comes into a room, sit next to her and encourage her to speak,' Gracie urged. 'She needs friends.'

Ada threw Gracie a grateful smile before she turned to the other residents. 'For centuries Mary Vale has opened its doors to welcome outsiders. Let's not stop now, ladies,' she begged.

Leaving the dining room, Ada slipped upstairs to Zelda's room on the second floor. After tapping gently on the door, she entered to find Zelda gazing out of the large bay window that gave wonderful views of the marsh, now washed clean by the outgoing tide.

'I've brought you something to eat, Zelda, dear,' Ada said, as she set down a bowl of jelly and a cup of tea on a small bedside table.

'Thank you, Sister,' Zelda replied shyly. 'You kind woman to me.' Picking up the bowl of jelly, she dipped a spoon into it, 'See, I eat,' Zelda announced. 'I listen to good doctor,' she added with a trace of a smile.

It was Gracie and kind Marie who led the vanguard to befriend Zelda. After Ada's ticking-off Gracie absolutely insisted that Zelda came down for ALL of her meals, while Marie, in the dining room, insisted that everybody behaved decently at the very least towards Zelda. Annie and Bessie remained predictably hostile, but, as they were now outranked by the majority, the general attitude towards Zelda slowly changed. Though hesitant to start with, the residents made a conscious effort, offering baffled Zelda 'a brew' or 'a butty', which Zelda, equally keen to make friends quickly, accepted, though she wasn't quite sure what she was agreeing to. Sitting at the dining table between Gracie on one side and Marie on the other, Zelda began to eat and drink healthily. Much to Gracie's amazement, once she even tried to join in a discussion about the sex of her child.

'Want boy,' Zelda said, pointing shyly to her still small tummy. 'Like husband.'

'I have no husband,' Marie replied.

With her deep, dark eyes full of tears, Zelda added, 'I also have no husband.'

'Bastard Nazis,' Marie muttered under her breath, as she poured out more tea for Zelda from the vast teapot Sister Mary Paul constantly replenished.

Zelda cocked her head as she considered Marie's words. 'Yah,' she agreed; then, with a sudden burst of anger, she repeated what Marie had said: 'Bastard Nazis!'

8. East to West

A fortnight had passed since Harry had left, but he still had not returned home. Though worried sick about the whereabouts of her fiancé and what he might be doing, Diana had no choice but to write an apologetic letter to the vicar, putting on hold all of his suggested wedding dates, after which, emotional and frightened, she wondered what on earth to do. Exhausted after a long day in the Ops Block, Diana cycled back to her cottage and slumped in the armchair by the Aga. After loosening the waistband of her skirt, she stared ruefully at her now large tummy and considered her options. With Harry still not back (and having absolutely no idea when he might return) Diana was beginning to realize that she couldn't afford to sit around waiting for her beloved to walk through the door. With him gone it was up to her to make arrangements for the months ahead, and one thing was clear: she certainly didn't want to give birth in the local cottage hospital.

'I have to get away,' Diana muttered out loud.

Only recently had she rather shame-facedly seen the doctor on the RAF base, who had confirmed her dates and given her the names of several mother-and-baby homes. Diana had rather randomly chosen a place called Mary Vale, on the edge of the Lake District, where, when she had made enquiries, she had been told there was an immediate vacancy for a fee-paying resident.

Though none of the officers in the Ops Block had alluded to her fiancé's prolonged absence, Diana had coerced one of Harry's pals on the base to meet her for a drink in the officers' mess. Knowing how vital it was that she left a line of communication open between herself and Harry before she left Duxford, Diana came straight to the point.

'I'm in a bit of a hole,' she had blurted out as soon as they had sat down with their drinks. 'You see, I'm pregnant.'

Gordon blushed to the roots of his short wavy hair, then gulped back a large mouthful of bitter from his pint glass.

'Harry and I were planning on getting married, but he's been gone for weeks now, and I can't afford to hang around here waiting for him; otherwise I'll start to show and that will create quite a scandal,' she added, as she lowered her eyes towards her swelling tummy.

Looking like a cornered animal, blushing Gordon averted his gaze. Determined to keep his attention, Diana rolled on. 'I'm just at my wits' end,' she said, and burst into tears.

Handing her his perfectly ironed handkerchief, Gordon nervously checked that nobody was listening in on their conversation before muttering nervously, 'What do you want of me, Diana?'

Diana quickly mopped her eyes before reaching into her handbag for a letter that she handed to him. 'When

Harry returns to base, please would you give him this letter, which contains the address of where I'm going to have our baby.'

Hoping to bring the conversation to a speedy end, Gordon gave an embarrassed nod. 'Of course,' he muttered.

'And here's a copy of my address for you too,' Diana added with a trembling lip. 'Please will you notify me of any news, be it good or bad?'

Gordon briefly glanced at the address she had written down on a piece of paper. 'Grange-over-Sands,' he had grunted. 'Bloody long way from Cambridge and the Fens!'

Diana smiled bleakly. 'A bloody long way from any-where,' she agreed.

The Ops Block team were surprised by Diana's sudden decision to transfer to a base nearer to her family home, a lie she had concocted one sleepless night that she clung to throughout all the awkward questioning she had to endure.

'Don't know how you managed a transfer quite so quickly,' one curious girl queried.

'Won't you miss being near your nice young man?' another had teased.

Up in the viewing gallery Harry's closest colleague, a man named Derek Robson, overheard the cross-examination going on around the mapping table and took pity on Diana. 'Enough chatting, ladies, we've got work to do.'

*

Though guilty about abandoning her war work, even though she knew she had absolutely no choice, Diana was ultimately relieved to leave Duxford; but when it came to leaving her sweet little thatched cottage she had wept. She had been so happy in Shelford, where she and Harry had spent so many happy times: walking by the river, cooking meals together, lying in bed wrapped in each other's arms listening to the rain pattering against the windowpane. Was her beloved alive and well? Was he suffering, cold and hungry? She could bear any amount of waiting if only she knew that Harry was safe. Desperately trying to blank out memories that would break her heart, Diana determinedly set off on her journey to the Mother and Baby Home two hundred miles away on the other side of England.

Ada was impressed by Diana's good manners and calm composure when, hours and hours after the exhausted girl had left Cambridge, she was welcomed to Mary Vale.

'Delighted to meet you, Miss Bishop,' Ada said warmly. 'How was your journey?'

'Very, very long,' Diana answered with a weary smile. 'Endless changes on packed troop trains. I felt so sorry for the weary soldiers and sailors; some of them were so tired they slept standing up in smoky corridors; a few even climbed into the luggage racks, where they dozed off,' she said, smiling. 'Poor souls, they didn't seem to have a clue where they were going.'

Diana glanced curiously around the sitting room with its comfy old sofas and summer blooms; the phlox and carnations arranged in vases along the windowsills gave off a perfume that the cool evening air intensified.

'Let's just say, I'm glad it's over,' she added, as she gratefully accepted a cup of tea and a slice of bread and butter from Ada.

'I gather from your letters that you worked as a WAAF on an RAF base in Cambridge,' Ada commented. 'Taxing work, I'm sure.'

Diana nodded. 'It was demanding work for sure, and pretty terrifying at times, but I loved every minute; it's where I met my fiancé – we worked in the Ops Block,' she said with a hint of pride.

Ada knew too well not to question further; a girl arriving on her own was on her own for the most obvious of reasons: her man was gone. Changing the subject, Ada explained that Diana would have her own single room on the second floor. Since Zelda and Gracie had bonded so well in the time that they had shared the big double room, Ada certainly didn't want to disturb their domestic arrangements, but she felt sure that Diana would enjoy being on the same floor as two women who were both due to give birth around the same time as herself.

'You have your own room just across the corridor from two other pregnant ladies,' Ada explained.

Diana gave a grateful smile. 'It will be such a relief to stop pretending,' she admitted. 'It's been quite a struggle hiding my condition from my colleagues at work.'

'You can relax all you want now,' Ada said with a reassuring smile. 'Everybody here is either expecting a baby or they've just given birth; you'll be no exception. When you've had enough time to think things over, we can discuss your plans for the future.'

Diana gave a polite smile. Right now she didn't even dare to think about the future; she was simply grateful for sanctuary, a place where, she prayed, she would soon hear from Harry; then, hopefully, if her prayers were answered and they were eventually reunited, they could discuss their future together.

After showing the newcomer to her room and the nearest bathroom, Ada bade her goodnight, then left her in peace. Diana washed the dirt of the day off her face and body, then gratefully snuggled down in her narrow single bed and closed her aching eyes. Listening to the soothing sound of the waves rhythmically breaking as the tide came in, Diana gave over her thoughts to Harry.

'God bless you, my darling,' she prayed. 'Wherever you are, stay safe and come home to me soon.'

The next morning, even though the blackout blind was drawn down, the light still managed to filter around the edges, giving Diana a chance to examine the room that would be hers for the coming months. Though it was nothing like the charming thatched cottage she had left behind in Cambridge, it was nevertheless clean and neat, with a high ceiling and a big sash window that, when she rolled back the blind, gave stunning views of a well-kept garden running down to a vast marsh, presently riotous with the calls of wading sea-birds.

Suddenly hungry, Diana slipped out of bed and dressed herself in a cool, roomy, cotton frock, then headed down the corridor to the bathroom, where she bumped into two girls busy cleaning their teeth.

'Hello! We've been expecting you,' a girl with beautiful thick brunette hair said through a froth of bubbles. Wiping her mouth on a flannel, she smiled and extended a hand to Diana. 'I'm Gracie, and this is Zelda.'

Gracie's companion was small and delicate with a mass of bright red curly hair and a pale complexion flecked with freckles.

'Pleased to meet you both,' Diana said, as she warmly shook hands with her new neighbours.

Smiling sweetly, Zelda said, 'Our room is close to you, we welcome you.'

Rather intrigued by her obvious German accent, Diana nodded enthusiastically. 'Thank you, I'd like that.'

'Pop in and see us any time you fancy a chat,' Gracie babbled on. 'Now, if you'll excuse me, I'm starving,' she said, as she gathered up her toilet bag. 'My advice to you as a new girl is, don't hang about in the morning or there won't be any toast left.'

Zelda giggled as she trailed after her room-mate, calling, 'You are always so hungry, *meine Liebe.*'

Heading towards the stairs, Gracie threw her a cheeky smile. 'Course I am, I'm pregnant!'

Sitting between Gracie and Zelda, surrounded by a noisy crowd of residents, Diana marvelled at her new social group. They could not have been more different from the highly educated, ambitious young WAAFs she had previously spent her time with. Here heavily pregnant women sighed and groaned with the effort of walking or standing for too long, and unashamedly supported their heavy tummies as they moved around the Home. Diana noticed that chattering Gracie, with her bright smile and lively expression, constantly attracted attention; she was surprised by how much the residents turned to her for advice.

'Are you doing Sister Ada's exercise classes this afternoon, Gracie?'

'Wouldn't miss it for the world!' came back the cheery reply.

'Should I write to mi mam and tell her I've had the baby?' another enquired.

'Why not?' Gracie retorted. 'It's not like she doesn't know you're pregnant!'

'Father Ben says he's found me some good folks who'd like to adopt my little boy – shall I accept?'

Gracie vehemently nodded her head. 'I'd trust Father Ben's judgement one hundred per cent,' she declared.

Observant Diana noticed that Zelda seemed quite happy to be in Gracie's shadow. Determined to draw her out a little, Diana patted her own tummy; then, speaking in German, she said, 'When is your baby due?'

Zelda's huge dark eyes opened wide in surprise. 'You speak German?'

Diana gave a modest smile. 'My school was keen on languages, French, Latin and German.'

Over breakfast, chattering away, the two women

learnt a little about each other's former lives. Diana's heart ached when she heard about Zelda's tragic loss; then suddenly, when gently questioned by Zelda, she found herself opening up about her own loss. Weepy with emotion, she confessed, 'I was supposed to be getting married not long ago; then my fiancé disappeared. I haven't a clue where he is.'

Zelda laid a cool hand over Diana's trembling one. 'I will pray for his safe return,' she promised. 'It breaks the heart to lose the one you love.' Casting her eyes around the room, she added quietly, 'I think many hearts are broken here.'

'Yours too, I'm sure,' Diana said gently.

Zelda dropped her voice to an embarrassed whisper. 'Diana, I have to ask you a favour. Though it is good to speak in my mother tongue with you, it is not good for the residents to hear me speaking German. It is the enemy's language and it upsets them.'

Diana gave an understanding nod. 'So, please, do you mind if we only speak German when we are in private?' Zelda finished.

'English it is!' Diana replied. Pushing back her chair, she rose to her feet. 'Now will you please show me the chores list?' she asked with a grin. 'I've been told I've got to earn my keep, so I'd better get started right away.'

9. Market Gardening

Ada was immensely relieved to see how much more at ease Zelda was in the dining room – sharing meals with her fellow residents, who now bade Zelda a cheery good morning when she walked into the room, to which blushing Zelda would reply: 'Good morning, how are you?'

'The situation's a lot better than it was,' Ada confided in Dora one morning, as they sterilized instruments in the delivery room.

Hollow-cheeked Dora, who had not returned to her former bouncing good health since her son's tragic death, sighed with relief. 'Thank God for that. I don't think the poor kid could have taken much more.'

As they worked side by side, Ada gave Dora a quick glance. 'Any news from your Jack?' she asked cautiously.

'We got a letter in answer to ours telling him about our Percy, no address of course.' She gave a long, shuddering sigh. 'He's utterly heart-broken, poor lad, says he can't imagine life without his twin brother. Oh, dear God, keep him safe,' she prayed out loud.

'Dearest,' Ada murmured, as she comforted tearful Dora, 'all of us pray for your Jack's safe return.'

Dora mopped her tears with the hankie that Ada handed to her. 'I suppose half the country's in the same state,' she continued sadly. 'Worried out of their minds and jumping every time they see the postman walking down the path.'

Ada smiled sympathetically. 'We're a nation of fathers, brothers, mothers, sisters and lovers, all praying for the same thing.'

'Peace,' Dora said with a yearning sigh.

Unfortunately, Dora's hope for peace was shattered by Italy's declaration of war on Britain almost immediately after the Germans started heavily bombing Paris. Though the sun shone down on Mary Vale, and the Irish Sea sparkled under a blue sky, these were undoubtedly dark times, with Hitler running roughshod over Europe.

One sunny morning Ada was surprised to find Zelda crouched down on the grass, apparently looking for something on the ground. She approached the girl, who was completely absorbed in her task.

'What are you doing?' Ada asked curiously.

Taken by surprise, Zelda jumped at the sound of Ada's voice; then, frowning, she tried to explain herself. 'I . . . er, this . . .' She demonstrated pulling up weeds growing around a clump of carnations.

'Weeding!' Ada laughed.

'Weeding,' Zelda repeated the word. 'I like flowers here,' she said.

Stretching out an arm to take in the wide sweep of the flowerbeds fragrant with the combined perfumes of lilies, roses, stocks, larkspur and daisies, she said to Ada, 'In

München I work in big beautiful *garten* – I make gardens.'

By the end of the conversation Ada discovered that Zelda had, in fact, been a landscape gardener in Germany, and it was clear from her unusually animated manner that it was something she was passionate about.

'You could always do some gardening here?' Ada suddenly suggested.

Zelda looked puzzled. 'Here, in Home?'

When Ada nodded, Zelda's face lit up. 'I like that,' she grinned. 'Yes, please!'

Ada grinned back at her. 'I'll speak to the gardener right away,' she promised.

The gardener willingly handed over a small plot of land at the side of the house, which was well sheltered by the neighbouring farmer's drystone wall.

'Lass will be doing me a favour,' the gardener said; then, after he'd given a rather embarrassed cough, he added, 'But should a lass in her delicate condition be diggin' in't garden?'

'I'm quite sure she won't be doing too much digging,' Ada assured him. 'Just a bit of pottering about, something to occupy her mind.'

But digging was exactly what Zelda had in mind. The next time Ada saw the plot it had been almost completely dug over, and Zelda, wearing a loose cotton smock and a floral scarf as a turban, was on her hands and knees grubbing up earth with her bare hands.

'Hello, Zelda!' Ada called.

When the girl looked up, Ada could see her face had caught the sun and her dark eyes were much brighter. 'Plant cabbages,' Zelda answered proudly. 'See.' She held up a packet of seeds. 'Cabbages.'

Ada peered at the picture on the packet. 'Sprouts,' she said, smiling as she corrected Zelda. 'Like little cabbages.'

Standing on the edge of the plot, Ada admired Zelda's hard work. 'I thought you were going to grow flowers?'

Zelda shook her head. 'Garden here has many beautiful flowers, but no cabbages. I grow food for mothers, and good food for our babies.'

Ada was incredibly touched by the girl's generosity; here she was slaving away, growing food for her fellow residents, who had only recently stopped treating her like a German spy.

'You're very kind, Zelda,' she replied. 'I'm sure the residents will appreciate it, and Sister Mary Paul always needs plenty in the kitchen.' She stopped as she gazed at the seed packets lying on the ground. 'Where did the seeds come from?'

'Farmer man,' Zelda explained, pointing to the farmhouse across the fields.

'Ah, yes, his name is Farmer Arkwright,' Ada told her.

Zelda wiped a muddy hand across her face. 'Tomorrow farmer man bring more seeds.'

It wasn't long before everybody knew about Zelda's garden, curiosity driving the residents outdoors to inspect her vegetables growing in healthy abundance in the sunshine.

'We're lucky,' Sister Mary Paul told Shirley, who was helping her with the daily bread-making. 'On top of our weekly food rations we get milk, eggs, cheese and the occasional rabbit or pigeon from Farmer Arkwright, and now we've got Zelda growing beautiful vegetables for the Home.'

'And it all disappears,' Shirley pointed out. 'There're never any leftovers.'

'The residents are always hungry,' Sister Mary Paul chuckled. 'Not surprising when you're eating for two.'

After Shirley had left the bread to rise, she made a flask of strong tea, then went to the garden shed, where she found a spade and a trowel. Tucking the flask under one arm and the tools under the other, she set off for Zelda's plot. She found the girl watering a row of tender tomato plants that she had only just dug in.

'Here, let me do that, lovie,' she said, as she relieved a sweating Zelda of a heavy watering can.

'Thank you, Sister,' Zelda muttered.

'Drink this,' Shirley said, and she handed over the flask. 'Go on, sit yourself down over yonder.' She nodded towards a line of shady fruit trees. 'Take a break – you look like you need it.'

Smiling gratefully, Zelda took the flask and went to sit on the cool grass under the trees, where she drank every last drop of the hot tea. When she looked across in Shirley's direction, she was astonished to see her on her haunches, grubbing up weeds in her crisply ironed postulant's blue smock.

'No, no!' Zelda cried as she rose to her feet. 'I do this.'

Shirley firmly held up a hand, which Zelda ignored; picking up her own trowel, Zelda smiled and said, 'We dig together, please?'

Shirley grinned and nodded. 'Two hands are better than one,' she agreed.

The women worked along the rows of vegetables, side by side, Shirley talking non-stop in her broad Lancashire accent, while Zelda, happy and contented in Shirley's company, smiled to herself. It was good to spend time with a friend.

When Dr Reid next came to Mary Vale to check on his patients, he was delighted with Zelda's marked improvement. He was also astonished when Ada told him about Zelda's market garden project.

'She's hardly strong enough to lift a knife and fork!' he exclaimed.

'You should see her with a spade,' Ada chuckled. 'She's a changed woman – and she's got Sister Shirley hoeing and weeding alongside her.' Ada's big blue eyes sparkled with merriment as she recalled various scenes in Zelda's garden. 'Now that the residents know she's growing food for the Home, half of them want to help,' she giggled. 'Not long ago, Zelda hadn't got a friend in the world; now she's got more than she can cope with.'

Jamie smiled. 'It must make a pleasant change to suddenly find yourself popular.'

'It's completely transformed her,' Ada agreed. 'She's sleeping better, eating better, plus her English is coming on in leaps and bounds with everybody talking to her all the time.' Ada suddenly burst out laughing. 'I even heard the gardener asking her in a broad Lancashire accent if she wanted a butty. I could see that Zelda hadn't a clue, but she politely said yes anyway. You should have seen her face when he handed her a great big cheese and onion oven bottom!'

Listening to Ada's spontaneous, full-throated laughter and gazing at her happy face, Jamie wondered how anybody could be so positive about life. Being crippled by polio as a child had left him feeling slightly marginalized. He had always come last in the running race; he couldn't walk fast enough to keep up with his friends in the playground; and he sensed people were talking about him, pointing at him, even when they weren't. As Jamie's strength slowly came back, a steely determination grew in him not to be crippled mentally as well as physically by the disease that had nearly killed him. In his teenage years at grammar school Jamie worked hard on building up his muscle strength; at university he refused to shy away from sporting activities and instead actively involved himself in walking, swimming, running and climbing. He never gave in and as a consequence he never felt ostracized or inferior in his later life. It was only when war broke out and he tried to enlist that he had felt the sense of failure for the first time in his adult life. The experience of a very public rejection had left him bitter and angry, feelings that were mildly assuaged by the vital work he did in Barrow and at the Home; but nevertheless there were too many times when he felt like only half a man.

Stunning, glowing Ada, all light and laughter, full of confidence, compassion and optimism, had clearly never been dismissed as an inferior human being. Losing himself in her sunniness, Jamie had an almost irresistible urge to touch the strand of golden-auburn hair that had wriggled free from the confines of her starched nurse's cap and kiss it. Shocked by his feelings, he said a little too briskly, 'Who's next on the list, Sister?'

'Diana Bishop, our latest arrival,' Ada told him. 'She's very bright and well educated, I thought she might come across as cool and a bit snooty, but she's mixing well with the other residents, mostly thanks to Gracie, who's turning into the Home's social secretary, organizing picnics and walks, swims even,' Ada chuckled as she opened the surgery door to call in the next patient.

As Jamie worked his way through the patient list that Ada had prepared for him, he was all the time aware of her presence: the way she smiled reassuringly at all of the girls as they entered his room; how she helped them settle comfortably on the examination table; the kind words and little jokes she shared with them; but above all the tenderness and concern she had for the vulnerable women in her care.

'No wonder everybody loves her; men must be lining up round the block to date her,' Jamie thought ruefully.

He fleetingly imagined Ada with a tall blond Viking

of a man, an RAF bomber pilot in a pale-blue uniform, goggles on his head, leather jacket thrown carelessly over his shoulders, striding across the tarmac crying out to his heroic team, 'Scramble! Scramble!'

Ada's imaginary lover would perform great deeds in his little Spitfire, popping off Jerry as they attacked him, and blessed with luck he'd return unscathed from every raid and walk straight into the arms of dazzling Ada, who'd welcome him home with warm kisses.

'Snap out of it, man!' he growled angrily to himself. 'You're becoming obsessed with the bloody woman!'

10. Butter and Chores

After her first examination with Dr Reid, Diana was relieved to discover that she was in good health and so was her baby.

'Your baby is a good size with a strong regular heartbeat,' the doctor announced.

Shortly after her arrival Diana had seen Father Ben. In the privacy of his book-lined study in the convent she had admitted with a shame-faced blush that she was worried about her ability to bring up a child on her own.

Father Ben had smiled sympathetically. 'No rush, my child,' he urged. 'Take your time, and God will guide you.'

After leaving Father Ben's office Diana did indeed pray to God to help her to make the right decision, not just for herself but also for her unborn child. Deep in thought, Diana walked into the dining room reflecting on the life she might have had if Harry had not gone away. Maybe they would have moved into the Shelford cottage as a young married couple? She saw herself as a young, happy mother, pushing her baby in a big old pram around the orchard that backed on to the farm, looking forward to her husband coming home in the evening, tired but eager to kiss his wife and cuddle his new-born baby.

Finding Diana looking miserably preoccupied at the dinner table, Zelda made a bee-line to sit beside her new friend and cheer her up.

'We have a treat today this dinner-time,' she brightly announced as she flourished a dish before Diana's eyes. 'Butter!'

Accustomed to the margarine regularly served up at meal-times, she gazed incredulously at the dish of mouth-watering golden-yellow butter.

'Where did it come from?' she gasped.

Zelda laughed. 'From Mary Vale's cow,' she replied. 'Good Farmer Arkwright he share some with us ladies. Is good, try,' Zelda enthused. 'Before all get eaten,' she giggled conspiratorially.

Unable to believe her luck, Diana thickly spread the butter on to her toast, then, sighing in anticipation, she raised the slice to her lips and sank her teeth into the salty butter, which melted in her mouth, making her groan with pleasure.

'Mmm . . .'

Zelda smiled at her ecstatic expression. 'Is good, yah?'

With her mouth full and her taste buds exploding, Diana slowly nodded. 'Is absolutely bloody brilliant!'

Gracie and Diana had been paired to work together on the chores rota, which was pinned up in the dining room.

'Look, here's the list of jobs,' Gracie pointed out as they gazed at the chart. 'We rotate laundry, kitchen work, cleaning and fires – this week the pair of us are on fires, a bloody mucky job!' she grumbled.

Not only was it a 'mucky job'; it was also (so Diana thought) a seemingly endless job too. Mary Vale, formerly a huge grand house that luckily for the residents could shelter numerous young women, had endless fireplaces. First, they had to sweep the ash from all the fireplaces in the Home, then, after laying fresh newspaper and kindling in the grates, they had to polish the fenders and the fire irons, and then (last of all) they had to fill all the coal buckets in readiness for the next time the fires would be lit. When their task was finally completed, Gracie slumped into the nearest chair.

'I suppose it beats working all day with a welding iron!' she joked, before soot got up her nose and brought on a sneezing attack.

After a morning's work and a heavy lunch of sausage and mash, Diana was inclined to have a lie-down, but there was no rest to be had; before Ada's exercise and breathing classes, Gracie insisted that they visit Zelda's garden.

'We mustn't let the poor kid overdo it,' she whispered conspiratorially to Diana. 'And you never know,' she added with a wink, 'we might get lucky and find some strawberries!'

Standing on the edge of the garden now teeming with potato plants, tomatoes, carrots, onions and a raised bed for lettuce, spinach, radishes and a vast array of herbs, Gracie marvelled at what was before her. Not only was the produce a sight for sore eyes, but the radical change in her room-mate was a joy to see. No longer a bag of bones, Zelda's body had rounded, and where before she had barely looked pregnant now her tummy was large and swollen under her smock. Her skin was freckled and tanned golden-brown by the sun, and her mass of long red curls was caught up in a colourful cotton turban.

'Zelda!' Gracie called out. 'We've come to help.'

Shirley's head popped over a row of potato plants. 'You two ladies should be resting,' she chided.

Ignoring her advice, Gracie led Diana along the narrow path that wound its way around the vegetable patch.

'What are you doing, Sister?' Gracie asked.

Wiping mud off her face, Shirley replied, 'Planting some seed potatoes for Sister Mary Paul.'

Gracie smiled. 'I see you've taken to wearing a pinafore,' she giggled as Shirley rose to stretch her aching back.

'I was washing my robes every other day until Sister Mary Paul made me wear one of her kitchen pinafores,' Shirley chuckled. 'It goes round me twice!' she added, as she flapped the spare material wrapped around her small, skinny frame.

Checking her little fob watch, Shirley quickly added, 'I'd better get back to the ward before Dora comes looking for me. See you out here at three for Ada's exercise class,' she called over her shoulder as she hurried away.

Diana shook her head in disbelief. 'I thought I might spend a lot of time resting here,' she joked. 'I can see now that clearly isn't the case!'

93

Grinning Zelda appeared from behind a row of young strawberry plants. 'You like my garden?' she asked proudly.

Gazing at the fertile plot Zelda had created, Diana exclaimed, 'I don't know how you do it.'

Zelda simply said, 'It makes me happy, for this I am glad.'

When the time came for Sister Ada's breathing and exercise classes, Diana joined the other residents (most vastly more pregnant than she was) out on the lawn. Lying with her eyes closed and the sun on her face, she soon relaxed as Sister Ada instructed her class on how to strengthen their muscles and control their breathing in readiness for the physical ordeal they would all have to endure very soon.

'Come on, ladies,' she called, clapping her hands to get the girls' attention. 'No drifting off!'

Some of the cheekier girls groaned good-naturedly. 'You're a task-master, Sister,' one teased.

Ada smiled as she continued patiently, 'When your body is fully relaxed, slowly inhale, and, as you do, feel the air expanding your ribcage, allowing your lungs to fill completely.'

Marie giggled. 'Heck!' she cried. 'I can feel my tummy button sticking out.'

'Concentrate on letting your navel area sink down and empty your lungs completely while preparing for the next breath,' Ada instructed. 'Inhale and exhale slowly and rhythmically; keep your breathing calm and steady. Well done,' she said, as her class relaxed on the warm grass. 'Take a breather before we repeat the exercise.'

A saucy young girl called out, 'Is it time for a fag-break, Sister?'

'Certainly not!' Ada laughed. 'It'll ruin your breathing. When you're ready, let's repeat the sequence all over again. Ready? Okay, inhale, and expand your ribcage.'

At the end of the session the girls dispersed, some to the house to wait for tea; others, like Diana and Gracie, went for a stroll. As they walked back into the Home, Gracie's bright-green eyes lingered on a Bedford van, propped up on bricks, that she had seen several times on her way back from Ada's classes. Smiling to herself, she gave the van an affectionate pat.

'What are you doing?' Diana asked, as Gracie stooped to peer through the dusty windows.

'I wonder who it belongs to?' Gracie murmured.

'Why? Are you thinking of borrowing it?' Diana joked.

Gracie smiled. 'I'd love to work on it, fix it up and get it running.'

Diana burst out laughing. 'It's a total wreck!'

Gracie gave a swagger. 'I'm a bit of a grease monkey, always have been. Me and my dad used to fix up old engines. If I could get permission, I'd work on it,' she said with a rush of excitement in her voice. 'It'd be something to pass the time.'

Diana grimaced. 'I'd rather you than me,' she chuckled.

*

Gracie discovered through Sister Mary Paul that the van belonged to the convent, and that it had been left standing in the yard for years.

'Waiting for a miracle,' the old nun had laughed.

A big smile lit up Gracie's pretty face. 'Will you ask the Reverend Mother if I can tinker with it?' she begged.

'For the love of God!' Sister Mary Paul hooted. 'What will you do with an owd heap of a thing like that?'

Gracie gave her a wink. 'Get it going and take you for a spin round Morecambe Bay, Sister!'

A few days later Ada, taking a brief walk in the garden, spotted Gracie's legs poking out from underneath the Bedford van. Alarmed, she called out, 'Gracie! Are you all right?'

Gracie wriggled and jiggled her body until she emerged with a smile on her face. 'Never happier, Sister,' she announced, as she sat upright and wiped her cheek with a hand smeared in thick black grease.

'What on earth are you doing?' Ada gasped.

'I've got the Reverend Mother's permission to play about with this old heap,' Gracie explained.

Ada gazed at the van balanced up on piles of bricks and, like Diana before her, shook her head in disbelief. 'Won't it topple over and hurt you?'

'It's more secure than it was – I propped up the back end with a couple of boulders,' Gracie assured her.

In professional mode Ada said firmly, 'You're in a delicate condition – you mustn't go straining yourself.' Unable to hide the smile that played about at the corners of her mouth, she added, 'Really, Gracie! You came to

Mary Vale to prepare for the birth of your baby, not to fix old cars.'

'It's very therapeutic,' Gracie explained. 'Takes my mind off things and stops me wanting to throttle the man who got me in the state I am now.'

Even under the black grease daubed all over her face, Ada could see the flush of anger that spread across Gracie's cheeks.

'Did he treat you badly, dear?' she enquired gently.

Gracie tossed her long, dark-brown curls, which had come loose under the turban she'd wrapped around her head.

'Not to start with – if anything he treated me like royalty, wined and dined me, took me out in his swanky car – it was him that taught me to drive, in fact. Unfortunately his so-called "driving lessons" led to other things.'

Ada nodded. 'I can imagine the rest,' she said quietly.

'It takes two to tango,' Gracie continued bitterly. 'I fell for him hook, line and sinker, so I've only myself to blame.'

'Is he still in the area?' Ada asked.

Gracie gave a hard, mocking laugh. 'No chance! As soon as he knew I was expecting, he scarpered back to London, to his wife and family, who, funnily enough, he'd never mentioned during our drives out.' She gave a heavy sigh. 'I suppose you've heard it all before?'

Ada nodded. 'Too many times, unfortunately. Men getting what they want, then leaving the girl high and dry. It still makes me very angry, but there's not much

I can do about it, other than care for Mary Vale's mothers and their babies.'

'Thank God you do, Sister,' Gracie said gratefully.

Ada gave a modest shrug. 'Believe me, Gracie, it's not just me: the staff are wonderful. The Reverend Mother and her entire staff are one hundred per cent supportive, and now we have a new and very good doctor. What more could we ask for?' she finished cheerily.

A deep male voice behind her made Ada jump. 'Did I hear my name being taken in vain?' Dr Reid asked.

'Heavens!' Ada cried. 'I didn't see you, Doctor.'

Dr Reid chuckled as he replied, 'You were so deep in discussion I didn't want to disturb you – well, not until I heard my name mentioned, then I thought I should make my presence known before you said something you might regret.'

Gracie beamed. 'I wouldn't worry about that; Sister here was just singing your praises.'

Going as red as a beetroot, Ada said, 'I was just saying how lucky we are to have such good and supportive staff.'

Looking her directly in the eye, Jamie responded with a warm smile. 'That sentiment goes both ways.'

Dragging his eyes away from Ada, he turned to the old van. 'Are you seriously working on this heap?' he enquired.

'I've just been tinkering with the crank shaft,' Gracie told him knowledgeably. 'I had to take the sump off to get to it. Once I've sorted out the main bearings, I'll refit the sump and then hopefully lift it off the blocks.'

Jamie's eyebrows shot up. 'Don't you go injuring yourself,' he warned. 'I can give you a hand with the heavy lifting.'

Gracie threw him her most dazzling smile. 'Thanks, that would be great.'

Jamie gave a sheepish grin. 'To be honest, I love old engines too. I'd be happy to work on the van when I have the time to spare,' he volunteered.

'The more the merrier,' Gracie giggled. 'I promised Sister Mary Paul that once I get it on the road, I'll take her for a ride round Morecambe Bay.'

'You know what they say?' Jamie joked. 'Never break a promise to a nun!'

Ada, who had barely said a word, listened in amazement to Jamie's lively exchange with Gracie.

'Really,' she wondered, 'is there no end to Dr Reid's talents?'

11. Therapeutic Work

Working on the Bedford van brought a thousand memories back to Gracie: a few sweet, some not so. When Zelda and Diana came looking for her, they found her in the driver's seat (the car having been lifted off the bricks by Jamie and the gardener) sobbing her heart out.

'Darling, what is it?' Zelda murmured, as she drew the weeping girl out of the car and held her in the circle of her comforting arms.

Diana hurriedly brought Gracie a glass of water from the kitchen, which Gracie gulped back; then, after taking a deep shuddering breath, she poured out her story to her friends.

'He was a sly sod, winning me over with his good looks and his posh silver Hillman car.'

Zelda couldn't resist a fond smile. 'Flowers and gardens, I understand; cars, I do not.'

'He had previously offered to take me to the pictures, the pub and the local dancehall, all of which I'd resisted, but after he dangled driving lessons before me I was like a kid after chocolate,' Gracie confessed. 'It was good fun to start with, even though I was a bag of nerves, panicking and stalling the car at every junction! Reggie would just smile and shake his head and we'd start off again.

Once I got confident, we started going further afield. Up to Windermere, driving round the lake, laughing and chatting; we'd walk hand in hand over the hills, stopping off for tea in Grasmere, watching the sun go down over Rydal Water – it was *so romantic*!' she exclaimed, as tears welled up in her eyes.

Though Gracie's outpouring was clearly painful, her friends could see from the emotional way in which she described the events that she needed to talk about what had happened to her.

Giving them a hard, level look, Gracie continued. 'I don't need to tell you what came next, do I? The kissing and cuddling in lay-bys led to picnics in isolated woods. Reggie started booking us into smart hotels for fancy meals; then one weekend he registered us as Mr and Mrs Ramsden. I spent just the one night with him, but that's, as we know, all it takes.'

Seeing Gracie's sweet, heartbroken face, Zelda cried fiercely, '*Meine Liebe*, you must stop this work – cars bring you too many bad memories.'

Gracie gave her a tearful smile. 'You were lucky, Zelda: your man loved you; mine certainly didn't.'

Tears swam into Zelda's eyes too. 'Oh, yah, my Izaak loved me very much.'

'Your memories, though sad, must be wonderful; mine are humiliating,' Gracie blurted out. 'I was a fool, seduced by a married man! How stupid do you think that makes me feel?'

Now it was Diana's turn to point out a few hard facts. 'Darling!' she cried. 'The man sounds a complete cad.

He calculated you were an impressionable young girl and set about seducing you.'

A slow smile crept across Gracie's tear-streaked face. 'Cad!' she laughed, savouring the word. 'I like the sound of that.'

'Seriously,' Diana insisted, 'he was an awful man who took advantage of your innocence.'

'I shouldn't have let him get away with it. I should've put up a fight, publicly shamed him with the truth, but he was off back to London before I could even think straight,' Gracie raged.

Diana shook her head. 'It's too easy to berate ourselves, Gracie. I certainly shouldn't have allowed myself to get pregnant, but I simply adore Harry. I forget about everything else when I'm with him – that's what passion does to you.'

Zelda gave a shy smile. 'Oh, this is true.'

'At least you've got a ring on your finger!' Gracie cried. 'Not like me, sleeping with a married man.'

'Mary Vale is full of girls who've made the same mistake,' Diana reminded Gracie. 'Stop beating yourself up; otherwise you'll drive yourself mad, and no man is worth that.'

Gracie dabbed away the tears on her face, thereby adding more greasy oil to her already streaky black face. 'Back to work!' she declared.

'No!' Zelda protested hotly. 'Forget this stupid van,' she implored.

Gracie shook her head. 'Don't worry, Zelda, I feel better for talking to you two. Friends help, especially ones in the same situation. Diana's right, no man's worth it – I'll make good regardless of rotten Reggie,' she vowed.

Gracie certainly didn't pour her heart out in the same way with Jamie, who regularly turned up to tinker with the Bedford's old engine. Nevertheless, they did have several easy, open conversations.

'So, what are you planning to do with this old lady if you ever get her up and running?' he asked, as they were cleaning the greasy spark plugs.

Gracie gave him a long, sideways look. 'Well . . .' she said slowly. 'I've been thinking.'

'Oh-oh! That sounds ominous.'

Unperturbed by his teasing grin, Gracie continued, 'Have you met Tom Arkwright, Mary Vale's farmer?'

Jamie shook his head. 'He takes his produce to Kendal Market every Saturday morning,' Gracie explained. 'He harnesses his horse to an old cart, and they set off at dawn, both of them looking worn out before they even start. If I can get this thing running, I thought I might drive Tom and his veg over to Kendal and give his old cart horse a break.'

Jamie looked impressed but a little doubtful. 'That's kind of you, Gracie, though he might take some persuading, if he's set in his ways.'

'I'll use the horse as a lever,' Gracie explained. 'Poor old Captain, he seriously looks like he might drop dead on the job.'

Jamie had another thought. 'With rationing as it is

surely the farmer's produce goes to the Home and the convent?'

Gracie shrugged. 'He must have a bit to spare because I've seen him heading off into town with a couple of crates of veg. I suppose it's a day out for him.' Dropping her voice, Gracie added, 'Zelda might have a bit to sell too.'

Jamie's eyes widened. 'Doesn't Sister Mary Paul need it?'

Gracie shook her head. 'At this time of the year there's often a glut of vegetables; if they can't be eaten or preserved, they just go off. Anyway, it might be bit of fun to take Zelda into Kendal.'

'It's a nice idea,' Jamie agreed. 'But she might be shy in public – you know how self-conscious she is about her German accent.'

'She's getting more of a Northern accent by the day,' Gracie giggled. 'She asked if I wanted a brew the other day and if she makes a bob or two, she could spend it on baby bootees!' irrepressible Gracie chuckled.

With a plan in mind, Gracie was indefatigable in her efforts to fix the Bedford. When she was confident it was in sound working order, she informed Farmer Arkwright that she could give him a lift to Kendal Market the following Saturday.

'Eeeh, lass, that'd be handy, 'owd Captain is knackered after yon journey to town.'

Gracie knowingly dropped a hint. 'Petrol allowing, of course.'

Farmer Arkwright gave a low chuckle. 'I think I might be able to lay mi hands on a drop or two of petrol I've been storing in the barn.' Giving her a sly wink, he tapped the side of his long nose. 'Keep thee trap shut, else I might get arrested.'

When Gracie told Zelda of her plan to go to market, Zelda's eyes widened incredulously.

'Sell my produce at a market. Really?'

'Only when you've got stuff to spare,' Gracie hastily explained. 'We don't want Sister Mary Paul having a heart attack at the thought of you flogging off all of her spuds!'

Though she was shy at the thought of meeting strangers, it was clear to Gracie that Zelda was also excited at the prospect of a change of scenery.

'What will the people say when they see two ladies with big tummies selling lettuces?' she asked nervously.

Gracie shook her lustrous brunette hair. 'We can't be the only women in Kendal who are pregnant; there are bound to be others who are expecting.' Glancing down at her own tummy, which had grown immensely since her arrival, Gracie added, 'Anyway we're not that big yet. Nothing like Annie, who's the size of a bus,' she giggled.

Zelda solemnly nodded. 'I hope her baby may come soon, then she get lost! As you say.'

Gracie smiled in agreement with Gracie. 'Aye!' she declared. 'The sooner we see the back of Annie the better.'

*

Their first excursion into Kendal was quite an event. All the produce had to be loaded into the back of the van early in the morning while the air was still cool.

'We don't want the sun wilting our fresh goods,' Farmer Arkwright grinned. 'The earlier we set off the better.'

With Zelda in the back, surrounded by crates of salad vegetables, the old farmer settled himself in the passenger seat beside Gracie, who was trying hard to conceal how nervous she was. This had all been her brainwave, based on the fact that the van was roadworthy. What if it conked out halfway to Kendal and they had to walk back to Mary Vale, leaving the produce by the roadside to rot? With her heart in her mouth Gracie put the key into the ignition and the van immediately bounced into life.

'Hold on tight, Zelda,' she called to her friend as they bumped their way along the drive.

To their surprise Ada and Sister Mary Paul came out of the house to wave them off. 'Good luck!' Ada called.

'Drive carefully,' Sister Mary Paul anxiously cautioned.

It was a lovely summer day, with the sun beaming down on the soft, rolling fells that surrounded Grange-over-Sands. The narrow, winding roads were almost empty until they approached Kendal, where they saw other traders transporting their goods by van or cart to market. Looking pleased with himself, Farmer Arkwright wound down the passenger window and proudly waved to friends as they drove by.

'They'll think I've gone up in the world,' he announced,

as his startled friends did an astonished double-take at the sight of the farmer being chauffeur-driven into town.

It was all hustle and bustle in the marketplace as the stalls were set up. Shy Zelda made sure she was partially hidden by a pile of spring greens, but bold Gracie, taking her cue from Farmer Arkwright, a veteran trader, was soon shouting out her wares. 'Come and buy your lettuces – fresh this morning, three for a tanner!'

Trade was brisk, and very soon their baskets of runner beans, pea pods, tomatoes, beetroot and salad onions had dwindled to barely nothing. Seeing the two girls sweating in the hot sun, Farmer Arkwright kindly said, 'You lasses go and get a mug of tea and summat to eat – I'll hold the fort till you get back.'

Grateful for a break, Zelda and Gracie linked arms and wandered around the pretty little town that nestled in green fields surrounded by rolling fells. Having barely been out since her arrival at Mary Vale, Zelda was thrilled by the shops they passed.

'So many nice things,' she murmured excitedly. 'I think I have enough money from market to buy wool to make warm coat for baby.'

Gracie, who would far rather fix an engine than knit a baby's layette, laughed. 'Good idea – you can knit one for me too.'

When they entered the haberdashery shop, the owner greeted the strangers somewhat coldly.

'What can I do for you?'

Seeing Zelda tense up, Gracie gave her most charming smile. 'We're looking for wool to knit some baby clothes.'

The woman's eyes flew to the girls' tummies; then she noticed that, though Zelda's wedding ring was very much in evidence, Gracie certainly wasn't wearing one. With a disappearing frown on her forehead, she produced from a drawer several samples of soft baby wool.

'Blue, yellow, pink and green,' she said, as she strewed the wool on the countertop.

Zelda's face lit up in delight. 'So beautiful!' she exclaimed before she could stop herself. 'But how do we know which colour is best for baby?'

Gracie shrugged. 'Neither of us know whether it's a lad or a lass, so best go for green or yellow.'

As Zelda muttered to herself trying to make a decision, the shopkeeper's eyes narrowed.

'Is that a German accent I detect?' she snapped.

Blushing, Zelda instantly stepped back from the counter, but Gracie did no such thing, standing before the woman defiantly. 'She's a refugee from Germany.'

'I'll have no bloody German in my shop,' the woman started to shout.

'For God's sake, woman, the bloody Nazis shot her husband,' Gracie cried indignantly. 'She's done now't to hurt you, or anybody else for that matter.'

Flushed with fury the woman snatched up the skeins of wool. 'Get out of my shop, the pair of you,' she screamed. 'Get out before I have you arrested!'

Terrified, Zelda scuttled for the door, but furious,

fearless Gracie held her ground. 'You should be thoroughly ashamed of yourself, missis,' she raged, before turning on her heel and joining trembling Zelda, who was waiting for her outside.

'Miserable old cow!' Gracie fumed.

Almost in tears, Zelda clutched her arm. 'I should not come into town.'

Gracie sighed wearily. Just when everything had settled down at Mary Vale, Zelda was yet again experiencing hatred and xenophobia.

'I'm sorry, sweetheart,' she apologized. 'I never imagined this would happen here in Kendal.'

Seeing all the colour drain from Zelda's face, Gracie guiltily said, 'You're as white as a sheet – come on.' She took her friend by the arm and walked her purposefully towards a café. 'Let's get you something to eat before the farmer comes looking for us.'

A slice of fresh apple pie and a mug of tea soon brought the colour back to Zelda's pale cheeks, but she barely opened her mouth in the café. She was clearly relieved when they got back to the market stall, where the farmer left them while he went off to the Crown for a pint. To Zelda's amazement he returned with skeins of yellow wool in a paper bag.

'Where . . . how you find this?' she spluttered incredulously.

Gracie gave a cheeky grin. 'I asked Farmer Arkwright to pick it up for you. I thought the old bag wouldn't refuse a local. It's not like we'll be going back to that old witch's shop any time soon, and you've got some knitting to do, lady!'

'She did not question you about *me*?' Zelda enquired.

'Nay!' Arkwright boomed. 'She doesn't even know that I know you and, if she did and dared protest,' he said with a steely glint in his eye, 'she would have a lot of explaining to do.'

By three o'clock they had packed up their empty baskets and crates and were heading back home with a few pennies in their pockets.

'Same again next Saturday?' Gracie asked.

Farmer Arkwright nodded eagerly. 'Aye, if you can spare the time, I'd be proper grateful. How about you, lass?' he asked, as he turned to Zelda sitting in the back of the van.

'I think, no, thank you, sir,' she said in a quiet, embarrassed voice.

'Eh, none of that!' Arkwright cried good-naturedly. 'I've got a son fighting the Nazis, but I don't hold it against you.' He grinned as he added, 'Anyway, your tomatoes went down a bomb, belting good English tomatoes.'

'Better not say English tomatoes grown by a German *Fraulein*,' Zelda said with a rueful smile. 'Peoples might choke to deaths!'

12. An Invitation

Gracie's wish for Annie's baby to be born soon came true. A few days after their visit to Kendal, Annie went into labour and Ada truly thought her ear drums would burst as a result of Annie's high-pitched screams, which continued throughout the whole of her labour.

'Thank God, Jamie's on duty,' she thought to herself as she tried her best to settle cursing and swearing Annie.

'It bloody hurts, Sister!' she wailed. 'Do something, I can't stand the pain.'

Ada sighed – if Annie was like this now when her contractions were coming only every five minutes, what on earth would she be like when they were coming every single minute?

'We're in for some drama with this one,' Dora muttered, as they prepared the delivery room for Annie, who was writhing on her hospital bed and threatening anybody and everybody in sight.

Ada gave a grim smile. 'I think my breathing and exercise classes went right over Annie's head.'

As another scream rent the air, Dora rolled her eyes. 'She's going to put the fear of God in all the other girls if she carries on like this.'

Luckily Jamie arrived and took control of the hysterical

woman. 'Now, Annie, he said calmly, 'you're wasting your energy thrashing about like this; you must conserve your strength for later.'

'How much bloody later?' Annie growled angrily.

'It's your first baby, so it will take some time,' Jamie answered truthfully. 'If the pain becomes intolerable, I promise you that I'll administer a painkiller.'

'Can't you do it now?' she snapped impatiently.

Jamie shook his head. 'No, not yet – first I have to examine you and time your contractions.'

When he joined Ada in the delivery room, Jamie said ominously, 'I've just examined Annie; I have to tell you her baby's a whopper.'

Ada couldn't help but grin. 'She's certainly been eating for two.'

'I think we're in for a long haul,' Jamie said, smiling.

As Jamie had predicted, Annie wore herself out well before she delivered; sweating and exhausted, she lay limp on the bed, wailing in between her ever increasing contractions.

Jamie sighed. 'Let's see if a whiff of gas and air might relax her.'

Fortunately, the drug quietened Annie, who moaned and groaned as she bore down and finally delivered a bouncing eight-pound baby boy just after tea-time.

'Thank God for that,' Dora said, as she washed down the strapping little fellow, who had clearly inherited his mother's lungs.

'Never again, God help me, never again, I swear,'

Annie vowed, as she heartlessly surveyed her son. 'You can take him away too.'

Dora muttered sadly, 'Poor little sod!'

Ada removed the baby from his mother's sight and, after bathing him clean and dressing him in one of Mary Vale's pretty little hand-stitched linen night frocks, she tucked him up in his canvas cot in the nursery.

'I'd say you're better off without a mother like that, sweetheart,' she soothed. 'I'm sure Father Ben will soon find you a nice mummy and daddy to love you.'

Tired and worn out, Jamie and Ada sat drinking tea and ravenously eating slices of fresh bread and butter in the ward kitchen.

'Thank God that's over,' Jamie said, as he topped up their teacups.

Ada giggled. 'My ears are still ringing.'

After taking a gulp of hot tea, Jamie said, 'With all the drama I forget to mention that I have to swap my hours next week – I'm taking Saturday off.'

'Can they spare you from the Barrow practice?' Ada asked.

Jamie gave a quiet groan as he guiltily shook his head. 'To tell the truth, if I worked round the clock, I'd never put in enough hours there. The workload is huge.'

Not wanting to add to his guilt, Ada sweetly said, 'I'm sure we can manage.'

'I'm taking the day off to drive over to Grasmere,' Jamie told her excitedly. 'The town holds a country show there every year and I'm keen to see it and do a bit of fell-walking too.'

Ada looked curious. 'I've never even heard of it.'

'I'm told it's been going for years. A bit of a quaint, old-fashioned event, with pole-vaulting, wrestling, a prize-cattle competition and the like. What I really fancy watching is the Guides Race – a two-mile run over the fells – that should be something.'

'With so many called up I wonder how many men will actually be fell-racing?' Ada asked in all innocence.

Jamie looked distinctly uncomfortable. 'It'll probably be a lot of crippled old codgers,' he muttered.

Realizing she might have embarrassed the poor man, Ada blushed as she tried to cover up her mistake. 'I should imagine the competitors are all local shepherds,' she rushed on. 'A couple of miles of running over boggy fells will be nothing to them – I don't know how they do it,' she laughed. 'I love fell-walking but fell-running is in another league altogether.'

Looking surprised, Jamie turned to her. 'You're a fell-walker?' he asked.

'Yes,' Ada told him. 'I walk the fells whenever I can, which isn't as often as I'd like. Nothing beats a good long walk on the mountaintops.'

Curious Jamie asked, 'Do you walk on your own?'

'I usually pick a popular walk so I'm not always on my own,' she replied. 'Though I do enjoy solitary walks, that's if I don't lose my bearings and get lost,' she joked.

Seeing the wistful smile on her face, Jamie impetuously

suggested, 'Why don't you come with me? I'm sure you would enjoy a day out.'

Ada's face flushed. Was Jamie asking her out on a date or was he just being friendly? Seeing her flustered expression, Jamie quickly added, 'That's if you can get time off, of course.'

Ada shrugged. 'I'm owed loads of time off, believe me.'

'Well, then?' he smiled. 'Why not?'

'I'll have to check with Matron,' she reminded him.

Feeling slightly flushed by his sudden decision, Jamie avoided eye contact by busily pretending to pack his doctor's bag.

'If you get the go-ahead phone me at the Barrow practice and I'll pick you up,' he said, as if it were of no consequence to him whether she came with him or not.

'I'll let you know,' she replied.

Outside in the privacy of his car, Jamie slumped back in the driver's seat and took several deep breaths.

'How did I have the nerve to do that?' he said out loud.

Always having assumed that lovely Ada had a string of handsome boyfriends, Jamie hadn't expected a positive response from her. He imagined that a woman as beautiful as Ada would have a dozen men lining up to take her out. Starting up his car, Jamie grinned to himself. If she agreed, he had something seriously marvellous to look forward to.

*

After Jamie had driven away from Mary Vale, Ada went about her work with a preoccupied expression on her face. She liked Jamie enormously, and she couldn't deny she found him very attractive – his long legs, broad shoulders and twinkling hazel eyes flecked with specks of gold certainly upped her heart rate – but she had to be careful – the last thing she wanted was to ruin what was turning out to be an excellent working relationship.

Shameful memories from the past drifted into her mind, making her anxious and uneasy. Up until she was twenty, she'd had a number of short-term relationships, but she certainly hadn't lost her heart to any man – not until she met Brian, a handsome young musician who toured the country playing with a swing band. Catching sight of him on stage at her local dancehall – swinging his hips as he played the trumpet with the glittering dancehall lights accentuating his good looks – had certainly made Ada's pulse race, and he was quick to notice the tall, shapely girl in a clinging red crêpe dress dancing to the strains of 'Little Brown Jug'. Dating Brian was an ideal arrangement as far as Ada was concerned: she could continue to concentrate on her nursing career while still enjoying the company of the handsome musician whenever he showed up in Manchester. Luckily for Ada she discovered from another member of the band, jealous of Brian's success with the best-looking girl in the ballroom, that Brian was, in fact, engaged to be married. Ada had felt utterly humiliated. The experience of being duped and openly shamed left her cautious. She realized that, unlike most of her friends, she was in no rush to start courting; for the present she was content to throw all her energy into her work, which she loved with an increasing passion.

When Ada approached Matron for permission to take time off, Sister Ann readily agreed.

'Of course, dear, you've hardly taken a day off in weeks. It'll be good for you to have a rest.'

'I don't think I'll be resting much, Sister,' Ada laughed. 'Dr Reid's taking me to the Grasmere Show to watch the fell-runners.'

Sister Ann, who had seen the look on Dr Reid's face when Ada appeared in a room, sincerely hoped that the handsome young man might have other more romantic intentions than fell-running on his mind. Keeping her thoughts to herself, the nun smiled as she responded, 'Have fun, dear, you deserve it.'

Ada phoned Jamie at his GP's practice in Barrow, and they arranged that he would pick her up outside the Home on Saturday morning. After he had put down the phone, Jamie punched the air.

'YESS!' he cried; then, fearful that people in the stuffy waiting room might have heard his jubilant cry, he took deep breaths in order to regain his composure. 'Beautiful Ada,' he murmured dreamily before he rang the bell for his next patient.

On the other end of the line thoughtful Ada also put the phone down. 'What do people normally wear for a country show?' she thought. When she went fell-walking, she would always wear her old tweed trousers, a cotton blouse, a woolly jumper if it was cold, boots and a rain-coat, but a 'show' sounded a bit posher than striding over the rain-soaked fells and wading through becks and gullies. At a loss, she confided in Dora, who responded in her characteristic blunt manner, 'From what I've seen in't newspapers women seem to wear suits, with a fox fur dangling round their necks, and fellas wear overcoats and bowler 'ats!'

Ada burst out laughing. 'You must be joking! I don't even possess a fox fur, and if Jamie turns up in a bowler hat, I'd have hysterics.'

'You'd be wise to dress for the weather,' Dora answered realistically. 'If it's pouring down, then it's wellies and a mac; if it's not, then summat prettier. Whatever, you always look right bonny, so thou's now't to fret about,' she concluded with a cheeky wink.

In the end, as Saturday dawned bright and sunny, Ada wore her favourite navy crêpe dress that was dotted with a pretty pattern of pink roses. She took her mac and a pair of stout shoes but set off up the drive in her court shoes. As she walked away from the Home, Ada looked over her shoulder to check that she had closed the front door, and, to her surprise, saw Sister Ann, Sister Mary Paul, Shirley and Dora all standing in the open doorway grinning as they waved her off.

'Go inside!' Ada begged. 'I don't want Dr Reid to see you watching me.'

'Don't do anything I wouldn't do!' irrepressible Dora called after her.

'God bless,' Sister Ann added on a quieter note.

'Be careful,' worried Shirley murmured.

'Don't get lost,' Sister Mary Paul fretted.

Smiling to herself, Ada walked towards the waiting car. She was truly blessed with friends, but there were times when she wished they didn't care about her *quite* so much.

13. Grasmere

Jamie smothered a gasp when he saw Ada approaching his car: he had never seen her with her hair down and was impressed by the length of her glorious Titian red-gold curls. He smiled when he saw the smart court shoes she was wearing.

'I don't think you'll be doing much fell-running in those,' he chuckled as he handed her into the car.

Laying the picnic basket that she was carrying on the back seat, Ada quickly put him straight. 'I've brought some walking shoes as well.'

Eyeing the basket, Jamie enquired, 'What have we got here?'

'Sister Mary Paul's convinced that we'll die of starvation up on the fells, so she packed us a picnic – there's enough to feed an army.'

Jamie and Ada talked easily as they drove along the twisting, turning, narrow lanes to Kendal, passing fields criss-crossed with ancient grey drystone walls. When they got on to the busier northern main road, Jamie apologized for the slowness of his car.

'It's my dad's old banger, as you can see: it struggles on hills.' He smiled as the car spluttered and wheezed its way along the Windermere Road. 'I should have asked

Gracie to give it the once-over before I set off,' he joked. 'She's an amazing mechanic.'

'I have to say I nearly had a heart attack when I saw her wriggling her big tummy underneath that rickety old Bedford van,' Ada admitted.

'Believe me, she knows exactly what she's doing,' Jamie replied. 'She actually admitted to me that she wanted to be the first woman in Barrow shipyard to drive a crane.'

'Knowing Gracie, she probably will be,' Ada laughed.

They briefly stopped chattering when the car laboriously breasted a steep hill that dropped down into Windermere, giving a breathtaking view of the vast lake dotted with sailboats.

'It's so lovely! Look at the little boats skimming across the water,' Ada exclaimed, as she eagerly leant forward to take it all in.

Happy as she was, Ada couldn't help feeling a twinge of nagging guilt. Was it right to feel so carefree when her country was at war? Seeing an anxious expression replace her eager, bright smile, Jamie guessed what Ada might be thinking. 'We have to take happiness where we can find it,' he said quietly.

'I know,' she agreed.

'How guilty do you think I feel?' Jamie declared. 'Here I am, an apparently hale and hearty young man who's not fighting for his country.'

Feeling awkward, Ada blushed as he continued, 'I see contempt and disgust in people's eyes when they look at me – I know they see me as a coward.'

Desperate to reclaim their happy mood, Ada said in a tight, quiet voice, 'Everybody who knows you, Jamie, has nothing but respect for you.'

Touched by her sincerity, Jamie's mood changed. 'That's the nicest thing anybody has said to me in months.' Straightening his broad shoulders, he dropped a gear and slowly drove down the hill that led into the little town of Windermere.

As Windermere gave way to Ambleside, then Grasmere, they drove through the wild, dramatic countryside. Suddenly on a steep road Jamie pointed to a high fell, etched dark and bold against the clear blue sky,

'Look!' he cried. 'The Lion and the Lamb – can you make out the rockface?'

Ada stared up at the humped mountains towering over them. Squinting hard, she said, 'There's a craggy rock formation at the top. Oh, yes!' she exclaimed. 'It really does look like a lion lying down guarding a lamb.'

Passing a tiny cluster of slate cottages just off the main road, Jamie pointed out another interesting feature. 'You'll never guess who lived in that cottage down that dark, narrow lane.'

Ada gazed at a tiny dwelling nestled under the mountain. 'I have no idea.'

'I'll give you a clue,' Jamie teased. ' "I wandered lonely as a cloud that floats on high o'er vales and hills . . ." ' he quoted.

Ada immediately picked up the poem: ' "When all at

once I saw a crowd, a host of golden daffodils" – Words-worth!' she laughed.

Turning to look over her shoulder, she was amazed by how poky the cottage looked.

'Heavens, I imagined he would have lived in a grand hall – that place looks more like a workman's hovel.'

'Wordsworth did eventually live in a much bigger house, Rydal Mount, down the road from here,' Jamie told her. 'But he and his wife and sister started off in Dove Cottage. I read that Samuel Coleridge from Devon often visited them: he used to jump over the wall and run down the fell to the nearest pub for a bit of local slap and tickle,' Jamie chuckled. 'Good for the muse, though: Wordsworth wrote some of his best works here in the Lakes.'

They followed the road signs that directed them to the showground and Jamie parked the car; then he eagerly checked the time for the start of the fell-race.

'Put your boots on, Ada,' he urged. 'We've got enough time to walk up to Butter Crag – it'll be a great vantage point from which to watch the fell-runners.'

Grabbing Sister Mary Paul's picnic basket and Ada's mac, Jamie set off through the bustling crowd with Ada by his side. After the drive it was good to stretch their legs, though Ada briefly dawdled by the prize cattle and sheep waiting in wicker pens to be judged. Jamie, as impatient as a child, hurried through an open farm gate, and then they both walked briskly along a stony path dotted with cairns marking the way up to Butter Crag.

As they climbed higher, the showground below grew smaller and smaller, until it looked the size of a child's toy farm. Cautious not to stride out and overtake Jamie, Ada thoughtfully let him set the pace, but she was soon astonished at the speed he went. Impressed by his stamina, Ada walked breathless in his wake.

'Clearly Dr Reid isn't the kind of man who lets the likes of polio get in the way of things he wants to do.'

After half an hour of brisk walking they reached a sunny crag, where Jamie set down the picnic basket.

'All we've got to do now is wait for the runners to appear,' he announced.

Leaning back against a big, warm, granite boulder, Ada gratefully accepted the tea that Jamie poured from the Thermos flask and a cheese-and-tomato sandwich too. After finishing his tea and hungrily polishing off several sandwiches, Jamie gave a deep sigh of contentment; then, carefree and relaxed, he folded his hands behind his head and stretched out luxuriously on the warm springy heather with his eyes closed. Ada's eyes swept curiously over Jamie's long, lean body, and through his open-neck shirt she caught sight of tanned skin and golden chest hair. She admired his thick tawny hair that fell in a boyish sweep over his eyes and the way his full lips parted over even white teeth. She was taken aback when her pulse suddenly started to quicken; she had always liked the new doctor and admired his skill in the workplace, but she had never before felt this sudden bolt of attraction blaze through her. Caught peeping, Ada jumped guiltily when Jamie lazily opened his hazel eyes.

'Penny for your thoughts?'

Ada smiled to herself – how would Jamie respond if she told him the truth? 'Oh, actually, Jamie, I was just going hot all over at the sight of you stretched out there.'

Fortunately, the first fell-runners appeared on the track down below, causing them both to rise to their feet.

'Here they come,' Jamie said, as he sheltered his eyes against the strong sunlight slanting down on to their vantage point.

The lead runners were already well out of the showground, and, surging forwards, they ran up the narrow path that wound its precipitous way around boulders and gurgling becks. Putting their hands on their knees to gain extra leverage, the experienced runners gained the trail first and sidestepped the rocks that lined the route, quickly putting a gap between themselves and the less experienced runners.

'Gosh! They're fast,' Ada cried.

Standing on the edge of the crag, Jamie clapped and cheered as the runners flashed by. 'Go! Go, lads! Well done!'

As the lead runners made the turn at the top of the course, marshals bearing clipboards shouted out names and numbers.

'They're checking to make sure nobody's cheating,' Jamie explained to curious Ada.

The tag end of the competitors soon followed; spluttering, they plodded along full of good humour. When they reached Butter Crag, they waved as they lumbered past Jamie and Ada.

'Good luck! I'm a doctor,' Jamie joked. 'Give me a shout if you need help.'

'How about another set of lungs, Doc?' one runner called out as he wheezed on his way.

Picking up the basket, Jamie and Ada set off quickly for the top of the pass, where they continued to watch the runners make their way down the steep track to finish the race. Marvelling at their strength and skill, Ada gasped. 'The way they skip and jump along – they look like they're almost dancing down the mountainside.'

When the race was finally over, Jamie hid the picnic basket behind a big gorse bush, then turned to smile at Ada. 'Shall we carry on up the fell?'

Nodding eagerly, she replied, 'Of course.'

After crossing a bubbling beck, they zigzagged over ground thick with purple heather. Breathless and sweating, they gained height until they reached a stretch of grassy upland where the walking got easier. Here they gratefully cooled their hot, flushed faces in a cool, sparkling beck that trickled over boulders worn smooth by the endless flow of water. Sighing, they both lay back, simply content to stare up at the clouds rolling across the blue sky and listen to the larks trilling as they rose higher and higher above the majestic mountains.

'On a day as perfect as this I sometimes think even

I could pen a poem,' Jamie said dreamily. 'Instead I became a doctor and thereby saved the nation from a load of ill-rhymed iambic pentameter.'

Ada smiled. 'When did you decide to become a doctor?'

'It was never a question,' Jamie replied. 'Dad was a doctor, and I always knew that was what I wanted to do; runs in the blood, I suppose.'

'Not in my case!' she giggled. 'My mum ran a chip shop; I can tell you that dream certainly didn't run in my blood.'

Impressed, he sat up and leant on one elbow. 'Really?'

Ada nodded. 'It was a little gold mine, situated between two mills and a pub,' she proudly told him. 'Mum opened every dinner-time and the mill workers swarmed in. It was a family affair – my granny and auntie both worked there – and in the school holidays my sister and I helped too, refilling the salt and vinegar bottles, cutting up newspaper to wrap the chips in, washing and chopping spuds – we loved it.'

'So what drew you into nursing?' he enquired.

'I always wanted to be a nurse,' Ada replied. 'Though my father wanted me to work in the mill – it was good money compared to training to be a nurse – but I refused point bank. Luckily Mother backed me, what she said went in our house, so I got what I wanted.'

Jamie plucked a blade of glass that he thoughtfully chewed on. 'How come you finished up practising midwifery at Mary Vale?'

Sitting up too, Ada laced her hands around her knees.

'I liked my work in Leeds, but I wanted to do something more, something that would make a difference. When I saw Mary Vale's advert for a senior midwife in the newspaper, I was curious and applied, but it was only when I got up here and met the residents that I knew for sure I wanted the job.'

'It's such an isolated place,' Jamie remarked.

'That was part of the attraction,' Ada replied. 'I've always loved the Lakes and wanted to spend more time up here; plus the girls in the Home were so trusting and needy, pretty ignorant sometimes too – can you believe some of them don't even know where their babies came from? Nobody had ever told them the facts of life until it was too late, poor kids. I really felt I could do something good and positive at Mary Vale.'

'Do you believe you have?' he asked.

'I certainly hope so,' Ada answered passionately. 'I always try to put the girls first, to prepare them not just for the birth of their baby but for what comes next when they leave Mary Vale.' She gave a sad sigh. 'Some of them are so young and ignorant, seduced by smooth-talking lads who only wanted what they could get, heartbroken young girls usually, shamed and rejected by their friends and families, cast out by society. What gives me the greatest pleasure is seeing a girl leave Mary Vale with a plan in her head and hope for a new future.'

Riveted by her passion, Jamie gazed at Ada's wonderful long hair blowing in the soft breeze; her dark-blue eyes were wide and sparkling all the time she talked; and her full, red, smiling lips revealed small white teeth. He was barely able to resist an overwhelming urge to pull her into his arms and kiss her.

'You really are a remarkable woman.'

Blushing, Ada shook her head. 'I wouldn't go that far, Jamie. I just love my job, and my patients and Mary Vale too.'

'The Home's lucky to have you,' Jamie said, as he rose and held out his hand to take hers. 'Shall we make our way down?' Smiling, he added, 'I'm dying for a pint.'

They ran down the fell, located the picnic basket that Jamie had hidden, then headed towards the showground, where they caught the end of the pole-vaulting competition and the wrestling, which Ada found fascinating to watch. After thirstily downing their beer in a crowded marquee, Jamie suggested they head back to Ambleside to get something to eat. Sitting in one of the local pubs, with a garden that extended down to the edge of Lake Windermere, they silently watched the slow-setting sun gild the high fells a deep burnished gold.

'Thank you for bringing me here,' Ada said gratefully, her eyes shining. 'I've had a marvellous day out.'

Jamie, who wanted the day never to end, could only murmur a response. 'Me too, the first of many days out on the fells together, I hope.'

And then, before he could stop himself, Jamie did what he had been longing to do all day long: leaning across the table, he gently lifted Ada's chin and kissed her long and deeply on the lips. As Jamie felt his world tip on its axis, he drew away in order to gauge Ada's reaction. He was delighted when Ada reached out and drew him back towards her.

'Jamie . . .' she murmured. 'Don't stop.'

14. Watendlath

Though Jamie and Ada tried their best to conceal their feelings for each other, it soon became evident to the staff that their relationship had moved on from professional to personal. Dora, typically, hit the nail on the head.

'I think you did a lot more at the Grasmere Show than watch beefy fell-runners!' she teased, when Ada breezed on to the ante-natal ward with her big blue eyes sparkling with happiness.

Studiously avoiding eye contact, Ada concentrated on tucking in the corners of the bed she and Dora were making.

'I've no idea what you're talking about,' she prevaricated.

'If you say so,' Dora chuckled. 'You know what they say, it'll all come out in the wash!'

And inevitably it did: working in such close proximity Ada and Jamie could barely tear their eyes off each other.

'I can't believe this has happened,' laughing Ada exclaimed as they sneaked a cuddle at the end of Jamie's morning surgery.

Laughing too, Jamie swept Ada's starched nurse's cap off her head so he could run his hands through her long, lustrous auburn hair.

'I can't think straight,' he declared. 'I open my eyes in the morning thinking of you and I go to bed in the evening only to dream of you.' Pulling Ada close, he kissed her deeply. 'You have completely bewitched me, Sister Dale!'

'Oh, Jamie,' she whispered dreamily, as she pressed her face against his white doctor's coat. 'I wish we were alone on the fells again.'

Excited as a boy, Jamie held Ada at arm's length. 'The whole of the Lake District is waiting for us!' he declared. 'Have you ever climbed Catbells or Scafell?'

Ada shook her head, reminding him she didn't have a car. 'I usually stay close to home for my fell-walking.'

'Then I'll take you further afield,' he announced.

A knock on the door made them both jump sky-high; blushing, Ada sprang apart from Jamie while he straightened his hair.

'Come in.'

Dora bustled in bearing a handful of patients' notes, but, sensing the charged atmosphere in the room, she quickly left the notes on the desk; then, before turning to leave, she gave a knowing wink.

'I'll leave you to get on with important business.'

When the door closed behind Dora, Ada covered her hot face with her hands. 'Oh, God!' she gasped.

Taking hold of Ada's slim waist, Jamie lifted her into the air and spun her around. 'Stop fussing, sweetheart,' he cried. 'Soon everybody in Mary Vale will know that Dr Reid is courting lovely Sister Dale – and he's the luckiest man in the world!'

As she went about her business, Ada gave up pretending when she next saw Dora. 'All right, you guessed,' she giggled, as they stood together swilling out dirty nappies in the sluice-room.

'Doesn't take Sherlock Holmes to solve that mystery,' Dora chuckled. 'Joking apart,' she added earnestly, 'I'm happy for you, lass, he's a good man and you're not so bad yourself. Be warned, though, no man other than St Joseph himself is ever going to be good enough to court you as far as Sister Mary Paul is concerned.'

Ada smiled fondly. 'She is such a sweet mother-hen.'

'And you're her precious little chick,' Dora reminded Ada.

Matron was thrilled when Ada confessed that she was going on a second date with handsome Dr Reid.

'We're all very happy for you,' she announced.

Ada gazed at her dear friend. 'All?' she enquired. 'Do *all* the staff know?'

Sister Ann burst out laughing. 'Yes – and everybody in the convent too!'

Before her date with Jamie something happened that brought Ada back to earth with a sharp bump. Just as she was about to go off-duty one evening, Diana asked if she could have a word in private.

'Of course, dear,' Ada immediately replied. 'Shall we sit in the garden? I've been cooped up on the ward all day long, and I'm in desperate need of fresh air.'

It was a lovely, late-summer evening, and, though the heat of summer still lingered, the sharpness of autumn was already in the air. Sitting side by side on a garden bench, both women watched the full moon throw a silvery bright light over the Irish Sea, now at full tide.

'I had a letter from Harry's friend at RAF Duxford this morning,' Diana started.

Ada tensed as she prayed the news would be good.

'Yes . . .' she asked tensely.

'Gordon said that his senior officer had recently managed to make contact with Harry.'

Ada gasped with relief. 'So he's alive,' she cried.

A smile spread across Diana's pale but lovely face. 'Yes, thank God.'

She took a deep, shuddering breath as she recounted her story. 'Only a few months ago Harry left the base for what was supposed to be a few days; we had made arrangements to marry just after he was due back.' Her head drooped. 'Obviously that never happened.'

Ada gave Diana's hand a sympathetic squeeze. 'I'm sorry, dear, it must have been hard for you.'

Diana's pale-blue eyes filled with unshed tears. 'It was agony, Ada,' she confessed. 'The very worst thing was that nobody – none of his friends or colleagues – even mentioned his name; it was as if Harry were dead. I was left thinking, "Did I dream this?" When, in sheer desperation just before I left Duxford, I plucked up the courage to talk to one of his pals, the poor chap clamped up.' She gave a bitter laugh as she recalled Gordon's terrified expression when she had spoken to him in Duxford's NAAFI. 'At least I got to leave my forwarding details with him, which is lucky, as otherwise I would never have got the wonderful news I'm telling you now.' Diana's voice trailed away before she continued. 'During one of the last conversations we had, Harry made it quite clear that he wanted me to keep our baby, but when he went missing and I was on my own I questioned my ability to bring up a child single-handed.' Diana stared at the stars, which were starting to prick the clear navy-blue sky. 'I was frightened, Ada. I wanted to get back to my old life, my war work, which I loved.' She gave a guilty shudder. 'I was even thinking of adoption, which is exactly what Harry didn't want.'

Ada gently patted Diana's hand. 'Dear, you've had good news today – concentrate on that for now.'

'You're right,' Diana agreed. 'Who knows?' she added wistfully. 'Harry might even come home soon.' She sighed. 'Oh, just to see him again, hear his voice, touch him,' she said with such yearning. 'I miss him so very much.'

The thought of her growing feelings for Jamie filled Ada's gentle heart with compassion – how would she feel if the man she was rapidly falling in love with should suddenly disappear from her life? She gave Diana a big hug. 'We'll all pray for Harry's safe return.'

Diana rested her tired head against Ada's strong shoulder. 'I'm glad I'm here at Mary Vale,' she said with a catch in her voice. 'It's such a support having you to turn to.'

'We'll always be here for you, Diana,' Ada replied. 'Now, come on,' she added, helping her patient to her feet. 'You've clearly been worrying yourself sick all day, and you need your sleep.'

*

After her talk with Diana, Ada felt almost guilty as she counted down the days to her next outing with Jamie; it seemed wrong to be so excited at the thought of seeing her sweetheart when so many women across the nation were missing their own loved ones. When the day dawned, Sister Mary Paul presented Ada with yet another picnic basket.

'Mary Vale Lancashire cheese, some fruit, a bit of rationing carrot cake and hot tea to keep your strength up,' she announced.

Touched by the old nun's generosity, Ada gave her a grateful kiss on the cheek. 'We're only fell-walking, Sister, not climbing Mount Everest!'

Always one to doubt the benefits of Mother Nature, Sister Mary Paul wagged a warning finger in the air. 'You can never take chances when you're facing the elements – a full stomach will keep you going in the wind and the rain,' Sister Mary Paul insisted.

'Thank you – we'll both be sure to enjoy it,' Ada assured her.

Reluctant to carry a cumbersome picnic basket up the fells, Jamie managed to pack most of the food into his rucksack. 'Off we go,' he cried, as he started up the ignition and they bounced down the drive and out of the gate. 'A whole day on my own with sweet Sister Dale!'

It was a hot, still-golden September day. The leaves on the trees seemed to hang suspended as if holding their breath, afraid of catching the first autumn wind that would hurl them into winter. As they drove along the

A66, Ada marvelled at the colour of the surrounding fells: burned by the summer heat, they were now dark sage-green, mottled brown and deep purple, with rolling stretches of tall bracken turning dark ochre.

Chatting companionably about work and patients, they drove through Kendal, where the hills bordered the road, giving tantalizing views of higher mountains just up ahead. They both fell silent as they began the steep ascent past Helvellyn, one of the most compelling mountains in the Lake District, which rose in majestic grandeur in the clear autumn light. Thirlmere loomed dark and forbidding against sheer scree-covered crags, with bristling pines reflected in the still, brooding waters of the deep lake. After they had driven by towering Blencathra, with emerald fields and neat little farms at its base, they were suddenly within sight of Keswick, a small grey stone town lying comfortably within the sheltering circle of mountains and fells.

Ada hungrily drank in the views. Smiling at her genuine delight, Jamie took the narrow, winding Borrowdale Road that ran beside Derwentwater glittering bright blue in the morning light.

'Pity we haven't got time to run up Catbells and say a good morning to Mrs Tiggy-Winkle,' he joked.

Ada's brow crinkled into a frown. 'Mrs Tiggy-Winkle – isn't she a hedgehog in a children's story?' she enquired.

'Indeed, she is,' Jamie agreed. 'And she lives on Catbells, the big fell over that way, towering over Derwentwater,' he pointed out. 'Sometimes you can see her scampering along the tops with her washing basket loaded with linen.'

'Stop teasing me,' Ada giggled.

'Mrs Tiggy-Winkle was my favourite bedtime story as a child,' Jamie confessed. 'Whenever Mum and Dad brought me to Keswick, I'd search Catbells and Newlands looking for a little hedgehog with a hat on.'

Stroking the thick tawny hair on the back of his head, Ada murmured, 'You must have been the sweetest little boy.'

'I was until I got polio, then I became a very grumpy little boy,' Jamie confessed.

Ada's indulgent smile faded. 'How did you contract the disease?'

'Apparently in the local swimming pool. I had to wear a calliper on my left leg due to muscle loss after being laid up sick in bed for weeks and weeks,' he explained.

'But you made a good recovery; you must have been strong and very determined.'

'I was nursed well by my attentive mother,' he said in a low voice. 'Poor dear, she was half mad with worry.'

Not wishing to dwell on the subject, unless he did, Ada waited for Jamie to continue. 'Going back to school was grim,' he continued. 'Children can be brutal.'

'Did the teachers keep an eye on you?' she asked softly.

'To a point, but I didn't want to come across as a softie, so I struggled on.'

'Poor darling,' Ada murmured with tears in her eyes.

Jamie shrugged as he took a sharp left-hand turn off the main road. 'Like all things, it passed.'

They made slow progress up the steep track that led to a narrow stone bridge: they'd had to pull over into passing places to allow a farm tractor and a cart wagon loaded with hay to get through. After parking the old Rover behind some farm buildings, Jamie helped Ada out of the car, then, holding her hand, he led her across the fields to the tiny hamlet of Watendlath. Ada caught her breath at the sight of an ancient grey-slate farmhouse that faced on to a small tarn nestling in the heart of the mountains.

'Perfect place for a picnic!' Jamie announced.

Taking a blanket from his rucksack, Jamie placed it close to the tarn, in which wild trout rose, then flipped back into the still waters with a loud *plop*. Smiling with pleasure, Ada made herself comfortable – but when she looked up Jamie was holding an old Kodak camera in his hands.

'Smile, darling,' he cried.

Blushing and feeling extremely self-conscious, Ada protested. 'Not now – I must look such a mess.'

Lifting her wonderful hair so it caught the breeze and floated prettily around her radiant face, Jamie took the shot, then settled on the blanket beside Ada, who cuddled up close to him.

'Thank you for bringing me here,' she whispered in his ear.

'I plan to take you to all my favourite places, where

I can kiss you all day, watched only by sheep and a few red squirrels,' Jamie whispered, as he lay back and pulled her into his arms.

For several minutes they lay in complete stillness, listening to little waves breaking in the shallows and the plaintive cry of ewes on the hillside; then, after giving Ada a final squeeze, Jamie sat up and started to unpack the picnic from his rucksack.

'I'm starving!' he declared.

Sister Mary Paul's sandwiches were delicious: tangy, crumbly Lancashire cheese combined with Zelda's delicious plump, ripe tomatoes were followed by flaky Eccles cakes and hot tea from Thermos flasks.

'I'm too full to move!' Ada groaned, as she lay flat out on the blanket and gazed up at the azure-blue sky.

'If only we could stay here forever,' Jamie sighed, snuggling up beside her. 'Sweetest Ada, you're bewitching me.'

Jamie's hands swept over the length of her long, slender body. 'God, you're gorgeous.'

Responding to his delicate touch, Ada pressed herself against his strong chest, slipping her hand inside his shirt. With the top buttons undone, she could feel the warmth of his skin and the steady beat of his heart. Nuzzling the soft, golden hair growing on his chest, she breathed in the smell of him, a heady combination of soap, antiseptic and sunshine. Locked in each other's arms, they lost track of time until a sheep dog barking from the nearby barn startled them.

'Lucky that happened,' Jamie chuckled. 'I was on the point of losing myself entirely.'

'Oh, Jamie,' Ada sighed, as she held him close. 'I can't remember a day when I've ever been so happy.'

Driving back in the cool of the evening with one arm around Ada's shoulder and the other on the steering wheel, Jamie gazed up at the glittering bright stars illuminating the fells they drove by. The day had been made up of all the things he treasured most: sunlight and stars, Watendlath, Derwentwater, Catbells and the beautiful woman by his side he was fast falling madly in love with.

'Could life get any better than this?' he thought with a contented sigh.

A dark-red fox flashing across the road caused Jamie to brake sharply. 'It was only a fox,' he told himself.

But the bubble of happiness that had cocooned him all day through was gone. Jamie shuddered as if somebody had walked over his grave. Little did he know that it would be months before he would spend another day such as this, on the mountaintops with his beloved, and, by then, he would have witnessed things that would change his life forever.

15. Alf Arkwright

Early one Saturday morning Gracie and Zelda drove over to Mary Vale Farm to pick up Farmer Arkwright as usual. They arrived to find crates and punnets of market produce neatly stacked outside the barn but no sign of Alf himself. Zelda and Gracie (who were now on first-name terms with the farmer) cast about the farmyard hoping to catch sight of him.

'Odd,' said Gracie. 'He's usually outside waiting for us.'

Though well into her pregnancy, Gracie lightly hopped out of the van and ran over to the farmhouse to knock on the front door. A few minutes later Alf appeared with a stricken expression on his face.

'We're just loading up,' Gracie said pleasantly. 'Will you be long?'

Arkwright shook his head. 'I won't be going to market today, pet.'

Gracie couldn't stop herself asking, 'Is everything all right? You don't look yourself.'

'It's not me, it's my son, Frank,' Alf replied. 'He's been badly wounded. The Army's sending him home – I just heard. I'm staying put at home in case any more news arrives.'

'I'm so sorry, Alf,' Gracie said softly.

The farmer gave her a brief smile, then patted her hand. 'Best get on your way, eh? You mustn't be late setting up your stall in the marketplace.'

Upset at the thought of leaving poor Alf on his own, Gracie hung back. 'Do you want any company?' she asked softly. 'I could put the kettle on for a cuppa if you like?'

Seeing her sweet young face clouded with anxiety, Alf shook his head. 'Nay, lass, be on your way,' he urged.

'I'll drop by later with your earnings,' Gracie promised, before she hurried back to Zelda waiting for her in the van.

After a busy market day Zelda and Gracie returned the farmer's crates to the barn, then dropped his earnings through his letter-box. 'I don't want to disturb him again,' Gracie told Zelda, as they drove back to Mary Vale, where they were just in time to catch a supper of spam fritters and salad served up by devoted Sister Mary Paul.

'Farmer Arkwright didn't come to market with us today,' Gracie said, ravenously digging into another salty spam fritter.

'He told Gracie that he'd had some bad news,' Zelda added.

After setting down a plate of bread and butter, Sister Mary Paul sighed heavily. 'His only son's been discharged from the Army.' Dropping her voice to a whisper, she added, 'The lad got shot in the head and has lost the sight in his right eye.'

On hearing the dreadful news, the colour completely

drained from Zelda's face; whenever she heard of wrong done by one of her countrymen she was filled with both guilt and fear. Yet again here was another German casualty, but this one had landed right on their own doorstep.

Though Zelda and Gracie continued to take Farmer Arkwright's produce to market every Saturday morning, Zelda, once she heard that Alf's son was now home, stayed firmly in the van, leaving Gracie to communicate with Alf.

'You're being silly,' Gracie chided.

Zelda went white. 'Please do not say that, Gracie,' she implored. 'Alf's son was shot by a German. He will not want to meet another German. Don't you see? I am his enemy.'

Seeing poor Zelda so pale and frightened, Gracie tried to comfort her. 'I'd have a word or two to say to anybody who upset you, lovie.'

Zelda smiled weakly. 'You are a good friend,' she answered quietly, but Gracie's staunch words of support did nothing to assuage her mounting anxiety.

Zelda's worst fears were confirmed a few weeks later when she was busy in her garden harvesting her herbs: basil, thyme, mint, marjoram, oregano and lavender. Smelling the neatly tied bundles, which she planned to dry out over winter, Zelda gave a sigh of satisfaction. In the peace of her teeming garden, with wildflowers and herbs growing alongside her summer vegetables, Zelda loosened the turban that she wore to cover her head and let her long curly red hair fly free. With the sun on her face and a soft breeze caressing her softly tanned cheeks speckled with golden freckles, she felt a surge of happiness that she could never have even imagined a few months ago. Her joy was suddenly shattered, and she jumped in fear as a loud, angry voice rang out from behind the drystone wall that adjoined Farmer Arkwright's field.

'Bastards, bloody bastards, all of them!'

On hearing the rage in the man's voice, Zelda dropped to her knees behind her tomato plants to avoid any possibility of being seen. She breathed a sigh of relief when she heard Farmer Arkwright calling across the field.

'Frank, lad! Where are you?'

Zelda's heart beat so loudly that she was sure the men over the wall would hear it.

'Just checking on't sheep, Dad.'

'I heard some shouting – is something wrong, son?'

'No, just me, yelling at sheep.'

It was clear from the proximity of the farmer's voice that Alf was standing close to his son.

'What's troubling you?' he asked tenderly.

Frank replied in a harsh, bitter voice, 'Apart from the fact that I'm half blind there's nothing much troubling me, Father.' Clearly ashamed of his cruel words, he faltered, 'Sorry, Dad, one of those days.'

'It will get better, lad,' Alf gently assured him.

'Good! Because it can't get any bloody worse. I hate the Germans that did this to me. I could shoot the bloody lot of them!' Frank growled moodily.

With her body half hidden by overhanging foliage, Zelda held her breath until she heard their voices receding across the field. Scrambling to her feet, Zelda wiped the dust from her face, then, rising to her feet, she walked slowly back to her garden shed, where she reran Frank Arkwright's furious words through her mind.

'I hate the bloody Germans . . . I could shoot the lot of them!'

What would he do when he found out that a German woman was living right next door to him? Take a gun to her too? Though she felt dreadfully sorry for Frank Arkwright, she would be mortified (not to mention terrified) if she were ever to find herself alone in his company. From now on, Zelda decided, she would be wise to avoid him at all costs.

In his desperation to speed up his son's recovery, Farmer Arkwright visited Mary Vale to have a chat with Sister Dale.

'It's not just his eye that's been damaged: the skin on the right-hand side of his face is badly burnt and weeping pus.'

Ada's smooth brow crinkled in concern. 'It sounds like the wound might be infected,' she said knowingly.

'That's what I'm afraid of,' the old man blurted out. 'It's bad enough Frank losing his sight in one eye but being scarred for life is quite another matter.'

'I thought he was under the care of the hospital in Lancaster?' Ada enquired.

'Aye, he is, but he can't always make the journey there,'

Alf sighed. 'To speak the truth, Sister, he's ashamed of his looks and hates going out in public, which is why I wondered if you might be able to keep an eye on him? You're only across the field from us, that's got to be an advantage.'

Ada gave him one of her brightest smiles. 'Bring Frank along to Dr Reid's morning surgery tomorrow,' she suggested.

Alf gave her an embarrassed look. 'Sorry, Sister,' he apologized. 'He won't want to be seen waiting with the lasses; he's proper embarrassed of his looks these days.'

Ada gave an understanding nod. 'I understand, Alf,' she said. 'Tell him to come after eleven o'clock – the doctor will have seen the residents by then and he'll be able to give Frank a bit of private time.'

Alf looked like a weight had been rolled off his shoulders. 'That's right kind of you, Sister,' he said, as he put the weather-beaten cap he had doffed back on his head. 'We'll see you a bit after eleven tomorrow, then.'

The following morning Zelda, who'd been the last patient on the list to see Dr Reid, got the shock of her life when she walked slap-bang into the man she was determined to avoid. Leaving the surgery, lost in her own thoughts, she cannoned straight into tall, dark, scowling Frank, who was accompanied by his father.

'Oh, *mein Gott*!' she had cried out in alarm.

Gasping, Zelda clutched her very large tummy, which had taken the brunt of the impact. Feeling Frank's brooding dark eye burning into her, Zelda turned to go, but Farmer Arkwright stopped her. 'Are you all right, lassie? Did you hurt yerself?' he asked in a concerned voice.

Desperate to get away, Zelda shook her head, still clutching her tummy, and all but ran up the corridor, leaving glowering Frank staring after her retreating figure.

'She just spoke German,' he muttered.

'She *is* German, lad,' his father told him.

'What the hell is she doing here?' Frank snapped.

'Waiting for her baby to be born like all t'other lasses in the Home,' Alf patiently explained.

'Why didn't she stay in her own damned country to give birth?'

Alf came closer to his son in order to whisper, 'Because the Nazis shot her husband and then they came after her – she's a Jew.'

Frank took a step back from his father. 'A Jew?'

Alf nodded. 'The Mary Vale nuns took Zelda in – she pays her way, mind, and she grows fruit and veg for the Home.' He smiled fondly before adding, 'She's a brave little lass.'

Frank remained unimpressed. 'I thought I'd seen the back of Germans when I got discharged.'

Alf gave him a hard stare. 'We're talking about a woman on her own, Frank. On paper she might be the enemy; here at Mary Vale she's just Zelda. Leave her be, lad, or you'll have me to answer to.'

After examining Frank's wounds James assured him that he would do what he could.

'I'm more than happy to take care of you, though I'm not a burns specialist.'

As Jamie and Ada treated the livid raw scar tissue on Frank's face, Jamie asked his patient how the attack had happened.

'We were in a Sherman tank in northern France, being chased by the Hun – everything suddenly went quiet and my senior officer instructed me to open the hatch and take a look outside. When I did a sniper shot me in the head – the bullet went through my right eye and out the other side,' he said grimly.

'My God!' Ada gasped. 'It's a wonder you survived at all.'

Farmer Arkwright, who had stayed with his son throughout the examination, nodded. 'Nothing short of a blessed miracle.'

'Believe it or not I was lucky,' Frank continued. 'The enemy lobbed a grenade into the Sherman, which exploded into flames. I was thrown clear but all my mates in the tank were blown to smithereens. I landed in a ditch where I lay semi-conscious, half dead, in fact, until a French peasant woman found me and helped me to hide in a barn.'

Sensing that his question about the attack might have sent his patient's heart rate sky-high, Jamie brought the conversation back to the ordinary by asking Frank how he spent his time now that he was back home.

'I try to do some work on the farm,' Frank replied. 'But I miscalculate distances and walk into the furniture all the time – it drives me mad,' he confessed.

'I tell him not to fret himself,' Arkwright protested. 'It will get easier.'

Ada, who was feeling increasingly sorry for Frank, suggested a course of physiotherapy. 'I'm sure Dora and I can spare a few hours a week to help you,' she volunteered.

'I'd like that very much,' Frank immediately replied.

After he finished cleaning and bandaging his patient's wound, Jamie said, 'I'll need to see you regularly to replace the dressing – we need to keep it fresh and clean to prevent infection.'

'I'm grateful for your help, Doctor, and yours too, Sister Dale,' Frank replied. 'See you next week.'

A combination of Jamie's treatment and regular bouts of physiotherapy slowly helped Frank to improve over the next few weeks. Without fail he regularly attended his appointments and worked hard alongside Ada or Dora, practising his walking, improving his balance and working muscles that had become weak due to protracted bedrest. The curious female residents talked about him over their meals in the dining room.

'I bet he were a right bonny before he copped it,' one girl said.

'He's got lovely dark hair,' another girl enthused.

Sister Mary Paul, who was clearing away the dirty dishes, clucked her tongue in disapproval. 'Leave the lad be,' she chided. 'He's got enough on his plate right now; the last thing he needs is lots of girls fussing over him.'

'You're right, Sister,' one of the girls agreed. 'Anyway,

who in their right mind would ever fancy a seven-month pregnant woman with swollen ankles and varicose veins?'

Gracie protested loudly. 'You can be bonny and pregnant!' she declared. 'As soon as I've had this baby I'm determined to get back to my original weight, seven and a half stone; then I'll start back at the shipyard and build warships to beat the bloody Germans!' she announced with passionate determination.

Zelda's face fell as she listened to Gracie. Did Gracie and Frank and the rest of the world want to kill her mother, sister, brother, aunt, uncle? She could not blame them, but neither could she live with the thought of always being the enemy. Catching sight of Zelda's flushed, embarrassed face, Gracie clutched at her hand. 'I'm so sorry, sweetheart,' she murmured guiltily. 'You know that I don't mean *you*.'

Saying nothing of her real feelings, Zelda squeezed her friend's hand. 'Don't worry, Gracie,' she lied. 'I understand.'

16. Leave

A few days later Dora came hurrying into work with an excited smile on her flushed face. 'You'll never guess,' she declared, as she took hold of Ada around the waist, then started to dance her down the ante-natal ward, where Shirley was busy helping out with the morning tea-round. 'Our Jack's coming home on leave; he'll be with us for his twenty-first birthday.'

'That's wonderful news!' Ada laughed, truly happy for her friend, when Dora finally let go of her. 'You'll have to have a party to celebrate his birthday.'

Dora's smile was suddenly tinged with sadness. 'It'll be our Percy's birthday too,' she added wistfully.

Hoping to keep Dora's mood up beat, Shirley said shyly, 'It will be very nice to meet one of your boys.'

Dora's expression visibly brightened as she beamed at Shirley. 'I just can't wait to introduce him to all my friends.'

When Jack visited Mary Vale, there was no doubting whose son he was. Unlike Dora, who was small and squat, Jack was tall and broad, but he had his mother's laughing eyes and her big wide-open smile. Sister Mary Paul bustled them into the dining room, where she'd laid on a special tea for Jack and the staff. The sight of lettuce and meat-paste sandwiches plus coconut cake and jelly and cream brought a grin to the young man's face.

'I've not seen grub as fine as this in months,' he chuckled. 'It's a sight for sore eyes.'

'I'm sure you're starving,' Matron said, as she set Jack, the guest of honour, at the top of the table and loaded his plate with cake and sandwiches.

'Save a bit of space for some pudding,' Sister Mary Paul added, before bustling out of the room to refill the teapot.

Surrounded by nuns, nurses and his mum, Jack enjoyed the warm female company, even though he was secretly longing for a fag. When Dr Reid appeared and suggested a stroll round the grounds, Jack was on his feet in a flash. 'Certainly,' he said, and followed Jamie into the garden.

He offered Jamie a Capstan cigarette, and, sitting smoking on the terrace bench, both men gazed out to sea.

'I should think you're sick of the sight of the sea,' Jamie mused.

After inhaling deeply on his cigarette, Jack replied, 'Not this sea: it's beautiful. It's the North Atlantic I'm not keen on – wind, rain, hail, mist, gales, mines – hell at times.'

'I really don't know how you lads stick it on board a mine sweeper,' Jamie said in all sincerity. 'Cooped up and throwing up.'

'I was terrible seasick to start with,' Jack told Jamie. 'It took me months before I found my sea-legs.' Casting around to make sure he couldn't be overheard, Jack continued in a low voice, 'We've just got wind that we might be moving south, to Italy. It's not official yet. The Navy's got to keep the supply line open for our lads in North Africa plus it'll hit the Wops hard if we start waging war on them from the sea.'

Jamie stared at the impressive young man beside him: for one so young he had a sensible head on his shoulders.

'You're clearly a brave set of chaps,' he said humbly.

'Just taking orders,' Jamie said, grinning. 'By the way,' he said, changing the subject, 'don't mention any of this to Mum. She worries all the time since our Percy died; the last thing I want to do is add to her grief.'

'I'll be careful what I say,' Jamie promised. 'It must be tough for you without your twin?'

'He was the eldest by five minutes,' Jack said sadly. 'Our Percy was always there for me. I know he's dead but sometimes, especially when I'm in danger, I feel him beside me, hear his calm voice, see the look he used to give me when I was frightened.' Tears filled Jack's eyes. 'He might be gone but my brother is still with me . . . I pray he always will be.'

Feeling a little choked by Jack's sincere outpouring, Jamie was relieved to see Ada walking towards them, smiling.

'If you two don't come and eat Sister Mary Paul's apple crumble soon, she'll have your guts for garters!'

While the men were outside, Dora had spoken in a conspiratorial whisper to her friends. 'I'm warming to this idea of a party for our Jack, though it is the day before he goes back, the thirty-first of October.'

'Halloween!' Ada cried.

Dora gave an excited smile as she turned to Matron. 'Might it be possible to borrow the dining room for the event?' she asked.

'Certainly,' Sister Ann replied.

'We could decorate the room with balloons and bunting to provide a bit of an atmosphere,' Dora continued. 'And I think my husband could lay his hands on a barrel of beer and some sherry,' she added with a mysterious wink. 'Some of Jack's pals might even be home on leave, and I'll ask all the lasses in the Home to come too, if they feel up to it. That should swell the numbers.'

As usual Sister Mary Paul's only query was about the food. 'I'll make a birthday cake, though with what I'm not quite sure,' Dora said, smiling.

'I might be able to get some cheese and a bit of ham from Farmer Arkwright,' Sister Mary Paul added.

'Let's keep it a secret?' Dora begged. 'Imagine our Jack's face when he walks in here on his birthday and sees the place decorated in his honour.'

The idea of a surprise party grabbed everybody's imagination. Gracie's face lit up as an idea dawned. 'Why don't we copy the Yanks? They go mad at Halloween. I saw it in a film once: nearly everybody dresses up and parades around in their spooky costumes. I could dress as the Bride of Frankenstein,' she joked. 'All I need is a big white nightie to look the part.'

'Maybe I could borrow one of the nun's habits and come as a ghost!' Diana giggled.

After they had received their invitations several of the residents got into the fancy-dress theme, but the majority said they couldn't be bothered.

'What's the point of fancy dress when you're as big as a house?' one girl grumbled.

Undeterred, Ada and Dora were determined to dress up for the event. 'I think I'll come as a little devil,' Dora announced.

'Very fitting,' Matron teased.

'I could make a devil's trident out of cardboard and paint it red, and stick some red horns in my hair,' Dora elaborated.

Ada was determined to dress up as a fairy. 'I'll see if I can find some old curtain material in the junk shops in Grange; lace netting would be even better. I could cut it up to make wings!'

Shirley, who was still a bit of a child at heart, asked if she could help with the sewing. 'Maybe I could find some sequins and make a fairy crown for you, Ada,' she said wistfully.

Ada gave her a long, knowing look. 'Shirley, dear,' she teased, 'I think sequins are the very last thing that you'll ever find in the convent!'

While Diana and Zelda declined dressing up, Zelda took things one step further. 'I won't be coming to the party,' she announced one night as she and her friends were preparing for bed.

Diana and Gracie stopped midway between cleaning their teeth. 'You won't be coming?' Gracie repeated her words.

'Why ever not?' Diana asked.

Zelda didn't dare tell the truth: that she was extremely uncomfortable being in the same room as Frank Arkwright.

'I suppose I'm just too shy.'

Seeing her blushing, self-conscious face, her friends didn't push it, but Gracie instinctively knew why Zelda was avoiding the festivities. She had seen the way the girl flinched whenever they stopped off at the farm these days. Before Frank's return Zelda had always liked visiting Alf; hopping out of the van to help him load up, she always used to laugh and chat with the farmer all the way to Kendal and back. These days she barely spoke a word a single word to him.

'Pity to miss out on the fun,' was all Gracie said as they bade each other goodnight.

Zelda didn't consider any time spent with Frank Arkwright would be 'fun', more like 'hell' as far as she was concerned. After switching off the light, Zelda lay in the darkness holding on to her tummy, where her baby turned and shifted position. Soon she would be holding him or her in her arms; soon she would be kissing Izaak's son or daughter. Her happy thoughts gave way to fear: where would she go, once she was discharged? Where would she and her baby be safe when she was forced to leave Mary Vale?

As the days passed and the party drew near, Ada and Shirley were busy in the little spare time they had cutting and sewing Ada's fairy dress. While picking up deliveries in town, Ada had tracked down some lace curtains in a second-hand shop, and some sequins and little crystal beads too. The material and decorations had delighted Shirley, who would never have worn such a frivolous outfit, but the thought of creating a magical garment clearly thrilled her. After taking Ada's measurements Shirley copied a dress pattern from a women's magazine on to sheets of newspaper.

'It'll be short and swirly, with a glittery bodice and wings!' she informed Ada, who couldn't help but laugh.

'You should make one for yourself,' she teased.

Shirley looked shocked. 'I'd never show my legs in public!' she exclaimed.

At the first fitting in Sister Mary Paul's kitchen Ada twirled around in front of the nun, who gave a disapproving snort.

'Heavens, it's a good inch above your knee – way too short!'

'Ada's got gorgeous long legs – she should show them off,' Shirley mumbled through several dressmaker's pins she was gripping in her teeth. 'What with her slim waist and long hair, Ada will look like the Queen of the Fairies on the night of the party.'

*

158

While the October days remained warm, Ada and Shirley stitched the dress in the garden whenever they had a moment to spare, but, as the evenings drew darker and longer, they removed themselves to the Home's snug sitting room, where Sister Mary Paul always kept a fire going on chilly evenings.

'It's lovely to see the pair of you stitching so peacefully – it's like something out of a fairy tale,' the old nun mused as she handed them both a mug of hot cocoa. 'I'd offer to help myself, but I'm better with a rolling pin than I am with a needle and thread.'

'Stick with the cooking,' Ada advised. 'We haven't all been blessed with your culinary talents, Sister.'

They passed the time chatting easily about work, the residents, the latest babies to be born, and then Frank Arkwright popped into their conversation.

'Dr Reid has done a splendid job,' Ada enthused. 'We're hoping the scar on his face will slowly fade, but it will take time,' she added cautiously.

Shirley gave a heartfelt sigh. 'The poor fella has enough to put up with, wearing an eye patch for the rest of his life; the last thing he needs is an ugly scar too.'

'Do you think he'll recover enough to work on the farm?' Sister Mary Paul enquired. 'His dad's not getting any younger, and he needs help these days.'

'Frank's strong,' Ada answered. 'There's no reason why he shouldn't get back to full strength; as for the state of his mind, that's altogether another matter.'

'Time is a great healer,' Sister Mary Paul said fervently. 'And prayer too.'

Ada smiled at the two sweet nuns, one old, the other young, both devout and trusting in their Lord; she hadn't the heart to tell them that Frank Arkwright hadn't ever given her the impression that he had any belief in God's goodness or for that matter in humanity either.

17. Party

Even though Ada was working flat out on her fancy-dress costume, Jamie refused point blank to dress up.

'I might be on call,' he pointed out. 'My patients would have a heart attack if I turned up looking like Count Dracula! But I will wear my best suit,' he promised, as he kissed the little freckles on the tip of Ada's nose. 'I'll even go so far as to buy a new shirt in honour of you, Fairy Dale, which by the way sounds like a scene from Walt Disney's *Snow White*,' he joked.

Lovely Ada threw her arms around Jamie's neck and kissed him full on the mouth. 'Won't it be wonderful to forget about the war just for a short time, to dress up and dance all night long?'

'Any excuse to hold your beautiful body in my arms,' Jamie murmured. 'Though it's been so long since I went dancing, I might well have forgotten how to foxtrot.'

When the party day finally dawned, Ada, Dora and the rest of the staff were in a lather of excitement.

'How are you going to get Jack over here without giving away the surprise?' Matron asked Dora, when she clocked in for work early that morning.

'Me and Mr Saddleworth have worked it out,' Dora explained. 'I'll say I'm working, and mi husband will bring our Jack over here later on for his supper; then, when he arrives, we'll all sing "Happy Birthday", pop a few beer bottles and let the fun begin,' she answered with a wide smile.

'And where will you change into your little devil out-fit?' Shirley giggled.

'In't sluice-room, of course,' Dora giggled back.

Matron and Shirley had kindly volunteered to work the late shift on the party night. 'But that's not fair, you'll miss all the fun,' Ada exclaimed.

'Don't you worry,' Matron chuckled. 'We'll take it in turns to come and check up on you all. Luckily nobody's due to give birth that night, though we can't bank on that, of course.'

'Though the sight of Senior Nurse Dale showing her knickers might bring on palpitations among some of the patients,' Dora joked.

'And you'll put the wind up some dressed as Old Nick!' Ada joked back.

'As long as nobody's waters break, we'll be fine,' Matron said calmly.

Ada was thrilled with the dress that Shirley had pains-takingly created.

'It's gorgeous!' she cried, and spun around in circles, sending the skirt swirling out around her thighs. 'The bodice is perfect,' she enthused. She stopped spinning in order to examine the neat lines of crystals and sequins Shirly had patiently sewn into place.

'It matches your tiara,' Shirley laughed, as she arranged

a sparkling band of crystals on top of Ada's tumbling golden-auburn curls. 'And here's a wand to complete the picture.'

Smiling Ada waved the wand, which was nothing more than a little star of silver paper stuck on the end of a stick. Enjoying herself, she grinned as she got into her theatrical role.

'Come on, Shirley: in gratitude for your wonderful work, I'll grant you three wishes!' she declared.

Thinking long and hard, earnest Shirley bit her bottom lip. 'I hope that Jack stays well and comes home safe and sound to Dora at the end of the war.'

Ada waved her wand. 'Granted!'

Shirley continued with a shy smile, 'I wish you and your young man have a happy future together.'

Ada frantically waved her wand. 'Certainly granted!' Ada laughed. 'And your third wish?'

Shirley blushed guiltily. 'I wish that God will forgive me for missing Mass this morning because I had to finish your dress.'

Ada twirled her wand before she pronounced. 'All your wishes will come true.'

Gazing into her friend's beautiful, glowing face, Shirley smiled wistfully. 'I hope so, for all our sakes.'

It was lucky for Ada that she didn't see Jamie arrive for the party; if she had, she would have immediately spotted his rather preoccupied expression. Fortunately, the sight of his glittering girlfriend distracted Jamie, who smiled when he laid eyes on her.

'Darling, you look enchanting!' he exclaimed.

'And you, Dr Reid, are undoubtedly the best-looking man in the room.'

At her remark Jamie burst out laughing. 'I'm the *only* man in the room, apart from Jack,' he pointed out.

Ada waved her wand before his eyes. 'If this room were full of men, you would still outshine them all, my darling!'

An expression crossed Jamie's face that caused Ada to stop smiling. 'What is it, dear?' she enquired. 'Is something wrong?'

Jamie quickly shook his head. 'Of course not, come on,' he said, as he grabbed her hand and pulled her into the centre of the dining room, now gaudy with balloons and red, white and blue bunting. 'Let's enjoy ourselves.'

When Jack arrived with his dad, Glenn Miller was blaring out on the gramophone, and several dancers, including Jamie and Ada, were dancing to the strains of 'In the Mood'. At the sight of Jack standing in the doorway with an astonished look on his face, Jamie briefly paused the music so they could all sing 'Happy Birthday', after which they toasted his good health in beer or sherry. When the music started up again, Jack swallowed down his pint before searching the room for somebody to dance with. It didn't take long before his eyes landed on Gracie. Wearing a loose white silk shift, with her lustrous dark hair curling around her shapely shoulders and her full, luscious lips painted carmine red, she was undoubtedly the best-looking girl in the room. Seeing Jack making a bee-line towards her, Gracie groaned.

'Oh, no!' she said to her friends. 'He's going to ask me to dance.'

When Jack held out his hand, Gracie hadn't the heart to refuse, but she knew that within seconds of holding her Jack would be a very disappointed lad. As they moved on to the dancefloor and their bodies bumped against each other's, Jack realized that he had been so captivated by his partner's lovely face that he hadn't registered the rest of her body.

'I'm sorry, I should have thought . . .' he muttered, struggling to express himself before clumsily blurting out, 'Are you all right to dance?'

Gracie threw back her head and laughed. 'Are you frightened I might give birth right here on the dancefloor?' she exclaimed.

Poor Jack blushed. 'Well, er . . .'

'Don't worry, if I wasn't dancing with you, I'd be dancing with one of the lasses,' Gracie grinned. 'And you're a lot lighter on your feet than any of them are.'

Seeing her cheeky smile and laughing eyes, Jack drew Gracie further on to the dancefloor, where he was astonished by her natural rhythm and her wonderful timing.

'Blimey! You can dance,' he gasped, as he struggled to keep up with her during a lively square tango.

'I've always loved it,' Gracie shouted over the music. 'Though to be honest I never expected to be dancing the night away here at Mary Vale,' she giggled.

When it came to the slow romantic numbers, Jack blushed and suggested that they sat the dance out and had a drink.

'Lemonade shandy for me, please,' Gracie requested.

After they'd finished their drinks, Gracie introduced Jack to several of her friends, at which point Dora joined them. 'Just checking you're not planning on kidnapping my lad,' she joked.

Jack, who had had several pints and was enjoying the attention of several (albeit pregnant) attractive young women, smiled. 'I wouldn't mind, Mam.'

Gracie nudged him in the ribs. 'Be a gentleman and ask your mam for a dance.'

Mother and son took to the floor, which gave Jack the chance to ask Dora a few personal questions about Gracie.

'How come a gorgeous young lass is in a place like this?'

Dora gave him a sardonic look. 'There's a lot of gorgeous young lasses in places like this, son.'

'She's just my kind of girl,' Jack added with a wistful smile. 'Lively, bright, young and really bonny. I wish her circumstances were different; otherwise I'd be asking her out on a date.'

'She's not going to be pregnant forever,' Dora pointed out. 'And don't run away with the idea that Gracie's just a pretty face – she's a shipbuilder at the yard in Barrow.'

Jack's jaw dropped. 'She's not the size of two penny-worth of coppers!' he protested.

'She might be small but she's a welder and a whizz with old engines too,' Dora informed him.

Over the space of a number of slow foxtrots, Dora told her son about Gracie's Bedford van and her visits to Kendal Market every Saturday morning.

'She always manages to wheedle a spot of petrol out of Farmer Arkwright – God knows where he squirrels it away,' she chuckled.

Jack gave a knowing wink. 'Best not to ask too many questions, Mam.'

'Any road up, thanks to Arkwright and a few petrol coupons from the convent, young Gracie ferries stuff all over the place. She's a sight for sore eyes bouncing along the road to Barrow or Grange in that rattling old van.' She gave a fond smile. 'I'll miss the lively little lass when she does leave here.'

Jack's ears pricked up. 'When might she leave?'

'When do you think, you great lummox?' Dora mocked. 'After she's had her baby of course. Gracie's made no secret of her plan to return to work as soon as her baby's adoption has been arranged.'

Jack gazed admiringly at the pretty dark-haired young woman now waltzing round the room with a protesting Shirley, wearing her blue postulant's smock.

'Come on, Shirley,' he heard giggling Gracie say. 'You might be a nun, but it doesn't stop you from having a dance. Follow me, one, two, three, one, two, three. Keep up, lass!'

Lighting up a Capstan, Jack watched Gracie painstakingly teach blushing young Shirley.

'Heck!' he thought. 'If she's this lively now, stuck in a Mother and Baby Home in the middle of nowhere, what will she be like when she's back working at the shipyard?'

Smiling to himself, he strolled over to the bar to help himself to another beer. 'I might look up Gracie Price next time I'm home on leave,' Jack thought. 'She's certainly a girl to keep track of.'

The party ended with a number of romantic waltzes, followed by a rousing chorus of 'God Save the King', after which the dancers and residents slowly drifted away. Hand in hand, Ada and Jamie strolled out into the garden, where a chill autumn wind whipped around them.

'You must be freezing in that fairy outfit,' Jamie said, as he drew Ada down beside him on their favourite bench on the terrace, and Ada nuzzled against his warm chest.

'You can warm me up,' she murmured, as she pressed herself close to his strong body. 'Mmm, I love the smell of you, soap and Dettol!' she giggled.

When he didn't respond to her teasing, Ada quickly glanced up at Jamie. 'Penny for your thoughts?' she asked softly.

Jamie let out a long sigh. 'I didn't want to spoil the evening, darling,' he finally admitted.

The moon, suddenly drifting out from behind a thick veil of scudding clouds, caught the crystal headdress in Ada's long, thick hair, making it glitter brightly against the velvet-dark night. Pausing to light a cigarette, Jamie inhaled.

'I received a letter this morning: I've been called up to join the Medical Corps.'

Ada stared at him in disbelief. 'But you can't,' she cried. 'Your leg,' she blustered.

'It seems the Army are less fussy than they were when I

first applied,' Jamie explained. 'They need more docto[r]
and suddenly I'm fit enough, which I am,' he staunchly
insisted. 'I'm ready to do my bit for my country; I always
have been.' He stopped short as he stared into her bewitching blue eyes. 'It's *you* that's changed things, my sweetest,
darling Ada.'

Though she felt like throwing herself on her knees
and begging him not to go, Ada instinctively knew how
much Jamie really wanted this. The Army's initial rejection had embittered and humiliated him; now he would
be exonerated. Holding him by both hands, Ada tried
her hardest not to cry as she looked him square in the
face.

'I know it's what you always wanted and I'm proud of
you . . .' Her voice wavered. 'I'll just miss you, and worry
about you,' she blurted out like a frightened child.

Seeing her face crumple, Jamie threw away the stub of
his cigarette and pulled Ada close. 'I love you so much,'
he said for the very first time.

Ada's heart lurched. How she had yearned to hear
those three precious words fall from Jamie's lips, but
never in these circumstances.

'I love you too, my dearest,' she whispered back.
Clutching each other and fighting back tears, Ada struggled for self-control. 'Here we are, thinking only of each
other, when all across the country lovers and families
have been saying their goodbyes for two years,' she said
bravely.

'You're right, darling,' he whispered, as he kissed her
again. 'If I'd been called up at the start of the war, as I

...ped I would be, I would never have met you. I have my wonky leg to thank for that,' he said, smiling.

Tense as she was, Ada couldn't help but laugh at his words. 'I love your wonky leg,' she told him. 'It's given us time together, here at Mary Vale and in the Lake District too.'

'Grasmere, Keswick, Catbells and wonderful Watendlath.' Jamie murmured the names dreamily. 'I'll carry those memories in my head forever.' Suddenly anxious, he whispered, 'You'll wait for me, won't you, my darling?'

Ada gulped hard as she firmly told herself, 'You cannot cry now. When Jamie's gone, you'll have all the time in the world to cry.'

Laying her head on his shoulder, Ada made a heartfelt promise. 'I'll be here waiting for you, my darling, no matter how long it takes.'

Ada accompanied Jamie on the train to Lancaster, from where he would go on to London. Because neither wanted to say their goodbyes on home territory, they had agreed on this arrangement as a good compromise; it also gave them just a little bit longer together. Sitting on the train and clutching each other by the hand, the young couple gazed out of the window at the sunny bay, where groups of toddlers, accompanied by mothers and grannies, looked up in wonder to wave at the thundering steam train as it passed by, skirting the coastline. Cuddling up as close as she could to Jamie, Ada inhaled the smells that she always associated with him: antiseptic soap, tweed and tobacco. Giving a long, yearning sigh she whispered, 'If only I could bottle your smell.'

Jamie gave her an incredulous look before he burst out laughing. 'I must smell like an old goat,' he cried. 'While you, my love, smell of mountains and sunshine,' he chuckled. Nuzzling her long hair, he whispered softly, 'When will we next go walking, my sweetheart?'

Lifting her face in order to gaze into his hazel eyes flecked with beguiling specks of golden light, Ada replied, 'The minute you're home we'll pack a rucksack and walk over Catbells into the Newlyn Valley.'

'It's lovely up there in the autumn. When the bracken turns gold and the heather glows purple.'

Giving him a teasing tap on the cheek, Ada said, 'Then you had better make sure you're back home with me soon.'

When it came to the dreaded moment of farewell, both of them feared saying too much in case their emotions got the better of them.

'Be careful,' Ada pleaded as she stood on the long platform at Lancaster Station, waiting for the train to leave. 'Take care of yourself.'

With the window wound down, Jamie leant out to grip Ada's hands, which he held to his lips. 'Write, please write,' he begged.

'I will, promise,' she assured him.

As the train hooted and started to shunt forward, they loosened their hold on each other.

'Goodbye,' she sobbed, as the tears she had struggled to hold back overflowed from her eyes.

A cloud of dark smoke belched from the train's engine, briefly obscuring all from view.

'Ada!' Jamie called through the smoke. 'I love you.'

'I love you too,' Ada called back. 'I love you *so* much.'

As the smoke dispersed and the train pulled away, Ada was able to see Jamie waving to her through the window; then, when the track rounded a sharp bend, the train and Jamie disappeared from view. Standing alone on the platform with tears streaming down her face, Ada was completely overwhelmed by sadness and despair. With every instinct in her body clamouring to follow the train bearing her beloved away, Ada forced herself to retrace her footsteps and, walking like an automaton, she made her way towards the train that would take her home. Duty called: she had vital work to do at Mary Vale, where friends and patients awaited her return. If Jamie on his way to the Front could put on a brave face, so could she; though her heart ached, life, unquestionably, went on.

18. Behind the Lines

A little of the sparkle in Ada's big blue eyes vanished the day that Jamie left for war. Though she smiled cheerily as she went about her work, it was clear to all of those who loved her that she was suffering. Dora, who had endured even greater pain, spoke to the staff behind closed doors.

'The girl's hurting right now – let her be. She'll come around in her own good time, God willing.'

Diana found it hard to follow Dora's advice and leave Ada alone; she instinctively knew what Ada was going through, and so she made a point of tracking her down after she had finished her morning rounds. Walking into the sluice-room, Diana said without any preamble, 'If you ever need to talk to somebody who knows what it's like, you know where to find me.'

Ada laid aside the bucket of sanitizing fluid she was in the process of preparing for the nursery and turned her sad eyes on Diana. 'How do you bear the waiting?' she simply asked.

Diana slumped against the side of the sink and leant against it to ease her heavy tummy. 'There's no choice,' she answered bluntly. 'At first, you're under some crazy romantic illusion that it's not happening, that your beloved will walk through the door and surprise you, or there'll be a letter in the post for you; but then, as time drags slowly by, you realize that they really have gone. And in my case,' she said, as she gazed down at her burgeoning tummy, 'you begin to wonder if you haven't just dreamt it all.'

Seeing Ada's alarmed expression, Diana quickly modified her words, 'Harry's situation is quite unlike Jamie's,' she assured Ada. 'Harry has disappeared in mysterious circumstances more than once. The base kept it all hush-hush, which nearly drove me out of my mind; nobody told me anything – least of all Harry.'

Ada's pretty arched eyebrows shot up. 'He must have a very important job.'

Diana gave a weary shrug. 'How would I know?' she exclaimed bitterly. 'I haven't a damn clue what's going on.'

Ada gently stoked Diana's slender arm. 'I'm so sorry, I had no idea,' she murmured sympathetically.

'To be honest,' Diana confessed, 'it's a relief to be able to talk to somebody; trying to get any information out of Harry's tight-lipped chums on the air base was like trying to get blood out of a stone. I shouldn't complain: at least monosyllabic Gordon let me know that Harry was still alive when I'd all but given up.' Continuing on a more optimistic note, Diana added, 'Lines of communication will be much better for you, Ada. Your boyfriend is a doctor, and, though he's fighting behind enemy lines, post will get in and out; you're bound to hear from him soon.'

Tears welled up in Ada's big blue eyes. 'Oh, I hope so,' she said with such yearning. 'I *really* hope so.'

Within ten days of Jamie's leaving, Ada received the letter she had been longing for. After Sister Mary Paul (with a concerned look on her face) delivered it, Ada held the envelope to her thudding heart; then she raised it to her nose and sniffed it to see if it smelt of Jamie, but there were no hints of his favourite soap or hospital disinfectant. Chiding herself for being a foolish romantic, Ada hurried to her office at the end of the hospital corridor. After closing the door, she leant against it before she opened the letter and read.

My dearest, sweetest, darling girl,

I'm looking at the photograph I took of you at Watendlath: though the picture is black and white I can imagine the beauty of your big blue eyes and the colour of your glorious long hair. God, how I love you! I hope you're well, my sweet, and all at Mary Vale too – please send them my best wishes. When I think of the Home, so secluded on the edge of that vast marsh washed by the Irish Sea, I marvel at how different it is to the hurly-burly of the casualty clearing station I've been posted to. I'm not allowed to give any details of my location – if I did my letter might be destroyed, and it would certainly be censored – but I can tell you about my daily routine. I'm one of four general doctors who work alongside two surgical specialists and a dentist; there are also quite a number of nursing orderlies and theatre assistants. We're a highly mobile clearing station, ready to move on at any time: our job is to accept the sick and the wounded, assess their injuries and carry out emergency treatment or evacuate them to general hospitals behind the Line. As I say, it's pretty hectic – we

*snatch a few hours' sleep whenever we can and usually eat
standing up. How I yearn for Sister Mary Paul's Eccles cakes
and Lancashire cheese sandwiches! When I'm not working or
sleeping, I think about you all of the time. I may be surrounded
by female nursing orderlies, but I have eyes only for my beloved
Sister Dale, who, as far as I'm concerned, outshines the stars.
Write back to me, sweetheart, with all your news, even if it's
only to tell me how many marrows Zelda has harvested. I'm
keen to hear if my post at Mary Vale has been filled by another
doctor. I think not, with all the shortages, which makes me
worry about how you're all managing.*

God bless you, my love, please, please write soon,
Jamie xxxxxx

Smiling dreamily, Ada kissed the letter. 'Thank God,
he's well,' she sighed.

Slipping the letter into the top drawer of her desk,
Ada resumed her duties, but hours later, at the end of her
long afternoon shift, she managed to find time to sit
down in her quiet office and write back to Jamie.

Darling Heart,

*Thank you so much for your wonderful letter, which filled me with
a mixture of both delight and relief. I can't believe that you've
been gone for nearly a fortnight – it feels more like a year. Every
time I hear car wheels scrunching on the gravel drive, or pulling
up at the entrance, I run to the front door thinking it's you
arriving to start your surgery. The residents miss you very
much – all of them regularly ask how you are and send their best*

wishes. Sister Mary Paul longs to send you a hamper full of goodies, but I've explained it might not get delivered to the right person, or, worse still, might even end up in the hands of the Germans, which really infuriates her. You're quite right, we haven't got a replacement doctor, and it's more than likely we won't get one either. I'm not sure what we'll do in emergencies, which, as you know, your ex-GP in Barrow is supposed to cover, but he must be working himself into the ground now that you've left his practice. We'll manage somehow — we have done in the past and we will do so again. When I think of you barely sleeping and eating on the hoof, I want to fly over to your side and take care of you, my own sweet Jamie, you're so very precious to me. Do you remember the rather elegant resident, Diana? She and I have become quite friendly since we now have something in common: our men are both posted somewhere overseas. She, poor girl, has not seen her fiancé in months, and she's carrying his child. I feel guilty when I compare myself to Diana. You've been gone barely two weeks and I've already heard from you, while she, poor girl, has heard nothing in months. War is so cruel. I try to stay strong, but when I think of you so close to the enemy my resolve breaks and I have to stop myself from crying. Write as soon as you can, my darling, and take good care of yourself.

I love you so very much,
Ada xxxx

Diana couldn't help but feel a stab of envy when Ada told her that she'd received a letter from Jamie.

'You must be so relieved,' she said, with a generous smile that immediately made Ada feel guilty.

'I'm sorry,' Ada quickly apologized. 'I shouldn't have mentioned it.'

'Don't be sorry,' Diana retorted. 'The machinery of war rolls on and we can't do a thing about it.'

Feeling overwhelmingly sad for Diana, Ada reached out to take her hand. 'If only you had an inkling of where Harry was,' she said wistfully.

With a catch in her voice, Diana replied, 'As long as he's alive, I can just about bear anything.'

Two hundred miles away, flying his single-engine Lysander light aircraft over France, Harry's thoughts were all about Diana. His present work, picking up SOE and SIS agents in Allied-controlled territories, was so top secret he couldn't speak a word of it to anybody, which meant that every time he took off on a mission he worried about what might happen if he didn't make it back – what if he 'bought it', as the chaps on the ground said? Now permanently posted outside of England, Harry had never had the opportunity to explain his treacherous war work to Diana, and he was sure the RAF wouldn't explain or apologize to her if he were suddenly to disappear on a clandestine mission. Risks were part of the job, and, as there were only a few experienced pick-up pilots available, Flight Lieutenant Harry Langham was in no position to say no to his senior commanding officers.

Patriotism aside, Harry's heart ached for the hurt he knew he must have caused Diana. She had been so determined, so tough; even when it was obvious that she was terrified, she had still kept a brave face just for his sake. His RAF colleagues in the viewing gallery had regularly (and in complete privacy) applauded him on his choice of a girlfriend who could clearly keep her mouth shut and not blab all over the mapping table to the other WAAF officers. Even now the poor girl didn't have a clue about his movements. Recently Harry had been so concerned about Diana he had bent the rules and got a message out to Gordon, who had been reluctant to do anything like passing on messages.

'For God's sake, man, you don't have to tell her where I am or what I'm doing,' Harry had pleaded over the phone to his stuffy friend. 'Just tell her I'm alive.'

Even now Harry had no idea if Diana had ever got his message.

Forcing himself to concentrate on his perilous landing in a dark field, Harry scanned the sky for Morse signals, which would be flashed from both the ground and the air signalling mutual recognition before he began his descent. This last leg was always short, just two or three minutes before he recognized a village, a bridge or a railway junction, and then, at the end, a friend in a field flashing the Morse letter he was expecting. He would only be on the ground briefly, long enough to pick up the returning agent and perhaps exchange a handshake with the undercover operator, who sometimes gave him a bottle of brandy; once he was given French perfume.

'For your wife,' the Frenchman had said with a wink.

His well-meaning sentence had cut Harry to the quick. He had never married the woman he loved, the woman who was carrying his child alone and unprotected. What kind of a man was he? Doing his bit in the war, fighting Hitler, was without a doubt the right thing to do, but Diana was paying the price for it. Things had not been going well recently; the Resistance ring with whom they had been liaising had recently been rounded up and executed. Harry knew that if any of the men and women in the ring had broken under interrogation, the Germans would be on his tail soon. He needed to be sure that if he was taken out by a sniper, Diana would be informed of his death, and hopefully told exactly what he had died for.

19. Novice

Apart from being Matron of Mary Vale, Sister Ann was also Shirley's spiritual mentor in the convent of the Sisters of Holy Mary. Under her tender care Shirley had been guided through her postulancy period by the older nun, who had monitored her reading of the scriptures and her understanding of the rules of the religious office she yearned to join. In that capacity she had been invited one grey misty November morning into the Reverend Mother's study in the silence of the convent to discuss Shirley's imminent future. Recalling Shirley's wild impatience some months ago when she had first approached the Reverend Mother for permission to join her order, Sister Ann said with an indulgent smile, 'The dear child was so full of passion she would have taken her final vows right there and then.'

The Reverend Mother returned her smile. 'Shirley's learnt patience during her postulancy; she's also learnt the routine of the convent from the inside, and she's been obedient to our daily timetable.'

'She's been so generous with her time,' Sister Ann said with a ring of pride in her voice. 'Insisting on cleaning the wards – it's her best time for prayer, she always says – and she's been a God-send in the kitchen, helping Sister Mary Paul, who is getting on in years.'

'I've had to insist from time to time that Shirley devotes herself to reading, prayer and getting to know our Sisters, as well as to scrubbing floors and baking bread,' the Reverend Mother chuckled.

'She has fully embraced all of that,' Sister Ann assured her superior.

'So now we need to talk to Shirley about the next stage of her training: becoming a novice in our order and living like a professed Sister,' the Reverend Mother continued. 'The timetable is fuller than she's used to, and she'll be introduced to more spiritual duties, particularly those that involve her taking part in Divine Offices.'

Sister Ann's eyes welled with tears. 'Shirley is a deeply spiritual young woman; I know she will embrace those duties with love and dedication to Our Lord. I have no doubt that she'll treat all with loving kindness and be a peacemaker, just like she is now,' she said confidently.

'She'll wear the white veil of a novice over our order's habit and will have the title "Sister",' Reverend Mother continued. 'And she can change her name if she wishes. At the end of two years, if Shirley feels ready and our order are in agreement, she could request to make her final vows.'

'This will be a testing time for her vocation,' Sister Ann commented.

'If it becomes too stressful, Shirley knows that at this novitiate stage she is free to leave at any time,' the Reverend Mother pointed out.

Knowing Shirley's overwhelming desire to dedicate herself to God, Sister Ann shook her head. 'With respect,

Reverend Mother, I believe that's highly unlikely. I've never known anybody more committed to becoming a nun than Shirley is.'

Sister Ann waited for a suitable moment to arise when she could speak in private with Shirley about the Reverend Mother's decision. On a chilly morning, as the sun struggled to pierce through the banks of clouds that loomed over the Irish Sea, Sister Ann spotted Shirley reading her prayer book on a bench in Mary Vale's garden. The gardener, sweeping up the leaves that were presently banked high around the edges of the lawn, greeted her gloomily. 'Morning, Matron,' he muttered darkly. 'If there's anything good to be said about a day when the Germans have done their worst.'

Sister Ann nodded in sympathy with him: the nation had woken up to the terrible news that Coventry and its beautiful cathedral had been destroyed by a Luftwaffe raid consisting of over one hundred bombers.

'It is dreadful news indeed,' she agreed.

'The Boche are trying to take the heart out of the nation,' the gardener growled. 'Burning and wrecking our beautiful cities and ancient monuments. Let's hope the RAF give 'em back as good as we got,' he added angrily.

Sister Ann, who couldn't go along with his vengeful thoughts, simply made the sign of the Cross.

'God help the poor souls who suffered,' she answered fervently.

'Amen to that, Sister,' the gardener said, and he went on his way.

*

Shirley laid aside her prayer book when Sister Ann sat down on the bench beside her.

'Good morning, Sister,' Shirley said fondly, and kissed her friend on the cheek.

'I have news for you, Shirley,' Sister Ann started. 'The Reverend Mother thinks the time has come for you to take your novice's vows.'

Shirley's eyes opened wide in delight. 'Oh, thank God!' she exclaimed, then, completely overcome with emotion, she threw her arms around Sister Ann's neck and wept. Struggling to control herself, Shirley wiped away her tears and stared incredulously into her mentor's beaming face. 'Who would ever have thought this blessing would come to *me*?'

'It is God's will, dear,' Sister Ann answered simply. 'He called you to do His will.'

Shirley, looking flushed and emotional, could only whisper, 'But am I worthy enough, Sister?'

'Yes, child,' her friend answered firmly. 'You are more than ready to begin the next part of your spiritual journey.'

Shirley went into retreat several days before taking the veil; and, as she prayed in silence for God's guidance, Sister Mary Paul began to completely overdo things in the kitchen. Helped by anyone who could spare an hour, the old nun cooked up pies and cakes for the guests and religious Sisters who would attend the meal after the ceremony. Meanwhile, in the convent, the mistress of robes completed Shirley's new habit and veil. On the night before the ceremony Sister Ann cut Shirley's chin-length mousy-brown hair; then, after helping her into her new habit, she showed her how to pin the veil to her head. The reflection of Shirley's pale face in the small mirror hanging on the convent wall showed an expression of sheer joy.

'I look like you, Sister Ann!' she exclaimed.

The older nun smiled proudly. 'Yes, Shirley,' she agreed. 'You look like a proper nun at last.'

The following morning Father Ben adorned the convent altar as for a solemn feast: dozens of candles in polished brass candlesticks flickered and glowed, their light reflected in the life-sized brass crucifix placed in the middle of the altar, now draped in starched white linen and adorned with a richly embroidered golden mantle. While the nuns sang harmonious Latin chants, the new novice was led into the chapel by Sister Ann. When she knelt at the prie-dieu holding a candle to her calm, peaceful face, there wasn't a dry eye in the house. Pungent incense, swung from a smoking thurible by a solemn-faced altar boy, floated up into the carved rafters of the chapel, which resounded to Shirley's sweet voice as she made her formal vows of Poverty, Chastity and Obedience. After the ceremony the Sisters of the order of which Shirley was now firmly a member led her through a metal grille into the privacy of a dark cloister, where they reverently dressed Shirley in her new robe. Carrying a veil and a wreath of white roses, the young novice was led back into the chapel, where she knelt before a smiling Reverend Mother. The nun covered

Shirley's head with the veil and secured the wreath of roses. With tears streaming down her face, Shirley stood to embrace her superior, while Father Ben prayed softly.

'By the symbolic shedding of clothes and dressing yourself in Jesus Christ you thereby lay aside the life of a lay person.'

Father Ben completed the moving service with the naming ceremony. 'Sister Theresa,' he said to Shirley, who smiled with joy at the sound of her new religious name, 'you no longer bear your father's name.'

Ada exchanged a knowing look with Sister Ann: they both knew exactly what the other was thinking. Shirley, now Sister Theresa, would be overjoyed to have severed all links with her father and the brutal life she had endured with him. Safe in the bosom of her Sisters, with the attribution of a new name symbolizing her new life, Shirley felt herself filled with blessings she never imagined herself worthy of.

It was a squash in Mary Vale's dining room: what with all the residents, the nuns and the visitors, the room was loud with chatter and laughter, and after the long ceremony everybody was desperately hungry and longing for cups of hot tea. Shirley had to be banned from the kitchen and from rushing around serving out cakes and egg-and-cress sandwiches.

'This is your day, Sister Theresa,' Sister Mary Paul exclaimed, as she added another cake to Shirley's plate. 'It's our turn to serve you.'

*

186

After the solemnity of the ceremony Shirley felt spiritually overwhelmed; now surrounded by so many kind, smiling, familiar faces, she felt emotionally overwhelmed too. It was almost a relief when the residents and the visitors said their farewells and she was left alone with her Sisters, who escorted her back to the chapel. Shirley was finally left alone to her own prayers and thoughts. It was well over an hour later that Sister Ann found her still kneeling at the prie-dieu, with her eyes closed and her hands crossed before her.

'Dearest,' she said in a whisper, 'it's been a long day; you must get some rest,' she urged.

Shirley's eyelids fluttered open, and when she turned to her friend Sister Ann smothered a gasp when she saw in Shirley's wide-open eyes the depths of her love and joy.

'This is the happiest day of my life,' the new Sister Theresa announced. She stood and walked back to the convent hand in hand with her mentor.

20. Salves and Poultices

Though Zelda had fled in fear the morning she bumped into Frank Arkwright in Mary Vale's hospital, she nevertheless could not fail to notice the hideous red raw scar on his right cheek. Even though she had not ventured anywhere near Frank, she had dared on a couple of occasions to poke her head out of Gracie's van window to peep at him when they were at the farm.

'Heavens!' Zelda exclaimed to Gracie as they drove out of the farmyard after collecting Alf's market produce. 'I never realized Frank Arkwright's face was so disfigured.'

Gracie nodded as she kept her eyes on the road. 'He was burned by a hand grenade that exploded in the Sherman tank he was travelling in. Alf told me that Sister Ada and Dr Reid have been treating Frank's scar, but, as far as I can see, there's not much improvement.' Suddenly struck by a thought, Gracie turned to Zelda. 'Why are you suddenly interested in Frank Arkwright?' she teased. 'You run a mile at the sight of the man!'

Looking self-conscious, Zelda answered her question. 'I just caught sight of him out of the window and felt sorry for him. I wonder . . .' she mused out loud.

'Wonder what?' Gracie enquired.

'When I was studying botany in Germany, we did some research on the healing benefits of herbal poultices and creams for burns and scar tissue.'

Gracie was so astonished she nearly drove into an unruly bunch of sheep a shepherd was herding to Kendal market.

'Really?' she exclaimed. 'You should definitely tell Ada – I suspect she needs all the help she can get, now that Dr Reid's left the Home.'

Leaving Gracie to concentrate on the market traffic gathering in the grey stone town square, Zelda thought to herself, 'Gracie's quite right. Ada might be grateful for a bit of help and, as long as I never have to come into direct contact with Frank Arkwright, I'd be happy to ease Ada's load.'

A few days later Zelda, with a pile of textbooks tucked under her arm (courtesy of Shirley and Sister Ann, who had borrowed them from the convent library), sat across the desk from Ada in the nurse's office just off the ward. Carefully opening the books at selected pages, Zelda repeated what she had recently told Gracie with surprising confidence.

'When I studied botany in Munich, we learnt about the benefits of herbal remedies for skin ailments and scars. Look.' Zelda pointed to pictures of flowering herbs, plant leaves and the roots of some spices. 'Chamomile, red clover, witch hazel, comfrey, chickweed, marsh marigold, cinnamon and turmeric. And honey and apple-cider vinegar.'

Though taken aback by Zelda's surprising announcement, Ada nevertheless gazed thoughtfully at the images as Zelda continued. 'All of these help in the healing of scar tissue caused by burning.'

Ada's eyebrows shot up. 'Really?'

'Of course, they have to be distilled and carefully blended into a paste,' she added. 'But they have been tested over time and have proved quite beneficial.'

Ada looked up from the images she had been carefully scrutinizing. 'I assume you're thinking of Frank Arkwright's wound?'

Zelda blushed. 'It might help him, and anyone else suffering from burn wounds,' she answered awkwardly.

Ada's gaze returned to the delicately drawn botanical images in the textbooks. 'It's very interesting,' she murmured. 'I've been using lavender oil, witch hazel and chamomile to soothe wounds and burns for years, but I had no idea of the benefits of honey, cinnamon and turmeric – and I must admit I've never even heard of apple-cider vinegar!' she laughed.

'The healing properties of some natural ingredients are astonishing,' Zelda enthused. 'Take honey: it provides a moist healing environment, clears infection and reduces inflammation too. Apple-cider vinegar accelerates the healing process and reduces scar tissue.'

'But how can you blend them?' Ada enquired. 'You would need to know the ratio of herbs to liquid before you could do any distilling.'

'I know some but certainly not enough,' Zelda admitted. 'I'd like to educate myself a bit more on the subject before I launch into making treatments,' she said with a shy smile.

'How would you go about it?' Ada asked curiously.

'I borrowed these reference books from the convent library, but what I really need is a good old-fashioned *Herbal*,' Zelda explained. 'There's a second-hand bookshop in Kendal where I hope I'll be able to buy such a book.'

Ada nodded in agreement with her. 'That would be a good place to start.' Looking Zelda in the eye she asked, 'Will you keep me posted on your findings?'

'Of course,' Zelda promised. 'As I said, I have some experience of the practice, but my research was done under supervision in a laboratory. I remember when I got excited about my experiments,' she said with a wistful expression on her sweet, heart-shaped face, 'my husband used to tease me and call me a white witch!'

'Well, if you could cast your spell over Frank Arkwright, I'm sure he'd be very grateful,' Ada said, smiling. Zelda did not return the smile; instead she replied somewhat abruptly, 'Sister, I have a favour to ask of you.'

Ada cocked her head.

'If I do succeed in making salves and poultices Frank Arkwright must never know of my involvement,' Zelda insisted.

'Why?' Ada gently enquired.

Blushing with embarrassment, Zelda blurted out her answer. 'I think if he found out that a German was mixing potions for his wounds, he would assume I was trying to kill him.'

Ada thought the notion so ridiculous she couldn't stop herself from bursting out laughing. With her face flushed and her hands trembling, Zelda protested. 'You may mock, but you haven't heard Mr Arkwright damning all Germans to hell like I have.'

Looking guilty, Ada quickly apologized. 'I'm sorry, Zelda. I had no idea.'

Zelda pressed on. 'So, if I do this work, you must promise never to tell Mr Arkwright.'

'I promise I won't say a word, if that's what you want,' Ada solemnly answered.

Zelda looked calmer already. 'I'd need a pestle and mortar to break down the herbs and spices.'

'That's not a problem – there are plenty of those in the hospital,' Ada replied. 'Anything else?'

'I have some herbs I dried over the summer,' Zelda continued. 'And I can search the countryside for others that might still be growing wild at this time of the year. Once I've got the essential essences, I'll be able to make up salves and creams with a carrier, like beeswax. It's essential that the salve is easy to apply,' she said thoughtfully. 'It must be soft and smooth; otherwise it will drag on damaged skin tissue.'

Ada looked excited. 'Do you really think it could work?'

'Yes, I do,' Zelda replied. 'I saw the beneficial effects of such salves on damaged skin when I was working in the laboratory; these traditional remedies have been tested over centuries.'

Ada quickly nodded, then had a thought. 'I see Frank

once a week. Maybe we could start your herbal treatments next week?'

'I'll do my best but first I have to find a *Herbal*,' Zelda reminded her.

'It's really kind of you to offer to help, dear,' Ada said gratefully.

Before she left the room, Zelda gave her friend a grateful smile. 'It would make me very happy to do something in exchange for all that you have given me.'

After she had gone, Ada thoughtfully tapped her long, slender fingers on her wooden desk. Initially it was the residents who intimidated Zelda; now it was Frank Arkwright. He had, albeit unwittingly, put the fear of God in the poor girl. Would Zelda ever find peace at Mary Vale, or anywhere else for that matter?

'What will she do once her baby is born?' Ada thought to herself as she walked down the corridor leading on to the wards. 'Where in England in wartime will a German woman with a new-born find a welcome?'

True to her word, Zelda set off on the local bus for the bookshop in Kendal, where she found not one *Herbal* but several. They were all old, leather-bound and reassuringly well thumbed. All had beautiful artwork, images of exotic herbs from foreign lands, and everyday common or garden herbs that grew in abundance in English hedgerows. Zelda excitedly bought two volumes, one written by Nicholas Culpeper, the famous apothecary of the seventeenth century. With her books tucked under her arm, she then set off for the old-fashioned chemist's shop in the town centre, where she studiously browsed along the shelves containing old-fashioned tonics, elixirs, oils and cordials all stored in elaborate glass bottles. Zelda started when she heard somebody just behind her say, 'May I help you?'

Turning, she saw a grey-haired gentleman with a moustache and round horn-rimmed glasses wearing an immaculate long white coat.

'I'm Mr Marsden, the chemist,' he said.

Delighted to meet him, Zelda shook him by the hand and, after introducing herself, she told him of her plan. 'I've just flicked through a few *Herbals*, and I can see already there are a number of ingredients that I won't be able to pick in the wild or grow myself; it would be useful to be able to purchase some of your oils and more exotic herbs,' she eagerly explained.

Mr Marsden beamed enthusiastically. 'I'd be happy to help in any way I can,' he assured Zelda. 'With medicines urgently needed by the troops, we should be thinking about genuine alternatives; in these days of increased rationing old remedies and treatments might prove very popular.'

Heartened by his encouraging words, Zelda bade Mr Marsden goodbye and got the bus back to Mary Vale, where she immediately set to work. Taking the pestle and mortar that Ada had supplied her with, Zelda hurried to her garden shed, where she stored her tools, seeds, onion sets and herbs that she had harvested earlier in the year when they were at their freshest. Now they dangled from bits of string attached to the rafters, filling the shed with the combined fragrance of basil, sage, fennel, chamomile, lavender and thyme. After lighting the little wood-burner that she had recently cleaned up, Zelda made a long list of ingredients that she would need; then, over the next few days, she wandered the surrounding countryside collecting any wild herbs that were still viable. During one of her Saturday market-day visits to Kendal, Zelda popped into Mr Marsden's shop and bought apple-cider vinegar, witch hazel and turmeric, which the chemist kept stored in old-fashioned pharmaceutical jars. Sister Mary Paul had already donated convent honey and cinnamon from her larder, and the nun in charge of the convent beehives had promised Zelda as much beeswax as she needed.

With all the ingredients now to hand, Zelda placed her precious *Culpeper's Herbal* alongside an old leatherbound volume entitled *Healing in the Herb Garden* on her workbench. Trembling with both nerves and excitement, she tucked her long red hair under a cotton turban, so it didn't get in her eyes, and donned her gardening apron. First she dropped little bunches of comfrey, St John's wort, chickweed, marsh marigold and witch hazel, the basic components for Frank's salve, into a small saucepan, which she covered with a lid and left to simmer on top of the crackling wood-burner, stoking it to get a good heat going. While the pungent mixture simmered, Zelda pounded borage, chickweed, lavender and chamomile in her mortar. After twenty minutes she removed the bubbling pan from the heat and strained the steaming liquid; then she removed the spiky stalks. Leaving the liquid to cool, she returned to grinding the herbs in the mortar.

'This is the moment of truth,' she said out loud, as she gazed intently from the herbal essences to the much reduced liquor. 'I've got to combine the two without making a complete mess of it,' she muttered, as she slowly added the liquor to the pounded herbs. At the end of the process she gradually added beeswax to the compound, until it reached the viscous consistency of hand cream.

Pleased that she had completed the delicate procedures, Zelda sank back on to her gardening stool and thoughtfully drank tea from a Thermos flask that she had brought along with her.

'I need to try it out before I give it to Ada,' she murmured, as she smoothed the salve on to her own hands, which bore no marks of burning or scarring. 'Who could I experiment with?' Zelda wondered out loud. Suddenly she smiled. 'Of course,' she exclaimed. 'The queen of Mary Vale's kitchen – Sister Mary Paul!'

The old nun was touched when Zelda presented her with a small pot of ointment. 'It's a natural hand cream made from herbs and honey,' she explained. 'It's an old remedy that's supposed to ease burns and blisters. I thought with all the cooking you do you might find it useful.'

Sister Mary Paul unscrewed the jar lid and cautiously sniffed the contents. 'It smells nice enough,' she said. 'And you're right, my hands are full of burns from that blessed old oven. Thank you, dear.'

Trying not to sound too eager, Zelda said, 'Please will you tell me how you get on with it? You know, if you see any improvement?'

'I most certainly will,' the nun assured her.

'Oh, and one more thing, Sister Mary Paul.' Zelda blushed as she told a bit of a white lie. 'Will you keep this a secret? If it's successful I could make pots of the same hand cream for the residents at Christmas.'

Sister Mary Paul beamed as she pocketed Zelda's gift. 'Let's see how I get on with this one first, shall we?'

Though Zelda was desperate to find out if her salve had worked on Sister Mary Paul's blistered hands, she reined in her impatience and waited for the nun to come to her. Her heart skipped a beat of excitement when one morning Sister Mary Paul came to find her in the garden, where Zelda was preparing onion sets. Breathless from hurrying across the lawn, the nun handed Zelda a steaming mug of hot tea before she made her announcement.

'It works!' She spread her hands before Zelda. 'The back of my hands were badly burned from catching the side of that old oven – it happens all the time when I'm moving big heavy trays and pans up and down on the shelves. I've been using your cream every night and, look, I can see a difference.' She turned her hands palms-up and then palms-down for Zelda to see. 'The skin's soft and moist and the burns are healing.'

Zelda carefully examined Sister Mary Paul's hands, which did look less inflamed.

'So,' she started cautiously, 'would you say that the cream helped heal the damaged skin?'

'For sure, and it's nice and soothing too,' Sister Mary Paul replied. 'The bad news is I've run out of it already so,' she chuckled, 'I'd be grateful if I could have another pot, please.'

Zelda gave her a bright smile. 'Of course, Sister, with pleasure.'

When the nun was safely halfway back across the garden, Zelda did a little jig of joy, which she was forced to stop when her baby protested with a hefty kick. Gently stroking her big tummy where her restless baby wriggled, Zelda murmured, 'Sorry, little one, your clever mama's feeling rather pleased with herself.'

As soon as she had time, Zelda repeated the whole process all over again, but made double the quantity. When she had finished, Zelda gazed thoughtfully at the two pots sitting on her bench: the smaller one for Sister Mary Paul, the larger one for Frank Cartwright. A tingle of excitement ran through her body: *if* this simple natural recipe was effective, there was a possibility that it could help other burn sufferers. Smiling to herself, Zelda dropped off Sister Mary Paul's 'hand cream', then she headed for the hospital, where she found Ada on the post-natal ward.

'Here,' she said, handing her the larger pot of salve. 'Apply liberally every night before bedtime for a week; hopefully you should soon see a difference. If it does work, I can make up more as you require.'

Ada peered at the label on the pot: Zelda had carefully listed all the natural ingredients. Impressed, she said, 'It's full of good stuff – let's hope it works for Frank.'

'I think it will,' Zelda replied. 'Please remember your promise, Ada: Frank Arkwright must never know that I had anything to do with this treatment.'

21. Shockwaves

Though Ada regularly received letters from Jamie, she had made up her mind that she wasn't going to mention them again to Diana, in whom she and her staff had noticed worrying changes: the weeks of unsuccessfully waiting for further news of Harry had taken their toll on her general health.

'She's pale and listless, and losing weight rather than gaining it,' Ada confided, as she and Sister Ann shared a pot of coffee (heavily mixed with chicory) in Matron's office early one dank November morning.

'She does look all baby,' Sister Ann agreed, stirring her coffee. 'But we know it's not unusual: babies often grow at the mother's expense, especially these days, when we're all existing on meagre rationed food,' she added, as she nodded towards the coffee pot. 'Does Diana show any other symptoms? High blood pressure, swelling of face and hands?'

Ada shook her head. 'No, I regularly check her blood pressure,' she said. 'Desperate as she is, she simply can't get any information out of anybody.' Ada gave a heavy sigh. 'You can see it's wearing her down.' Looking annoyed, Ada replaced her coffee cup in its saucer. 'Why can't one of those wretched RAF men whom Diana worked with take pity on the poor girl? Just a little word or two to ease her misery?'

Sister Ann gave her a thoughtful look. 'It might well be top-secret information that it's too dangerous even to talk about.'

Ada's dark-blue eyes opened wide. 'Heavens!' she cried. 'I don't know how she endures it. The waiting and uncertainty would kill me!'

When a letter with RAF Duxford stamped on the back arrived for Diana, Ada's heart skipped a beat.

'Please God let it be good news,' she prayed, as she personally delivered the letter to Diana, who was on light kitchen duties.

'For you,' she said.

In seconds all the blood drained from Diana's face, and she grabbed the edge of the sink, where she had been washing up, for support.

'Sit down,' Ada urged and pulled up a chair; then she quickly got Diana a glass of water. 'I'll leave you in private,' she murmured, but Diana grabbed her by the hand.

'No, Ada, please stay with me.'

Hardly daring to breathe, Ada tensely watched Diana open the letter, which she clutched with trembling hands; suddenly she gave an anguished cry and thrust the letter at Ada.

'It's from Derek Robson, Harry's RAF Commanding Officer in Duxford: he's a friend of Harry.' Looking terrified, she begged, 'Read it.'

Dear Miss Bishop,

I know how devoted Harry was to you, which is why I feel it is my duty to inform you that he has been reported missing in action. Please understand that for reasons of national security I cannot go into details. All I am able to say is Harry disappeared on a flying mission over two weeks ago, and we have had no contact with him from that date. His plane was discovered grounded in central France. We can only assume that Harry is missing in action and pray for his safe return.

I will continue to keep you informed.

Yours faithfully,
Flight Commander Derek Robson
RAF Duxford.

Shocked rigid, Ada put on her bravest, most optimistic face. 'It's bad news,' she babbled. 'But missing in action could mean he's in hiding until it's safe to make his way home.' Ada scrambled around in her mind, trying to think of something positive to say, something – anything – that poor Diana could hold on to, but Diana didn't seem to be listening to her.

They were disturbed by Sister Mary Paul bustling into the kitchen bearing an empty tray. When she saw Diana doubled over in a chair with her head in her hands, the nun didn't ask any questions but immediately filled up the kettle, which she popped on to one of the Aga hot plates.

With tears coursing down her face, Diana became hysterical. 'The Germans could have picked him up, they could have tortured him – Harry could be dead by now!'

Ada tried her best to calm and placate Diana, who was fast losing control. Glad of the cups of hot sweet tea that Sister Mary Paul quietly handed over, Ada urged Diana to take a few sips to steady her nerves.

'He could be any of those things, dear,' Ada soothed. 'He could also be alive and well; for all we know he could have linked up with Resistance workers and be making his way back to England.'

'Oh! Why can't they tell me more?' Diana wailed. 'I can't bear it,' she cried in an agony of despair.

Seeing her patient becoming severely distressed, Ada led the poor trembling girl upstairs to her bedroom, where she helped her undress and get into bed. Sitting by her side, Ada stroked Diana's long, silky blonde hair until Diana fell into a mercifully deep sleep. Desperate that nobody should disturb her, Ada quickly slipped downstairs to warn Zelda and Gracie not to enter Diana's bedroom. Both women were horrified when they heard the bad news, Zelda especially so.

'I am happy to sit close by,' she gently suggested. 'It might be good to have a friend there when she does wake up.'

Ada gave Zelda a grateful smile; if anybody knew about loss it was Zelda.

'Thank you, dear, that would be most kind.'

Ada noticed Gracie looking slightly panicked. 'The best thing we can do until we know more is to be as normal as possible, Gracie.'

The girl's big green eyes filled with tears. 'I know, Sister, I'll do my best, I promise – but,' she muttered with a catch in her voice, 'poor Diana . . . as if she's not been through enough already.'

Diana was taken off all the duty rotas, including feeding the babies in the nursery.

'You need plenty of bed rest,' Ada said when she visited Diana in her bedroom the next day.

Her patient gave a wan smile. 'Don't you start, Sister,' she murmured. 'Zelda's on a mission to make me a herbal tonic – honey, spices, beeswax, and God knows what else.'

Ada smiled. 'You'd be surprised by how much Zelda knows about natural remedies. She studied their beneficial effects for a while at university; she's not making it up,' she assured her patient. 'And don't worry, Zelda does a lot of research before she even starts the distilling process.'

'That's a relief. I thought she stuck two twigs in a teapot and gave it a good shake,' Diana joked.

Pleased that Diana's sense of humour was returning, Ada smiled too. Ada had spoken the truth about the benefits of Zelda's products: she had seen first-hand the improvement in Frank Arkwright's skin since he had started using the ointment that Zelda had prepared for him. During his weekly check-up Frank announced that he actually preferred the latest lotion to the previous one he had been using.

'It doesn't sting or congeal on my skin like the other stuff,' he told Ada. 'Due to my poor eyesight I can't really see how improved my skin is, but it certainly feels a lot better.'

After examining Frank, Ada agreed that the scar tissue was much improved.

'It's certainly not as inflamed as it was,' she said cautiously.

Frank then asked the question that Ada had been secretly dreading. 'Do you get it delivered from Lancaster Infirmary?'

Remembering her promise to Zelda, Ada blushed guiltily as she replied, 'No, it's easier to pick it up locally.'

'Well, I'm grateful to you,' Frank replied.

After Frank had left the surgery, Ada assuaged her conscience by reasoning that Zelda (working in her garden shed) was a kind of chemist, and nobody could argue that, for the moment at least, she was very local.

Zelda's herbal tonic for Diana required ingredients she could buy only at the old-fashioned chemist's shop in Kendal, which Gracie kindly drove her to. When Zelda appeared with powdered garlic and ginger in her shopping basket, Gracie burst out laughing. 'Honest to God!' she exclaimed. 'You come out of that shop smelling a lot different than when you walked in.'

'If it makes Diana just the tiniest bit stronger, I don't care what I smell like,' Zelda retorted.

Gracie's smile fell from her pretty face. 'You're right, Zell,' she replied using the nickname she'd given her room-mate. 'Anything is worth trying, as poor Di's in such a state.' Dropping her voice to a whisper, she asked, 'Do you think her boyfriend could be dead – I mean, really, it does sound likely, doesn't it?'

Zelda looked Gracie square in the eye. 'Do you want the honest truth?'

Gracie nodded.

'We can only hope and pray he is alive and can find a way to safety, wherever he is.'

Clearly obsessed, Gracie continued, 'But if he really is dead, do you think Diana might decide to have her baby adopted?'

Zelda spoke from experience. 'The child could be the last link she will ever have with her beloved.'

Back in her garden shed, Zelda worked up quite a sweat, grinding and pounding herbs and spices in her mortar for Diana. After simmering them in a pan of water until they were reduced by a third, she let the liquor cool before she bottled it. When she presented it, Diana stared sceptically at the golden-brown liquid.

'Thanks, darling, I know you mean well –' she said nervously.

'Stop being polite, Di,' she exclaimed. 'Just try it – I swear it will do you no harm.'

In fact, Diana rather took to Zelda's honey-rich tonic. After several large doses she started to sleep better, and her appetite improved to such an extent that she developed a passion for jelly and custard. Ada allowed herself to give a sigh of relief; hopefully Diana had turned a corner and would soon be strong enough to endure the ordeal of childbirth. She prayed nightly that Diana would receive positive news about Harry. But, contrary to her hopes, a

206

week after Diana had received the letter from Flight Commander Robson in Duxford, the officer himself made a personal phone call to the Home.

'May I please have a word with Diana Bishop?' he asked Sister Mary Paul, who scuttled off to find Diana, bumping into Ada along the way. 'There's a gentleman on the phone asking to talk to Diana – he said he's from the air base where she used to work.'

'Oh, no!' Ada murmured fearfully. 'I'll fetch her, Sister.'

Standing by Diana's side, Ada hardly dared breathe as she watched her pick up the phone with white, trembling hands.

'Hello,' she whispered in a quavering voice.

'Hello, Diana, Flight Commander Derek Robson here, from Duxford.'

Gripping the desk Diana murmured, 'Yes, sir.'

'Miss Bishop, I'm sorry to have to tell you Harry is no longer assumed missing, I'm sorry,' Robson, clearly upset, repeated himself as he struggled to continue. 'Reports have just come in . . . I thought you would want to know immediately . . .' His voice broke as he clearly tried to steady his emotions. 'Harry has been killed in action.'

As the phone slithered out of Diana's shaking hand, she fell to the floor in a faint. Ada quickly replaced the phone in its cradle, then called out for help. Sister Ann appeared, flushed and breathless, and between them the two women managed to get Diana on to the ward, where they quickly drew the curtains around a vacant bed.

'I'll get her some water,' Ada said, as her colleague settled their patient on to the bed.

Sister Ann stopped Ada in her tracks. 'She'll need more than water, dear,' she said, lifting Diana's wet skirt. 'Her waters have broken.'

Diana had a long, hard birth. The weakness and lethargy that she had suffered throughout the latter part of her pregnancy meant that what strength she had was very soon exhausted. Her cervix was slow to dilate, and the grief and stress that had recently preoccupied her dominated her emotions throughout her labour.

'She needs to calm down,' Dora whispered to Ada, as they took it in turns to monitor Diana's progress. 'She's not relaxing in between contractions, just constantly fretting and working herself up.'

Ada nodded grimly. 'I know – Matron said the same thing too. My heart aches for her, poor lamb, going into labour early due to the terrible shocking news she's had,' Ada swiped her hand across her worried brow. 'I'm concerned that if labour drags on her baby could suffer foetal distress.'

'We'll have to keep checking her blood pressure,' Dora added. 'The last thing we want is for Diana to get pre-eclampsia.'

Gradually Diana's contractions started to quicken, at which point Ada asked Zelda and Gracie to take it in turns to sit with her, as she and Dora were suddenly needed by Marie in the delivery suite.

'Wouldn't you know it?' Dora said as she rolled her eyes. 'Two births in the same day!'

Ada smiled. 'Well, at least Marie's as strong as a horse.'

Gracie's big green eyes all but rolled out of her head when Ada asked for her to sit with Diana in Ada's absence.

'What if she gives birth right there in front of me?' horrified Gracie cried.

Ada couldn't help but chuckle at her reaction. 'Giving birth is never that quick, Gracie,' she assured the startled girl. 'Anyway, we'll be just along the corridor, not in Timbuctoo!' she joked. 'All you have to do is talk to Diana and reassure her, or, if you're really worried, just come and get one of us.'

Gracie gave a nervous nod. 'All right,' she agreed, then quickly added with a self-deprecating smile, 'But can Zelda sit with her first? She's a lot calmer than me.'

Zelda was a natural: soothing Diana with her soft voice, she sat by her bedside giving the patient little sips of water and cooling her hot face with a damp flannel. Zelda's heart ached for the poor stricken girl, whose anguish brought back many painful memories, though Zelda realized, as she reflected on her past, that remarkably she was starting to heal. Not that she could ever forget her beloved Izaak or her family in Germany – they were part of her, her life's blood – but she had found peace and security in England. Mary Vale and her wonderful friends were intrinsic to the unexpected happiness of her new life, and for that she would never stop giving thanks. In return for what she had so freely received, Zelda made a vow: she would do everything in her power to help others who were suffering – whether it was mixing tonics, making salves, growing veg or sitting by a woman in pain. They were small, grateful gestures to the Home and staff who had saved her from falling into an abyss of utter hopelessness.

Meanwhile, in the delivery room, Marie's contractions were fast and furious.

'You're doing very well, sweetheart,' Dora said, as Marie took deeps breaths in between her contractions.

Ada quickly took the opportunity to check the baby's position before Marie's next contraction. Placing her cool hands on Marie's huge tummy, she deftly traced the shape of the baby's back. Concentrating hard, she said, 'Baby's in the correct position: its back is towards the front of your tummy, Marie,' she explained. 'Exactly where we want it, allowing easy movement through the pelvis and the birth canal.'

'Oh-oh! Here comes another,' Marie grimaced.

Dora checked her fob watch, then looked across the bed at Ada. 'They're coming every two minutes,' she said.

'You'll have your baby soon, Marie,' Ada reassured her patient. 'Big in-breath, go with the contraction, good girl.'

'Arghhhh!' Marie howled.

'It's passing,' Ada soothed. 'Well done, dear,' she said, as Marie slumped back on to the bed.

In no time at all Marie was bearing down. Panting in

between the contractions, she conserved her energy; then, tucking her chin on to her chest, she pushed her baby out into the world.

'A boy!' Dora exclaimed as the baby slithered out from between Marie's beefy thighs. 'A big boy too,' she added, holding him out for Marie to see.

The young new mother's eyes filled with tears as she stared into her son's puckered-up face.

'The image of his father,' she murmured, as she cradled him naked in her arms. 'Beautiful silky dark skin and big brown eyes.'

'He's lovely,' Dora agreed. 'Have you thought of a name for the little lad?'

Marie gazed into her new baby's face. 'George,' she announced. 'Just like the King!'

Suddenly the baby opened his mouth and started to wail.

'Hand him over,' Dora urged. 'I need to wash and weigh him, then I'll get you a nice cup of tea.'

Marie grinned. 'A pint pot mug, if you please, Nurse Dora, and a packet of fags!'

22. A Breakfast of Ashes

Hours after George (who weighed in at a bouncing nine pounds) was born, Diana delivered another little boy into the world. Unlike George, Diana's son was pale, underweight and listless after his long, protracted birth. As soon as her ordeal was over, Diana slipped into a deep, exhausted sleep, which lasted until dawn, when she woke up to the sound of a wailing baby. Turning instinctively towards the sound, she opened her eyes to find Ada by her bedside bearing a little bundle in her arms.

'This little boy would like to meet his mother,' Ada said gently.

Tears slid down Diana's face as she stared into her baby's face. 'His mouth is like Harry's,' she murmured. 'And he has his hair too,' she said incredulously, running her fingers through her son's sparse blond hair.

'I've brought a bottle so you can feed him,' Ada explained. 'He's only had a bit of sterilized water so far.'

Diana gazed intently into her baby's blinking eyes. 'I want to feed him myself.'

Ada gave her a hard look. 'Are you sure?'

Opening her nightie, Diana answered simply, 'Quite sure.'

'Here, let me help you,' Ada said, as she positioned the

baby in the crook of Diana's right arm. 'Let him nuzzle your breast – he'll find his own way from there.'

The little boy snuffled, then, when he found the nipple, he latched on and started to suck.

Surprised at his strength, Diana let out a little cry. 'Ow! He's pulling.'

'He's hungry, poor chap,' Ada said, smiling. 'He slept on and off through the night; he must be starving by now.'

As Diana gazed at the child in her arms, she remembered what Harry had said when they had discussed their baby before he left.

'Have you thought of a name?' Diana had asked one night as they were sitting comfortably on the sofa.

Harry's handsome face had grown serious as he considered the options. 'What about Margot if it's a girl and Teddy if it's a boy?'

At the time Diana had smiled indulgently, but, thanks to that conversation, she knew for sure the name of their son.

'Hello, Teddy,' she whispered, as she stroked his soft, warm cheek. 'Welcome to the world.'

From the day they were born George and Teddy slept side by side in identical snowy white canvas cots lined up in the nursery, where all of the other Mary Vale babies slept. Marie bottle-fed her little boy, while Diana continued to breast-feed. Well aware of Diana's fragile state, Ada sat with her as Teddy, now nearly a week old and already visibly bigger, suckled on her breast.

'Are you sure this is wise, dear?' Ada tentatively asked.

Diana turned her cornflower-blue eyes on Ada. 'I know what you're really asking me,' she smiled. 'Is it a good idea to feed the baby you're about to have adopted?'

Ada nodded. 'I'm thinking of both of you, to be fair,' she pointed out.

'I completely understand that,' Diana acknowledged. 'To be perfectly honest, Ada, I can't think straight. I've lost the love of my life and found the love of my life,' she confessed. 'I weep in my sleep for Harry, yet I smile when I wake up and hold this little treasure. I *never* thought I would feel like this. Before I gave birth, everything was cut and dried: with Harry gone the only sensible thing to do was to return to my war work, which, by the way,' she added with a modest smile, 'I was rather good at.'

'I'm sure you were,' Ada agreed. 'You're a clever woman, Diana.'

'That's sweet of you to say so,' Diana said, grinning. 'Before I met Harry I was very focused and professional, but he, dear man, turned me into a bag of emotions and desires. I loved him very, very much, Ada. It's so unfair that we had so little time together.'

Her son wriggling fretfully at her breast momentarily claimed Diana's attention. When he had settled back down to feeding, Diana continued.

'I am *not* giving Teddy up, Ada. He's all I have of Harry.'

Because their babies had been born on the same day, Diana and Marie instinctively sought each other out.

214

They couldn't have been more different: tall, elegant, clever Diana and chubby, chatterbox Marie, who loved to eat, gossip and smoke, preferably all at the same time. Diana was grateful to Marie for not asking too many personal questions; Marie on the other hand had no hesitation in telling Diana of her passionate romance with Canadian Air Force Corporal Cody Buchan.

'His unit was posted over here at the start of the war,' she said, as the two of them sat in the nursery feeding their babies. 'I met him at the Palais de Danse in Bolton. Gorgeous fella,' Marie sighed dreamily. 'He was the tallest man in the room, broad-shouldered, handsome in his blue uniform. He was by far the best-looking.'

George, who had drained his bottle in no time, wailed as he wriggled uncomfortably on his mother's knee.

'All right, all right,' Marie soothed. 'You wouldn't have wind if you weren't so greedy.'

She confidently lifted him on to her shoulder and patted his back until he gave a loud burp.

'George is the spit of Cody,' Marie continued, lowering her son into the crook of her arm, where she rocked him to sleep. 'The same big brown eyes and smooth dark skin. Cody was a great singer,' she recalled with a laugh. 'He'd sing anywhere – walking down the street, in the pub, up on't moors – he never stopped.'

Diana, who was thinking she would be rather embarrassed by Cody's extrovert nature, asked, 'How long did you know him?'

'Best part of a year, all the time he was stationed in the North,' Marie replied with a nostalgic sigh. 'As soon

215

as Cody found out I was pregnant, he said he'd marry me, but mi dad put a stop to all that. He said he was having no daughter of his marrying a foreigner.' Marie gave a derisive snort. 'When I told him that Canada is part of the British Empire and the Canadian Air Force are over here fighting on our side, he just laughed in my face. Cody even came to our house to ask for my hand in marriage, but mi dad kicked him out, said he was having nothing to do with a mixed-race marriage.' Marie gently lowered sleeping George into his little white canvas cot. 'By the time I arrived here at Mary Vale, Cody's unit had been posted overseas. Not long after I got a letter from a friend in Cody's unit who told me that Cody had died on active service.'

Tears welled in Diana's pale-blue eyes. 'Seems like we both lost the man we loved,' she murmured.

'Bloody rotten war,' Marie seethed. 'Snatches your life away and leaves you with nothing but a breakfast of ashes.' Gently rocking George's cot, she continued bitterly, 'I'd like to keep George, but mi dad wouldn't even contemplate having him in the house. Only white fellas who work in the local mill and drink in the local pub are acceptable in his book, ignorant bloody fool that he is.'

Feeling very sorry for Marie, who clearly loved her son, Diana asked a question she almost immediately regretted. 'Could you manage to live on your own and keep your child?'

'I wish!' Marie exclaimed. 'I'm not clever and educated like you, Diana. I left school the day I turned fourteen and I've been working in the spinning room at Johnson's Mill ever since. I've no money, no savings, and nowhere to go but back to Bolton and the mill. God help me!'

Wiping tears from her eyes, Marie gazed lovingly at her sleeping baby.

'Anyway, what kind of a life would George have even if I could take him back home? I'd be out at work, and he would be brought up by my rotten family, who would resent him, just because of the colour of his skin. I want a much better life for my sweet, innocent little baby than that!'

A few days later Marie arrived in the nursery sobbing her heart out.

'What is it?' Diana exclaimed. 'What's happened?'

'I've agreed to George being adopted!' she wailed. 'Oh, God, how will I leave him here, all on his own?'

Diana caught Marie by the arm. 'Listen to me,' she said firmly. 'As long as I'm here, I promise I'll look after George, I'll write you weekly reports on how he's progressing.'

Marie smiled wanly. 'That's nice of you, Diana, but then what happens when you leave?'

'To be honest I don't think I'll be leaving very soon,' Diana replied frankly. 'The man I love is dead, and right now Teddy and I both need looking after; I've already talked to Ada about staying on a bit longer.'

'Lucky you,' Marie sighed. Seeing Diana's hopelessly sad expression, she quickly apologized. 'Sorry, stupid me and my big mouth,' she exclaimed. 'I know you're anything but lucky, losing your fiancé the way you have, but at least you're not going to be given your marching orders when your baby's six weeks old.'

In an attempt to cheer her sad friend up, Diana said, 'You know, Marie, times are changing. With all the men called up, things can't go on the way they always have done. The government will soon be turning to us women to help them run the country. We could be quite a force in the nation.'

The idea of change and empowerment brought a bright smile to Marie's tear-stained face. 'Aye, you're right,' she agreed. 'Somebody's got to drive the buses, build the bombs and work the land. I fancy us women have a big part to play in our country's future!'

In early December Ada, Matron and Diana had a consultation about Diana's plans for the future.

'I know I said I was champing at the bit to get back to the Ops Block,' Diana started. 'But I'm not any more,' she said flatly. 'I feel weak, depressed, aimless, heartbroken – and I desperately don't want to be apart from Teddy. My emotions are all over the place. I don't even know how I'll feel tomorrow, never mind next month,' she tearfully confessed.

Seeing poor Diana struggling with her emotions, Ada gently said, 'That's perfectly natural in your puerperal condition, dear: many new mothers feel exactly the same.'

'And now you have your son to think about too,' Matron softly added.

Ada gave a slow nod.

'How I ever imagined I could give him away, I'll never

know,' Diana blurted out. 'Teddy is my lifeline: apart from my memories, he's all I've got of Harry.'

Matron nodded. 'Zelda says the same thing: that the baby she carries gives her hope for the future.'

Diana took a deep breath before she asked the question that had been on her mind for some time.

'I was booked into the Home until after Christmas, but, as a result of Teddy being born earlier than expected, will I now have to leave before then?'

Ada reached out to squeeze Diana's hand. 'Dearest, you must leave when you and Teddy are ready – nobody's pushing you out,' she assured her anxious patient. 'We want you fully recuperated before you return to normal life.'

'That's a huge relief,' Diana confessed. 'It gives me some time to think about what I'll do next and where we'll go.'

'I'm delighted to hear it, Diana,' Ada said, beaming. 'None of us wants you to leave Mary Vale until you're strong enough to do so.'

Poor Marie was in pieces when her turn to leave the Home came around. Ada and Diana saw the weeping girl to the station. Almost hysterical with grief, she clung to Diana.

'I thought I had longer with George,' she wailed. 'Mi bloody dad's forcing me to go back home earlier so I can start back at the mill. Look after George for me,' she implored. 'Kiss him every night before he goes to sleep and tell him how much his mam loved him.'

Her anguished words reduced Diana to tears too, and, worried that the two women might both become hysterical, Ada was relieved to see the big cloud of black smoke issuing from the approaching steam train's tall chimney. Slowly pulling the weeping girls apart, Ada led Marie along the platform, then helped her on to the train. Stumbling up the steps that she could barely see for the tears streaming down her face, Marie waved sadly out of the open window.

'Keep an eye on my boy,' she implored.

'I will, I promise,' Diana replied. 'And I'll write,' she cried, as she waved goodbye and the train shunted slowly away from the platform. 'I won't forget you, Marie. I'll look after George!'

Waving until the train was swallowed up in a dark cloud of sea-mist and smoke, Ada and Diana retraced their steps along the platform. The sound of the rumbling train receded, to be replaced by the murmur of the outgoing tide and the raucous cry of sea-birds wheeling overhead.

23. Frank Exchanges

Though heavily pregnant, Zelda was filled with an amazing amount of energy and spent as many hours as she could in her garden shed, which was now almost like her second home. Though it was frosty and cold, Zelda, muffled up in a thick cardigan with a long, hand-knitted scarf wrapped around her neck and a woolly hat on top of her mass of thick red curls, was warm enough. Every morning, before she began work on her remedies, Zelda stoked up the little wood-burning stove that threw out a surprising amount of heat.

Apart from brewing up another batch of salve for Frank (which Ada had told her he continued to use with some success), Zelda was on a mission to improve Diana's herbal tonic. Teddy's long, arduous birth had left Diana anaemic, and, combined with breast-feeding, her hungry son reduced her energy levels to virtually zero. Zelda hoped to produce a stronger herbal brew that would strengthen Diana's blood and hopefully stimulate her appetite too. Zelda's interest and curiosity in herbals had led her to buy even more old, dog-eared, leather-bound *Herbals*, which now sat in a neat row on one of the shelves over her workbench.

On one particular chilly December morning, with the heavy grey sky threatening snow, Zelda heaped logs into the wood-burner and set to work on boiling up pungent herbs for Frank's skin salve. Concentrating hard on her task, Zelda was completely unaware of the shed door swinging open; it was only when she felt a draught whipping around the back of her calves that she stopped and looked up to see if the door had been blown open by the wind. When she saw Frank Arkwright towering over her, his big bulky body almost blocking out the light that streamed in from the garden, Zelda almost fainted with terror. Clutching the bench for support, Zelda turned a deadly white. Thinking she would fall to the floor in a faint, Frank dashed forward to catch her before she hit the ground. Holding her firmly in his arms, he led her to the battered old armchair by the wood-burner and gently lowered her down.

'Rest yourself,' he said softly.

Gazing into his face dominated by the large black patch over his left eye, Zelda couldn't help but notice (even in the midst of her panic) that Ada had spoken the truth: the salve had indeed helped to heal and reduce the scar tissue on Frank's face.

'What are you doing here?' she finally managed to ask the intruder.

'I was tending the sheep over yonder wall,' Frank replied in his deep rolling Lancashire accent. 'All of a sudden I smelt summat right powerfully sweet and strong like, I was curious as to where it were coming from, so I popped o'er wall to find out.'

Zelda closed her eyes as she anticipated the worst. 'Oh, God. He's going to find out the truth about the salve.'

'This might sound daft, but whatever it is you're brewing up in here smells exactly the same as the ointment that Sister Ada gives me every week.' He inhaled deeply and with obvious pleasure. 'Lavender ... and some herbs.'

As he spoke, Frank turned around to stare at Zelda's workbench, on which were ranged the row of little pots that she had been in the process of filling before Frank had walked in and interrupted her.

Turning back to Zelda, who he seemed to have forgotten he had briefly met after she had collided with him in the hospital corridor some time ago, Frank said incredulously. 'Them's the very same pots as I get from Sister Ada.'

Knowing that she was cornered, Zelda didn't even try to lie. 'It *is* the same stuff,' she admitted. 'I make it for you.'

'YOU make it!' he spluttered.

Unable to respond, Zelda could only stare into Frank's mystified face. 'Why would you do that?' he demanded.

Beyond lying, Zelda shrugged. 'Because I can, and I wanted to help you. I studied botany and the benefits of herbal remedies when I was at university in Munich –' She stopped as she caught her breath. Why in God's name had she mentioned Munich to this man who hated Germany?

Frank took a step backwards. 'So you're the German lass Sister Ada told me about. The one whose husband was shot by the Nazis?' he asked bluntly.

Just hearing the words fall from his lips made Zelda's

eyes well up. 'Yes, I am German, and, yes, my husband was killed by the Nazis,' she said with as much dignity as she could muster. 'I apologize for the cruelty my fellow countrymen have inflicted on you, sir,' she added tremulously.

The air around them seemed to spark with the intensity of their joint emotions. Mercifully Frank defused the atmosphere by picking up and reading one of the herbal remedy books he spotted lying on the bench. He seemed genuinely curious.

'So . . . what is this brew that you make for me?'

Feeling heavy and uncomfortable, Zelda supported her burgeoning tummy as she struggled to rise from the armchair and approach her workbench.

'I use natural products,' she started cautiously. 'Herbs which I grew in the summer and dried for later use.' She pointed at the numerous bunches hanging from the shed rafters. 'Thyme, basil, dill, marjoram, oregano. I also pick herbs from the local woods and meadows.' She pointed at the bunches of mint, horseradish, bay leaf and stinging nettle lying on the bench. 'I follow remedies that have been tried and tested over centuries.'

Frank continued with his questions. 'But how do you mix all these herbs into a cream?'

'Well,' she smiled patiently, 'I distil some in boiling water, then reduce them to a liquor; others I grind.' She nodded towards the heavy mortar on the bench. 'To extract their essential oils, it takes a lot of pounding,' she explained. 'Then I blend the two components together with a carrier ingredient like beeswax.'

Frank shook his head as if he couldn't believe that he was hearing correctly.

'I consult with the chemist in his shop in Kendal if I can't find the right herbs and spices,' Zelda went on. 'Fortunately, Mr Marsden has a well-stocked pharmacy, as he mixes tonics and cough syrups for some of his customers.'

Picking up a blob of beeswax that was lying on the bench, Frank rolled it between his thumb and fingers. 'Where do you find this stuff?'

'The convent,' Zelda told him, as she dipped her finger into one of the little pots, then gently rubbed the salve into her hands. 'One of the Sisters keeps bees and kindly gives me surplus wax from her hives.'

'To think, all this time you've been making ointment for me,' he marvelled. 'If I hadn't got a whiff of it this morning I'd never have known.'

'I didn't want you to know,' she confessed. 'I asked Ada to keep it a secret between me and her.'

Frank gave her a hard look. 'If you trust the remedies you make, why would you want to keep it a secret?'

Zelda blushed. 'I am from the country you are at war with. I was sure you would distrust my motives.'

Frank considered her words. 'To be honest I might have done,' he answered. 'But now, after seeing what you do and how good your stuff is, I don't. In fact, missis, I'd say I was in your debt, and I thank you for your troubles.'

Turning on his heel, Frank headed towards the door. 'Good-day to you,' he barked over his shoulder.

Zelda gazed in astonishment at Frank, who walked out of the shed, scaled the old drystone wall and dropped completely out of sight.

Covering her face with her hands, she gasped in astonishment. 'Oh, my God!'

Not bothering to put on any of her warm woollies, Zelda rushed across the frozen lawn into the hospital wing, where she tracked down Ada cleaning the delivery room.

'You'll never believe this!' Zelda cried.

Ada couldn't help but laugh out loud when Zelda finished her breathless story.

'Thanks heavens!' she exclaimed. 'I never liked lying to Frank.'

Completely overcome, Zelda shook her head. 'I never for a minute imagined he would be *grateful* to me,' she exclaimed. 'When he walked in and stood over me like a dark giant, I almost collapsed with fear. He actually had to support me,' she confessed.

'He can be quite the gentleman,' Ada said diplomatically.

'I'm glad you think so. I've just never seen that side to him before,' Zelda reminded her.

'Whatever Frank was ranting on about the day you overheard him wasn't meant for your ears, Zelda,' Ada said in Frank's defence. 'I'm quite sure he would never do something as cruel as that on purpose.'

Zelda shrugged. 'Well, it's all out in the open now.' Her cheeks flushed with pleasure as she recalled his words. 'He actually thanked me for my salve.'

'Of course he did,' Ada cried. 'You've thoroughly researched the product and gone to a lot of trouble to get it right – and it works!' She burst out laughing, as she had a sudden amusing thought. 'You know what, Zelda? You could bottle the stuff and make a small fortune.'

Now it was Zelda's turn to laugh out loud. 'Don't be silly, Ada! I do this work for you and your patients; nobody else would be interested.'

Ada gave a wise smile. 'I wouldn't be too sure about that, dear.'

While Zelda was busy mixing her salves and tinctures, Gracie, now hugely pregnant, spent a lot of time with Diana, who was slowly regaining her strength if not her spirits after the birth of her son. Worried Ava regularly found Diana feeding Teddy with silent tears streaming down her face. Taking Gracie into her confidence, Ada asked a favour.

'Keep an eye on Diana, will you? I'm concerned about her spending too much time on her own and getting full-blown post-natal depression.'

Gracie looked anxious. 'I'm good at telling jokes and making people laugh, Ada, but this is serious. What should I talk to Diana about that won't upset her? Should I mention her boyfriend, or should I avoid the subject altogether?' she blurted out.

'If Harry naturally comes into the conversation, you should pursue it,' Ada advised. 'Don't avoid it, or blank it: it would do Diana good to talk about him.'

'I see her brooding all the time,' Gracie said sadly. 'I just don't know what to do for the best.'

'Spend some time with her and you'll find out,' Ada predicted.

One bright, clear December afternoon, while Teddy was sleeping in the nursery alongside George, Gracie suggested that she and Diana went for a walk on the marsh. To her surprise Diana eagerly accepted her invitation.

'A brisk walk will blow the cobwebs away,' she said with a smile.

Out on the vast marsh the wind whipped in from the Irish Sea, buffeting the two women, who walked somewhat unsteadily along the sandy path left by the outgoing tide. At first it took all their breath just to stand up straight in the face of the wind, but, as it dropped, they were able to hear each other speak.

'I can't believe I'm ever going to have this baby,' Gracie groaned as she held on tightly to her tummy. 'I sometimes think I'll look like a barrage balloon for the rest of my life.'

'You've not long to go now, Gracie,' Diana assured her. 'You've been so fit and lively throughout your pregnancy – just a few more weeks and it will all be over.'

'I know I've been lucky compared with some of the girls who've been sick and weak –' Gracie stopped short and blushed. 'Heck! I've gone and put my foot in it,' she muttered with a self-conscious blush.

Diana laughed. 'If you're talking about me, don't apologize. I know I didn't handle pregnancy very well.'

'You had a nightmare time, Di,' Gracie said sympathetically. 'I thought when your fella was reported missing, then dead, you would give up the will to live.'

'It's true, I wanted to die,' Diana confessed. 'I have no idea how I'm going to face the future without Harry, but my son has given me a reason to get up every morning. For his sake I put a smile on my face and eat enough food to feed him and help him grow big and strong. It's one day at a time for me, Gracie. If I can do that, hopefully Teddy and I will both survive.'

Gracie gulped in a breath of fresh air before she had the nerve to ask, 'What was he like, your young man?'

'Harry.' Diana smiled as she said his name out loud. 'Tall, handsome, clever, brave, the strong, silent type. I never knew where he was or what he was doing when he was alive.' Staring out at the churning grey sea where roaring waves seem to vie with the raging wind to create the loudest noise, she murmured, 'Now he's dead, and I don't even know where he's buried.'

Feelingly achingly sorry for her friend, Gracie laid a hand across her shoulders. 'You're such a brave woman, Di. I don't know how you bear it.'

Diana turned her cornflower-blue eyes on Gracie. 'There's nothing brave about me; I bear it because there is *absolutely nothing* else I can do,' she explained in a voice that was hollowed out with grief.

Walking back as the sun began to slide like a flaming ball of fire over the dark horizon, the two women stopped to watch the brilliant colours of the setting sun blaze dark crimson and purple on the crashing waves. As the winter light faded, the northerly wind seemed to be even colder.

'Let's get back to Mary Vale,' Gracie urged.

Turning towards the big old building standing on a promontory overlooking the sea, Diana smiled. Teddy would be waiting for her, and so would George, both with smiles on their dear little faces, both desperate for her return.

'Yes,' she said, as she quickened her pace. 'Let's go home.'

24. Ditched

In the period that Harry was 'Missing, assumed dead', he was, in fact, struggling to survive in the German occupation zone in France. As Diana, nursing her new son, grieved for the man she had lost, Harry had been secretly transporting Special Ops agents in and out of France. Harry's sudden disappearance off the radar happened on a dark, cloudy night when his Lysander aircraft crashed just as he had been airborne again after discharging a passenger.

Gliding the Lysander soundlessly down, Harry felt as if he had been floating for ages in a strange, silent world, with no way of telling what sort of terrain the Lysander might land in. Grateful that the drifting moon was presently obscured and therefore not able to throw light on his descent, Harry brought the aircraft down with an alarming bump, followed by loud bangs and rattles that shook the plane as it shuddered to a stop in what looked like a field of sugar beet. Knowing he had only hours to disappear, before the German soldiers with their dreaded sniffer dogs were on his trail, Harry unbuckled his seat, then wrenched open the cockpit. Breaking into a run, he stumbled over fallen logs and trailing blackberry bushes, until the sky paled and he was forced to stop to catch his breath.

'Oh, God,' Harry groaned. 'I'll be picked up at first light if I'm spotted in this wretched RAF uniform.'

Forcing himself to concentrate, Harry spotted a gap in a hedge, which he wriggled through, then found himself standing on a narrow track that led to a small farmhouse. As Harry dithered by the roadside, he heard children's laughter coming from inside the house; reassured by the sound, he took a deep breath and rapped on the door. The door slowly creaked open to reveal a couple in their early thirties and their two young children, who were in their nightclothes. Grabbing his wife by the shoulder, the farmer pushed her behind his back and stepped boldly in front of Harry, who babbled in his rather poor French that he was desperately in need of assistance. Knowing full well the consequences of harbouring the enemy, the poor woman covered her mouth with her hand to suppress her fearful cry.

'I'm so sorry to put you in danger,' Harry cried in the best French he could muster. 'If you could just tell me where I am,' he added, as he produced a little silk map the size of a handkerchief from his pocket and laid it on the table. Pointing to it, he asked in French the position of the hamlet he was presently in.

'*Ici*,' the man said, jabbing a finger at the map. 'Near Nantes.' Obviously keen to get rid of Harry, the harassed farmer all but pushed him out of the door. 'I will take you – *vite*!'

Directing Harry to an ancient pickup truck, the farmer pointed at a large, smelly tarpaulin sheet in the back and indicated that Harry should hide under it. Just as her husband was about to drive away, the farmer's wife came running out of the house.

'Stop!' she cried. 'Take these,' she said, as she handed Harry a pair of grubby dungarees and a rather threadbare jacket. *'Bonne chance,'* she whispered breathlessly before she rushed back to her children.

As the taciturn farmer rumbled along the narrow lanes, Harry wriggled out of his uniform and donned his grubby disguise. His shiny RAF shoes were far too smart for the ragged clothes he had been given but hopefully he would be able to sort that out when they reached Nantes.

'*If* I get to Nantes,' Harry thought grimly.

In the back of the rattling truck Harry tried to observe through a rip in the tarpaulin any significant landmarks, but no matter how hard he tried to concentrate his eyes drooped; the effects of a night without any sleep finally caught up with him and he lost consciousness. He awoke with a start as the truck ricocheted to an abrupt stop. Suddenly he felt a hard hand on his leg.

'Nantes,' said the farmer, as he helped Harry out of the truck. *'Bonne chance.'*

Mercifully the farmer had dropped Harry off in a quiet side street that was dominated by a rather splendid large sandstone church. Desperate to be out of the public eye, Harry walked briskly towards the church and slipped inside, grateful for the gloomy quietness that met him. Only a few people were there: mostly the old, kneeling at prie-diex and muttering prayers to statues of the saints with stony-cold expressions. Seeking out the darkest part of the church, Harry hid in the shadows, where he slowly felt his pulse return to normal.

'Well,' he thought to himself, 'I've survived a plane crash and a lift in a truck with a total stranger who's dumped me in a town I now have to figure out how to get out of.'

Though his tummy rumbled with hunger – he hadn't eaten since before the Lysander crash-landed – Harry remained where he was. Staring out across the long nave, Harry's eyes were drawn to the beautifully carved altar, built of the same soft stone as the rest of the church and dominated by a massive crucifix vividly illuminated by tall candles that threw out a soft, glowing light. Feeling his body grow limp with fatigue, Harry laid his head against the back of the wooden pew and half closed his eyes. Though this church was five times bigger than the Shelford church where he had planned to marry Diana, he could nevertheless allow himself to imagine her walking down the aisle towards him.

'Would she have worn a white wedding dress?' he wondered. 'God,' he thought. 'Diana would look stunning in white satin with a long lace veil over her silky blonde hair, covering her beautiful smiling face.'

He imagined Diana arriving at his side at the altar steps, where he would raise her delicate veil to smile into her cornflower-blue eyes, then kiss her pouting pink lips. The sound of close-by shuffling feet snapped Harry out of his fantasy, bringing him back to reality; quickly casting a glance around, he sighed with relief when he saw it was only an old lady stopping to light a candle in front of a statue of the Virgin Mary. Keeping his head down, Harry pretended to be deep in prayer, only relaxing when the old lady, leaning heavily on a walking stick, hobbled away.

Alone once more, Harry's thoughts returned to Diana, whose wedding day he had succeeded in ruining.

'I should have moved heaven and earth to get back to her,' he charged himself. 'What an utter bastard I've been to the poor darling girl.'

How would Diana ever know that he had sworn an oath to keep his clandestine missions secret? It wasn't just his life that was at risk; if he were to blab dozens of other men would be in jeopardy too.

'Who could blame the poor girl for thinking I had walked out on her, abandoned her when she needed me most?'

Slipping to his knees, Harry put his head in his hands and this time he genuinely did pray. 'God forgive me for what I've done,' he pleaded. 'Please God help me find my way home to my darling Diana.'

As his hunched body shuddered with emotion, Harry suddenly felt a hand on his shoulder. Smothering a cry of fear, he whirled around and looked straight into the face of a priest wearing a long black cassock.

'Can I help you, my son?' the priest murmured.

For the second time in less than a few hours Harry took his life into his hands: again speaking in halting French, he told the gentle-eyed priest what had happened to him.

'Follow me to the sacristy,' the priest replied to him in good English. 'Wait for five minutes before you join me,' he warned.

Checking his watch, Harry did as instructed; though terrified of being spotted, he slipped down the dark side aisles to the sacristy, which smelt of candles and sweet communion wine.

'Father, I do not want to get you into trouble,' he immediately started. 'If I can just hide in your church until nightfall, then I'll be on my way.'

The priest answered him with a knowing smile. 'I think I can do better than that: stay here, lock the door and wait until I get back'

In the silence that followed his departure, Harry locked the door, then sat cross-legged on the tiled floor, waiting for the priest to return. When he did, he was accompanied by a short, stocky man whom the priest introduced as one of his parishioners.

'My friend here,' the priest explained, 'tells me you might have to go undercover for some time, but once the coast is clear he will link you up with a guide who has some experience in helping prisoners of war out of the country.'

Harry gratefully shook the stranger's hand. 'Merci, monsieur. I am in your debt.'

As they slipped out of the church, Harry dipped his hand into the holy water font and blessed himself – at least some of his prayers were being answered.

25. Cartmel Forest

Back at Mary Vale, Zelda cuddled Harry's son in her arms. Marvelling at his silky soft hair and big blue eyes, she kissed his warm pink cheek. 'He is so beautiful!'

Diana smiled indulgently. 'He's the spit of his father.'

Holding the gurgling baby up so she could smile at him, Zelda marvelled at how much Teddy had grown. 'Aren't you a lovely little boy?' she cooed.

Teddy, who couldn't quite smile yet, blew bubbles instead. 'Cheeky!' Zelda teased as she hugged him. 'Oh, to think I'll have my own baby to cuddle soon.'

'Better get plenty of sleep: night feeding is a nightmare,' Diana warned.

'I plan to breast-feed, just like you,' Zelda announced.

'It's the best thing to start with, if you can,' Diana agreed. 'Apart from the cracked nipples,' she said with a grimace. 'Sister Ada has some marvellous cream for that particular problem, but I'm sure you, little herb-mixer,' she teased, 'will whip up a salve to solve the problem.'

Fed up with being dangled and admired, Teddy turned towards the sound of his mother's voice. 'Oh-oh! He's getting restless,' Zelda said, as she passed the fretful baby back to his mum, who quickly unbuttoned her blouse so Teddy could suckle. Twirling his little feet in the air, the baby latched on and sucked noisily.

'Heavens!' Diana laughed, as she readjusted him in her arms. 'Take it easy, darling, or you'll be sick.'

Zelda gazed fondly at her friend, who now had a little colour in her cheeks and, though still on the thin side, had put on a little weight despite her son's lusty appetite. As if reading her thoughts, Diana turned to Zelda. 'Joking apart, Zel, I can't thank you enough for the tonics you've made for me,' she said with a grateful smile. 'At first I thought, how can a bunch of herbs make me feel any stronger, but now I really think they have made a difference.' At that, Teddy gave a loud hiccup. 'And Teddy thanks you too.'

Modest Zelda blushed, but it was clear from the sparkle in her eyes that she was, in fact, delighted by Diana's kind words.

'Ada and Sister Mary Paul have been looking after you too,' she reminded Diana.

'I know! Sister Mary Paul slipped a meat pie into my room the other day, and a little piece of cake too, dear sweet woman that she is.' Diana sighed as she again rearranged her baby on her breast. 'I honestly don't know how I would have survived without Mary Vale,' she admitted with tears in her eyes. 'Having you, Gracie, Ada, and all of my friends, and the babies too, I feel like I have a real family here. God knows how Teddy and I will survive struggling along on our own.'

Zelda laid a hand on Diana's arm. 'Don't think about that now,' she advised, purposefully changing the subject. 'How is baby George?'

'Adorable!' Diana declared. 'They've been sleeping

side by side in adjacent cots since the day they were born.' She gave an amused smile as she continued, 'Now that they're a bit bigger, I lay them down on the nursery rug for a little roll around; you wouldn't believe how much noise they make, or how they try to grab hold of each other with their little fingers. It's so sweet.'

Zelda laughed. 'When they're bigger and stronger, they'll be rolling around on the floor like naughty lion cubs.'

Diana gave a wistful smile. 'Sometimes I have the pair of them in my arms, one on the breast, the other on the bottle – it's a bit of a juggling act – but I actually like the feel of two little boys in my arms.' She paused before she added, 'To be honest, I'm worried sick about what will happen to George.'

'Has Father Ben found anybody suitable for him?' Zelda asked.

Diana shook her head. 'Not so far. He told me several couples were interested but had decided against it: they felt it was unfair to place a child of colour in an environment that was predominantly white. I can see his point, but I'd absolutely hate little George to go into an orphanage.'

'Have you been in touch with Marie?' Zelda enquired.

Diana nodded. 'I write occasionally, but not as often as I promised; it seems wrong to keep going on about how adorable her baby is, like rubbing salt in a wound.'

Zelda nodded in agreement. 'It might be painful to hear news of George if she's in the process of trying to let go.'

'Ada said more or less the same thing,' Diana confessed.

'She thought that Marie needed time to get over her loss, not to be constantly reminded of it.'

'Poor Marie,' Zelda said, as she rose to her feet, checking the time on the wall clock. 'I'd better get back to work.'

'What are you brewing up now, little Miss Magic?' Diana teased.

'I've just made a new salve for Frank that I need to pot and deliver to Ada,' Zelda replied.

Diana smiled. 'Who would ever have thought you would be on first-name terms with Frank Arkwright? You used to run a mile at the sight of him!'

'We've settled our differences,' Zelda said. 'He even brings me logs for the wood-burner these days.'

Seeing Zelda grimace as she struggled to her feet, Diana frowned. 'Is your baby sitting on a nerve? Towards the end Teddy always lay somewhere uncomfortable,' she recalled.

'And this one too!' Zelda chuckled. 'Right where it hurts the most.'

'Take care, dear. Don't go overdoing it,' Diana warned. 'You've not got long to go now.'

Zelda supported her burgeoning tummy. 'I'll be careful,' she promised.

After putting on her coat, Zelda hurried to her shed, where she collected the basket that she kept for gathering herbs. Feeling a little guilty that she hadn't informed Diana that she was going for a walk in the woods, where she hoped to find the freshest stinging nettles for her tonic brew, Zelda set off down the back lane. It was a cold, bright clear morning, with perfect views of the surrounding fells. Feeling energized by the low-lying sun, Zelda lengthened her steps as she considered what other fresh herbs she might find in the nearby woods and meadows. Though the hedges were stark and bare at this time of the year, Zelda knew they would soon be teeming with primroses and snowdrops, and she had been told by Ada that the woods in the springtime were an ocean of shimmering bluebells.

Reaching the woods just under the shadow of Cartmel Fell, Zelda cautiously made her way along the winding pathways to a particular patch of comfrey, or knitbone, as the locals called it, which grew in abundance throughout the winter months and was marvellous for the treatment of burns, scalds and bruises. After snipping off a large number of comfrey stalks with her scissors, Zelda moved on along the path. Progressing beneath a canopy of majestic chestnut and oak trees, the shade from which made the narrow path slippery wet at this time of the year, Zelda carefully balanced her basket against her big tummy. Plodding on, determined to get to a bed of nettles that grew just further up the path, Zelda suddenly felt a little light-headed. Stumbling awkwardly, her foot slipped on a tree root and she tumbled to the ground.

'*ZUT!*' she exclaimed.

After getting to her feet, Zelda felt even more light-headed, and, chiding herself for overdoing it, she decided she would return another day to collect the nettles; but, as she turned to retrace her steps, a gush of warm water ran down her legs.

'Oh, no!' Zelda cried in horror.

Knowing she was a long way from the road and even further away from Mary Vale filled Zelda with alarm.

'I have to get back,' she frantically muttered as she hurried as fast as she could back up the path. 'Oh, why did I come here in the first place?' she raged at herself.

For months she had done her best to keep her baby safe, and now with only days to go before her due date she had decided to go for a long walk alone.

'Stupid! Stupid!' she scolded herself, stopping dead in her tracks as a pain in the small of her back literally took her breath away.

Unable to stand upright, she crouched low on the ground, waiting for the pain to pass; then, hardly daring to breathe, she rose and very cautiously set off again. She had gone no more than a few feet when another pain shot through her belly. Now truly terrified, Zelda placed herself firmly against the vast trunk of an ancient oak tree, which she pressed against as the pain surged through her pelvic region.

'ARGGGHHH!' she groaned.

Not daring to move, Zelda stayed exactly where she was.

'What on earth am I going to do?' she said out loud.

It was clear that walking increased the probability of starting off the pains, so, cautiously sliding down the tree trunk, she sat at its base and desperately tried to compose herself.

'Oh, God,' she groaned.

Even if she yelled for help nobody would hear her here in this wild wood.

Though she was panicking, Zelda took deep breaths to steady her nerves; then, feeling a little calmer, she slowly rose to her feet and almost crawled along the path. Just when she thought she might make it to the edge of the wood, another pain seized her, and this time she knew that she could simply go no further. An animal instinct gripped Zelda; casting her eyes frantically about, she spotted two huge oaks under which was a heap of dry autumn leaves. Feeling hot and starting to sweat, Zelda dragged herself to the spot and unbuttoned her winter coat, which she laid loosely over herself. Lying back looking up at the winter sky through the filigree of remaining leaves fluttering in the treetops, Zelda was startled by the flight of a Great Spotted Woodpecker, which flashed its bright red feathers at her before landing on a bough just above her head. Listening to the rhythmic tapping of the bird's pointed beak, Zelda was gripped by another contraction that caused her to cry out. 'ARGHHH! Help me!' she wailed. 'Please help me!'

With Sister Mary Paul's measurements for this year's Christmas tree clearly written down, Frank Arkwright attached Captain to the old farm cart and set off at a slow pace along the road that led to the forest. Frank smiled to himself as he recalled the old nun's description of a perfect Christmas tree. 'It mustn't be too tall, or it will catch the ceiling, and it mustn't block the front door, and cut it fresh so I don't have to sweep up pine needles every five minutes. Oh, and it must have enough space around the base for all our presents.'

'I'll do mi best, Sister,' Frank had good-naturedly promised.

Enjoying the clear bright winter day and the nearby smell of a bonfire burning damp leaves, Frank felt a pang of guilt. He knew he had done his bit for the war effort when on active service: nobody could have been more committed than him and his unit. He had lost an eye serving his country, but he was always haunted by the thought that he should (even now) be fighting at the Front, something he had confessed to his commanding officer before he was discharged.

'I don't think so, son, not with only one good eye,' the officer had barked.

His answer may have been brutal in its delivery, but Frank knew that the officer was right – his eyesight wasn't good enough to aim a rifle and kill a man – nevertheless guilt was always there.

'Looking on the bright side,' he thought to himself, 'thanks to the talents of clever little Zelda I look a damn sight better than I used to.'

The lass had come up with an amazing ointment that had slowly healed his inflamed skin, and to this day Frank could never understand why she had gone to so much trouble for him. Over time, as their friendship grew, Zelda had blushingly admitted to Frank that she had initially been petrified of him.

'So why put yourself out to help a miserable bugger like me?' he had teased.

'I have the knowledge right here,' she had exclaimed as she tapped her head. 'So why not use it? Also,' she had added guiltily, 'somebody in my country caused you this terrible injury. If I can change things for the better, then I will feel less responsible.'

Seeing her bright, little earnest face aflame with emotion had touched Frank deeply.

'I think you've got a heart of gold,' he had told her gruffly. 'A right proper little Florence Nightingale!'

As old Captain clip-clopped down the lane, Frank lit one of his roll-up cigarettes; then, just as he was settling himself more comfortably on the wooden seat, he heard a high-pitched cry that caused Captain to shy and shake his harness. Clicking the horse into a trot, Frank wondered if the sound was that of an animal in pain.

'Perhaps it's a hare caught in a trap,' he wondered.

Another loud cry coming from the nearby woods convinced him it was not an animal but a person in trouble.

'Eh up, boy,' Frank urged the horse, which responded to its master and trotted on even more quickly.

When Frank reached the forest, which he had explored daily as a boy and knew like the back of his hand, he tethered the horse to a tree before setting out along the forest path that Zelda had taken less than two hours earlier.

*

Meanwhile poor Zelda, half crazed with pain, was lying on a soft bed of leaves, gasping for breath. When another contraction engulfed her, she simply hadn't the energy to scream any more; instead she rolled on to her side and grunted like an animal. And that's how Frank found her.

'Jesus Christ!' he cried, as he rushed towards her writhing body.

'The baby's coming,' Zelda gasped. 'Help me, please help me, Frank.'

The sight of her small pale face and her enormous dark eyes full of pain brought tears to Frank's manly heart. Leaning down, he gently stroked her damp, tangled red curls.

'Don't you go fretting yourself, lass, I'll have you back home in no time,' he soothed.

'No!' she yelled. 'The baby's coming *now*, you've got to help me,' she implored.

Frank gazed at her in horror. He was a soldier and a farmer; how could he deliver a baby in the forest all on his own?

'I'd be better off facing a shooting squad,' he thought grimly.

As Zelda stiffened and her back arched to ride the pain, Frank gripped her hand in his; barely noticing the blood she had drawn with her fingernails, he smiled and said, 'You're a natural. Almost as good as my best ewe.'

Zelda smiled weakly. 'I've never been compared to a sheep before.'

'You're bonnier,' he said kindly.

In the brief time they had before another contraction

246

consumed her, Zelda asked Frank to lay her coat underneath her body so that she didn't give birth in a bed of leaves. As he tenderly arranged the coat, Zelda gripped his hand hard.

'Do you think you can do this, Frank?'

Looking her straight in the eye, Frank didn't flinch as he spoke the honest truth. 'I've delivered puppies, kittens, a couple of foals and about a hundred lambs. I can do this, lass, I promise.'

Seeing his steady gaze and trusting completely in him, Zelda lay back and for the first time relaxed; if she were going to give birth in a forest with Frank Arkwright acting as midwife, then so be it, she thought to herself. Less than an hour later Zelda, under Frank's vigilant care, pushed her baby into a world loud with the call of woodpeckers and blackbirds. Gathering the little wet bundle into his arms, Frank almost wept with relief when the baby flailed its tiny arms in the air and wailed.

'A girl!' he sobbed as he handed her to Zelda.

'A little girl,' Zelda sobbed too. 'Izaak's beautiful daughter.'

26. Baby's First Gift

Having successfully delivered Zelda's daughter, Frank now had to make sure that he got both mother and baby safely back to Mary Vale, and as quickly as possible. Shrugging off his old work jacket, he removed his jumper, which smelt of sheep's wool and tobacco, and tenderly wrapped the new-born in it.

'I'm going to take the little 'un to the cart I left tethered by the wood,' he told Zelda, who struggled to sit upright.

'I'm coming with you,' she cried.

'You can't walk in your condition,' Frank answered gruffly.

Gazing down at her sprawled legs smeared with blood, Zelda hadn't the strength to argue.

'I'll get the little lass settled and come back for you.'

Looking alarmed, Zelda cried, 'Why can't you take us both? I can hold her.'

'You're weak, woman, and the path's narrow and slippery with mud. I'm not taking any chances,' he said firmly. 'It's safer to take you one at a time.'

Having just given birth to the most precious thing in her life, Zelda was almost hysterical at the thought of parting with her. Seeing the look of sheer panic on her face, Frank took control of the situation and without further ado he lifted the baby from Zelda's arms.

'Don't fret – I'll be back in a tick.'

Before Zelda could protest, he carefully descended on to the track and then, when he was under cover of the trees and well out of Zelda's sight, he ran as fast as he could, bearing the little bundle in his arms. When he reached the road where he had left Captain tied up, the old horse neighed shrilly and impatiently stamped his feet.

'All right, lad,' Frank said softly.

Fortunately, the base of the cart was scattered with hay, the remnants of a bale Frank had fed the sheep that morning. Scooping the hay into a cosy bundle, he gently laid the little girl, who was now gazing in wide-eyed wonder at the arching blue sky overhead, on to it.

'Now, listen, lassie, stay right where you are.' Frank spoke to her as if he were talking to one of his collie dogs. 'I'll be back before you know it with your mam.'

When the baby made weak little mewling noises like a kitten, Captain started and whinnied as he turned to peer at her.

'And you, mate,' Frank said firmly to the patient animal, 'stay right where you are too!'

With his heart pounding in his chest, Frank raced back to Zelda, who, though weak and feeble, was desperately trying to clean the blood left by the afterbirth off her thighs. Feeling dizzy with the effort, she cried out with relief when she saw Frank. Without any preamble he spoke quickly. 'Come on, put your arms around my neck and I'll carry you.'

Zelda protested.

'But . . . I'm covered in blood.'

'So am I,' Frank said bluntly as he lifted her into his arms.

Carefully negotiating the muddy patches on the path, Frank cautiously made his way back to the road, where Captain, who had not budged an inch from the spot, was patiently waiting for him.

Frank gently laid Zelda in the cart beside her daughter.

'*Liebling, meine Liebe*,' Zelda murmured as she cuddled her baby, who lay like the Infant Jesus on a bed of sweet-smelling hay.

With his cargo safely stored, Frank untethered the horse's reins, then leapt on to the driver's seat.

'Giddy up, lad,' he called.

The old horse, eager for his warm stable, set off at a brisk trot. Though desperate to get mother and child safely home, Frank resisted the temptation to whip Captain into a gallop. He knew from experience that the rutted road would cause the cart to bounce, which might disturb the baby and alarm the mother. Reining in the horse, Frank kept up a smooth, steady pace that belied the state of his jangling nerves. When Frank arrived at Mary Vale, he drove the cart right up to the front door and frantically rang the bell.

'Hello!' he yelled.

The welcoming smile on Sister Mary Paul's face fell when she saw Frank Arkwright standing on the doorstep with his clothes stained with blood and flecks of hay in his dark hair.

'Frank!' she cried. 'What's happened to you?' Then, looking at the empty cart, she exclaimed, 'Where's our Christmas tree?'

'There's summat else in the cart,' Frank said abruptly. 'Take a look.'

The old nun flew to the back of the cart, which she had to grasp in order to support herself when she saw Zelda lying there with a baby in her arms.

'Glory be to God and all the angels in heaven!' gasped Sister Mary Paul.

Leaving her to deal with Zelda, Frank ran into the Home, then headed for the hospital area.

'SISTER ADA!' he bellowed.

Hearing his cry, Ada rushed out of the ward where she had been busy making beds.

'You're wanted – urgently. Come quickly!'

Breaking into a run, Ada followed Frank outside, where they found Sister Mary Paul clutching Zelda's baby.

'Zelda's daughter,' she said with tears in her eyes.

Looking thoroughly alarmed, Ada looked around for Zelda. Frank pointed to the girl struggling to sit up in the back of the cart. Seeing her deathly white face and wildly dishevelled hair, Ada cried out in alarm, 'Don't move – we'll carry you indoors.'

'I'll take her,' Frank said, as he tenderly lifted Zelda once more into his strong arms.

'Where do you want her, Sister?'

'The post-natal ward,' Ada answered.

Seeing Frank's blank expression, Ada hid a smile: how silly of her to assume that Frank Arkwright would know where the post-natal ward was.

'Follow me,' she said quickly. 'I'll lead the way.'

With her head cradled against Frank's warm shoulder, weary Zelda was taken on to the ward, where she was laid on a hospital bed. Knowing she was now in safe hands, Frank gave a brief backward glance at mother and daughter, then fled.

Driving back in the crisp, cold winter twilight, Frank reran the dramatic events of the day as he smoked one roll-up cigarette after another. Captain, keen to get back to a warm stable and a manger full of hay, trotted briskly towards the farm, where lights shone out of the kitchen window.

'Thank God we're home, lad,' Frank fervently said, as they entered the farmyard, before adding even more fervently, 'And thank God I'm not a woman!'

On the post-natal ward Zelda, now bathed and wearing a warm nightdress, sat with her back against a bank of pillows, gratefully sipping a cup of hot sweet tea that Ada had just brought to her. Her tired face lit up when she saw Dora approaching with a tiny bundle in her arms.

'She's all cleaned up and tidy,' Dora told the radiant mother. 'I weighed her too: six pounds, a little 'un but tough, I'd say.'

Zelda gazed in wonder at her daughter, now wearing one of Mary Vale's pretty little nighties and tiny white woolly bootees. Quickly laying aside her teacup, Zelda held out her arms.

'Let me hold her,' she begged.

'That Frank Arkwright,' Dora declared. 'He's a natural-born midwife – I couldn't have done a better job myself.'

'She's a little beauty,' Ada cooed as she too fussed over the baby.

'Even if she was born under a bush,' Dora chuckled.

Zelda smiled as she corrected her: 'Actually, she was born under an oak tree.'

Returning her gaze to her daughter, Zelda closely scrutinized her little face and tiny hands. 'She's perfect,' she sighed.

'And I think she may be hungry,' Ada said knowingly.

Zelda quickly undid the buttons on the bodice of her nightie so she could place the baby on her breast.

'Is this right?' she anxiously asked the nurses.

'She might take a moment or two,' Ada replied, as she keenly observed the baby's response. 'Help her find her way to the nipple,' she suggested.

Gently supporting the baby's little wobbly head in her hand, Zelda steered her daughter's sweet, rose-bud pink mouth towards her nipple.

'There, *meine Liebe*, there . . .' she soothed.

The baby feebly nuzzled the nipple, then she opened her mouth and started to suck.

'She'll soon get the hang of it,' Dora assured the nervous new mother.

'Now,' said Ada, smiling as she sat down on the chair

beside the bed, 'can you please tell us what on earth pos-
sessed you to do such a reckless thing as to go walking
in the forest on your own, young lady?'

Embarrassed. Zelda smiled. 'I felt so lively and ener-
getic this morning, and it was such a lovely day, so I
decided to go to Cartmel Forest to pick some stinging
nettles and knitbone for Frank's ointment.'

'Cartmel Forest!' Dora declared. 'I ask you!'

'My waters broke when I stumbled and fell on the
forest path.'

Dora rolled her eyes in complete horror. 'I was in such
a state,' Zelda continued. 'But luckily for me Frank heard
my calls and came to my rescue.'

'Lucky!' Dora scoffed. 'It's nothing short of a bloom-
ing miracle.'

A deeper blush spread across Zelda's face. 'Frank was
so calm. He told me not to fret, as he had delivered
puppies, kittens and about a hundred lambs in his time.'
She smiled tenderly. 'Somehow that made me feel confident that he could deliver my baby too.' Looking down
at her now sweetly sleeping daughter, Zelda spoke with
a catch in her voice. 'Frank did a wonderful job.'

Not wanting to overtire her patient, Ada rose to her
feet. 'You must rest now – here, let me take her,' she said,
as she lifted the drowsy baby off her mother's breast.
'Has this little girl got a name yet?'

Zelda slowly nodded her head. 'Constanza Cartmel,'
she said proudly. 'Constanza after the wife of Mozart,
who was my husband's favourite composer, and Cartmel
after the forest where Frank brought her into the world.'

Dora grinned. 'A grand name for such a tiny little baby.'

Snuggling down into her bed, Zelda dreamily repeated the name of her daughter. 'Constanza Cartmel,' she whispered before she fell into a deep and peaceful sleep.

News of Zelda's baby's birth swept round Mary Vale. When Diana and Gracie heard what had happened to their close friend, they were momentarily struck dumb with shock.

'She had her baby in Cartmel Forest?' Gracie spluttered in a very high voice.

Ada nodded. 'It's true,' she said.

'On her own?' Diana gasped.

'Frank Arkwright turned up just in time to deliver the baby,' Ada informed the thunder-struck women

Gracie slumped weakly in her chair. 'I've heard it all now. The man Zelda thought was a monster turns out to be her knight in shining armour!'

With an amazed smile on her face, Diana cried, 'I can't believe Frank brought mother and baby back to Mary Vale in his horse and cart!'

'Are they all right now?' Gracie asked anxiously.

'Yes, they're both fine,' Ada assured her.

'What in God's name was the girl doing out there?' Gracie cried.

'Looking for stinging nettles for one of her remedies,' Ada smiled.

Diana giggled as she swept her blue eyes over Gracie's big tummy. 'Take care you don't go wandering into the forest looking for stinging nettles,' she joked.

Gracie vehemently shook her long, dark hair. 'Don't fret yourself. I'm staying put right here in Mary Vale.'

In the days that followed Constanza's birth, Zelda literally bloomed with joy and love. Her thick red curls seemed deeper and richer in colour, her dark eyes sparkled with happiness, and her sweet, heart-shaped face glowed with health. Lying in her hospital bed one freezing cold morning, Zelda stared dreamily at the flakes of snow drifting by her window. She was startled from her reverie by Ada, who popped her beaming face around the door.

'You've got a visitor,' she said.

Zelda looked up in surprise. 'It's not visiting time yet, is it?'

Ada gave an indulgent smile. 'No, but we can make exceptions for this one.'

Stepping aside, she made way for the visitor, who was none other than Frank Arkwright. Zelda cried out with pleasure at the sight of him.

'Frank, how lovely to see you!'

Frank shuffled awkwardly from foot to foot.

'I'll make you both a nice cup of tea,' Ada offered.

Tapping the chair beside her bed, Zelda smiled. 'Please, sit down.'

When he did, Zelda noticed how clean shaven and smart Frank looked; he had abandoned his usual woolly jumper and thick tweed working jacket in favour of a well-brushed coat and shiny polished boots.

'Where's the little lass?' he asked gruffly.

'Constanza's asleep in the nursery,' Zelda explained.

'Is that what you've named her?'

'Constanza Cartmel,' Zelda told him with a proud smile.

'Them's proper bonny names,' Frank beamed in approval.

'Some have already shortened her name to Connie,' Zelda informed him.

'And is she hale and hearty?'

With grateful tears brimming in her brown eyes, Zelda answered warmly, 'She's a bundle of health, thanks to you.'

Frank shrugged this off as if delivering a baby in the middle of a forest were of no consequence at all.

'It were now't,' he mumbled.

Zelda stretched out her hand in order to take hold of Frank's big hand, which was creased with calluses from rough farm work.

'We could have died out there on our own,' she whispered. 'I will be grateful to you till the day I die.'

And before she could stop herself, tears began to run down Zelda's cheeks. Frank, initially startled, solemnly drew a perfectly white handkerchief from his pocket. Wiping her face as tenderly as if she were a child that had just fallen over, he murmured gentle words of comfort. 'There, there, pet. Thee mustn't go upsetting yourself,' he warned. 'I've seen it happen with cows – it turns the milk.'

Zelda stopped crying and started to laugh out loud. 'Frank Arkwright! You are a wise man as well as being a kind one,' she giggled.

Clearly embarrassed by all the high emotion in the room, Frank could only mumble, 'I've got summat for the little lass.'

'That's very thoughtful of you,' Zelda replied.

Another embarrassed moment followed as Zelda wondered where 'the summat' he had mentioned could possibly be.

'It were too big to bring indoors so I left it outside on't path,' Frank explained, as he pulled the curtains aside in order to give Zelda a better view from her bed.

Sitting up straight, Zelda strained her eyes to make out through the falling snow what Frank's gift might be. She gasped in surprise when she spotted a big navy-blue pram on the path outside her window.

'A pram!' she exclaimed in delight.

'Aye, a new one too,' Frank told her with a proud ring in his voice. 'One of them fancy Silver Cross jobs, with a hood and cover to keep out any bad weather and proper sprung wheels too.'

Completely overwhelmed, Zelda grasped Frank's hand for the second time, raising it to her lips to gently kiss it. But this time it was Frank Arkwright who had tears in his eyes.

27. Babies

As the snow continued to fall, creating a beautiful but icy-cold landscape, Mary Vale's baby nursery was comfortably snug even if it did ring with the loud cry of new-borns. George and Teddy, now strong, wriggling little boys, seemed to compete with each other as to who could make the loudest noise, while tiny Constanza surprised everybody with the strength of her lusty cries. Reticent Zelda, who was quietly spoken, blushed with embarrassment when her daughter's cries rang out.

'She's often the loudest in the nursery,' she told Dora, who gave a philosophical shrug.

'That's what babies do, lovie. How else are they going to claim our attention?'

'She cries even when she's just been fed,' Zelda pointed out.

'She's just exercising her little lungs, exploring the world,' Dora said knowingly. 'Stop fretting, lass, she's feeding well enough – little yet often, though that will change as she grows and gets into a regular routine.' Stooping over one of the little white cribs, she lifted baby George into her arms. 'How's this lovely little lad doing?'

'He's so big,' Zelda exclaimed.

Making herself comfortable in one of the changing

chairs, Dora laid the heavy baby on to her wide lap. Giving George an affectionate tickle, she playfully chided him. 'Stay still while I sort out your dirty nappy.'

When George was clean and changed, Dora warmed up a prepared bottle of formula milk for him and, holding him securely in the crook of her arm, fed the little boy, who sucked loudly as he hungrily drank his milk. Sitting beside Dora and breast-feeding Constanza, Zelda asked if there were any more news on George's adoption.

Dora sadly shook her head. 'Nothing. According to Father Ben, everybody who comes to see George loves him to bits, but they feel he should grow up in a mixed environment, with other kiddies of colour.'

Zelda frowned. 'Are they in fact saying they're afraid of bringing up a child of mixed race?'

Dora gave her a knowing look. 'Probably. Look at Maria's own father,' she snorted derisively. 'He wouldn't even have George's father in the house – imagine what his feelings must be towards George's baby?'

'But he's so lovely,' Zelda cried with tears in her big brown eyes. 'People are so cruel, so judgemental.'

'There's plenty of them in the world,' Dora answered bitterly.

'How long can you keep him at Mary Vale?'

Dora gave a sad shrug. 'We don't have the facilities here for babies beyond three months; anyway the younger a baby is when it's adopted the better the bonding between the baby and the new parents.'

'What if Father Ben can't find the right family for George?' Zelda asked fearfully.

Dora gave a heavy sigh. 'Then he would have to go into an orphanage.'

'Oh, God,' Zelda murmured sadly. 'He's such a delightful little boy.'

'He's that all right,' Dora agreed, as she laid the sleepy baby over her shoulder and lovingly patted his back. 'He's a little champion.'

After his feed Diana popped George into one of Mary Vale's big old-fashioned prams. Tucking him up beside Teddy, she set off for a walk around the snowy garden, accompanied by Gracie. Walking along the garden path, Diana smiled indulgently at George and Teddy, snuggled up together under a warm woolly blanket.

'Bouncing these two along in a pram seems to send them off to sleep better than anything,' Diana told her companion.

'As long as they're well wrapped up, the fresh air will do them good,' Gracie replied.

'Are you all right?' Diana enquired. 'I would have thought you'd prefer to stay indoors on a day like this.'

'I'm a bit like the boys, in need of fresh air. 'I've been feeling so cooped up recently – I feel like I've been pregnant ALL my life,' Gracie groaned. 'Sometimes I think I'll never see my feet again!'

'From the look of you I'd say you've not got long to go,' Diana remarked.

As she stopped briefly in order to rearrange the blankets around the slumbering babies, she said adoringly, 'Just look at these little cherubs. Even in their sleep they clutch on to one another.'

Gracie, who had often watched the boys lying on the nursery rug, chuckled at the sight of them. 'When they're awake they're like two little boxers, grabbing hold of each other, usually by the ears and squeaking. Heaven knows what they'll be like when they're toddlers; they'll probably tear each other's hair out.'

A sad expression clouded Diana's pretty face as she continued pushing the pram along the garden path.

'They won't be toddlers together, Gracie,' she quietly pointed out. 'Eventually they'll go their separate ways. We'll be in one place, God only knows where, and George will be in another, probably hundreds of miles away from Teddy. They'll grow up not knowing each other at all.' Not wanting to linger too long on a subject that was becoming increasingly painful even to think about, Diana quickly said, 'What about you, Gracie, still keen to get back to Barrow?'

Gracie replied without a moment's hesitation. 'I can't wait to get back to the shipyard; hopefully if there's a shortage of men on the ground I might get to do what I've dreamt of for years.'

Diana threw her a quizzical look. 'What would that be?'

'To drive one of the shipyard cranes,' Gracie announced.

'I imagine that's still a man's privilege?' Diana queried.

'Aye, but there's bound to come a time when there'll be no choice but to ask us lasses to do the job,' Gracie cried. 'Who else is going to work the cranes if all the fellas are away at war?'

'You're right,' Diana agreed. 'And we all know what a good driver you are,' she teased.

Gracie threw back her shoulders as she added with complete conviction, 'I'll convince the gaffers just as soon as I'm back in the yard that I can do as good a job as any fella,' she said passionately.

Diana couldn't help but laugh at Gracie's complete conviction that it would happen. 'What about romance, men, marriage?' she teased.

Gracie rolled her sparkling green eyes. 'Bugger that! Once I get out of Mary Vale, I'm going to be a career girl with HIGH ambitions,' she joked. 'Anyway,' she continued on a more serious note, 'I want to make up for all that I've put my poor parents through. I want to make them proud of me for a change.'

'Dora's son, Jack, seemed to notice you when he was home on leave,' Diana remembered. 'I thought he might be keen to keep in touch'.

Gracie stopped in her tracks before she gave a reply. 'He is keen,' Gracie agreed. 'But you've got to admit, Di, it's a bit rum: me pregnant and him writing to me, not love letters but about things that we might do together in the future when he's home on leave.'

'Perhaps he just likes writing to a pretty girl,' Diana suggested.

'Maybe,' Gracie sounded unconvinced. 'By the way, Di, don't mention his letter-writing to Dora: I don't want her getting the wrong impression.'

'I won't say a word,' Diana promised. 'Though in truth I think Dora would be pleased if she knew you were cheering her son up.'

'The truth is, Di, I'm *not* cheering Jack up,' Gracie told her bluntly. 'I've never replied to any of his letters and I know full well that Dora really wouldn't appreciate that.'

Diana nodded her head in agreement with her friend's wishes, while at the same time thinking how extraordinarily unexpected life was at Mary Vale: before her stood a determined young woman with ambitions to drive a shipyard crane; in the nursery was a baby girl born alive and well in a forest, sleeping alongside her own dear Teddy and precious George, who might well end up an orphan. War was forcing radical changes everywhere, quite rightly challenging old beliefs. Nevertheless, a cold shiver shot down Diana's spine: change brought fear and uncertainty, both of which she had had more than her fair share of recently.

When they walked back into the Home, both women were delighted to find Frank Arkwright and his father erecting a splendid fir tree, still speckled with snow, in the entrance hall.

'Oh, it's beautiful!' Gracie exclaimed in delight.

Frank gave her a cheeky wink. 'I set off t'other morning to chop one down but got side-tracked by Zelda in't forest,' he joked. 'I thought I'd better make amends before I get a roasting off Sister Mary Paul.'

*

264

After helping Diana with the babies, now wide awake and starving hungry, Gracie wheeled the pram back into the storeroom, where the big nursery equipment was kept. Deep in thought, she mulled over Diana's words. Was Jack keeping in touch with her simply because it was pleasant to have a bit of feminine company, or was there more to it than that? She liked the lad well enough – he was warm, open, straight and funny, just like his mam – but right now the thought of anything beyond friendship with men repulsed Gracie. After her shaming affair with flighty Reggie and the consequences of getting pregnant, Gracie had no sexual appetite. The cheeky young flirt of a girl had been replaced by an older, more cynical woman who would never make the same mistake again.

Everybody loved the Christmas tree, which generated excited festive plans.

'We should decorate the dining room,' Gracie suggested.

'And bake cakes,' Zelda suggested, before quickly adding, 'That's if we can get enough rations and Sister Mary Paul will let us use her kitchen.'

'We could hang little Christmas stockings by the fireplace for the babies,' Diana added.

Ada and Sister Theresa, who had joined the girls around the Christmas tree, had their own suggestions too. 'There's a lovely carol service in the chapel on Christmas Eve,' Sister Theresa informed the group. 'You're all warmly invited.'

'Fate always conspires to make me work on Christmas Eve,' Ada said with an apologetic smile. 'Somebody always goes into labour just as the carol service starts, so, seeing as I'm on duty that night, I'm not making any firm plans to attend the service. But nothing will keep me away from Sister Mary Paul's Christmas dinner. Last year Farmer Arkwright supplied the Home with two geese – nobody dared ask where they came from,' she added with a wink. 'We were just grateful to have them.'

'This will be my first Christmas with my Sisters in the convent,' Sister Theresa said happily.

Ada yet again marvelled at the change in Shirley. This happy, confident, articulate young woman dressed in her nun's habit and wimple was hardly recognizable as the same sad, wretched girl who had arrived at Mary Vale in need of sanctuary. Ada missed not seeing Shirley as frequently as she used to in former days – her life as a nun obviously meant that the convent and her religious life came first. When she did see Shirley, or Sister Theresa as she must remember to call her, it was always a joy, especially when she turned up on the ward with a mop in one hand and a bucket of hot soapy water in the other.

Though none of them had much money, the Mary Vale residents started to think of little gifts they could leave for each other underneath the Christmas tree. Zelda for one had quite ambitious plans, which would only come to fruition if she could spend time in her garden shed. Waiting until Constanza had had her feed, Zelda settled the sleepy baby in the Silver Cross pram with its sparkling chromework and smart waterproof hood and cover one morning. Gently bouncing the pram, Zelda made her way carefully along the snowy path to the shed, which was freezing cold. Putting the brake on the pram, Zelda hurriedly made a fire in the wood-burner, which crackled into life and heated the shed in no time. Knowing full well she could not go foraging in the nearby woods and fields for wild herbs, Zelda skimmed through her existing collection of precious *Herbals*.

'Marigold hand cream!' she exclaimed when she had found what she had been searching for. Scanning down the list of ingredients, Zelda muttered out loud, 'Marigold petals if in season, otherwise combine dried lavender, rosemary and sage and a pint of good oil, sim-mer ingredients in a pan until a satisfying consistency is reached, strain off the herbs, cool the mixture and bottle when cool.'

Zelda was so engrossed in her reading she barely heard Constanza whimpering in her pram, and by the time she became aware of her baby's cries the child was wailing indignantly – at which point Frank Arkwright came striding into the shed. He called out in his charac-teristically direct way: 'Everything all right?'

Zelda smiled at his anxious face. 'Yes, thank you, Frank,' she answered calmly.

'It's just that I heard a baby crying and I thought I'd better check like . . .' he mumbled, before peering under the bonnet of the big pram and winking at Constanza, who gazed up at him with the same beautiful dark eyes as her mother.

'I'm afraid I didn't respond immediately she sum-moned me,' Zelda admitted. 'I was lost in my Herbals.

I want to try to make some Christmas presents,' she confided in him. 'None of us have any money so we're all racking our brains trying to think of gifts that are inexpensive but a little bit unusual.'

Frank stared curiously at an open page in one of the *Herbals*. 'Face and hand cream,' he said. 'If you come up with summat as good as what you brew for me, lass, your gifts are bound to be much appreciated.'

Zelda coloured at Frank's kind words. Since he had delivered Constanza, their relationship had reached another level: previously she had jumped at the sound of his voice, but now she found it warm and comforting. In the past she would have fled at the sight of him, but now she gave a welcoming smile at the sight of Frank, who always grinned back at her like a big cheeky boy. Frank's kindness had generated trust and love in her heart, which she knew was fully reciprocated. Nowadays he was unquestionably one of her dearest friends, a man she could truly rely on.

'I'll take the little lass for a walk in her pram,' Frank generously suggested. 'Give you a bit of peace.'

Looking at the glittering bright frosty day outside the shed window, Zelda had a change of mind. 'I'd like to walk with you, if you don't mind?'

Frank nodded and, taking hold of the pram, he pushed it outdoors and bounced it several times. 'Damn good springs if I say so myself,' he mumbled gruffly.

As they set off, Frank was suddenly struck by an idea. 'If you don't mind,' he started nervously, 'I'd like to take the little lass to meet mi father down at farm?'

Zelda smiled her agreement. 'I'd like that; he might like to see the new pram you bought Constanza.'

'Aye, he might well,' Frank agreed.

The farm track was rutted and filled with drifts of snow, but Frank thoughtfully steered the pram on to smoother patches, so he didn't disturb the baby.

'We should have resurfaced this blasted road years ago,' he grumbled.

'Well, now is definitely not the right time of year for road-laying,' Zelda laughed as she manoeuvred her way around the banks of snow.

Frank was surprised at how much slimmer she looked these days; he was used to seeing Zelda big and pregnant, but now she walked with a quick lightness in her step. Her hair looked longer too; he liked the way it sprang in bright red curly tendrils around her delicate, heart-shaped face. Gazing at her with pleasure, Frank, sensing a tell-tale blush of embarrassment creeping up his cheeks, quickly looked away.

Farmer Arkwright was thrilled to see the 'Babby', as he called Constanza. 'She might need feeding,' Zelda said, as the baby began to stir again after her long walk in the cold.

The farmer sensitively showed her into a little parlour, where a warm fire crackled in the hearth.

'We'll leave you in peace,' he said softly. 'When you've done, there'll be a cuppa tea waiting for you in't kitchen.'

Zelda felt strangely peaceful sitting by the fire feeding her baby in Farmer Arkwright's parlour, a place she would never have expected to find herself in her wildest dreams. After Constanza had fallen asleep on her breast, Zelda buttoned up her blouse, then made her way to the kitchen, where a collie dog lay flat out in front of the old black grate, while a kettle merrily whistled on a hot plate.

'Father's just gone out to milk the cows,' Frank said, as he laid a tray on the table.

Zelda was touched by the trouble he had gone to: dainty china crockery on a pretty embroidered white linen cloth, a pot of tea and slices of cake.

'That looks very pretty, Frank,' she commented.

'Me and mi father don't normally dine in such a genteel lady-like fashion,' he chuckled, as they sat down together. 'Though Sister Mary Paul, bless her heart, does make us a cake every week, from the eggs she gets from the farm,' Frank explained as he poured her tea.

'Delicious,' Zelda exclaimed, sipping her hot tea and nibbling the nun's coconut and carrot cake.

Sitting on either side of the grate, they ate in a comfortable silence, broken only by the collie's loud snores. It was the closest Zelda had felt to home in many, many months.

28. Basque Country

The parishioner of the kind priest in Nantes kept his word. After smuggling his charge safely out of Nantes, Harry was passed on to another worker, who guided Harry south. After many weeks of being on the run, Harry met the Resistance worker who would lead him and other escapees over the Pyrenees. Though thoroughly daunted by the journey that lay ahead of him, Harry knew that if he had to scale every mountain between France and Spain to be reunited with Diana, he would do it – even if it killed him.

That night before his journey into the Basque Country, Harry dreamt of his first meeting with Diana. She had been wearing her pale-blue WAAFs uniform but had removed the jacket in order to sit more comfortably in the chairs ranged around the wide mapping table that dominated the Ops Room. Even from the gallery, as he puffed thoughtfully on his pipe, Harry could see Diana's long, slender legs, narrow waist and full bosom. When she stood up to rearrange the position of the markers, her shoulder-length silver-blonde hair fell in a silky curtain over her pale, intense face and, as she turned towards him, Harry noticed how big and blue her eyes were.

'The colour of summer cornflowers,' he thought dreamily.

It soon became perfectly clear that Harry wasn't the

only officer on the base who rated beautiful WAAF Officer Diana Bishop. She had only to walk into the NAAFI and all heads turned her way.

'Best-looking girl for miles,' Harry's immediate boss and best pal, Flight Commander Derek Robson, remarked. 'Bright too – doesn't natter away like most of the other girls and always gets the map locations spot on.'

Seeing the effect Diana had on men in the NAAFI, their smiles and wolf whistles that she assiduously avoided, caused Harry to wonder if she was, in fact, already married or engaged. So convinced was he that Diana was spoken for Harry decided it would be wise not to pursue her. It was only after bumping into her crouched down pumping her bicycle tyre in a dark alley-way outside the Ops Block that his opinion started to change.

'May I help?' he asked rather formally.

Even though it was getting dark, Harry could see the gleam of Diana's perfect white teeth as she smiled up at him.

'I'm afraid I've got a puncture,' she told him.

After several minutes of trying to inflate the back tyre, Harry agreed with her. 'It's as flat as a pancake.' Seeing her pretty crest fallen face, he quickly added, 'Come on, I can give you a lift home.'

'I wouldn't dream of it,' she protested.

'Where do you live?' he insisted.

'In a little village called Shelford – it's miles away.'

Harry laughed. 'It's hardly any distance at all. Wait here while I go and fetch my car.'

*

On the drive to Shelford, Harry kept peering at Diana out of the corner of his eye. Though he had to pay close attention to the road, particularly as he had his headlights dipped, he could not resist taking sneaky peeks at her perfect profile and glowing blonde hair. She talked easily about her work and enquired after his too; she appeared so cool and relaxed, while Harry felt uncharacteristically nervous. Much later, when he told Diana that he originally thought she hadn't fancied him, she had burst out laughing. 'I most certainly did!' she exclaimed. 'I thought you were the cleverest and most handsome officer in Duxford.'

'Well,' he had grumbled, 'you managed to hide it pretty well.'

Diana gave a cheeky shrug. 'You can blame my posh upbringing for that.'

As Harry drifted into sleep, he smiled as he remembered their first date at the Regal Cinema in Cambridge, where *Rebecca* was showing. When he had nervously whispered, 'May I kiss you?', Diana had replied without a hint of coyness, 'I would love that.'

There was no going back after that first kiss: beautiful Diana Bishop was all that he had ever dreamt of.

When morning dawned Harry and his fellow escapees embarked on the most dangerous journey of their lives. As they gained height and walked higher and higher into the mountain range, Harry shivered, not with cold but with the memory of his guide's words before they departed.

'This is a perilous journey that brave men have died doing,' he had warned. 'You all know what will happen if any of you are caught.'

If Harry was to return home he had no choice but to take chances; nevertheless, as he gasped for breath in the high altitude and slithered on the frozen mountain tracks, he prayed with all his heart: 'Please God, guide me safely home to the woman I love.'

29. Christmas Eve

Christmas Eve dawned bright and frosty. As Ada's working day began, she paused briefly on her way into the hospital to gaze up at the mountains. The light was so crisp and clear she could see the snowy peaks of some of the northern fells etched sharply against the sparkling blue sky. Her thoughts immediately flew to Grasmere and Keswick, to the fells where she had walked hand in hand with Jamie, whom she missed so much it sometimes physically hurt her.

'Darling, darling Jamie,' she sighed.

His letters were no longer quite as regular as they had been when he was first called up. He had mentioned in a recent letter that all correspondence had been heavily censored now that his unit was 'moving in deeper'. It certainly didn't take a genius to interpret what he meant. His clearing station was obviously moving closer to enemy fire, the thought of which terrified Ada.

'He's a medic,' everybody said to comfort her. 'He'll be a lot safer than the men fighting on the Front Line.'

Unfortunately, Ada knew quite the opposite: just because Jamie was a doctor didn't mean that he was safe; she had read too many newspaper articles about first-aid ships and casualty hospitals being bombed and destroyed during an attack. There were some days when she felt paralysed with fear and apprehension, and the only person she could share her worries with was her close friend, Sister Ann.

'I feel so guilty making a fuss,' she blurted out one day as they shared a pot of tea in the Matron's office. 'Diana has lost her fiancé, Zelda is a young widow, and Dora's son is dead. I should thank my lucky stars that Jamie is alive, at least as far as I know, and that I still receive letters from him.'

Sister Ann laid a gentle hand on Ada's arm. 'Child, how can you not worry?' she reasoned. 'There are thousands of women all over the country enduring the same pain as you.'

Ada swiped the tears from her eyes. 'I feel like I've waited all my life for a man like Jamie, and just when I've found him, he's been snatched away from me.' She gave a shuddering sigh. 'I know it's what he wants: he was miserable and ashamed when he felt he wasn't doing his bit. I really have no right to complain,' she finished determinedly.

Seeing Ada struggling to regain her composure, Sister Ann tactfully changed the subject. 'Tell me, how is Zelda progressing?'

'She's a wonderful mother,' Ada replied, as she pocketed her damp handkerchief. 'Totally besotted by little Constanza, who is thriving. I have difficulty keeping Zelda out of her garden shed,' she smiled. 'Now that she's back on her feet, she's busy once more mixing her healing salves and poultices.'

'She's a wonder with those herbs,' Matron replied.

'Diana seems to be thriving too. Whenever I see her, she has George in one arm and Teddy in the other.'

'Is there any news from Father Ben about George's adoption?' Ada enquired.

Sister Ann shook her head. 'Nothing, and to be honest it's becoming a source of concern to all of us. Such a lovely little boy whom we can't seem to place.'

'I worry about him being parted from Teddy,' Ada admitted. 'The pair of them are like two peas in a pod. They sleep side by side, roll around on the nursery mat together. Diana occasionally manages to feed them together, one on the bottle and one on the breast. It's quite an achievement,' she chuckled.

'Diana has been wonderful with George,' Matron acknowledged.

'I think taking responsibility for both boys has occupied all of her waking moments and saved her sanity in the process,' Ada said. 'I was worried sick she would go to pieces, but she put her baby's needs before her own and now she's taken on George too.'

'We must leave it in God's hands and trust that he'll find the right parents for George.' Matron held Ada's gaze. 'I would hate to send the little boy to an orphanage.'

Back in the Home the atmosphere was charged with excitement. Little colourful bootees and baby socks decorated the black-marble fireplace surround, and the home-made red, green and blue crêpe paper decorations that the residents had made were draped across the ceilings of the sitting room and dining room. Boughs of holly heavy with red berries were artfully arranged behind mirrors and pictures along with bunches of mistletoe that dangled over doorways.

'Any excuse to get a kiss,' Gracie joked, as she posed under a bunch of mistletoe with her full red lips pursed for a kiss. 'Though to be honest I'm in no mood for kissing fellas,' she admitted. Supporting her huge tummy with her hands, she gave a weary sigh. 'Surely it can't be long now: I'm well past my due date.' Eyeing Diana's slender figure, she added enviously, 'You're lucky: at least you're the other side of childbirth, I've got it all to come.'

'I would have preferred it if my labour hadn't been brought on by grief and heartache,' Diana sadly reminded her.

Gracie blushed with shame. 'Sorry, Di, when will I ever learn to keep my big mouth shut?'

Eager to make amends for her slip-up, Gracie struggled to her feet. 'Fancy a cuppa?'

'Not right now, thanks,' Diana replied. 'I need to check up on the boys in the nursery then I want to put the last of my presents under the Christmas tree in the entrance hall.'

'Me too,' Gracie replied. 'I'll meet you there later.'

Diana found her boys rolling around on the soft playmat in the nursery. Dora, who had been keeping an eye on the babies, smiled when she saw her. 'They've been having a little boxing match, grabbing each other by the nose and ears. Teddy even had hold of George's hair a few minutes ago, little rascals,' Dora said fondly.

Diana gazed down at them: Teddy tall and pale with serious blue eyes; George dark and smiling, with a strong, muscular little body. She had given birth to one child, but she had enough love in her heart for the two of them. George and Teddy, Teddy and George: she couldn't say one name without immediately thinking of the other.

'Are you okay to look after them for a little bit longer, Dora?' Diana asked. 'I want to put the last of my gifts under the tree.'

'Fine, lovie, off you pop,' Dora answered cheerfully.

'I'll be back in time to feed them,' Diana said over her shoulder, as she hurried out of the nursery.

With one eye on the gurgling babies wriggling on the playmat, Dora continued changing the cotton sheets that lined the babies' white canvas cots. With Percy gone and Jack posted overseas, she had been dreading Christmas: the thought of just her and her husband on their own all day with only their sad thoughts for company was simply unbearable. Matron's generous invitation to spend the day at Mary Vale had cheered both of them up considerably. Dora would happily lend a hand in the kitchen or on the wards if necessary, while she knew that her husband would be content to chat to the residents and to the Arkwright men, who had also been invited to the Home for Christmas dinner.

Relieved that she was on her own, Dora let her tears fall unchecked. Christmas was a terrible time of the year when you were mourning the loss of a loved one. No matter how hard she tried to stop the flow of memories, they flooded back, bringing with them wave after wave of grief. How could she ever forget the sight of little Percy, his big brown eyes huge with wonder on the Christmas morning when he had found a red-and-yellow scooter propped up beside his bed?

'Santa's been,' he said in an awed voice. 'Mummy, look what he gave me for me.'

He and Jack, her sweet twin boys, had rushed into the garden in their bare feet to see if Rudolph had eaten the carrot they had left out for him on Christmas Eve. When they saw all that remained of the carrot, their eyes had sparkled with excitement. It had unquestionably been one of the happiest days of her life: her boys small enough for her to watch over and protect, young enough to show their unconditional love, and innocent enough to believe in Father Christmas.

George's loud scream when Teddy once more gripped his nose distracted Dora from her sad thoughts. Picking up a wailing George, she held him close to her heart. 'What would I do without my babies to care for?' she asked George, who immediately stopped crying at the sound of her soothing voice. 'I don't think I could have lived through these past few months without you, young man,' she added, as she planted a kiss on the top of his silky dark curls. 'Come on,' she said, and walked into the little kitchen attached to the nursery. 'Let's warm up your bottle – then it's nap time for you, young George.'

Gracie and Diana arranged their few presents under the tree alongside Zelda's interesting packages, which were wrapped in brown paper and tied with pieces of old ribbon she had ironed and reused.

'Whatever's in there smells gorgeous,' Gracie said as she sniffed a package with her name on it. 'I can't wait to open it.'

'I haven't got much for Zelda, or for anybody, in fact,' Diana murmured guiltily. 'I've given Zelda one of my silk scarfs – I thought she might use it to tie her hair back when she's gardening – and I managed to find a little rattle for Constanza.'

'I bought her some bath salts,' Gracie giggled. 'To ease her back ache after mixing her brews all day.'

'It's the thought that counts more than anything,' Diana insisted. 'When I think of the Christmases we celebrated at home before the war . . . always lots of guests for dinner, chilled champagne in front of the fire, while we unwrapped our presents and the food!' she exclaimed. 'I can't believe we ate so much in those days.'

'Roast turkey, sausages wrapped in bacon, stuffing and potatoes, Christmas pud, mince pies, creamy Lancashire cheese, port and bottles of ale,' Gracie said dreamily. 'How did we put all that lot away?'

'It's so different these days,' Diana sighed. 'But I'm sure Sister Mary Paul will work a miracle or two.'

Gracie gave a confidential wink. 'I saw Frank Arkwright walking into the kitchen with a brace of pheasants the other day,' she said.

Diana grinned. 'He's a changed man these days, isn't he? I never imagined him to be a natural with babies.'

Gracie burst out laughing. 'One particular baby,' she pointed out. 'Little Constanza, he's besotted with her.'

'For good reason: he did bring her into the world,' Diana laughed.

'Who would think big, gruff Frank, who could barely crack a smile, is more than happy to push a pram around the garden?'

Diana gave her a deep meaningful look. 'Who would ever have imagined that shy, retiring Zelda would be the one to bring out the softer side of Frank?'

Gracie looked thoughtful too. 'Do you think it might be serious? You know, like he's falling for her?'

Diana didn't hesitate for a moment. 'I think it's very serious,' she answered honestly. 'The only thing is,' she added as her voice dropped to a whisper, 'I don't think either of them knows it yet.'

It grew dark early on Christmas Eve, but the chapel was lit with dozens of candles and fragrant with the perfume of blooms grown in the convent's greenhouse. Sister Theresa had polished the pews until they glowed and she greeted the residents as they trooped in.

'Welcome, welcome,' she cried as she rushed to greet Zelda, Diana, Gracie, Ada and Dora. 'Take a seat – the service will start soon.'

Grateful to take the weight off her feet, Gracie sat down in one of the narrow pews, which just about accommodated her tummy.

'Are you comfortable?' Ada enquired.

'Just,' Gracie grinned. 'It's nice that you managed to get here, Ada, and Dora too.'

'We'll take it in turns to nip back to the ward,' Ada replied in a whisper. 'It's quiet at the moment – let's hope it stays that way. I've never yet got through a carol service without having to rush away to deliver a baby.'

Everybody fell silent when the nuns, led by the Reverend Mother, walked into the chapel in solemn procession; with their long dark veils sweeping the aisle behind them, they took their places and the ceremony began. Ada could barely take her eyes off Sister Theresa, whose face glowed with joy as she approached the high altar. From her radiant expression, nobody could doubt that her days in the convent had transformed her: from a scrap of a girl Shirley had blossomed into a young woman with a true vocation.

After singing the opening carol, 'Oh, Come All Ye Faithful', the chorus of which the nuns sang in Latin, Father Ben began the Mass. During the service, as the congregation stood up, knelt down, then stood up again, Gracie began to feel hot and slightly sick. Maybe it was the heat of the candles combined with the smell of incense that filled the chapel, or maybe she had eaten too much of Sister Mary Paul's delicious rabbit-and-leek pie? Whatever the reason, Gracie wasn't quite able to keep up with all the bobbing up and down, so she stayed seated until communion, when she felt she ought to kneel. Struggling awkwardly, she manoeuvred her enormous tummy into position; then, just as Father Ben consecrated the host and the communion bell rang out, she felt an acute stabbing pain in the lower part of her back.

Hearing a suppressed gasp, Ada quickly turned towards Gracie, who was now sitting doubled over clutching her belly. Ada discreetly waited a few minutes until the consecration was over, then she took hold of Gracie by the elbow and gently helped her to her feet.

'Can you walk?' she whispered.

Gracie nodded. 'Yes, but slowly, and not far,' she said, as she bit back the pain that was gripping her tummy.

'Hold on to me,' Ada whispered as she gently ushered Gracie out of the chapel.

Wide-eyed, Zelda, Diana and Dora grinned at one another. 'Perfect timing,' Dora chuckled. 'Gracie's baby will have the same birthday as Jesus!'

30. Surprise

Young and strong, Gracie seemed to breeze through her labour. Experienced as she was, Ada marvelled at her patient's stamina, even as the contractions ratcheted up. Coming more and more frequently and with greater ferocity, Gracie continued to breathe well through most of them. However, it wasn't until nearly past midnight that she finally started bearing down. Dora, who had returned from the chapel to assist Ada, cautioned her patient. 'Try and hold on so that you make the most of your pushes,' she advised. 'Ada and I will be watching baby's progress from the other end – we'll let you know when it's time for the really big pushes.'

Even though she was officially off-duty, Ada stayed with Gracie, who finally gave birth well after midnight.

'A girl!' Dora announced as she held Gracie's bouncing seven-and-a-half-pound daughter in her arms. 'A fine healthy little girl.'

Ada always held her breath at this particular moment; even though Gracie had been clear all along that she was having her baby adopted, nothing ever prepared a new mother for the first sight of her new-born child. Gracie cradled her daughter and admired her, but she nevertheless remained detached.

'She's lovely,' she said, as she stroked the little girl's

mop of dark hair very much like her own. 'But I'm not going to change my mind. She'll be better off with parents who really want her, not with the likes of me,' she said with a realistic sigh.

Ada nodded. 'Shall we let Dora clean up baby while I make you a cup of tea?' she suggested. 'If you don't mind, once you're comfortably settled, I'll love you and leave you, dear. I'm dog-tired.'

Just after Ada had delivered a strong, hot cup of tea and a few slices of bread and butter to Gracie, the front doorbell rang out.

'Who on earth can that be calling so late?' Ada thought, as she hurried to open the door.

Fearing it might perhaps be bad news for one of the residents, Ada peered into the darkness with an anxious expression on her tired face. In the gloom she made out the shape of a tall man standing on the doorstep, but when he stepped over the threshold and stood in the light Ada had to grasp the door for support.

'JAMIE!' she cried, and all but fell into his open arms.

'Darling,' he murmured, as he gathered her close and held her tightly to his chest. 'My darling . . .'

His lips reached for hers, and for several minutes they clung on to each other, kissing long and hard, only stopping to gaze at each other before kissing again. James lifted Ada's starched cap from her head so that he could run his hands through her rich, golden-red curls.

'I've missed this,' he said, as he smothered her hair with kisses. 'And this,' he said, kissing her nose. 'And this,' he said, kissing her chin. 'But, more than anything, your lips,' he declared, planting another kiss on her smiling mouth.

Ada drew him into the hallway so she could close the door. 'Come and get warm,' she urged, and led him into Sister Mary Paul's immaculate kitchen, where the nun had left loaves of bread raising on top of the Aga. Unable to take her eyes off Jamie, she threw herself once more into his arms.

'Why didn't you tell me you were coming home?'

'I didn't even know myself till two days ago,' he laughed. 'Our commanding officer suddenly announced that a couple of us medics could go home for Christmas, and I was one of the lucky ones. I was out of that casualty hospital before you could blink.' He stopped his excited explanation in order to hold her at arm's length. 'Sweetheart, you look exhausted.'

Ada grinned. 'I was but I'm not any more,' she declared. 'Not when I've got you, my love,' she whispered, as she nuzzled his warm neck and inhaled the rich smell of tobacco and antiseptic soap.

'I'm astonished you're still working,' Jamie continued, as he stroked her silky skin. 'I thought everybody would be in bed, but, when I saw the light on, I thought I'd risk Sister Mary Paul's wrath and ring the bell. I need a bed for the night,' he added. 'I've come straight from London.'

'We'll find you a bed,' Ada assured him. 'You could even use the single one in your old office,' she suggested.

'Pity you won't be lying in it with me,' he teased.

Ada blushed. 'I was thinking exactly the same thing,' she said with a guilty giggle.

The kitchen door opening wide made them both jump apart. 'Ada, there you are,' Dora exclaimed. She stopped short when she saw Jamie. 'Dr Reid! What a nice surprise.'

Seeing the lovers' radiantly happy faces, Dora quickly excused herself.

'I just needed to fetch some milk,' she said, grabbing a bottle from the pantry. 'Merry Christmas,' she added as an afterthought, as she closed the door behind her.

Suddenly aware that Jamie had been travelling for several days, Ada said, 'You must be starving?'

'Yes, I've only had a couple of stale sandwiches all day.'

Ada cast her eyes around the kitchen. 'I could make you an omelette?'

'Three!' he laughed. 'And if you could find some strong drink, that would be all the better.'

Sitting at Sister Mary Paul's vast scrubbed kitchen table, Ada watched Jamie wolf down everything she put in front of him: Lancashire cheese, omelette, a slice of bread-and-butter pudding left over from supper and autumn apples that had been overwintered in the cellar. After Jamie had satisfied his hunger, they sat side by side with their backs to the warm Aga. Holding little glasses of whisky, the couple toasted each other.

'Happy Christmas, my darling,' Jamie said, as he kissed Ada on the lips.

Leaning her head against his strong shoulder, Ada dreamily closed her eyes. 'This is the happiest Christmas of my life,' she sighed. 'I've got everything I need right here beside me.'

When she turned to look at her beloved, she gave him a tender smile. Jamie, worn out by his long, arduous journey and their emotional reunion, was fast asleep. Unable to wake him, Ada made up a bed of coats that she arranged in front of the Aga; then she lay down and slept the night through beside him.

They both woke with a start when Sisters Mary Paul and Theresa, who had volunteered to help in the kitchen throughout Christmas Day, walked in just after seven o'clock.

'Glory be to God!' the old nun cried, when she saw what looked like a heap of clothes piled up on the floor.

Seeing Ada slumbering with her arms clasped around Jamie's neck, Sister Theresa took charge of the situation.

'Sister, you go and check who's in the dining room, and maybe pop on to the ward to see if Dora needs anything.'

With her eyes still on the heap that was starting to stir, Sister Mary Paul bustled out of the room. The second the door closed behind her, Sister Theresa shook her friend awake.

'Ada!' she cried. 'Get up!'

Completely bemused as to where she was and what time it was, Ada rubbed her eyes and straightened her long, dishevelled hair.

'Shirley . . .' she mumbled blearily.

'It's morning!' Shirley cried. 'Quickly, wake Dr Reid.'

Grabbing her uniform, which she held to her chest, Ada shook Jamie. 'Darling, wake up,' she urged.

In a daze Jamie staggered to his feet, then smiled joyfully at Ada, who stood with her hair falling around her face and shoulders. As he reached out to kiss her, Sister Theresa ushered the pair of them out of the back door.

'No time for that now,' she giggled. 'Off you go.'

Ada left Jamie in his old office, where he instantly fell asleep again on the narrow hospital bed. Ada tidied herself up as best she could, then hurried on to the ward to relieve Dora.

'You look like you've been dragged through a hedge backwards,' cheeky Dora chuckled.

Ada gave her friend a guilty smile. 'We fell asleep in front of the kitchen Aga.'

Dora chuckled even louder. 'As long as that's all you did,' she teased.

Ada blushed. 'It would have been mortifying if Sister Mary Paul had found me sleeping beside Jamie. Thank God, Shirley had her wits about her. She shooed us both out of the kitchen like naughty children.'

Seeing Dora smothering a yawn, Ada quickly added, 'You head off now, dear, it's been a long night.'

Before Dora departed, Ada enquired after the new mother.

'Gracie slept the night through,' Dora told her. 'Her baby's presently being fed in the nursery.'

'I'll check on Gracie just as soon as I've seen her baby – now off you go,' Ada urged.

'See you later,' Dora said, as she reached for her bag, which she kept under the desk at the nurse's station. 'Me and Mr Saddleworth will be here in time for dinner; we're looking forward to it too,' she added sleepily.

Ada squeezed her arm. 'Get some rest, dear, and come back in good time for a glass of sherry.'

Dora winked. 'I could do with a couple right now, if I'm honest,' she joked.

Though hospital and the Home were loud with cheery calls and happy laughter, Ada was far too busy to join the residents under the glittering Christmas tree in the hallway, but Zelda and Diana went along with their babies in their arms.

'Can you manage those two big boys?' Zelda anxiously asked as Diana tucked Teddy under one arm and George under the other.

'I'm used to it,' Diana answered with a happy smile. 'Anyway, they'd make a fuss if they were separated,' she added knowingly. Smiling, she lifted the boys up so they could get a better view of the tree, the tip of which almost swept the lofty hallway ceiling.

'Look, darlings, look at the pretty tree.'

With their eyes wide open in wonder George and

Teddy gazed at the glittering decorations that sparkled when the light caught them.

Holding Constanza close to her chest, Zelda reached under the tree and drew out Diana's gift, which she slipped into her friend's cardigan pocket.

'You might want to open it later when you've got a free hand,' she suggested. 'I'll give Gracie her gift later too; after last night she might be glad of a bit of a lie-in.'

Diana smiled as she nodded at a brightly wrapped square package. 'That's from me to you, Zelda. Merry Christmas.'

When the boys in her arms started to wriggle and complain, Diana headed back to the nursery to feed them, leaving Zelda rocking Constanza under the Christmas tree. Gazing out at the sunny, bright garden, Zelda, on a whim, decided to take her daughter for a walk. After popping Constanza into her rather grand pram and covering her with warm blankets, Zelda slipped into her coat and headed for the front door. Passing the tree, she spotted Diana's present, which she was now free to open. She gasped in delight when a bright, emerald-green silk scarf slipped from the wrapping paper along with a pretty little rattle for Constanza. Quickly knotting the scarf under her chin, Zelda checked her reflection in the hall mirror; delighted that the emerald-green fabric brought out the richness of her thick red curls and emphasized the honey darkness of her big brown eyes, Zelda set off with a skip in her step.

Gently rocking the pram, Zelda made her way along

the garden path that wound its way past her garden shed; stopping at the back gate, she glanced from left to right, then took the left turn that led to Arkwright's farm. It would be good to see her friends this morning and wish them both a very happy Christmas.

31. Mary Vale Farm

As news of Jamie's surprise visit spread through the Home, Sister Ann insisted that Ada, who was scheduled to do the Christmas Day afternoon shift, should spend the rest of the day with her boyfriend.

'He'll be gone before you know it,' Sister Ann said earnestly. 'You must make the most of your time together.'

Ada, who could only think of her beloved, was in no mood to argue: the thought of spending time alone with Jamie made her giddy with happiness.

'Well, if you're sure . . .' she asked.

'Get away with you,' Sister Ann exclaimed. 'It's not like we're rushed off our feet. There's nobody else due to give birth. Sister Theresa has volunteered to lend a hand with the feeding rota so you're as free as a bird.'

'Will you make sure that Gracie gets her Christmas dinner on a tray in the ward?' Ada fretted. 'I don't want her tiring herself out walking up and down all those long corridors.'

'Of course,' Sister Ann promised. 'I'll see to it myself.'

Ada was feeling rather guilty that she had barely seen the new mother since she had given birth. 'I popped in to see her earlier: she seems to be thriving, though her breasts are sore with not feeding, but that will pass.' She smiled as she added, 'Gracie's called her little girl Daisy – she's a sweet little thing.'

Sister Ann gave her friend a gentle shove. 'Don't hang about here wasting precious time. Off you go – there's a handsome young man waiting for you!'

Smiling excitedly, Ada hurried to Jamie's former surgery, where she expected to find him soundly sleeping, but when she got there Jamie was nowhere to be seen. Standing in the corridor wondering where he might have gone to, Ada heard loud, clear whistling coming from the staff bathroom.

'Jamie, is that you?' she called, as she pushed open the door.

Waving his razor in the air, Jamie answered with a cheerful smile. 'Morning, darling. Come and join me,' he said, and he beckoned her over to the sink.

Giggling Ada wiped soap from his stubbly chin and then mischievously dabbed it on his nose.

'Did you sleep well?' she asked.

Disregarding his soapy face, Jamie pulled Ada to his chest and kissed her long and hard on the lips.

'I most certainly did,' he announced, as he rubbed his stubbly face against her silky-soft cheek.

'OW! Stop,' she exclaimed, as she struggled free of his grip. 'Listen, darling,' she added urgently, 'Matron's given me the rest of the day off.'

'Wonderful!' he declared. 'Let's go fell-walking, just you and me on the mountaintops on Christmas Day,' he added romantically.

'Oh, yes,' she exclaimed. 'I'll go and get changed right away.'

'Try and scrounge some food off Sister Mary Paul,' Jamie called after her. 'I'm ravenous again.'

'Okay,' Ada called over her shoulder. 'See you in the kitchen in ten minutes.'

Ada found Jamie sitting at the kitchen table with a mug of tea and a plate of fried eggs and beans before him. Clucking like an anxious mother hen, Sister Mary Paul popped another plateful of food and another mug of tea on the table for Ada.

'Eat!' she commanded. 'Dr Reid tells me you're going fell-walking in this freezing cold weather. Glory be to God, you could catch your death up there,' she fretted.

Ada playfully rolled her eyes at Jamie, who gave her an indulgent smile.

'It's a fine day, Sister,' he insisted. 'The ground will be hard after the frost, which makes for good walking – better than slipping and sliding on ice and mud. We should enjoy a full day's walking if we set off soon,' he added, as he wiped his plate with a slice of toast and downed his tea.

Sister Mary Paul presented them with several greaseproof packages. 'There's some cheese-and-pickle sandwiches and a Thermos of hot tea: that should keep the pair of you going until you get down from the fells. And I'll keep your dinners warming in the Aga – it would be a terrible shame to miss Christmas dinner.'

'Thank you, dear,' Ada said, as she rose to give the old

nun a big hug. 'We'll survive till dinner-time on your picnic and we'll be down before it goes dark.'

'You'd better be, or I'll have the mountain-rescue team out looking for you,' Sister Mary Paul threatened.

As Jamie and Ada drove away from Mary Vale, Zelda was pushing Constanza's pram into the Arkwrights' farmyard, where father and son greeted her with smiles of pleasure.

'Hello there,' Alf exclaimed.

Zelda gave a bright smile. 'I thought I'd drop by with Constanza to wish you both a Merry Christmas.'

'Merry Christmas to you too,' Alf replied warmly. 'How is the little lass?' he enquired as he peered into the pram, where the baby lay peacefully sleeping. 'My, she's growing proper fast, right enough,' he enthused.

Frank also fondly peered into the pram. 'Sleeping like an angel,' he whispered. Still smiling, Frank turned to Zelda. 'I were just leaving to walk down to the bottom field to check on the sheep – fancy stretching your legs and coming with me?'

Zelda looked uncertainly at her sleeping daughter. 'I'll keep an eye on the babby,' Alf kindly volunteered.

'Are you sure?' Zelda asked.

'Aye, as long as she doesn't need feeding,' Alf joked.

'I fed her just before I left Mary Vale, so she should be fine for another few hours,' Zelda explained.

'Well, then, off you go, enjoy your walk,' Alf urged. 'Get back in time to walk over to Mary Vale for Christmas dinner,' he reminded them with a chuckle. 'I can almost smell Sister Mary Paul's dinner roasting in the oven.'

Zelda gave the old man a grateful smile, then set off at a brisk pace with Frank, whose long legs were twice the length of hers. Breathing in mouthfuls of cold fresh air, Zelda smiled as she climbed over the stile that led into the fields skirting the edge of Cartmel Fell. Catching her breath, she chatted to Frank. 'I feel like I've been indoors for too long,' she admitted. 'The only time I go out these days is when I push Constanza's pram to the garden shed.'

Frank smiled at her flushed pink cheeks and bright sparkling eyes. 'You've had your hands full recently,' he conceded.

'What are you going to do with the sheep?' she asked, as she all but ran to keep up with him.

'Just checking how they're getting on,' he told her. 'We need to keep an eye on them, as they'll be lambing soon; then we'll have to bring them into the barn.'

Looking around at the beautiful landscape of wild forest and rolling green hills that steadily rose to meet the higher, more majestic peaks of the Lake District, Zelda asked something she had been curious about for some time. 'There aren't many farms around here, apart from yours – do you ever get lonely?'

Frank shook his head. 'There's barely time to get lonely on a farm,' he replied. 'I've got friends in the area, but they're presently away fighting. It's only the likes of me who's been signed off,' he said flatly.

An indignant light flashed in Zelda's eyes. 'You've done your bit,' she exclaimed protectively. 'You can't possibly be thinking of wanting to return to the Front?' she hotly demanded.

Seeing her face, usually so sweet and calm but now inflamed with passion, Frank couldn't stop himself from bursting out laughing. 'It's me that should be angry with the situation, not you, lass,' he soothed.

'War makes me angry,' she blurted out.

'Aye,' he agreed, before changing the subject. Wanting to see her smiling again, Frank said, 'So what are your plans for the future, now that you've got a kiddie?'

'I have to admit I've been asking myself that same question,' Zelda replied.

Turning her eyes towards the hills and mountains that had become so familiar to her and that she had learnt to love over the months she had lived at Mary Vale, she said thoughtfully, 'I've found peace and happiness in this beautiful valley.'

Catching the emotion in her gentle voice and seeing the tears welling up in her large dark eyes, Frank's heart ached for the brave little woman standing before him. 'I'd like my little girl to grow up here,' Zelda added wistfully.

Frank gave a gruff cough. 'It's a grand place to bring up kiddies: plenty of space to run around, trees to climb, mountains to walk. Little Constanza would do well to grow up in this valley.'

Zelda gave a helpless shrug. 'I agree with you, Frank, but I'm not sure how it could possibly be achieved.

I mean, how would I make ends meet, what would I live on?'

'Don't be so daft, lass,' he smiled. 'You've got your market garden and your tonics and ointments. I'm sure you could make a go of things.'

'I doubt it,' Zelda replied.

'Why not give it a go?' he urged. 'You stand a better chance of making a go of things in an area where you're already well established than moving to a strange town where you don't have any friends.'

'I can't deny that's a good point,' she agreed.

Determined to push the idea home, Frank quickly added, 'There are cottages in the valley that sometimes come up for rent; they might need a bit of patching up, but between us Dad and I could sort that out for you. Neither of us would like to see you and the little lass go,' he concluded in a rush.

Zelda smothered a cry of astonishment. In all her wildest dreams she had never imagined that Frank or Alf would miss her! Moved by his kind offer to help, she was momentarily lost for words. Luckily the loud noise of bleating sheep claimed Frank's attention, and for the next half-hour they were both fully occupied with herding the sheep into a fold, where Frank was able to examine them one by one. Finally satisfied, Frank guided Zelda out of the fold, with the sheep bleating plaintively after them.

'Dad will have a fit if we're late for Mary Vale's slap-up Christmas dinner,' Frank said, smiling. 'He's supplied most of the grub.'

Zelda checked her watch and quickened her pace. 'Constanza will be waking up any time now,' she announced.

Amused at the thought of his dad handling a hungry baby, Frank chuckled low in his throat. 'Another good reason why Dad might have a fit!'

32. Sour Milk Gill

Ada and Jamie were also enjoying a beautiful Christmas day, driving through Keswick alone and blissfully happy. Empty of visitors and with its shops closed for the holidays, the little grey-stone town with its ancient Moot Hall looked charming as they drove through on their way to Derwentwater. In the morning light waves broke on the shore of the vast lake, while meandering streams the colour of lapis lazuli threaded their way through a network of marshlands.

'I feel like we're the only people in the world,' Ada said, as she gazed at the empty shoreline, where a flock of swooping seagulls screeched crossly at each other.

'The Christmas-morning services will be over by now,' Jamie mused. 'Time to get out the sherry bottle and open gifts while dinner cooks in the oven.'

Ada gave him a curious look. 'You sound almost envious.'

Jamie pressed his warm hand on her slender thighs, which he softly squeezed. 'I wouldn't want to be anywhere in the world but right here with you, my darling.'

Ada laid her head against his shoulder. 'I wish we could hide in the mountains until the war is over,' she sighed, tears forming in her eyes. 'I just can't bear the thought of your going back.'

'Let's not think about that just yet,' Jamie begged. 'We've got all of today and some of tomorrow.'

'I feel guilty that I've taken up most of your leave. Your mother will be feeling very neglected.'

'Don't be silly, sweetheart. My sister will be at home with her three noisy children – I wouldn't get a word in edgeways even if I were there.'

Cuddling up close to him, Ada leant over to kiss Jamie's cheek.

'We must seize the day!' Jamie cried, as he pressed down hard on the accelerator, and the car sped along the winding lanes. 'Just for now, let's forget all about tomorrow.'

A few miles down the road Jamie halted at a little grey-slate village surrounded by sheepfolds and barns.

'Seathwaite,' he said, grinning. 'The wettest place in England!'

As they laced up their walking boots and put on raincoats, Ada asked where Jamie was planning on walking.

'We're going to Sty Head, another of my favourite places.'

Ada laughed at his boyish enthusiasm. 'You say that about everywhere we go,' she teased.

'That's because they're all perfect places when I can share them with you,' Jamie laughed.

Walking hand in hand, they crossed the boggy fields and began walking over slabs and rocks that skirted a fast-flowing stream.

'This route up the fell is called Sour Milk Gill,' Jamie said, as he watched Ada sprint like an athlete up the steep upward-curving path. 'You can cool yourself down if you get too hot – the water's delicious,' he said, dipping his hand into the freezing cold gill. 'Sweet and cold and fresh.'

Following the course of the cascading stream, they climbed higher and higher, until they reached the peak of Green Gable, where they stood buffeted by a strong wind. Gazing in awestruck silence at the majesty of the landscape, Ada caught her breath.

'That's Sty Head Tarn,' Jamie explained, pointing towards a small lake twinkling in the slanting sunlight like a bright jewel. 'Up above Sty Head you can just make out the blue waters of Sprinkling Tarn and beyond that the Langdale Range.'

'Oh, my goodness, I don't think I've ever seen anything quite so beautiful in my life,' Ada cried, as she flung her arms wide. 'I want to catch it all and hold it forever,' she said, and turned to kiss Jamie full on the mouth. 'I'll remember this always,' she whispered in his ear, as the wind whipped her hair around her face.

Smiling, Jamie pulled her close and kissed her cold cheeks, now bright red because of the cold wind.

'Fancy having our picnic down there by Sty Head Tarn – it'll be more sheltered from the wind than up here?' he asked.

Ada nodded. 'I'm starving!'

*

By the time they reached Windy Gap, the wind roaring up from Honister Pass was strong enough to almost blow them over.

'It's wild,' Ada laughed, as she struggled to keep her balance.

'It'll be fine once we drop down on to the other side,' Jamie replied.

Keeping to the stony pathway that followed the course of Sty Head Gill, they made their way down Aaron Slack, where the wind did indeed drop until they were finally able to hear themselves speak. Once they'd reached the relatively flat area surrounding the tarn, they settled down with their backs against a great granite slab that kept them sheltered from the wind as they ate their picnic.

'Thank God for Sister Mary Paul,' Jamie mumbled, as he ate his cheese-and-pickle sandwiches with relish.

'Here, have some tea,' Ada said, handing him the Thermos.

Replete after eating, Jamie sighed as he lifted his face to the weak sunshine. 'This is a world away from where I've been,' he said quietly.

Ada held her breath as Jamie started to speak. She had been longing to talk to him about his time in the casualty clearing station but had held back for fear of spoiling their happy mood, but now he seemed relaxed enough to open up about his work.

'The bombing seems to go on all day long,' he started. 'The shells zip over in batches every fifteen minutes. No matter how hard and long we work, the casualties just keep on piling up. We're constantly shifting the operating theatre, which is lit by only one pretty feeble electric lamp, to a safer place. On one ghastly occasion the operating theatre, in some grand room in an abandoned French chateau, was hit by a shell. It was grim sorting out the patients from the masonry in order to get the injured outside. Everybody was shouting for help and water; some poor chaps were crawling, wounded and bleeding, on the lawn with shells bursting around them.'

Seeing the lines around Jamie's jaw thicken with tension, Ada reached out to take his hand, which she kept hold of.

'It must be heartbreaking working in such terrible conditions,' she murmured.

'It's great when you can help to alleviate a patient's pain or evacuate the casualties to a general hospital behind the lines – what's hell is seeing men suffering and not being able to do anything.' He swallowed hard. 'I'm a doctor, dedicated to saving lives, but I've had to watch sick men die and it feels so wrong.' Squeezing Ada's hand hard, he added, 'Don't misunderstand me, darling, I want to be there, I just wish there were better conditions in which to treat the wounded, and more equipment too. There's simply never enough. Civilians send us socks and soap when what we really need is scalpels, lamps, bandages, beds, blankets and stretchers.'

'Surely as the war intensifies the authorities will provide more essential equipment?' Ada asked.

'I hope so,' he agreed. 'But how can we possibly operate effectively with German shells landing so close to our clearing stations? It's not just lives that are lost; it's the loss of all the equipment too.'

Taking a deep breath, Jamie replaced the lid on the Thermos. 'Enough of that,' he muttered apologetically. 'I've said way too much.'

Ada looked at him indignantly. 'Why shouldn't you tell me what you're going through over there? I would prefer to know the truth,' she hotly insisted.

Jamie laid his head on her full, rounded breasts. 'I wish I could stay here forever, here in the country that I love with the woman I adore.'

Ada stroked his cheek as she kissed the top of his head. 'Come back to me safely, won't you, my darling?'

Jamie looked up into her lovely but anxious face. Tracing the line of her luscious pouting lips with his index finger, he whispered his reply. 'It's the thought of you, my love, that keeps me alive.'

By the time Jamie and Ada got back to Mary Vale, Christmas dinner was over and a party was in full swing in the dining room. With Dora on the piano leading the singing, the Home resonated with the happy sound of carols. Alf's and Frank's deep voices sounded out, while Sister Theresa's and Sister Ann's sweet, pure voices accompanied the residents, who were all wearing paper hats. Sister Mary Paul had kept her promise to save Jamie and Ada dinner, which they ate sitting at the kitchen table.

'There's a glass of port, a little gift from the convent, to go with it,' the nun said with a wicked smile. 'Now I'll leave you in peace to finish your meal before I start clearing up.'

It was lovely to sit by themselves in the cosy kitchen, which smelt of spices and baking bread.

'The perfect end to the perfect day,' Jamie said, as he finished off every single scrap on his plate. Picking up his glass of port, he raised it to Ada, 'Here's to us, my darling, happy days.'

Smiling, Ada clinked her full glass against his. 'Here's to many more days walking beside you in the Lake District.'

After Jamie had helped her to wash up their dishes, Ada turned to him. 'Would you mind if I just popped on to the ward for a moment? I'm keen to see Gracie.'

'Of course,' Jamie answered. 'But before you go can I ask you something?'

Hanging up the tea towels with her back turned to him, Ada replied in a matter-of-fact voice. 'Yes, of course, what is it?'

'Come and sit by me – there's something I want to show you,' Jamie said, smiling.

Returning to the table, Ada sat down beside him; he gently took her left hand in his.

'Will you marry me, my darling, wonderful Ada? Will you be my wife?'

As he spoke, Jamie slipped a glittering diamond ring out of his pocket. Shocked, delighted and overwhelmed, Ada was completely lost for words and could only stare in disbelief at the beautiful ring.

'Really?' she finally blurted out before bursting into floods of tears.

'I've never been more serious in my entire life,' Jamie assured her.

Sobbing and laughing all at the same time, Ada cried out her reply. 'Yes, yes, oh, yes!'

Laughing with joy too, Jamie eased the ring on to her wedding finger, then pulled her into his arms.

'I was going to propose to you at Sty Head Tarn,' he confessed. 'But when we got there, I realized I had left the ring back here. What a chump I am!'

Ada clung on to him; with her head pressed into his chest, she tried to stop the flow of tears that threatened to overtake her completely. How could she be so happy, so unbelievably lucky? She had met the sweetest man in the world, whom she longed to spend the rest of her life with. And yet her bubble of joy burst at the thought that tomorrow he would pack up his bag and return to the Front, to fight for all that they believed in. How would she bear being separated from her beloved all over again? Jamie was no longer her dashing, handsome boyfriend: he was her future husband; the man with whom she would spend the rest of her life, she hoped.

'Please God,' she prayed in the silence of her heart. 'Look after my Jamie, keep him safe and bring him home to me. Amen.'

33

1941

The post-Christmas lull hit hard. The atmosphere wasn't lightened by the snow, which, before Christmas, had seemed magical, but now, melting in slushy pools as grey rain persistently fell day after day, was nothing more than an eyesore. The fields flooded in low-lying areas close to the river caused a lot of problems for Frank Arkwright and his father, who were just starting the lambing season.

It seemed that the only resident who went happily about her daily life was Zelda. Every morning, after bathing and feeding Constanza, who grew sweeter and more charming with every passing day, Zelda pushed the baby in her pram down the garden path to her shed. Though the earth was still in the grip of winter, Zelda nevertheless peered closely at the damp soil, eagerly searching out for signs of new growth. Tightly curled small buds were in evidence on the trees in the wood that extended as far as Mary Vale's garden, and in the garden borders Zelda could just about make out tiny spears of green coming through, promises of snowdrops and aconites soon to come. The thought of new life, new growth bringing herbs and flowers that would soon be available to harvest, brought a smile to Zelda's face. After a busy winter of making tonics, lotions and salves, Zelda had almost depleted her stocks of dry herbs. Mr Marsden, the chemist in Kendal, had been her salvation over the winter months, supplying her with all the dried herbs she had run out of, and more besides. Though grateful Zelda had offered to pay from the money she had earned from her market produce sales, Mr Marsden simply wouldn't hear a word of it.

'Away with you,' he had chuckled. 'I refuse to make a profit from your good works.'

After pooling their information and sharing remedies, Zelda had become quite good friends with Mr Marsden, who surprised her one day by suggesting that, on the back of her success with her herbal remedies, she should think about branding them and selling them on a larger scale. Zelda had been flabbergasted. 'I couldn't do that!'

'Why not?' the chemist enquired. 'They've done no harm – quite the opposite – and they have all proved successful.'

Seeing Zelda blushing and uncomfortable, he gave her a kindly pat on the shoulder. 'Think about it,' he concluded.

As baby Constanza slept in her pram or gurgled as she played with her tiny pink fingers, Zelda worked on at her bench, warmed by the cheerful glow of the crackling wood-burner. When Constanza wailed with hunger, Zelda lifted her lovely, warm body from her cosy bed of blankets and, after settling herself comfortably in the battered old armchair by the wood-burner, she fed her baby. During these contented tranquil moments, Zelda's thoughts ranged far and wide. Her major preoccupation was how long would she and her dear friends remain at Mary Vale? She was quite certain that Gracie would be the first to leave; in fact, she knew that Mrs Price was visiting this coming weekend to discuss the adoption of her granddaughter, Daisy, with Father Ben. Diana was reluctant to leave the Home, mostly because she was dreading leaving baby George behind. She was already talking about returning home to her parents in Suffolk, which meant that out of the three of them Zelda would be the last to leave. Much as Zelda loved Ada and the staff, the prospect of staying on longer than her friends held little appeal.

Gazing down at her sleeping daughter, Zelda smiled. Constanza was so beautiful! Small and delicate, with the daintiest little heart-shaped face, deep, dark, inquisitive eyes and pink cupid-bow lips. It was all she could do not to kiss her sleeping baby, which would surely wake her up, so Zelda firmly resisted.

'Where will I go next?' she spoke out loud to her baby, who yawned as she snuggled under the blanket in her pram.

Zelda had been excited when Frank had suggested that she rent locally; she would have liked nothing better than to stay in the Grange area, as she loved living so close to the forests and mountains that always reminded her of home. Most of all she loved the proximity of the vast Irish Sea, with its ever changing seasonal moods and tidal shifts, its incoming and outgoing tides bringing a peaceful, calming rhythm to her day that she already knew she would sorely miss.

Unfortunately, Frank hadn't mentioned rental property again since they had discussed the subject on Christmas Day. Zelda was cautious about troubling him further; she knew too well how busy he and his father were right now, dealing with the winter floods and lambing too. From the plaintive bleating coming from the sheepfold on the other side of the drystone wall, Zelda knew that more lambs were being born in quick succession. With the Arkwright men working around the clock, this certainly wasn't the time to bother them with her problems.

'Where on earth will we live, *meine Liebe*?' she asked slumbering Constanza.

As she sat staring dreamily at the sparks flying up the wood-burner's chimney, Mr Marsden's idea drifted into her head. What if she were to market her potions and creams – might she make an income? Straightening her narrow shoulders, Zelda rose slowly from the chair and laid her sleeping child back in the pram before turning to the *Herbals* laid out on her bench. Could these ancient remedies really sell over the counter? Would people really want to buy marigold and knitbone skin cream?

'I'll make it work,' said Zelda determinedly. 'If it means I can stay close to Mary Vale, I'll work until I drop to make a living,' she vowed.

*

Mrs Price arrived from Barrow on Saturday morning, keen to see her daughter and her granddaughter too.

'She's a right bonny lass,' Mrs Price announced, as she gazed at Daisy sleeping in her white canvas cot in the nursery.

'For God's sake, don't wake her up,' Gracie begged, when her mum made to touch the little girl. 'She's got a voice like a fog-horn; she'll have the entire nursery bawling in less than a minute.'

'Just like you,' Mrs Price remarked. 'You could stop a bus once you got going!'

Gracie hurried her mother out of the hospital wing and into the sitting room, where a log fire crackled in the enormous hearth.

'We've got a few minutes before we go to see Father Ben,' Gracie explained. 'Do you want a brew?' she asked.

For once Mrs Price shook her head. 'No, not till we've got this appointment over with.'

Gracie suddenly realized her mother was nervous. 'Mam, what's up?' she asked softly.

Mrs Price gave an awkward shrug. 'Are you quite sure this is what you want?'

Gracie gave her mum a long, steady look. 'I've been over this a hundred times in my head,' she started. 'I've talked about it over and over again with my friends here in the Home and the staff too. I am absolutely crystal clear that I want to have Daisy adopted.'

'I know that's what you've always said,' her mother interrupted. 'But now you have a daughter, aren't you in two minds about your decision?'

'No, I'm not,' Gracie declared. 'How many times do I have to say it? Maybe one day I'll be ready to be a mother, but right now I know I would make a bad job of bringing up Daisy. I'm not ready, Mam. How could someone like me give a little baby a good settled home?'

Her mother gave an understanding nod. 'Don't get me wrong,' Gracie continued. 'I really care about Daisy's future; I want my child to be happy,' she added with tears in her eyes.

Not wanting to push Daisy further, Mrs Price let the matter drop. 'You told me that Father Ben had been really helpful.'

'He has,' Gracie agreed. 'That's why I wanted you to see him for yourself, before I leave the Home, and Daisy too.'

'Right, then,' said Mrs Price, as she checked the time on the clock on the mantelpiece. 'Let's not keep the man waiting.'

Father Ben's office in the convent was calm and quiet after the hurly-burly atmosphere in the Home, where girls constantly chattered, babies cried and visitors came calling.

'Nice to see you again, Mrs Price,' said the priest, as he held out a chair for her to sit on beside his desk.

After a few polite preliminaries Father Ben started his update. 'I think the best choice for Daisy is a couple who are in their thirties and live in the North-East.' He glanced down at the notebook on his desk before he continued. 'After suffering several miscarriages, they gave up on the idea of having any children at all until they read about Mary Vale in their church magazine. You can imagine there are quite a few procedures we have to work through, Mrs Price,' he said to Gracie's mother. 'Matching a baby to the right family is vital to all of us. Anyway, the couple I refer to fell in love with Daisy at first sight and can't wait to take her home and start their life as a family with her,' he concluded.

Mrs Price wiped a tear from her eye. 'As long as our Gracie's happy with the arrangement, that's all right with me,' she said as the meeting concluded. 'Thank you, Father, for all your help.'

As they walked back along the silent corridor that connected the Home to the convent, Gracie gave her mum a squeeze.

'Sorry to put you through that ordeal, Mam,' she said, with an emotional catch in her voice.

'Don't go fretting yourself, lovie,' her mother staunchly replied. 'I understand it's the right thing for you, and, after hearing about the couple who want to adopt Daisy, I feel a lot easier.'

'But you're still upset?'

'Aye, what mother wouldn't be? I want the best for you, and for your baby too,' she answered with a resigned sigh.

Before she left, Mrs Price clearly had something else on her mind. 'Would you mind if I didn't say goodbye to the child?'

Gracie shook her head. 'It's all right, Mam, I understand.'

'I need to put a distance between her and me for both our sakes,' Mrs Price explained. 'She's starting out on a new life that doesn't involve me and I'd prefer to leave it like that.'

'I know the feeling,' Gracie answered quietly. 'I've been doing the same thing myself. It's not fair on Daisy to do otherwise. I'm the one that made the mistake; the poor little mite shouldn't be the one to suffer for it.'

'Aye, lass,' her mother agreed sadly. 'The sooner life gets back to normal the better.'

On a gloomy, dank day in January 1941 Diana announced that she was leaving Mary Vale.

'My parents have offered me and Teddy a home. They're not happy, but they'll do the right thing by me, for which I am truly grateful.' She gave a heavy sigh. 'The thought of that long, ghastly journey to Suffolk with a new baby is bad enough, but what's worse is the idea of being cooped up in that rambling, draughty old house overlooking the North Sea with barely any company. I'll miss you all so much!' she cried.

'Hopefully it's only short term,' Gracie suggested. 'Until something better comes up.'

'I shouldn't be so bloody ungracious,' Diana said guiltily. 'At least I've got a bolt hole to go to. I've arranged to leave the Home at the end of the month,' she added with no excitement in her voice. 'Hopefully George will have found a family to adopt him by then.'

Ada gave a bright smile that belied her own anxious

feelings about the little boy's future. 'We will miss you so much, dearest Diana,' she admitted.

Diana gave her a warm smile. 'You must get so used to women coming and going in this place,' she commented.

Ada threw Diana an affectionate look. 'Yes,' she agreed. 'But there are some women that you *never* forget.'

34. Coming Home

Harry's prayers were miraculously answered as one freezing cold January morning, after weeks of arduous and hazardous travel, an airplane lifted him and twenty other prisoners of war off the Rock of Gibraltar. As they took off over the Atlantic, Harry's eyes followed the coastline until it receded into a vast blue shadow; then he turned his eyes westwards. Harry was going home.

Massively underweight, Harry arrived back on home soil a shadow of the man who had left it. Walking through the capital to his debriefing, he barely recognized London, with barrage balloons floating over the Thames and St Paul's and sandbags piled high outside shops and hotels. After his rigorous debriefing Harry's commanding officer took him to one side.

'Well done, old man, you got out and you've been able to pass on vital information that will assist further reconnoitres.' After giving Harry a hefty slap on the back he continued. 'Time you touched base with the family and got some rest. I'll be in touch in a week or two to discuss your future.'

Having no idea where his fiancée and baby might be, Harry decided his best move was to start where he left off, so he wasted no time in getting the train back to Cambridge, from where he hitched a lift to Shelford. His heart lifted at the sight of Diana's charming, picturesque cottage with its pale-blue front door, though he was saddened when he peered through the grimy windows to see the rooms empty and dusty: clearly nobody had occupied the place since Diana had left. Not finding the farmer (who rented out the cottage) at home, Harry hitched another lift, this time to Duxford, where he sought out his chum, Derek Robson, in the Ops Block. The man was visibly stunned at the sight of Harry.

'Oh, my God!' he exclaimed, as he sprinted down the flight of stairs that led up to the viewing gallery. 'Sweet Jesus!' he gasped in total shock. 'You're alive!'

Taking hold of Harry's arm, he added in an urgent whisper, 'Listen, old man, we urgently need to talk.'

In the Officers' Mess, over two stiff whiskies, Robson wretchedly told Harry about his most recent communication with Diana.

'She thinks you're dead,' he gulped.

Harry slumped in despair. 'Poor Diana,' he groaned. 'God knows what I've put the poor girl through.'

Stricken with guilt, Robson apologized. 'Believe me, Harry, I would never have written to her with such bad news if I hadn't been informed at the highest level.'

Harry stared miserably into the bottom of his empty glass before reassuring his friend that he quite understood.

'Knowing how desperately fond you two were of each

other, I thought notifying your fiancée of the situation was the right thing to do, especially given her circumstances. I'm sorry, old man,' Robson muttered. 'I seem to have got it all bloody badly wrong.'

'Stop beating yourself up, man,' Harry exclaimed. 'I'd have done exactly the same thing. But I need to put things right. I need to go to her right away.'

Robson quickly wrote Diana's address on a piece of paper that he handed to Harry, who was already on his feet.

'You can't leave now,' he protested. 'Diana's on the other side of England – you'll be travelling all night.'

'I need to go to her right away,' Harry repeated frantically. 'That's if she'll ever talk to me again.'

Harry did indeed travel all through the night, sleeping standing up in packed, smoky corridors where airmen, soldiers and sailors jostled for a space in which to lie down. When the train finally disgorged most of its passengers at Lancaster, Harry flopped on to a carriage seat that a number of noisy soldiers had just vacated. Falling into a deep, exhausted sleep, he was jolted awake as the train shunted into Kents Bank Station, where Harry disembarked. Blinking, Harry stood on the empty platform, trying to get his bearings. As the train chugged away and the smoke lifted, Harry got his first view of Morecambe Bay, and the wide, dramatic sweep of the Irish Sea over which the weak winter sun cast a pewter sheen. Following the porter's instructions, Harry left the station and, after walking through a small wood, he emerged in the gardens of Mary Vale with his heart starting to race. Would Diana still be here? If so, would she still want him after all he had put her through? Was his baby in the building he stood before, or would Diana, thinking Harry was dead, have had their child adopted?

Feeling sick with fear and apprehension, Harry took a deep breath before he rang the front doorbell and waited, hardly daring to breathe. A few minutes passed before a rather beautiful nurse with deep, dark-blue eyes opened the door.

'Good morning, may I help?' she said pleasantly.

Tongue-tied, Harry was momentarily lost for words. 'I'm Harry Langham,' he finally blurted out. 'Diana Bishop is my fiancée. Is she here?'

Ada visibly paled. Gripping the door handle for support, she gasped in shock. 'Oh, heavens!' she cried, and repeated exactly the same words that Harry's Duxford pal had said on first sight of him: 'You're *alive*!'

Now almost frantic, Harry repeated his question. 'Yes, yes, I'm very much alive,' he spluttered. 'I beg you, please tell me, is Diana still here?' he implored.

Ada gave a quick nod and smiled delightedly as she beckoned him inside. 'Yes, yes, Diana's here. She's in the nursery.'

With butterflies whirling in her stomach, Ada led the visitor along the corridor. Before they reached the nursery, she paused to lay a warning hand on Harry's shoulder. 'This is going to come as a terrible shock to Diana,' she said anxiously. 'A good shock, of course, the best thing that could possibly happen, but nevertheless . . . you'll need to be *very careful* with her,' Ada said in her firmest professional voice.

Harry gave her a curt nod, his eyes anxious and questioning.

'The baby came early; she's really only just getting her health back after . . .' Ada explained, unable to summon up in a sentence quite what her patient had gone through over the past few months. 'Well, after everything that happened,' she finished limply.

'I promise I'll be careful, only please,' he begged once more, 'just let me see her.'

Totally unaware of what was taking place only around the corner, Diana was stooping over the canvas cot, where Teddy lay squealing in delight at her smiling face.

'Come here, you little rascal,' Diana laughed, as she lifted her son into her arms and covered his smiling face with kisses. 'Mummy's darling boy,' she murmured into his ear just as Ada walked into the nursery, followed by Harry in his blue uniform. As his eyes locked on to hers, Diana went absolutely still, hardly daring to believe her eyes, before letting out an animal noise that brought a sob into Ada's throat. Harry walked slowly towards his fiancée, who clutched her son tightly to her chest. The uncomfortable squeal of her little boy seemed to bring Diana to her senses, and, standing wide-eyed, she felt Harry's arms wrap around her body, and then she smelt him; tweed, soap and tobacco. Still unable to speak, she leant her head against his warm chest, where she listened to the steady beat of his heart. Teddy's second indignant squeal made them both start in surprise.

Anxious Ada stepped forward. 'Shall I take him, dear?' she asked softly.

Diana shook her head. 'No thanks, Ada,' she murmured. 'It's time Teddy met his father.'

Laying the baby in Harry's arms, Diana watched and waited.

'Teddy,' Harry whispered, as he gently rolled his hand over his son's soft, downy hair, then stared into eyes exactly the same colour as his own. 'My little boy.'

As tears rolled unchecked down Harry's face, Ada guided the little family into the empty dining room.

'You can have a bit of privacy for the time being in here,' she told them. 'I'll just go and make you both a cup of tea.'

Closing the door softly behind her, Ada all but ran to the kitchen, where Sister Mary Paul and Sister Theresa were rolling pastry for an onion-and-mincemeat pie for lunch.

'Oh, my God!' she exclaimed, as she rushed into the room. 'You're never going to believe this.'

In the dining room Harry and Diana clung to each other as much as was possible, given that wriggling Teddy was in between them.

'I thought you were dead,' she cried.

'I know, I know, forgive me,' he begged, and kissed her over and over again.

'I thought I'd never see you again,' she murmured, as

she traced the line of Harry's nose and mouth with her free hand.

'Darling, I'm sorry, I'm so very sorry. What you must have been through . . .'

'And you too, Harry, I have so many questions. Where have you been all this time – why did Robson write and tell me you were dead?'

'It's not his fault, darling. He went off the information he was given; he acted with the very best motives,' Harry told her.

'I wanted to die too!' Diana exclaimed. 'There was nothing for me to live for without you.'

Squealing Teddy, who was both hungry and restless, interrupted her passionate outburst.

'I've got to feed him,' Diana told Harry, as she settled herself in an armchair close to the fireplace.

Standing with his back to the fire, Harry watched with tears in his eyes as the love of his life unbuttoned the top of her blouse and put Teddy to her breast.

The noisy contented sound of his son made Harry laugh with joy. 'You look like an image of the Madonna and Child,' he exclaimed in wonder.

'It doesn't feel like that with this little one tugging hard at me,' Diana said, grinning. 'But I love it,' she murmured, bending to kiss her baby's head. 'He's a hungry chap,' she added with a proud smile.

Watching Harry gazing at his son, Diana beckoned for him to come closer. As he settled on the arm of the chair next to her, she lovingly leant her head against his chest. 'There are so many, *many* questions I want to ask you.'

Harry laid a finger softly on her lips. 'Later, my darling, I'll tell you everything,' he murmured. 'For now, just being here, with you and my son, is everything I want. It was all that I've hoped and prayed for, and sometimes wondered if I would ever experience,' he finished with a catch in his voice.

She nodded tearfully and they sat in sweet, peaceful silence: a little family reunited after months of sorrow, and, just for now, there was nothing in the world either wanted more than this perfect moment.

When Ada returned with a loaded tray of tea and bread and butter, she found Harry with his arms encircled around his fiancee and his son. Leaving the tray on the table, Ada swiftly left the room. Closing the door behind her, Ada stood and smiled – Diana and Harry had a lot to catch up on.

While Teddy slept in the nursery, Diana's many questions were gradually answered.

'Poor Diana,' he groaned. 'The agonies I must have put you through.'

'I can't deny it wasn't hard, especially when you didn't come back and I was faced with a solid wall of silence in the Ops Block. I felt very, very alone,' she confessed.

'But you found this wonderful place!' exclaimed Harry, who had had a brief tour.

'Sheer luck,' Diana told him. 'But you're right, it is a wonderful place. I've felt happy and safe here, and I've made wonderful friends – Zelda, Ada and Gracie, people I would never have mixed with in ordinary life – but they're women who have changed my life. I know that we'll be friends forever,' she admitted with tears shining in her cornflower-blue eyes.

'I was helped by so many wonderful people too: we've both been fortunate, so blessed by strangers.' Harry shook his head as he recalled the bravery of the very many men who had helped him navigate his perilous journey home.

Gazing into Harry's smiling face, poor Diana, still shell-shocked, simply couldn't hold back her tears. 'Oh, my darling,' she said, as she started to cry all over again. 'I was so frightened without you.'

'Shhh, my love,' he soothed as he gently rocked her in his arms and stroked her hair.

'I didn't know where to go, or what to do, or what I would tell Teddy about you when he was older. I was such an utter mess,' she sobbed.

Harry waited quietly until she was calmer. 'We'll be fine now, my darling, I've been granted leave and I promise I'm going nowhere without you and my son.'

Diana looked up fearfully. 'How much leave?' she asked tremulously.

'Enough time to marry you and get to know my boy too,' Harry replied with a lump in his throat.

'Marry me?' Diana said the words tentatively. 'Remember what happened last time we made plans to marry?'

'This time will be different,' Harry promised cheerfully.

'I won't let you out of my sight for a second,' she told him with a determined smile.

'I don't want to be out of your sight,' he answered

passionately. 'I want to be able to touch you, feel you, kiss you, turn around and see you – I'll never be able to get enough of you, sweet Diana Bishop.'

Kissing her long, slender fingers, Harry asked nervously, 'Are you sure you still want to marry the wretched man who put you through so much misery?'

Diana gazed into his eyes that were full of uncertainty. 'There's nothing more in the world that I want, Harry. A lifetime with you and Teddy was something that I thought I had lost forever.'

35. Arrangements

Harry was given a guest room in the convent, where he was fussed over by all the nuns, while in her kitchen Sister Mary Paul made Harry nourishing meals 'to put a bit of flesh on his bones'. Harry's time in the convent proved useful in more ways than one. He quickly introduced himself to Father Ben, who was a mine of useful information when it came to Diana and Harry's forthcoming wedding.

'The nearest church is St Mary's in Allithwaite Village,' he told Harry, as they took a stroll round the convent gardens. 'I know the priest there, Father Peter, and I'm sure he'll be able to accommodate your wishes. You'll need to have the banns read, of course,' he added. 'They're usually read on three separate Sundays in the three months before the ceremony takes place.'

Harry's face dropped. 'I'm on compassionate leave but I might be called back to London at any time. I was hoping we could get married immediately; then I can settle my family in a new home before I'm posted elsewhere.'

'We live in strange times. I'm sure Father Peter has had many an anxious groom asking just the same question,' Father Ben assured Harry, who gave the priest a grateful smile.

'When I next part from Diana, I want to leave her and

Teddy in a secure place,' Harry said earnestly. 'We're a family now and I never want her to feel abandoned again.'

'I quite understand,' Father Ben said. 'We'll need to get you a Special Licence,' he added. 'While we're waiting for it to come through, let Diana have this happy time with you, my son – God knows, she deserves it.'

Diana was eager to introduce Harry to Teddy's best friend, George.

'They were born the same day, a few hours apart, and they've slept side by side in the nursery ever since. Look at them now,' she laughed, as she pointed to the two little boys rolling around on the nursery mat, gurgling as they made grabs for each other's tiny fingers.

Harry watched the boys in delight. 'They're so strong,' he exclaimed. 'They can't leave each other alone.' He laughed as Teddy yanked at George's glossy dark curls.

When it came to feeding time, Harry popped George on to his knee and fed him with a bottle, while Diana breast-fed Teddy. Seeing Harry cradling George in one arm while he tried to steady the bottle in the other brought a smile to Diana's face.

'Heavens!' Harry exclaimed as hungry George drained the bottle in no time. 'This chap can put it away.'

'Now burp him,' Diana instructed.

'How do I do that?'

'Put a cloth over your shoulder in case he's sick,' Diana advised. 'Now lay him against your shoulder and gently rub his back until he burps.'

Looking as if he were holding the crown jewels, Harry

cautiously rubbed George's back, then chuckled as the little boy gave a series of burps.

'Thank you for helping, darling,' Diana said. 'I try to feed them both together, but the bigger they grow the more demanding they get; sometimes it's quite a juggling act,' she admitted.

Holding sleepy George close to his chest, Harry gazed into his big dark eyes. 'Where's his mother?' he asked quietly.

'She left when George was six weeks old; she hasn't seen him since,' Diana answered.

'She must have been devastated?'

'Oh, she was,' Diana assured Harry, as she set about burping Teddy. 'She adored George and would have kept him but for her family, who refused to have anything to do with a child of mixed race.'

'Poor little chap,' Harry murmured. 'What will happen to him?'

'Marie left him here to be adopted . . . but it's not happened yet,' she added sadly.

'But he's gorgeous,' Harry cried. 'Strong, healthy, bright and as good as gold.'

'He's all of those things and many more,' Diana said passionately. 'But prospective parents thought it only right that a child of colour should be brought up by parents of colour. Actually,' she hotly blurted out, 'I would happily raise George beside Teddy and call myself proud to be the mother of such a wonderful little boy – whatever the colour of his skin!'

*

The Allithwaite vicar, who had been advised by Father Ben as to the urgency of Harry's circumstances, agreed to marry the couple by Special Licence. Once Harry was sure of the wedding date, he suggested to Diana they went into Grange for a walk on the vast beach that stretched way out to the Irish Sea. Diana had been worried about leaving the babies, but Dora had allayed her fears with a wave of her hand.

'Away with you! If I can't handle two extra babies for a few hours I shouldn't be in the job,' she teased. 'You've been cooped up here for weeks on end; take a break and have some fun with your handsome young man.'

Hand in hand, the couple walked the short mile along the track into Grange, which, by comparison with quiet, isolated Kents Bank, was buzzing with activity. It was pleasantly exhilarating to be out among people going about their business, popping in and out of shops and stopping on street corners to pass the time of day with friends and neighbours. After walking along the esplanade in the gusty wind that brought colour to Diana's high cheekbones, they hurried into the warmth of the Smugglers' Arms Inn, where Harry ordered tea.

Sitting by the crackling log fire, Harry mused, 'This is the first time we've been really alone since the day I left you in Shelford.'

Diana cocked her head as she reflected on the last year.

'I suppose it is,' she agreed.

'We were happy in Shelford, weren't we?'

Diana gave a radiant smile. 'Very happy,' she assured Harry, who took a deep breath before unfolding his plan.

'So, my darling girl, how would you feel about going back there?'

'I would absolutely love to go back to Cambridge!' she exclaimed. 'It would be like going back home.'

Harry waited for the waitress to set down her tray loaded with tea and toasted tea cakes, before he continued with a twinkle in his eye.

'We'll carry on where we left off,' Harry said happily.

Diana's smiling face suddenly tensed as a thought occurred to her. 'But your work?' she asked fearfully. 'Where will they send you next?'

Harry gave a playful wink. 'Derek Robson in the Ops Block is in the process of pulling a few strings; he's hoping to recall me to Duxford's viewing gallery. It's not firmed up yet,' Harry added hastily. 'But Derek's hopeful that it might be soon.'

'So, you won't be sent away?' Diana gasped.

'Not immediately,' he assured her. 'Oh, and there's just one more thing about moving back to Cambridge,' Harry said, smiling.

Diana gave him a teasing look. 'You seem to have covered everything, darling. '

'With your permission I'd like George to join us in Cambridge too!'

In floods of tears, Diana, completely overcome with happiness, had to be taken out of the cosy inn, where the drama of their intense conversation was attracting too much attention. Once outside, Harry swung his fiancée into his arms, wiping away her tears with his kisses.

'The last thing I wanted to do was to make you cry, my love.'

Clinging to him, Diana laughed with joy. 'I've never felt happier in the whole of my life. It's exactly what I wanted!'

'I know,' he smiled. 'I'd only got to look at you to see that.'

'I was dreading parting them,' Diana confessed. 'Teddy and George love each other like brothers.'

'Father Ben is already working on the adoption papers,' he told her.

Now that she was able to process what was going on, Diana's brain started racing. 'I'll need to phone the farmer to see if the Shelford cottage is still vacant.'

'It was when I was last there quite recently,' Harry said. 'It will need warming up. It might be a bit damp after being empty for so long.'

Diana shook her head as if she could not quite take everything in. Tipping her small chin so he could smile into her cornflower-blue eyes, Harry said, 'Invite everybody in the Home and the convent to our wedding, sweetheart – let's make it a day of real celebration!'

With her wedding day fast approaching, Diana went into a flat spin. She would have been content to walk down the aisle in her pale-blue WAAF uniform if Gracie, Ada and Zelda hadn't taken her to one side.

'I was going to leave the Home next week but now I'll

leave the day after your wedding – I wouldn't miss you getting wed for the world,' Gracie announced. 'My last gift to you before I rejoin my mates in the shipyard is to do your make-up and hair on your wedding day.'

Before Diana could open her mouth to protest Ada joined in. 'And mine is to help you sort out what you're wearing.'

'And I'm doing the bouquets, corsages and button-holes,' Zelda chipped in.

Diana smiled at the three women who had become her best friends during her stay at Mary Vale. 'Thank you,' she said. 'I gratefully accept all of your kind offers.'

'When you've got a spare ten minutes, let's go through your wardrobe,' Ada suggested.

Diana laughed in excitement. 'No time like the present.'

The contents of Diana's wardrobe were hardly inspir-ing. There was an assortment of baggy outfits that she had worn through her pregnancy, and a couple of pairs of trousers. But Ada gave a cry of delight when she spot-ted a silky blue crêpe two-piece suit tucked away at the back of the wardrobe.

'That looks nice,' she said.

Diana shrugged. 'It's just an old suit,' she replied.

Ada pulled it out of the cupboard to take a closer look. 'It doesn't look old,' she protested.

'I've not worn it for ages,' Diana said dismissively. 'I'm sure it won't fit me any more.'

'Of course it will fit you,' Ada cried. 'You're as slim as

a wand these days. Here, try it on,' she urged, as she pressed the suit into Diana's reluctant hands.

Diana wriggled into the silky crêpe suit, then stood in front of the mirror, staring at her reflection.

'It's too big if anything,' she said, as she tugged at the loose waistband.

'Breast-feeding is a sure and certain way of losing weight,' Ada said knowingly. 'Turn around.'

Diana obediently spun in a circle.

'It just needs a nip and a tuck, and it will fit perfectly,' Ada told her friend. 'And the colour is wonderful on you,' she enthused.

Diana paused to take another look at herself, 'It is rather pretty,' she conceded.

Ada gave her a hug. 'Harry's bound to love you in it!'

Sister Mary Paul and Sister Theresa were working out a menu for the wedding breakfast.

'If Farmer Arkwright could supply me with a pheasant or two, I could make a tasty game pie,' the old nun suggested.

'I'm sure Zelda's got enough winter veg in her garden to go with it,' the younger nun replied.

'And I've got some fine potatoes stored in the cellar; we could roast those with some parsnips,' Sister Mary Paul added.

'A feast!' Sister Theresa exclaimed excitedly.

'No cake, though,' Sister Mary Paul grumbled.

'I'm sure cake is the last thing on Diana's mind,' Sister Theresa teased.

'I think we could stretch to a nice meringue,' Sister Mary Paul added with a hopeful smile. 'If I could get extra eggs off the farmer.'

Sister Theresa grinned as she shook her head. 'What on earth would we do without Frank Arkwright and his dad?'

Sister Theresa was absolutely right: cake or food of any kind was the very last thing on Diana's mind. Grateful that all arrangements were under control, Diana concentrated on the practical details of returning to the cottage with two babies in tow. When she received a letter in response to her own from the Shelford farmer, she was relieved to hear that the cottage was indeed vacant, though in need of warming up.

'I'll get the Aga going,' the kindly farmer wrote. 'The place should be nice and snug by the time you arrive here.'

Diana, in a daze of excitement, simply could not believe that after all her heartache and sorrow life was suddenly so wonderful. To complete her happiness, Father Ben had drawn up the adoption papers for George for her and Harry to sign. He had also been in touch with Marie, informing her by letter that her son, George, had found a perfect home.

'I didn't think it was appropriate that I should name you and Harry as the child's new parents,' he told the prospective parents.

Diana nodded. 'We can follow that through at a later date when we think the time is right,' she agreed.

'God works in mysterious ways,' the smiling priest told Diana. 'Teddy will have a brother and you will have another wonderful son.'

Hugging herself, Diana left Father Ben's office chanting joyfully, 'George and Teddy — Teddy and George — our own little boys!'

36. St Mary's, Allithwaite

Zelda made sure that all the important guests had a corsage of evergreen entwined with fresh flowers, courtesy of the convent's greenhouse, to wear on Diana's wedding day. Harry had paid Zelda good money to source a spray of white roses that would complement his future wife's wedding outfit.

Wearing his smart blue RAF uniform, Harry arrived at Allithwaite's pretty little church with his best man, in fact, the *only* man he knew in the area, Frank Arkwright. Farmer Arkwright, dressed up in his Sunday best, had driven both men to the church in his freshly cleaned-out farm cart, pulled by Captain, looking especially smart for the occasion in his recently polished harness.

It was usual on wedding days for the best man to ease the groom's nerves, but on this occasion it was quite the other way around. Frank turned out to be nothing but a bag of nerves. Although he had repeatedly pressed his best suit to within an inch of its life and polished his shoes until he could see his reflection in them, Frank still felt awkward and uncomfortable.

'Honestly, man,' Harry said after Farmer Arkwright had dropped them off, then returned to Mary Vale to pick up the bride, 'anyone would think it's you that's getting married.'

Frank fiddled with the buttonhole corsage that Zelda had so painstakingly made up for him.

'I've never felt so nervous in mi life,' he confessed. 'Facing the enemy was a whole lot easier than this.'

'Just so long as you've got the ring, that's all I'm bothered about,' Harry said with a cheerful smile.

For the hundredth time Frank groped for the ring, which was carefully stored in the top pocket of his jacket. Smiling with relief, he nodded at Harry, who was gazing at the pretty church nestled within the fold of the valley, surrounded by rolling fields that looked surprisingly green in the sharp winter sunshine.

'Tomorrow,' Harry thought. 'Diana and I will leave here to start married life together.'

They had already made up two little beds in the back seat of his car: two cardboard boxes lined with blankets in which George and Teddy could sleep, with their mother in the middle keeping an eye on them throughout the long journey south. Harry had tried to calculate how long the journey from the north-west of England to the extreme east would take, but with the country at war there was no way of telling. It would depend on the state of the roads and how many diversions they came across. Even if they left early in the morning, he was quite sure they wouldn't arrive in Cambridge until late evening. Though Harry knew Diana was happy, he was nevertheless anxious about how she would feel when it came to actually leaving the loyal friends who had supported her in her darkest hours. Of course, they had all been urged to visit them down south, but travelling long distances was hard and complicated in war time. Who knew when Diana would meet up with Zelda, Gracie and Ada next?

Harry's wandering thoughts were brought back to the here and now by the sound of the church bells peeling out as the first of the wedding guests started to arrive.

'Best get inside,' Frank anxiously urged.

As the organist played out Widor's Toccata, the church rapidly filled up and all eyes constantly turned to the door, eager for their first sight of the bride. The music changed to 'Here Comes the Bride' as radiant Diana processed slowly down the aisle with her bridesmaids, Gracie and Zelda, keeping in step behind her; behind them, smiling Ada pushed Zelda's smart new pram in which George and Teddy lay peacefully sleeping. Though the babies were quiet for the moment, Ada knew full well that if they started screaming blue murder, she would immediately reverse the pram back down the aisle and wait for the newly-weds outside. As it turned out, George and Teddy were perfectly behaved. Apart from an indignant squeak when George grabbed Teddy's nose, they lay still throughout the exchange of marriage vows. During the signing of the Register, when Harry and Diana disappeared into the registry, Ada and Dora sat side by side in a pew, each with a burbling baby on her lap. When the organist struck up the final hymn, the bride and groom progressed down the aisle, waving happily to their babies as they passed them by.

Once the ceremony was over and the wedding party was outside in the churchyard, home-made confetti was showered on the bride and groom, who clambered into Alf Arkwright's farm cart. Waving and smiling, Diana and Harry were driven away by Alf, while the rest of the party followed on foot. When the newly married couple arrived back at Mary Vale, Harry gathered his bride into his arms. Blowing confetti from her silky blonde hair, he held her close.

'Happy, my love?'

In answer Diana stood on her tiptoes in order to lace her fingers around the back of her husband's head, which she pulled down to her level so she could kiss him full on the mouth.

'Unquestionably the happiest day of my life,' she replied with tears in her eyes.

By the time the guests arrived, Harry and Diana were on their second glass of sherry, kindly donated by the convent from their fine cellars. A mixture of friends, residents, staff and Sisters from the convent formed quite a crowd in the dining room, but eventually everybody found a seat and the wedding breakfast got under way. The meal so lovingly prepared by Sister Mary Paul and Sister Theresa was served by them too. If they ever needed thanks for the long hours they had spent in the kitchen, the grateful smiles on the guests' faces said it all. Alf Arkwright was especially fulsome.

'You've excelled yourself, Sister.' He beamed at Mary Paul who was busy trying to eke out seconds of the succulent game pie.

The nun gave a modest smile. 'Thanks are due to you, Farmer Arkwright, the game you brought was –'

Nervously pressing a secretive finger to his lips, Alf muttered, 'Least said soonest mended, Sister.'

Quickly getting the drift of his message, the old nun went red in the face. 'Quite so, Farmer Arkwright,' she hurriedly agreed, as she loaded the last piece of pie on to his empty plate.

Seeing her flustered, Farmer Arkwright swiftly changed the subject and turned to his son, nodding in the direction of Zelda, who was seated next to Frank.

'Zelda's done grand with the veg,' he boomed.

'Oh, aye,' Frank agreed. 'There's nobody grows spuds like Zelda does,' he announced to the whole table.

Shy Zelda paled at his praise. 'Shhh, Frank,' she pleaded quietly.

Out of his one good eye Frank gave her a tender look. 'You're a wonder, lass,' he said warmly, taking a gulp of beer from the glass in front of him. 'You can set your hand to anything and make it come good – salves, tonics, herbs, babbies, gardening – where do your talents stop?'

Though she felt like sliding under the table with embarrassment, Zelda nevertheless held Frank's gaze.

'That's kind of you,' she replied. 'But you shouldn't forget how generous people have been to me – you, Alf, Ada, Mr Marsden. I have been very fortunate.'

Emboldened by the beer, Frank spoke his mind. 'That's because we all love ye, lass.'

At which point, if it hadn't been for Constanza

waking with a loud squawk, Zelda was quite certain Frank would have kissed her.

'I'd better see to her,' she muttered, as she lifted her daughter from the pram recently vacated by George and Teddy.

Leaving the dining room later for the privacy of the sitting room, Zelda sat in a cosy armchair by the crackling log fire with her head in a spin.

'Frank Arkwright has just told me that he loves me,' she told her daughter, as she settled her on the breast.

Admittedly, Zelda thought to herself, it had been a collective acknowledgement, a mark of people's affection for her; nevertheless she had never thought to hear the word 'love' fall from Frank Arkwright's lips. Gazing into her child's big honey-brown eyes, Zelda considered her feelings for Frank. Over time, terror of the man had given way to deep affection and respect, which in turn had deepened into a relaxed and easy friendship. She actively looked forward to seeing Frank and spending time with him; she totally trusted him with Constanza, whom he had brought into the world, and she regularly turned to him for advice. But now she realized something was changing. Recalling the steady look Frank had given her, the warmth of his smile, his full lips and strong body, Zelda felt her insides turn to water, and with a shock she recognized what she was feeling. Desire. She no longer wanted Frank as a friend to rely on; she wanted him as a man she could love.

*

344

In the dining room, after the speeches had been said and the toasts made, much to everyone's surprise Diana rose to her feet.

'I know this might seem slightly unorthodox,' she said, smiling at her guests. 'It's usually the father of the bride who would speak at this point, but he's not here so I will instead. Tomorrow I'll leave Mary Vale, where I've been so safe and so happy.' With a catch in her voice she fought back tears. 'I have made the best of friends in Mary Vale, darling Gracie, and Zelda.' She nodded in the direction of Zelda, who had just re-entered the room with Constanza asleep in her arms. 'How would I have survived these last few months without Ada, Dora, Sister Mary Paul, Sister Theresa and Father Ben? No words can ever express my gratitude to all of you for your guidance and prayers.' Reaching out to Harry, she clasped his hand in hers. 'I leave here with my wonderful husband and not one but two sons. Please, raise your glasses to Mary Vale!'

A loud chorus of 'Mary Vale' followed, as guests chinked their glasses and Diana's friends rushed to give her a hug.

'I can almost forgive Reg for getting me in the family way,' cheeky Gracie joked. 'If I hadn't got pregnant, I'd never have met any of you.'

'Oh, Gracie, you never change,' giggled Ada. 'Mary Vale will be a far quieter place without you.'

As the guests dwindled away and the table was cleared, Harry's eyes sought out his wife's dreamy blue ones and she immediately knew exactly what he was thinking.

'When can we be alone?'

In answer she kissed him softly on the cheek. 'I'll see to the babies if you could finish the packing?'

'And then will you know where to find me?' he whispered.

'I'll know *exactly* where to find you, husband,' Diana answered with a long, lingering smile.

The following day, just before their departure south, Harry decided to walk his boys by the sea.

'Last time, lads,' he announced to the babies, who had rolled on to their sides and, with their thumbs in their mouths, were drifting off to sleep.

With the tide rushing in, Harry wheeled the pram down the path that ran alongside the railway track. The glimpse of bright sunshine that had blessed their wedding day had given way to a dark stormy sky, where grey clouds loomed, threatening rain. Listening to the cry of the gulls on one side of him and the bleating of lambs in the fields on the other side, Harry passed hedgerows bright with snowdrops, aconites and crocuses pushing their way through the cold earth. A mistle thrush perched in a tall beech tree overhead sang his song, which Harry stopped to listen to; the bird repeated the song twice, as if it couldn't quite believe it, then burst into a rapturous melody that filled the sky with a piercing sweetness. Harry smiled to himself as he continued walking his sons; it really was the perfect day on which to start the rest of his life with his new family.

37. Good Luck! Goodbye! Farewell!

The mood in the dining room that morning was very different to that of the previous day. The usual buzz of chatter around the room was subdued; apart from the odd greeting as residents sat down, the loudest noise to be heard was the clatter of crockery or the tinkle of cutlery. Knowing that two among them would soon be gone made the diners all too aware of what they themselves would soon face.

Ada and Dora comforted each other in the privacy of the sluice-room, where Dora pummelled the nappies soaking in the sink, while Ada refilled two large galvanized buckets with cold water and sanitizing fluid.

'No matter what they're like, you can't help but worry about the girls,' Dora chatted. 'I've tried not to get attached, but it doesn't work: living beside them and bringing their babies into the world ties you to them, even the horrible ones, like Annie,' Dora laughed.

'I often wonder whether Annie's life is better or worse since she left Mary Vale,' Ada said, as she set down the heavy buckets on the tiled floor.

'There's one girl I won't be worrying about,' Dora smiled. 'And that's Diana. Have you ever seen a woman happier than her?' Giving a naughty wink, she dropped her voice to a whisper. 'Gracie told me that she and

Zelda had offered the bride and groom their big bed-room. Apparently the two girls pushed their single beds together to make a whopping big double and left them in peace to enjoy their wedding night.'

'How very thoughtful,' Ada cried.

'They made up the bed with clean sheets that Zelda sprinkled with some of her special lavender water,' Dora added.

'So where on earth did the two girls sleep?'

'Gracie slept in Diana's room and Zelda bunked down in a spare bed on the ante-natal ward,' Dora explained, before she started to giggle. 'The newly-weds looked like the cat that had got all the cream when they came down to breakfast this morning.'

Ada covered her mouth with her hand to try to stop herself from giggling too. 'I bet they hardly slept a wink!'

'Harry has been in the convent since he arrived,' Dora chuckled. 'He can't have got up to much mischief there.'

Ada gave an envious sigh. 'How nice for them to have time alone together.'

Seeing a sad look come into her friend's lovely big blue eyes, Dora spoke cheerily. 'It'll soon be your turn, missis.'

Ada blushed. 'One day soon, please God,' she murmured wistfully.

'It'll be tough saying goodbye to George and Teddy.'

'It would be tougher still if George was left behind,' Ada pointed out. 'I'm sure he'll have a wonderful life with Harry and Diana.'

In a sentimental mood, Dora wiped a tear from her

eye. 'Then there's little Daisy,' she sighed. 'She'll be gone soon too.'

Ada gave her colleague a comforting pat on the shoulder. 'Father Ben assures me that Daisy is going to a loving couple: a vicar and his wife in Durham, who are desperate for a child.'

'God love her,' Dora said fervently. 'And we've got Constanza for a bit longer,' she said on a more cheerful note.

Ada looked grave. 'I worry how Zelda will manage once her friends have gone.'

'Aye, I've been thinking the same thing too,' Dora agreed. 'It won't be easy, being the one left behind in the Home.'

Sitting upstairs in their bedroom, which had been restored to its former two single-bed status, Zelda was blinking back tears that threatened to overwhelm her any minute. She was supposedly helping Gracie pack her suitcase, when all she really wanted to do was to hurl the clothes out of the suitcase and lock the door so Gracie wouldn't be able to leave. Feeling like a five-year-old in the middle of a panic attack, Zelda simply couldn't hide the misery in her dark-brown eyes. Catching sight of her friend's expression, Gracie sat down on the bed beside her and gripped her trembling hands in her own.

'I know what you're thinking, sweetheart, so stop trying to be brave.'

'I'm sorry, I should be stronger,' Zelda apologized. 'I should be happy for you, rejoicing in your freedom, but

I'll miss you more than words can say,' she said, as her tears flowed. 'Cooped up in this place, you've been like a beautiful caged bird, you've kept us smiling and entertained with your spirit and determination —' Zelda broke off as something made her smile. 'You even managed to pick up a boyfriend!'

Gracie burst out laughing. 'Catching a fella when you're six months pregnant *and* living in a Mother and Baby Home too is quite a coup,' she conceded.

Seeing Zelda's sweet face brighten briefly with a tremulous smile, Gracie continued earnestly. 'Sweetheart, you really have got to start thinking of your own future now.'

Zelda's head drooped. 'I know, it's all I do think about these days.'

'I'd invite you and Connie to come and live with me in Barrow, but all we've got is a two-up, two-down, though to be honest that wouldn't stop mi mam – she'd welcome anybody in need.'

'That's sweet of you, Gracie, but I must be independent,' Zelda answered honestly. 'If I had a choice, I would dearly like to bring up Constanza in this lovely area.'

'Aren't Frank and his dad looking out for a cottage for you?' Gracie enquired.

'Yes, but so far they've found nothing that I know of,' Zelda replied. 'I could stay on a bit longer at Mary Vale, but without you and Diana it just doesn't seem right,' she confessed.

Making a huge effort to pull herself together for

Gracie's sake, Zelda rose to her feet. 'Come, let me help you with your case; it's time you were on your way, my friend.'

When Zelda and Gracie walked outside, they saw Harry was busy packing up the car while Diana was arranging the little boys in their cardboard beds on the back seat on either side of her.

'They've just been fed,' Dora chatted, as she helped Diana tuck blankets around the wriggling boys. 'They should drop off soon, with a bit of luck.'

'Hopefully they'll sleep until we get on the A1,' Diana said excitedly. 'Heaven only knows where we'll stop for their next feed.'

'You'd best get on your way while they're both quiet,' Dora urged. 'You've a long journey ahead of you.'

Diana caught the nurse's hand. 'I'll never forget you, Dora,' she said, with an emotional catch in her voice. 'You have a heart of pure gold.'

They were interrupted by Sister Mary Paul bustling forwards with a hamper packed with as much food as she could spare from her kitchen.

'Something to keep you going on your journey,' the nun said. 'Hot tea, barley water, Farmer Arkwright's Lancashire cheese sandwiches with my apple chutney and a pastie apiece – only onion and mutton, but it'll keep you going until you get down South.'

'Darling Sister Mary Paul, I'm going to miss you so much,' Diana cried, as she wriggled forwards in her seat to hug the old nun.

'God speed, dear girl,' Sister Mary Paul answered tearfully.

Harry climbed into the driver's seat and wound down the window. 'Cheerio!' he called.

The group of well-wishers standing on Mary Vale's doorstep waved goodbye, as Harry started up the engine, at which point Ada, who had been held up on the ward, came rushing towards the car.

'Take care of yourself, dearest girl,' she called out to Diana. 'Promise you'll come back and be chief bridesmaid on my wedding day?'

Winding down her window, Diana blew kisses back to her friend. 'Promise!'

'Goodbye,' her friends chorused after the departing car. 'Good luck . . . God bless . . . Goodbye.'

Gracie was determined to make the journey home on her own. No fuss, no bother, and this time she wouldn't need her mother as an escort. Certain that she would pick up where she left off, Gracie (having learnt her lesson the hard way) would take her time when it came to courting the opposite sex. Well aware of the pain she had caused, not just to her family but to her innocent little daughter, who would grow up never knowing her birth mother, Gracie's resolve was unshakeable. She wasn't going to waste time having fun; she had heard enough of Hitler first-hand from Zelda, and she had seen what a monstrous dictator he was on the cinema news reels. Now, Gracie wanted to fight back, do her bit for the war effort, either by joining the forces or repairing warships to fight the enemy at sea;

she was determined that come what may she would work for peace until she dropped.

Gracie quietly left the Home by the back way. She had said her goodbyes; she didn't need to wring it out even longer. After one lingering backward glance, Gracie headed for Kents Bank Station. With a skip in her step and a smile on her face, she set off for the new life that awaited her just around the corner.

38. Business Matters

After her two best friends had left, Zelda spent more and more of her time in her garden shed. With Constanza either sleeping peacefully or gurgling contented in her big posh pram, Zelda pondered on her future. Casting her eyes around the shed, she spotted the few remaining little pots of lavender-scented hand cream that she had made as Christmas presents for the residents. Taking them down from the shelf, Zelda set them on the bench before her and scrutinized the prettily decorated labels on which she had hand-drawn pictures of wild lavender and beehives. They looked nice enough, but could she really make a living out of selling hand cream? Her eyes strayed to her trusty *Herbals*, lying open on the bench. There were so many amazing remedies that she longed to try out. Gazing through the window at the gloomy February garden, Zelda knew that life was stirring underneath the damp earth. Very soon daffodils, tulips, irises and bluebells would come bursting through the sodden ground; blossoms would be riotous in the convent orchard; and herbs would once more grow in wild abundance.

It was time for making and planning, but Zelda felt she had nobody to make or plan for, not until she heard the gentle sound of Constanza happily sucking on her little pink thumb. Smiling adoringly at her baby, Zelda was suddenly galvanized – she had a child, a beautiful daughter, whom she was totally responsible for – she had to get hold of her life and *do* something.

Frank had promised to look out for a vacant cottage that she could rent, but she couldn't keep nagging the poor chap; it simply wasn't reasonable. This was one of the busiest seasons in the farming year: Frank simply hadn't got time to go running around the countryside looking for vacant properties, and it was her responsibility to do that anyway. If the truth were known, Zelda had seen little of Frank since Diana's wedding day. She had tried not to take it personally, blaming lambing for Frank's absence. Nevertheless, it couldn't be denied that since his emotional outburst at the wedding breakfast Frank Arkwright had certainly made himself scarce.

Impatient and now on a mission, Zelda decided there was no time like the present to turn thoughts into actions. After she had fed Constanza and settled her down in one of the little white canvas cots in the nursery, she caught the bus into Kendal. As the bus rumbled through the narrow, winding streets of the pretty town built of local grey slate, memories of happy market days with Gracie came flooding back. Sadly, the old Bedford van that Gracie had so painstakingly restored now stood idle in Mary Vale's garage.

Hurrying down the main street to the chemist's shop, Zelda passed several locals whom she recognized and smiled at. Even the granite-faced woman who ran the wool shop cracked a smile as their paths crossed. Zelda found Mr Marsden in the back room of the shop, where he was preparing a bottle of cough mixture for a customer. Curious, Zelda gazed at its intense black colour, then (after asking permission of the chemist) she sniffed the contents.

'I can smell blackcurrant and liquorice.'

Mr Marsden nodded. 'I know it looks like a witch's brew but it's extremely effective when taken regularly.'

After he had completed his task, the chemist made a pot of tea for his guest, which they drank as they sat by the spluttering gas fire.

Laying down her cup, Zelda took a deep breath before making her announcement. 'I've been thinking over your suggestion.'

Mr Marsden raised his thick eyebrows in a quizzical expression. 'I want to give it a go, to try to market my herbal products,' Zelda blurted out.

Reaching into her shopping bag, she pulled out her precious old *Herbal*.

'There are so many wonderful remedies in this book – maybe you're right that there could be a market for good old-fashioned products?'

'Zelda, you don't need to convince me of the benefits of herbal remedies,' the chemist responded. 'With the war worsening by the day and medical provisions at an all-time low, there's a real need for alternative medicines.'

Zelda's pulse started to quicken with excitement.

'Mind you,' he added, 'I wouldn't encourage quacks

and charlatans, but I've seen your work and how effect-ive it has been.'

Zelda blushed with pleasure. 'You've given me a lot of your time, Mr Marsden,' she reminded him. 'I don't think I would ever have had the confidence even to start this venture without your advice and support.'

'I've enjoyed the challenge; it keeps me on my toes,' he chuckled. 'You shouldn't heap all the praise on me, young lady,' he continued. 'You've come into this busi-ness as a qualified botanist, your research is thorough and well-grounded, and, so far, your products have proved to be successful and reliable.'

Zelda smiled to herself as she recalled her far-off student days, working in the botany laboratory in Munich. It was there that her interest in herbs and healing had started – strange to think she was now pursuing that same interest hundreds of miles away from her homeland. The chemist broke through her reverie.

'How many products were you thinking of market-ing, Zelda?'

For the second time she reached into her shopping bag, this time producing the scented hand creams and restorative tonics she had made.

'I was thinking of starting with these,' she said, as she handed them over for the chemist's inspection.

'They look very attractive, nicely packaged,' he remarked.

Flushing with excitement, Zelda explained her plan. 'I thought I might widen my range to face creams, and ointments for acne and rosacea, hair restorers and salves for aching bones. All of them would be genuine remedies from my trusty herbal,' she assured him.

Mr Marsden stared thoughtfully at the products in his hands. 'If you cost them sensibly and keep up with the market demand, they could be a winner.'

Hardly daring to ask the question, Zelda breathlessly said, 'Would you consider stocking them?'

The chemist nodded firmly. 'Certainly. We could have a three-month trial run and see how it goes. It might be a good idea to give your products a brand name to pull the sales concept together. Have you thought of one?'

Without a moment's hesitation, Zelda replied with a bright smile. 'Mary Vale – that's where it all started.'

'Pretty name, with a nice local ring. So,' Mr Marsden enquired, 'how soon can you get started?'

Zelda's sweet face glowed with excitement. 'As soon as possible,' she exclaimed.

The chemist's face became serious. 'I hope you don't mind my asking, but how much longer can you practically continue to work out of Mary Vale's garden shed?'

'I've been asking myself exactly the same question,' Zelda admitted. 'The shed is only part of my worry: it's not right for me to be in the Home any more,' she confessed. 'I should free up my room for somebody who needs it more than I do. The problem is, I have nowhere else to go.'

The chemist thoughtfully scratched his bald head. 'There's a little flat over the shop that I used to have before I got married and moved out of town. I've not bothered trying to rent it out – it's small and a bit old-fashioned – but if you don't mind that, it might do for you and your daughter pro tem,' he suggested. 'In fact,' he continued as he rose to his feet and reached for a key hanging on a hook by the door to the stairs, 'why don't you take a quick look at it now?'

'I'd love to,' Zelda exclaimed.

'I'll leave you to it,' Mr Marsden said, as he handed over the key. 'I've got to get back to work.'

Zelda slipped up the narrow flight of stairs that led to the flat, where she switched on the electric lights to familiarize herself with the place. There was a very small kitchen with a gas stove and an old-fashioned sink, a sitting room with an open fireplace and a bedroom that was big enough to take a single bed and a cot, plus a little bathroom with a gas water heater.

'It will do well for Constanza and myself,' Zelda said out loud.

It would need a good airing and a good clean, but apart from that it was completely habitable. A lick of paint and some bright new curtains would cheer it up too. Hurrying back downstairs, Zelda nervously asked the chemist what rent he would charge.

Kind Mr Marsden gave her a reassuring smile. 'Let's talk about that when we know the profit margin on your products,' he said kindly.

Zelda was so excited she had to stop herself from flinging her arms around him. 'Thank you so much,' she cried. 'I'm very grateful to you.'

The chemist shook her by the hand. 'I wish you luck with your new enterprise, Zelda. I'm quite certain we'll work well together in the future.'

Once back at Mary Vale, Zelda rushed into the nursery, where starving hungry Constanza protested loudly at her mother's absence.

'I'm sorry, my darling,' Zelda soothed her cross baby as she put her to the breast. 'Mama had important business to attend to in Kendal. Next time I'll take you with me, I promise.'

Once Constanza had been fed and changed, Zelda rocked her off to sleep in her little white canvas cot, before hurrying away to look for Ada, whom she found writing reports in her office.

'Ada, I'm so sorry to interrupt you,' Zelda cried, as she burst into the office without even knocking.

Seeing Zelda's wide eyes and flushed cheeks, Ada jumped up from behind her desk. 'What is it, dear?' she cried in alarm.

Zelda filled her dear friend in on all the morning's developments. Ada shook her head, astonished. 'Really?' she gasped.

'*Really, really*,' Zelda giggled excitedly.

Though Ada was delighted to see her friend so happy, she was nevertheless a little concerned about the suddenness of Zelda's decision.

'I hope you're not leaving Mary Vale because you feel you've overstayed your welcome?' she asked anxiously.

Zelda vehemently shook her head. 'I feel the time has

come for me to vacate my room; there are others in far greater need of it than me.'

Ada couldn't argue with what she said. Mary Vale was rapidly filling up with new residents; there was no doubting that Zelda's big double bedroom would be most welcome.

'I need to think of my future beyond Mary Vale too,' Zelda said frankly. 'I want to make a life in this beautiful part of the world for Constanza and myself.'

Delight that Zelda and her little girl would be close by brought a smile of relief to Ada's worried face. 'I'm glad you'll be near,' she admitted. 'After saying goodbye to Gracie and Diana, it would be very hard to say goodbye to you too.'

Tears swam into Zelda's big dark eyes. 'I would hate to be far away from you, dearest Ada. I want Constanza to grow up knowing you and Dora, and Sister Mary Paul and Sister Theresa too.'

Ada gave her a warm smile before asking another question. 'So when are you thinking of moving to Kendal?'

'As soon as the flat's been aired and cleaned,' Zelda replied.

'Is there enough room there for you to make your herbal products?' Ada enquired.

'The kitchen is small, but it has a stove and hot water – I'm sure it will be fine.' Suddenly Zelda's face dropped as a worrying thought occurred to her. 'My garden!' she exclaimed. 'What will happen to my lovely garden when I leave here?'

'I'm sure you'll be able to keep an eye on it,' Ada assured stricken Zelda.

'If only I could drive,' Zelda cried in a frustrated voice. 'Gracie's old Bedford van is sitting out there in the garage doing nothing.'

'Maybe you should learn to drive,' Ada suggested. 'It would make life a lot simpler for you.'

A smile lit up Zelda's face. 'If I could drive, I could transport my herbs and flowers in the back of the van,' she said thoughtfully. 'I could even take my products further afield, to Lancaster and Grange, and try to sell them there.'

'You'll have an empire before you know it,' Ada laughed.

'Mary Vale Health and Beauty Products,' Zelda proudly proclaimed.

Ada slowly repeated the name. 'Mary Vale Health and Beauty Products, I like it,' she declared. 'It has a lovely ring to it.'

39. February

Ada was desperately missing Jamie, whom she was lucky enough to still get letters from, though in recent weeks their tone had changed. His former letters had been chatty and informative, but his latest missives were hurried, and she instinctively sensed he was holding things back from her. Was he trying to protect her from the gory details of his work in the casualty clearing stations on the Front Line? Baffled and frustrated, she wished he would be more straight with her.

'For goodness' sake! I'm not squeamish – I'm a nurse. I can take it.'

The more she thought about it, the more Ada realized that Jamie was, in fact, just trying to protect her. The wartime principle of keeping up civilians' morale would be uppermost in his mind; there was enough fear and uncertainty circulating in the country without demoralizing the spirits of vulnerable women and children.

One morning, when Ada was at her lowest ebb, Dora didn't report in for duty.

'She's as reliable as clockwork,' Sister Ann puzzled.

'She must be ill,' Ada insisted.

'We can't get in touch; she's not on the phone,' Matron remembered.

'Maybe Mr Saddleworth will phone us from his works?' Ada suggested.

After receiving no phone call all day, and after Dora failed to appear for work the next day, Sister Ann and Ada asked the Mary Vale gardener if he would give them a lift in his old van to the nearby village where Dora lived. Mr Saddleworth's grim expression when he opened the door confirmed the visitors' worst fears.

'Won't you come in?' he said.

After ushering them into the kitchen, where a fire burnt in the grate, Mr Saddleworth offered his guests a cup of tea, which they politely declined.

'We've come to see Dora – is there something wrong?' Sister Ann said quietly.

Slumping into an armchair, Mr Saddleworth said, 'It's our Jack – we've had terrible news, the worst news.'

Ada's hand flew to her mouth to suppress a startled cry.

Sister Ann dropped to her knees so that she could lay a comforting arm around Mr Saddleworth, who looked hollowed out with grief. 'I'm so, so sorry,' she murmured gently.

'What happened?' Ada asked softly.

'His mine sweeper was torpedoed; the entire crew went down with it,' the poor man murmured, as if he still couldn't quite take it in. 'We had a letter from Jack's commanding officer.' He gave a sigh that seemed to come from his soul. 'Both our lads gone now, together, up there in heaven,' he sobbed, as tears rolled unchecked down his haggard face.

Sister Ann and Ada exchanged a tense look.

'How's Dora?' Sister Ann enquired.

Rubbing a hand through the grey strands of his wispy hair, Mr Saddleworth shook his head. 'Terrible — she's kept to her room since the news came through, not eaten a thing, hardly spoken . . .' His voice wandered off.

'May we see her?' Sister Ann murmured.

'Aye, front bedroom, top of the stairs.'

Leaving Mr Saddleworth blankly gazing at the crackling fire, the two women crept upstairs, and, opening the door, they slipped into the bedroom, lit only by a flickering light on the bedside table, beside which stood a small bottle of pills.

'Dora, dearest,' Ada whispered softly.

When Dora didn't stir, Sister Ann checked the label on the bottle of pills. 'Sleeping tablets,' she told Ada.

Looking at their friend with her eyes closed and her face racked with grief made them both feel utterly wretched.

'She might not survive this,' Ada said as she started to cry. 'She always said that if she lost Jack, she would have nothing left to live for.'

Taking Ada by the arm, Sister Ann steered her out of the room and down the stairs.

'We'll leave you in peace, Mr Saddleworth,' she told Dora's wretched husband.

'Peace,' he said the word blankly. 'Without our lads, Dora and I will never know peace again.'

Mary Dale was bereft without Dora. The babies desperately missed her, and the staff were devastated.

'We must stay hopeful,' Sister Ann insisted. 'We must

keep Dora and her son, Jack, constantly in our prayers, we must *never* give up hope.'

Behind Zelda's back Ada had a chat with Frank about giving Zelda driving lessons.

'I know you're grateful to her,' she started.

'I am that,' he assured her.

'She's keen to learn to drive; it would help with transporting her herbs and flowers, and maybe she'll continue to sell her veg on Kendal market. It's such a waste, the van standing there empty.'

'Not a problem, Sister, it'll be a pleasure.'

'She might be a bit taken aback,' Ada warned. 'She thought you might be too busy.'

'I am busy, but I'd like to help the lass; she's been proper good to me in the past,' Frank answered with his usual characteristic honesty.

Zelda was flabbergasted when Frank strode into her shed and suggested they went for a spin.

'Sister Ada thought it was about time you learnt to drive the Bedford van,' he announced.

'She did?' Zelda gasped.

'She thought you might be too shy to ask me yourself,' he grinned.

Blushing to the roots of her red hair, Zelda was tongue-tied. 'Just wait till I see Ada,' she thought to herself.

'I'm between lambing shifts right now, if you're free?' Frank suggested.

'*Now?*' flustered Zelda gasped.

'If you want?' he answered calmly.

'Can you wait while I see to Constanza?' she asked.

Frank nodded. 'I'll take the van for a spin down the lane, get her warmed up for you. Take your time.'

Zelda quickly fed and changed Constanza, then, after rocking her off to sleep in her little canvas cot, she hurried to get her coat and scarf. With butterflies fluttering in her tummy, she ran outside, where Frank was waiting for her.

'In you get,' he smiled, holding the car door wide open.

Settling herself in the driver's seat, Zelda gripped the steering wheel so tightly her knuckles went white.

'Can your feet reach the pedals?' Frank asked.

Zelda wriggled her small feet. 'No, not quite.'

'Hold on, I'll push your seat a bit further forwards – is that better?'

'Yes,' she answered, as she felt the brake pedal underneath her foot.

'Right, then,' Frank grinned. 'Let's get started.'

Frank had grown up driving a tractor, and while he was in active service in northern Europe, he had been driving either Army trucks or tanks. But he had never actually taught anybody to drive. He knew full well that driving teachers had been redeployed since the start of the war; petrol was too precious to waste, so driving tests had been suspended until peace returned. However, people were still driving, and still needed to learn to drive if the country were to continue to function and, more to the point, if they could get their hands on any petrol.

There was little traffic on the valley roads; apart from farm wagons transporting livestock, the lanes were virtually empty. Surprisingly the Bedford van was running well, and Zelda soon relaxed behind the wheel. With solid-as-a-rock Frank at her side, directing and guiding her, Zelda began to enjoy herself. After she had driven the van back to Mary Vale, Frank suggested that they went out for a short drive every day.

'Can you really manage that, Frank?' breathless Zelda asked.

Looking into her flushed, sweet face, Frank would have agreed to anything just so long as it meant he could spend time with her.

'Wouldn't offer if I didn't mean it,' he said gruffly, but the smile in his eyes belied his tone.

'Thank you, Frank,' Zelda replied, and, before she could stop herself, she leant over to peck him on the cheek that her salves had healed so well. 'See you tomorrow.'

Zelda's driving lessons took them all over the beautiful Cartmel Peninsula, and, though the weather was cold, with a biting wind blowing off the churning Irish Sea, Zelda loved their outings. When she had the confidence to look around while driving, she was able to see signs of spring breaking through everywhere. Catkins dangled from hazel and silver birch trees, daffodils in all shades from creamy white to golden yellow blazed in the hedgerows, along with brilliant blue crocuses and wild anemones.

They usually stopped for a break in the countryside, to stretch their legs and drink the strong tea that Frank always brought along in his Thermos flask. During these brief moments Zelda's eyes would rake the surrounding fields and woods for signs of wild herbs shooting into life.

'You're supposed to be concentrating on the *Highway Code*, young lady,' Frank teased. 'Not conjuring up new potions.'

'I'm so excited,' Zelda confessed. 'My mind is full of plans for the future, I fall asleep reading my *Herbal* every night – there are so many remedies I want to try.'

Frank gazed at her with a fond smile on his face. 'If your new products are anything like as successful as the ointment you made for me, you'll be a rich woman in no time,' he predicted.

Zelda gazed at his left cheek, where healthy skin now grew. 'It gives me such pleasure when I think that my salve helped to heal you.'

Frank appreciatively rubbed his hand over the fresh new skin. 'I use a bit every day,' he informed Zelda. 'In fact, that reminds me, I'll be needing a new pot soon.'

'I can't keep up with you and your demands, Frank Arkwright,' she teased.

Stubbing out his cigarette, Frank drained his cup.

'Right, lass, back to work,' he announced, as he reached out his hand to help Zelda back into the car.

Keeping hold of Frank's warm hand, which looked enormous in her own delicate white hand, Zelda gazed up at him.

'Thank you for doing this for me,' she said with genuine gratitude.

'Being with you is always a pleasure, Zelda,' Frank answered with a shy smile.

One afternoon, as Zelda was feeding Constanza in the nursery, Ada came rushing to find her.

'A letter from Diana,' she announced excitedly. 'Shall I read it out?'

Zelda gave an eager nod. 'Yes, please.'

Dearest Friends,

I must apologize for not writing sooner but life has been hectic since we got back to the cottage in Shelford. Mercifully the farmer had the Aga going full blast, so the place was snug and warm for our arrival. There are two connecting bedrooms upstairs: Harry and I have the double room, while the boys have the little room, which just about accommodates their two cots. I can't tell you how sweet they look when they're tucked up at night and in the morning; we wake up to the sound of them giggling together. It is such a joy to see them growing up together.

I never imagined that Harry would make such a wonderful father; you should see him proudly pushing the boys, still sharing one big pram, around the village. They both adore him and make such a fuss when he arrives home from Duxford, where, thank God, he's stationed for the time being. It's an enormous relief having Harry so close by. I lived in terror that he would be transferred to flying planes again, but for the moment he's here with us, which makes the four of us very happy.

I miss you all so much and long to hear your news. I hope
that Zelda's garden continues to flourish, and you're not rushed
off your feet, dearest Ada? Please do give my love to Sister Mary
Paul, Sister Theresa and Sister Ann too.

Lots of love,
Diana, Harry, George and Teddy xxx

'What happy news,' Zelda enthused. 'A new family
and a lovely new home.'

Ada cautiously approached the subject that had been
troubling her since Zelda had announced her plans to
move to the chemist's shop in Kendal.

'Have you set a date for your move?' she asked.

'I'm hoping to speak to Mr Marsden about dates this
week,' Zelda replied.

'And does Frank know about your plans?' Ada asked
as casually as she could.

Zelda blushed as she switched breasts so Constanza
could carry on feeding.

'Actually, I haven't even told Frank I'm moving,' she
confessed.

Seeing Ada's surprised expression, she quickly added,
'It's just that not long ago, Frank said he would look out
for a cottage for me and Constanza, something here in
the valley. I was very grateful to him for even thinking
about it, but he hasn't mentioned it since. To be honest I
don't think I could even afford anything he found. It's a
bit of an awkward situation,' she admitted.

'It would be nice if Frank heard the news from you

first, dear,' Ada urged. Seeing Zelda on the verge of tears, she added, 'Out with it, what's really troubling you?'

'Oh, Ada!' Zelda cried. 'My country has done him so much harm – he doesn't want to be saddled with helping me when I must be such a reminder of all that he has suffered. I just need to make my own plans and leave the poor man in peace,' she finally blurted out.

In a serious quandary Ada wondered what was the right thing to do. For only recently Frank had nervously taken Ada into his confidence.

'There's a house come empty just by Cartmel Forest,' he had told her. 'It's a bit dilapidated, but between us, me and Dad could do it up for Zelda and the little 'un.'

'But how's she going to afford it?' she had enquired.

'The farmer who owns the place has gone to live with his daughter in Kendal. He's prepared to rent it out for a low price so long as the tenant accepts a long lease on the property.'

Ada smiled to herself. She knew how big-hearted Frank was and how he would always want to help Zelda, but she also sensed that he wanted to keep Zelda close. It had been obvious to her for months that the man was falling in love with the lovely young woman. Interrupting her wandering thoughts, Frank said, 'Do you think it's a good idea, Sister?'

'I think it's a lovely idea, Frank.'

Shuffling awkwardly, he muttered, 'Can you keep it to yourself till the time's right to tell Zelda? I wouldn't want the lass seeing the house until it's proper smart and up to scratch for a fine lady such as her.'

'I promise, Frank,' Ada assured him.

Ada knew she absolutely could not break her promise to the earnest young man, but if Zelda didn't inform Frank of her situation soon, she could finish up breaking Frank's very fragile heart.

40. On Top of the World

Gracie's return home was a joyous occasion. Her parents welcomed her back with open arms, and the neighbours were discreet enough not to ask too many awkward questions. Though happy to be back with her family, Gracie suddenly saw things in a different light. The home she had grown up in seemed small and cramped; she had forgotten all about the draughty outdoor privy in the backyard, and after spending months at Mary Vale the lack of gardens and fresh sea-air was quite a shock. Of course, Gracie soon slipped back into familiar old ways, but she nevertheless realized what a huge impact Mary Vale had had on her, in more ways than the obvious one.

Back at the shipyard, Gracie was welcomed with hugs and kisses from her female workmates. The men (so many fewer than there had been when she was last there) wolf-whistled or winked at Gracie as she passed by, but Gracie had eyes only for the majestic cranes that dominated the Barrow skyline. When would she get the chance to operate one, she wondered impatiently.

The call-up from the management for women with experience of driving came faster than Gracie could ever have imagined. When she was being interviewed, Gracie told the bosses of her driving experience, while carefully sidestepping her stay in a Mother and Baby Home.

'I've been driving for well over a year now,' she informed them. 'In fact, when I lived previously in Grange, I did a market run every weekend and ran a delivery service during the week.'

Seeing the two bosses exchanging looks, Gracie talked up her passion and ability in the hope of impressing them.

'I'm quite capable,' she insisted. 'And it's something I very much want to do,' she added boldly. 'It's vital war work and essential to the running of the shipyard.'

The two men nodded in approval.

'You're right there, lass,' the senior man said. 'With able-bodied crane drivers whipped off to drive tanks, we've been pushed to find anybody remotely qualified.'

'Who'd a tho'wt we'd see the days when lasses were doing a fella's job,' the other man moaned.

Though Gracie thought his remark inappropriate in these times of crisis, she kept her mouth firmly shut. She was on the verge of getting what she wanted; now was not the time to rock the boat.

'There'll be a training period before you're left in sole charge of any of the giant cranes,' the older man told her.

'I would expect that, sir,' Gracie answered earnestly. 'Driving a shipyard crane is serious work.'

The older man smiled; she could see that he liked her.

'You're right there, pet – be back first thing in the morning to start your training.'

'Yes, sir,' Gracie replied, trying to control the bubbling

excitement that threatened to overtake her as she virtually skipped out of the manager's office.

After her intense training Gracie was passed as fit to operate a mobile crane with a twenty-five-foot jib. Her heart skipped several beats as she stood underneath it, staring up with a slack jaw and wide eyes.

'My dreams have come true,' she murmured to Maggie, who, though immensely proud of her friend, was left unimpressed by the sight of the towering crane.

Battling back tears, Gracie gulped, 'I'm the first woman in the yard to drive a crane.'

Maggie grinned as she gave her old pal a dig in the ribs. 'Isn't that what you always wanted?'

'YES!' deliriously happy Gracie cried, as she hugged her astonished friend.

'Then you'd best make a good job of it – you know what fellas are like?' Maggie pointed out. 'Quick to judge, especially where us lasses are concerned.'

In order to start work Gracie had to climb 160 feet up the crane on a series of ladders. When she finally arrived in her cabin, hot and flushed, what little breath was left in her lungs was lost in a wild gasp of delight.

'No wonder these machines are called giants,' she thought to herself. 'I feel like I'm on top of the world.'

Spread out below her were the yard, the docks, the berths and the slipways, with hundreds of bustling workers, looking like little ants, going about their business. The town lay beyond, rows and rows of terraced houses and long, narrow streets; and beyond the urban sprawl was the vast expanse of the sparkling Irish Sea, which stretched westward into a shimmering blue infinity.

Dragging her mind back to the job in hand, Gracie settled into her seat, where she started to tackle her first task: to load a boiler on to a battleship that was in the process of being rebuilt. Trembling with both nerves and excitement, Gracie took her time to complete the task of lifting and of unloading tons of equipment. With practice and experience she was soon able to place the goods that she was responsible for within an inch of where they were required to be, whether it was moving material off the ships that had come into the yard for repair work or loading them with vital equipment needed overseas.

As the war progressed, it was a huge relief to see American convoys arriving at the shipyard. Safely escorted across the Atlantic by frigates and destroyers, they were regular, welcome visitors loaded with cargo that was vital to Britain: anything from food supplies, coal, medical equipment to ammunition, tanks and planes in sections ready to be assembled. It was at moments like these, when Gracie offloaded hundreds of tons of precious goods, that she truly felt that she really was part of the war effort. From Barrow, American goods deposited in the yard would be quickly dispatched across the country to feed the hungry, heal the sick, build bombs, warm homes and fight off the enemy. With only the wheeling seagulls overhead to hear her Gracie often would cry out her heartfelt thanks.

'Thank you, Yanks! Come back soon.'

*

Though Gracie missed her friends, she barely had time to catch her breath since starting her challenging new job. She hadn't written to Diana or caught up with Zelda, so when she saw Dora in Barrow town centre Gracie was overjoyed.

'Dora!' she cried, as she rushed across the street to give her friend a hug.

It was only when Dora turned in her direction that Gracie saw how dramatically changed the older woman looked. From being a strong, robust woman with sparkling eyes and a ready smile always playing at the corners of her mouth, Dora was now drawn and thin, with vacant eyes and unkempt, greasy grey hair.

'Hello, dear,' Gracie said in a softer voice. 'Do you remember me from Mary Vale? Gracie, Zelda and Diana?'

A spark of recognition briefly lit up Dora's haggard face; then, sounding confused, she demanded in a slurred, tired voice, 'What's your name?'

Desperately wondering how she could reach out to the woman who had been one of her strongest allies only months ago, Gracie was uncharacteristically lost for words. She was hugely relieved when she caught sight of Mr Saddleworth hurrying towards his wife with an anxious expression on his face.

'Lovie, what're you doing?' he asked gently.

'I got lost and this woman here says she knows me,' Dora answered in a frail, quivery voice.

Mr Saddleworth smiled as he recognized Gracie. 'We've just been to the doctor's,' he explained, filling Gracie in on their recent devastating news.

'She's been on tranquillizers since we heard – no interest in anything, not even the work that she used to live for.'

'She'll be badly missed at Mary Vale,' Gracie murmured. 'Everybody loved her, especially the babies.'

'I wish she were back there,' Mr Saddleworth said with real longing in his voice. 'These days she just sleeps or weeps all day.'

Seeing Dora getting agitated, he took her by the arm. 'Come on, lovie, let's find the bus stop and get you home.'

'Bye, Dora,' Gracie said softly. 'God bless you, sweetheart.'

Standing by the roadside watching them walk away brought a sob to Gracie's throat. Dora was one of the strongest women she had ever known. Tough, funny, compassionate and generous, she had been a great support to everyone at the Home, nun, nurse, resident or neighbour. Yet here she was, broken in the prime of her life by the horrors of war that were just too painful to bear. Seething with anger, Gracie continued on her way home.

'It's not bloody fair,' she swore out loud, causing passers-by to throw odd sideways glances at her.

Jack, laughing, joking friendly Jack, who had asked her to dance when she was the size of a house; who planned to take her to the pictures when he was next home on leave. If she hadn't been pregnant, she might have flirted with him, kissed him and sent him off with a smile on his face; as it was, she hadn't ever answered one of his letters.

She stopped on the corner of her street for a moment and turned to look at the sea. Her heart lifted at the sight of her crane, which she immediately made out from the others berthed in the yard. By God, she had got what she wanted, more than she had ever dreamt of. She was alive and young, her life stretched out before her, but what had those thousands upon thousands of young lads fighting for their country got? The thought made Gracie both angry and sad. It also galvanized her further: she would work until she dropped to fight the war the only way she knew how – driving cranes at Barrow Shipyard, where beating the enemy motivated the entire workforce.

41. Cartmel Cottage

After the conversation she had recently had with Ada, Zelda decided she would inform Frank of her plans to move to Kendal. Anxious that she may have already left it too late, Zelda hardly slept that night. When morning eventually dawned, she was up with the lark to feed and bathe Constanza; then, after playing with her in the nursery, she set off for her prearranged driving lesson. Sitting in the driver's seat, Zelda watched Frank walk through the back gate of Mary Vale and approach the van with a broad grin on his face. He looked so tall and broad in his dark winter coat, his black hair contrasted against his tanned outdoor skin; even his eye patch added a touch of dare-devil glamour to his sharply chiselled face. As he came closer, Zelda could see he was giving her a somewhat concerned look. In his usual, forthright manner, he came straight out with his concern.

'You look right peaky, lass.'

'I didn't sleep well,' she prevaricated.

'Something troubling you?' he asked, as if reading her thoughts.

'You could say that,' Zelda replied, as Frank settled himself in the passenger seat beside her. 'I'll feel better after a bit of fresh air,' she said with feigned cheerfulness.

'Right, then,' he said. 'Where shall we drive today?'

'Not too far,' she quickly said. 'I need to get back for Constanza and . . .' She dithered as she tried to think of another excuse. 'I'm beginning to feel guilty about wasting your dad's precious supply of petrol.'

Frank shrugged. 'That's for me to worry about. Let's head towards Cartmel, see how good your reversing is in those narrow little streets.'

They stopped by the clear bubbling beck just outside the pretty village of Cartmel, dominated by its ancient eight-hundred-year-old Priory, whose long history went far back to the monks of Lindisfarne Island. Here Frank clambered out of the van to stretch his legs and smoke one of his roll-up cigarettes, while Zelda drank tea from the Thermos he had brought along with him. Though it was a bitterly cold spring morning, songbirds warbled in the overhead treetops and a weak sun shone down on the nodding daffodils lining the riverbank. After stubbing out his cigarette on the gravel path, Frank reached out for the Thermos that Zelda was clutching. He poured himself some tea.

'Spit it out, lass, I can see something's up.'

Zelda took a deep, trembling breath; the polite sentences she had been running through her head all morning disappeared, and instead she simply blurted it out.

'I'm leaving Mary Vale, Frank – I'm moving to Kendal.'

Looking like he had been punched in the solar plexus, Frank stared at her for several long seconds before speaking bluntly. 'Why?'

'The chemist in Kendal has offered me his flat over the shop,' she explained.

'I see,' he murmured. 'And is that what you want? You'll be happy, the two of you, in a flat over a chemist's shop?' he asked pointedly.

Blushing, Zelda could only mumble, 'It's a start.'

Replacing the top on the Thermos, Frank climbed into the van, but this time he sat in the driver's seat.

'Please don't be cross with me, Frank,' she pleaded.

'I'm not cross with you,' he told her straight. 'There's just something I need to show you.'

Feeling hot and self-conscious, Zelda sat quietly beside Frank, wondering what on earth he planned to show her.

After they had left the village behind them, they drove along the winding lanes that skirted Cartmel Forest, where Constanza had been born only a few months ago. Zelda couldn't help but smile when she saw the tree that Captain had been tied to while poor Frank had run back and forth on a mercy mission to rescue a frantic mother and her new-born baby girl.

She was taken aback when Frank turned up a track that led to a pretty white-washed house that looked exactly like a doll's house but life-sized. Standing firm and square in a large but very overgrown garden, it had a delightful east–west orientation that made the house look bright and light. When Frank pulled up outside the front door, Zelda glanced around. 'Have you come to pick something up?' she asked.

Frank gave a curt nod. 'I left some tools here the other day.'

Stepping out of the van, he opened Zelda's door and helped her out. 'Come and have a look round.'

Rather bewildered, Zelda followed him inside. 'The kitchen's nice,' she said, as she admired the recently painted black grate and a fine old pine dresser that covered one entire wall.

'Wait till you see the sitting room,' Frank said, as he ushered her into the spacious but empty front room.

'It's very pretty,' Zelda exclaimed. 'Lovely views,' she murmured, as she gazed out on to the garden, where, between the brambles, Zelda was sure she could make out a large abandoned rose bed. 'Pity it's so neglected,' she said sadly.

Following Frank up the stairs to the carpeted landing, she asked who lived there.

'It belongs to a farmer who has gone to live with his daughter Keswick way,' Frank replied.

Opening one of the bedroom doors, Frank led Zelda into a sweet little room that had a cot in one corner and a chest of drawers in the other, with several framed photographs placed on the top of it. Zelda visibly stiffened as she looked along the line of photographs, which were all of Constanza. A shiver ran down her spine as she suddenly understood the purpose of their visit to this house. Feeling faint with shock, Zelda gripped the edge of the windowsill for support.

'I don't understand,' she eventually managed to say.

Frank shyly took hold of her trembling hands. 'If you

want it, it can be your house, sweetheart: me and Dad have been doing it up for you and Constanza.'

'But, but,' she spluttered as she burst out laughing, 'it's such a nice thought but I couldn't possibly afford a lovely big house like this.'

'Well, it so happens that I have a plan for that, but let's talk about that later,' he urged.

With her emotions flying all over the place, Zelda turned around to admire the newly painted room with its polished floors and rag carpets.

'You did all of this for *me*?'

'Aye,' he said, with a proud ring in his voice. 'I was hoping to finish the job before I gave you a tour, but, since you went and jumped the gun by announcing your imminent move to Kendal, I thought it might be wise to show you around sooner rather than later.'

'It's gorgeous!' she cried. 'Just beautiful.'

Touched beyond words at the trouble he'd gone to on her behalf, Zelda stared up at him. 'You are the most wonderful man,' she declared before she could stop herself.

'There is just one thing I haven't explained yet . . .' Pausing to take a deep breath, Frank continued in a low, trembling voice, 'The thing is, I'd like to live here with you, if I may?'

Zelda gulped. 'You want to live with *me*?'

'Nay, little lass,' he gulped. 'I want to marry you.'

Zelda gazed up at him. '*You* want to marry *me*?'

'I most certainly do,' Frank answered robustly.

Flabbergasted as she was, Zelda could not stop herself from bursting out laughing.

'Even though I'm *German* – and a Jew too?'

Pulling her close to his chest, Frank did something he had been longing to do for months: after running his heads through her glorious rich red curls, he tilted her small chin and bent to kiss her soft pink lips that opened to his.

'I love you, lass,' he murmured. 'I really don't think I could live without you.'

Smiling and crying all at the same time, they stood locked in each other's arms until Frank whispered in Zelda's ear, 'You've not said yay or nay yet, sweetheart.'

Smiling up at him, Zelda was almost beyond words; this giant of a private man with one eye and a scarred face had become her companion and help, but now, after baring his soul, Frank was suddenly her beloved. Standing on tiptoes so she could reach up to him, she pressed her lips to his and kissed him deeply.

'Yes,' she sighed.

'Yes!' he gasped. 'You're quite sure?' he gabbled. 'I won't take the house away from you if you say no, I'll just go back home and leave you in peace.'

'I can't think of anything I would love more! I'd be happy to live with you *anywhere*, dearest Frank,' she smiled, before kissing him long and hard again.

'Well, then, in that case,' he chuckled, 'it's time you inspected the master bedroom.'

Zelda stared with pleasure at the big room that overlooked the front garden and contained only one article of furniture – a big old double bed. Drawing Zelda on to the bed so they could sit beside each other, Frank stared at his wife-to-be.

'I've got summat else,' he said shyly. 'I didn't want to bring it out until you'd agreed to my proposal.'

Zelda smiled. 'I can't believe you ever thought I would turn you down?'

'I hardly dared to hope, I wanted it that much,' he answered with a searing honesty that brought a lump to her throat.

Drawing a little velvet box with a gold clasp from his pocket, he handed it to Zelda. 'It was mi mother's ring.'

Flipping open the lid, Zelda gasped when she saw a cluster of emeralds set in a vintage gold ring.

'It's beautiful,' she murmured.

'I thought the stones would go with your lovely hair,' Frank said as he slipped the ring on to Zelda's small wedding finger.

'Darling,' she murmured, laying her head on his warm shoulder, as they both lay back on the bed, holding each other tightly, overcome with love and emotion.

'I could lie here all day,' Frank murmured, nuzzling her silky soft neck.

'Me too,' she sighed. 'Think of it, dearest, after our wedding we'll lie here together every night,' she whispered with a small seductive smile.

Frank gave his happy boyish grin that always melted Zelda's heart. 'Who knows,' he murmured. 'Maybe one day soon there'll be another little cot besides Constanza's,' he said with real yearning in his voice.

Zelda began to giggle. 'If I should ever give birth

again, believe me it will be right here in this lovely house – not on a bed of leaves in Cartmel Forest!'

Later, before they left Cartmel Cottage, Zelda completed a quick tour of the garden.

'Don't worry,' Frank said knowingly. 'There're acres of space for your herbs, sweetheart.'

As Zelda stood in the middle of her new home, with the weak winter sun beaming down on her head, she suddenly felt a benign presence at her side. Shivering like somebody had walked over her grave, she turned, but it in a blink the sensation was gone. Nevertheless, Zelda knew in her heart that Izaak had, from beyond the grave, reached out to her. She knew he wanted this for her: to live in the country that had given her sanctuary, with a man who loved her and Constanza. The knowledge filled Zelda with great peace; at last she had come home.

42. Spring Weddings, 1941

Zelda and Ada ended up getting married on the same day, though not in the same church. Zelda and Frank got married in the local Register Office; in attendance were Alf Arkwright, cradling little Constanza in his arms, and Gracie, who had turned up that morning from Barrow and drove the small wedding party to the venue in the Bedford van that Frank had polished until it gleamed.

'I hope you didn't mind marrying me in a Register Office, my darling,' Zelda whispered after the brief ceremony.

'Stop thy fretting, little lass,' Frank answered tenderly, as he kissed the bright gold wedding ring on her finger. 'I told you right from the start, I understand your reasons for choosing the Register Office – why would a person of the Jewish faith marry in the Church of England?' He grinned at his new wife before adding, 'I'm quite sure God doesn't mind either way.'

'Oh, Frank, thank you,' Zelda murmured as she stood on her tiptoes in order to reach up and kiss him. 'Thank you for loving me,' she added, as tears welled up in her gentle brown eyes.

'All that matters is we're married, man and wife,' Frank added proudly. A squeak from hungry Constanza, still in Alf's arms, caused Frank to smile before rearranging his sentence. 'Sorry, little lady, who could ever forget you? Man, wife and *baby* – a right proper little family.'

'Let's get a move on,' a grinning Gracie urged, as she unlocked the Bedford van for her passengers. 'We've another wedding to go to, and that's up the 'ill in Allithwaite.'

Allithwaite Church, beautifully decorated by Sister Theresa with fragrant flowers from the convent's greenhouses, was packed with smiling guests – nuns, residents, relatives and friends. Even Dora had rallied to attend the ceremony, and, though the poor woman was a shadow of her former self, it was a joy to see her sitting in a pew beside her devoted husband.

Jamie had been granted five days' leave, which he and Ada planned to spend walking in the Northern Fells, first stop Scafell Pike; their decision literally put the fear of God in Sister Mary Paul, who predictably announced the young couple were 'completely out of their minds'.

'We'll be fine, Sister,' a laughing Ada had assured the agitated nun.

'But you can't sleep on top of a mountain,' Sister Mary Paul had chided. 'And what will you eat?'

'We have accommodation organized at a farm,' Ada explained. 'I promise you we won't starve.'

What Ada didn't tell the old nun was that her thoughts weren't on eating either; passion and desire chased away any interest in food. The thought of spending all night long in bed with Jamie took Ada's mind off everything but him. She could not wait to be Mrs Ada Reid and wake up every morning of her honeymoon wrapped in her beloved's arms.

Walking down the aisle, bearing the lily of the valley bouquet that Zelda had made up for her, radiant, smiling Ada approached her beloved Jamie. She was followed closely behind by her bridesmaids, Gracie and Diana, the latter showing no strain from the two-hundred-mile journey she had made across England in order to be with Zelda and Ada on their wedding day. After the touching service enhanced by the chapel choir, who sang sweetly throughout the ceremony, the happy couple was showered in confetti before everybody headed back to Mary Vale for the wedding breakfast.

A few hours later, replete with food, sherry and good wishes, the two couples went their separate ways. Mr and Mrs Reid drove north to the highest mountain range in England, while Mr and Mrs Arkwright set off, with Constanza cradled in her mother's arms, for Cartmel Cottage. As Jamie carried his young bride over the threshold of their bedroom, which overlooked Watendlath Tarn glowing like a jewel in the sunset light, Frank carried his wife and her daughter into their new home. For two young couples very much in love, life was beginning, and, though war raged all over the world, just for now the world stood still.

Acknowledgements

I would like to thank Jane and Selwyn Image from Cambridge for all their help and advise. Selwyn's knowledge of cars, planes, dates and the timeline of the war years were invaluable, while Jane's gardening tips, particularly on 'Digging for Victory', were brilliant.

Thank you to Clare Bowron, Donna Poppy and Rebecca Hilsdon at Penguin – putting a book together during a pandemic can't be easy!

The biggest thanks of all goes to my loyal readers – enjoy. x

He just wanted a decent book to read ...

Not too much to ask, is it? It was in 1935 when Allen Lane, Managing Director of Bodley Head Publishers, stood on a platform at Exeter railway station looking for something good to read on his journey back to London. His choice was limited to popular magazines and poor-quality paperbacks – the same choice faced every day by the vast majority of readers, few of whom could afford hardbacks. Lane's disappointment and subsequent anger at the range of books generally available led him to found a company – and change the world.

'We believed in the existence in this country of a vast reading public for intelligent books at a low price, and staked everything on it'
Sir Allen Lane, 1902–1970, founder of Penguin Books

The quality paperback had arrived – and not just in bookshops. Lane was adamant that his Penguins should appear in chain stores and tobacconists, and should cost no more than a packet of cigarettes.

Reading habits (and cigarette prices) have changed since 1935, but Penguin still believes in publishing the best books for everybody to enjoy. We still believe that good design costs no more than bad design, and we still believe that quality books published passionately and responsibly make the world a better place.

So wherever you see the little bird – whether it's on a piece of prize-winning literary fiction or a celebrity autobiography, political tour de force or historical masterpiece, a serial-killer thriller, reference book, world classic or a piece of pure escapism – you can bet that it represents the very best that the genre has to offer.

Whatever you like to read – trust Penguin.

read more
www.penguin.co.uk